SILENT IS THE SWORD

SONG OF INK

EVELYN GRIMALD STONE

TARNEY BRAE CREATIVE ENDEAVOURS

❀ Formatted with Vellum

For those who understand the power of silence,
And for those who were forced to speak

CONTENTS

PREFACE

This book is an epic fantasy with romantic elements. There are no open-door scenes, nor any language that might be considered cursing. However, this book does contain dark themes, including child abuse, severe anxiety and panic attacks, depression, torture, murder, imprisonment and violence. Please, be aware of these elements and read with care.

The main character of this book has selective mutism. This depiction is merely one form of selective mutism, and there are many other people with different experiences. Selective mutism is more common in neurodiverse people, but it is by no means exclusive. I did not write Elyria as a neurodiverse character, but if you would like to see her that way, then by all means, you are welcome to do so!

The sign language depicted in this book is not based on any one particular form of sign language.

I hope you enjoy *Silent is the Sword*!

at plains

ral

vazen

Imara

ira

PART I
THE QUIET

PROLOGUE

There was a silence to winter that I loved. It sank into the bones, the emptiness after a swell of music, the pause after a release of breath indicating peace. The moment between heartbeats. The waiting. The anticipation. When the snow draped itself like a feather blanket over the boughs of leaf-bare trees and evergreen fronds, I would bundle myself up in my best woollen cloak, pull on my boots, and run outside, breathing heavily until I reached a grove well away from Summerfell manor and all its constant noise. Its constant demands on the shape of my life. There, in the grove, I closed my eyes, tilted my head up to the sky and let the silence fill me with its potential, draining away the rest.

Summerfell was the holding of the Baron of Summerfell, the Keeper of the Northern Passes, and to a girl of eight, who was too young to be of any real import, yet too old to be bound to a nursery, it was difficult not to be underfoot. I had no interest in the soldiers who passed through in the warmer months, either heading back to the lowlands after a gruelling winter's patrol, or heading into the Passes bundled in fur, even in summer. Nor did the gruff manners of hunters and trappers who ventured into the forests tinged with magic appeal to me. The servants were in a constant bustle, either seeing to the guests or preparing for the harsh colds of winter. My father and mother were usually off managing their own affairs, leaving me to the care of my uncle, the Baron, who was busy always. Occasionally, my cousin Alar was allowed to come away from his tutors and play, but it was rare. Nor was I allowed to join him in his lessons; he was heir to Summerfell and I was a girl without title, despite being of noble blood. Our lessons were vastly different.

So I was left often alone, surrounded by noise and unable to escape except in the deepest winter in a grove of trees.

On this particular day, the changing of the watch was happening earlier than anticipated, meaning the keep was all but frantic. Our weather seer had predicted a storm that would block the passes for months. We usually got them, cutting us off from the lowlanders to the south, but this one was early. The unexpected storm had the servants doing their best to salt and dry every bit of meat, preserve every vegetable, unpack the furs, stuff forest moss into the crevasses of the keep for insulation, bundle in wood for fuel, and more things that I didn't care much about.

Even Alar was excused from his lessons to spend time

with his father while the Baron saw to the change in the watch, so he could learn that important task. Those who had served the summer were being sent down south while their replacements—only arrived yesterday—were being loaded up with supplies for the various small outposts in the passes or settled into quarters at Summerfell for the watch.

I didn't really understand what all the fuss was about, given that we hadn't had an attack from the raiders in the north, beyond the magic of the boundary mountains, since I'd been alive, but as I'd been told many times, I was a girl and wouldn't understand. The servants sometimes whispered about monsters and fell beasts that threatened from the farthest icy fingers up north, but they never did so when they could see me.

I made sure they often couldn't see me.

I tilted my head back and watched a bright blue jay hop its way from tree branch to tree branch, picking at the bark for insects. A squirrel chattered at it as the bird drew too close to a stash and the clearing erupted into noise for a brief moment.

"Elyria Trevain, what are you doing out here by yourself?!" A hand grasped me around my upper arm and yanked. I cried out and tried to wrench away, but the large, stern woman at the end of the hand glowered at me. She was hastily bundled in a cloak and her hood was askew, fur trim nearly hiding her eyes from me. I knew her and didn't want to see her eyes.

"I'm sorry, Nissa," I said, lowering my gaze and halting my struggles. I didn't want a caning for fighting the chief of the servants after she came out all this way to fetch me. "My lessons were cancelled for the afternoon, and I didn't want to be in the way."

Nissa clicked her tongue and started dragging me across the clearing, ruining the fresh coat of snow by her heavy steps. I stumbled along beside her, my arm still held in her grasp.

"You should know better than to run off on your own in the forest. Especially in winter. Especially with the change of the watch!" She looked like she wanted to strike me, but settled for wrenching my arm instead. I frowned; she'd never hesitated in the past. Why would she do so now?

"I *am* sorry," I said. Sorry I got caught, that is.

"Well, at least you'll learn better apologies where you're going. That one is pathetic." We left the clearing and fell onto a well-worn path through the snow, one of many that the watch carved on their various patrols around the keep. From there, the walk back to the stone fortress was a matter of moments.

"Where am I going?" I couldn't help the question that slipped out and flinched in expectation. But once again, there was no rebuke for my insolence. Instead, Nissa just glared at me.

"Somewhere you can finally curb those questions and learn to be a lady," she said, dragging me through the doors and ignoring the smiles the two guardsmen threw us. I tried to smile back, but was pulled forwards. I didn't see if the guards watched our progress, looked at me with fondness or pity. I sometimes preferred it when they didn't look at me at all.

Before I could ask more questions, or consider Nissa's words, she had my cloak undone and yanked roughly off. She threw it at a waiting maidservant, then examined me. Her expression hardened as she reached out for my hair.

White-blonde, it was a common Trevain trait, one I shared with my cousin and the Baron, though it was difficult to tell whether the Baron's hair was white with age or with family history. I wore mine in a ragged braid, one I'd done myself only that morning. Nissa undid it swiftly and without care for my sensitive scalp and pinned back the strands at the front, leaving my hair loose. She adjusted my dress and scowled at the hem, which was two inches too short. I'd grown again.

"You have much improvement to achieve," she sneered, "but you will suffice."

"For what?" I asked, and this time I got my ear twisted for my impertinence.

"Ask no questions!" Nissa reminded me. "How many times have I told you? A lady—"

"A lady is quiet and cunning," I recited, eyes firmly on the stone floor through the rushes. "She asks no questions unless she knows the answers. She is able to steer a conversation by word and look alone, with no one the wiser."

Nissa inhaled sharply. I squeezed my eyes shut, bracing for the strike. Instead of striking me, or scolding me, she made a sound in the back of her throat that was one part exasperation and another part disappointment. "The Baron

17

is waiting for you in his library," she said, prompting me to open my eyes.

The Baron never called for me, not unless I was with Alar already. And the *library*? That was for official business. Keep business. Not family business. Excitement fluttered in my belly at the thought of finally being involved in Keep business.

"Go!" Nissa snapped. I went, fleeing the chief of servants with as much grace as I could muster. I slowed my quick steps to a smooth walk as I approached the door to the library. It was at the back of the fortress, with wide windows that looked onto the vale below the Northern Passes and every wall covered in shelves upon shelves of books. It was a room that thrilled me. And, despite my excitement, a room that terrified me.

Maybe you won't hear them, I told myself, then shook that thought away from me. I wouldn't even think about it. If I thought about it, that made it real, and I did not want it to be real. No, it was just a room full of books. The important thing was to not make a fool of myself in front of the Baron. My parents would be disappointed when they next received a letter from my uncle. I would make sure they weren't disappointed. Maybe then they would come home. Or take me with them next time they left.

The library door was closed, heavy ironwood doors looming over me. I wished I were grown and taller, so that doors wouldn't intimidate me. I closed my eyes and shook that thought from my mind, too.

Then, taking a deep breath, I lifted my shoulders, held

my head high in the posture my teachers had drilled into me, lifted my hand with as much smoothness and grace as I could, given the trembling, and knocked.

"Enter." The deep, bass voice rang out almost before the sound of my knock had faded. I didn't hesitate, lifting the latch on the door and pushing it open. Without even looking at the room or its occupants as I slipped in, I lowered into a curtsey and waited to be acknowledged.

"Rise." The Baron's voice was dismissive, almost disinterested. But I knew that was a ruse, since he had called me here. Summoned me.

I rose and lifted my eyes. To my surprise, there was someone else in the room with the Baron. Seated in a simple wooden chair by the fire was a woman, one so beautiful I could barely keep from gaping at her.

Every line in her body was smooth and elegant, from the way her dress draped about her knees to the small movements of her fingers stroking a fur muff. Her gaze was soft but intelligent, and her smile quiet, easy.

"This is she?" the woman asked, and even her voice was musical, almost delicate.

"Yes," the Baron said, a picture of gruffness in comparison. My gaze moved to my uncle. He was ruddy skinned from so much time out under the winter sun. His beard was closely shorn, but it did little to hide the three parallel scars that ran down his left cheek, one running right through where his eye had been. He wore a bear skin about his shoulders, clasped with the claws of the great beast. Alar told me that a bear had given the Baron those scars and that the Baron had killed the beast with his bare hands; I believed it.

The Baron looked at me, mouth twisting in the familiar line that it took when I was near. He waved vaguely at me. "Go stand by the window, where we can see you."

I curtseyed again and did as he asked, walking over the rushes as quietly as possible and standing by the window, my back to one of the bookshelves. My heart thudded in my ears as I heard a faint rustle of pages.

"And you are sure about this?" the woman asked, never looking away from me. "It is not an easy thing to become one of our order."

"But the benefits...?" the Baron prompted.

"She will be taught all manner of thing, certainly," the woman raised a hand, the gesture graceful. Like a dancer, I thought. "Accomplishments. Instruments. Singing, if she has a voice for it. Poetry. Art. Dance. All the standard requirements for a lady of good bloodlines in this age." The woman sniffed, as if such things were below her. "The Order of Ter Avest will provide more, though. A thorough understanding of politics. Languages. She will learn strategy. She will—"

"Be an asset," the Baron said, nodding firmly. The woman's expression didn't change at the interruption, but I would have sworn she was irritated.

What was the Order of Ter Avest? Was I being sent away to school? This was my home; I didn't want to be sent away. Why weren't my parents here to decide my fate?

The paper rustling behind me intensified. I stiffened.

"Any woman of noble blood is an asset, my dear Baron,"

the woman said in that same musical tone. "A woman of the Order is more than an asset. She can ruin a country with the right poem. She can ratify a peace treaty by her marriage. She will be worth more than her weight in gold."

"Fine. That's fine," the Baron said. The woman blinked, a flicker of something dark touching her eyes for that brief instant. "So long as she is useful."

Wasn't I useful here? I was being taught to do important things. I knew my figures and my letters. I was helping Nissa with the balance books for the kitchens. And I *could* play the harp, even if I didn't like practising much. I was doing all the things a lady was expected to do.

You could be doing more. The voice was a whisper in my ear, rich and dark. I gasped and clenched my hands into fists. The Baron glared at me, and I quickly lowered my gaze.

"She will be useful," the woman assured him. "*If* the Order accepts her."

"Why wouldn't you accept her?" the Baron asked, anger creeping into his voice. "She's the right age. She knows her place. She has all the qualities you want!"

The woman tilted her head, much like the blue jay back in the clearing. "She is eye-catching. White hair is so uncommon, even here in the north. And her face is well formed. She will certainly turn head when she grows, so long as her expressions can be controlled. Pity about her brown eyes, but at least they're pleasant enough."

I drowned in the blue of her eyes, another voice said, high and reedy. *Her step was but wind on the grass, and her smile could outshine the sun. To win the honour of her heart, I would slay dragons and—*

"Quiet," I breathed, a single bead of sweat dripping down my spine. At my plea, another voice, this one reciting the history of a battle long past, started speaking, voice monotonous, boring, impossible to ignore. My breath caught in my throat and I barely managed to swallow back a whimper.

The woman, who had still not once taken her eyes from me, raised her brows ever so slightly. "The concerns that the Order have is regarding her parentage."

The Baron scoffed, but I heard nervousness in his laugh. "You came all the way here at the start of winter to see her. Surely you have no *real* concerns."

The woman smiled, though her expression somehow didn't change. "My lord, braving the danger of the early snows is little concern for one of the Order. I am content to return south without the girl, if she is not suitable."

"Elyria Trevain is the only child of my brother," the Baron said through gritted teeth.

"Indeed," the woman said. "And her mother?"

Motherless child, left in the hands of one who could not take her. It became my responsibility to raise the get. I will not have her near my son. I will not see her grow here, coveting what will never be hers.

This new voice, so deep and sharp like the Baron's, filled my head so that I could barely hear the conversation between the woman and my uncle. Sweat formed on my brow. My hands were clammy. My knees shook beneath my dress. I tried to push the voices back and remain still, remain tall and proud, but they only became louder. More voices joined in, and words scrawled in ink flew through my mind.

I tried, I really did. I knew the beating I would take for moving, for being so weak, but I didn't care anymore. I couldn't take another second of the voices dancing around my mind. I cried out and put my hands over my ears.

"Make them stop," I begged. Through the haze of my tears, I saw the woman stand abruptly, startled, though her expression smoothed a moment later.

The voices only grew louder.

And in the year 189, following the magical war, a great famine spread across the land, rendering the fertile forest lands of the middle continent into barren wastelands. The trees were felled for farmland, and when nothing grew, the people of those new plains starved, leaving behind only relics of their cities and—

"Make them stop!" I yelled, turning to my uncle, my family, for help. "Make the voices—"

"SILENCE!" The Baron screamed, raising his hand and striking me across the face, his ring cutting my cheek open. In an instant, the words were stolen from my throat. The voices fell silent, leaving dead, empty space in their wake. I dropped to my knees, leaning against the bookshelves. They were cold now. They should have been warmed by the fireplace nearby, but they were cold. The tears in my eyes fell without my bidding.

"A pity," I heard the woman say as the world wavered around me, the edges fading to black. "I know no one can predict when magic will appear, but it is always a shame to see it in one such as her. Unfortunately, Baron, the Order of Ter Avest can no longer take your ward. We have nothing to do with magic, and she is full of it. A shame, for she had such potential. You'll have to find some other place to dispose of her."

The world disappeared, and with it the pain in my cheek where warm blood flowed, the fear of the voices and words I couldn't control. With it went my own voice, too. Silence was asked for, and silence I gave.

CHAPTER 1

*L*emon *trees are fruiting trees of the tropical variety,*
requiring—

"Elyria!"

I looked up from the book I was shelving, blocking out
its whispers on the various properties of lemon trees. This
book was more insistent than most, trying to tell me about
its tricks for growing trees. I was far from interested in such
things as gardening—given my background as someone
from the north, no one in the entire city of Vazeri would be
foolish enough to trust me with their garden. Still, as I
handled the book, the ink in its pages whispered its
contents to me. Mostly, I could block out the constant whispers unless I was touching a book; then its ink sang the song
of scribe magic.

I turned to see Archivist Rosaria hurrying towards me.
Well, as much as any Archivist hurried. She was taller than
me by at least a full head, had skin the colour of walnut

wood, and was months away from being promoted to Central Archivist. She didn't have scribe magic like me, but that hadn't stopped her from making a name for herself in the Great Archives.

I set my stack of books down and smiled, trying not to show too much enthusiasm at being sought out. I was polite and pleasant and perfectly helpful, not desperate for interaction. I lifted my hands, fingers dancing as I signed, *"How can I help you, Rosaria?"*

She stopped before me, looking flustered. That was never a good sign. "The triumvirate was working through a council meeting on the provisions being made for the garrisoning of Makhierian soldiers here. You know, to deal with the potential Imaran situation? Which is ridiculous, since they can't cross their mountains, and everyone knows they wouldn't dare invade by sea, given how steady our trade is. Anyways, the council was looking for old laws on the keeping of horses and can't find them. Anywhere. I've had Tavio searching all morning, and even Central Archivist Mariam was searching! Can you…would you mind?"

I smiled and shrugged. *"No problem,"* I signed, my fingers flying through the simple answer. *"Let me get to the atrium."*

Rosaria sagged in relief. "Thank you, Elyria. I owe you a dinner at the very least. From that little place down the hill. You know how the triumvirate can be when we can't find information for them."

I did know, though I would have helped, regardless. The triumvirate ruled the city-state with no small amount of bickering and bureaucracy, and if they or the council couldn't find information, the Great Archives were usually to blame. Our budget had been cut once already in the two years since I'd been there, and it had been threatened at least thrice more for simple misfilings.

Thankfully, they needed us, not only for their paperwork and to keep track of records, but because we were the largest library in the entire group of harbour city-states. Vazeri controlled the information, and therefore we were considered the most powerful. That, in turn, drew skilled mages and craftsmen here, which only increased the influence of Vazeri. All because of the Great Archives.

I moved my stack of books to a cart at the end of one of the massive shelves for a novice to sort through later. Rosaria led me through the Great Archive building, slipping through hallways floored with marble and trimmed in decadent wood and metal. The entire city was built similarly, with stone carved into intricate designs making up the exterior of most of the buildings and the interiors done with beautifully worked plaster, trimmed in wood, floored in marble or smooth riverstone, and furnished with the best that could be had.

It was a dramatic shift from my time as a noviciate to the Archives in Liral, at the edge of the Great Plains. There, it had been wattle and daub, rare pieces of wood salvaged for shelves, and what stones could be dug from the earth piled into walls. Simple, austere. Nothing like the grand decadence of the hilled city.

I thanked the gods often for bringing me to Vazeri. A place where, maybe, I could truly belong.

The atrium was in the process of being painted with scenes depicting the legends of dragons and angels, their battle playing out in grand scale. The artists had set up scaffolding, and one of the art mages was calling paint from his palette to shade the tip of a dragon's claw. Seeing the beauty they created, I was sometimes jealous of art mages. My own drawing skills were poor at best, art not being made of words and therefore impossible to influence with my magic. But, then, if I had art magic, I wouldn't have the company of ink and books and paper. Having a thousand friends was better than being able to paint with a flick of my fingers.

And, as I'd been told by my teachers in Liral, scribe magic was rare. Art magic was not. Hence the various starving artists that every city boasted.

There had been no artists in the north, I remembered unbidden. Immediately, I shut down that line of thought, instead turning to Rosaria. She flapped her hands at a few novices carrying scrolls and gossiping.

"Clear the room, if you please," Rosaria said, her voice never rising above a smooth dulcet, though there was an urgency to it that had the novices scrambling. The artists climbed down from their scaffolding. The youngest, a boy of perhaps fifteen, gaped at me as he walked by. While there were many people from the north in the harbour cities, having fled the harsh winters for a chance at prosperity, there weren't many with my white-blonde hair. It was impossible to dye. I'd tried.

I smiled at the boy, all olive skin and dark curls, and he

flushed fiercely before scrambling off to stand next to his companions.

"*The others are prepared?*" I asked, fingers waving. This flurry of movement earned more stares from the artist boy, who had likely never seen anyone use the signed language before. It wasn't common, though it was more so in the Great Archives, where silence was valued in times of study. I often received stares when signing. I tried to ignore the familiar flush to my cheeks and focused my attention on Rosaria, keeping my smile pleasant and interested.

I was safe in the Archives, I reminded myself. The people here liked me. They didn't care that I didn't talk since I made myself valuable in other ways. I was safe here.

Rosaria nodded. "They're prepared," she said. Her hands fidgeted with the dark blue wool of her dress, the standard Archivist uniform. My own dress was banded at the cuffs with red trim, a sign of my status as a scribe as well as Archivist.

I raised my hands, ink-stained and with one paper cut that I got that morning, and closed my eyes. Slowly, so as not to overwhelm me, I lowered the walls in my mind, brick by brick. Whispers began to fill the empty spaces, some too quiet to understand, others all but shouting as they tried to convey their information. I mentally hushed them. Words swam before my eyes, an endless stream of ink in a thousand different hands and some in the new typed-face pieces that were coming out of the presses invented a handful of years ago.

I slowed the stream of words, calling for quiet from all

the written words in the Great Archive. The entire building fell quiet, even more than usual, as the books lapsed into silence. I heard a gasp from a young girl as the unnatural silence fell over the building. An Archivist shushed her, and I returned my thoughts to the books.

Laws, please, I murmured in my thoughts. *Regarding the stabling and keeping of horses. Also, information on the garrisoning of troops not of Vazeri. Supply lists, dates, where the troops were from.*

The books rustled and shifted. I felt a tug at the back of my mind and turned to face that part of the building. Raising my hands higher, I beckoned with my fingers. Deep in the Great Archives, the ink on the pages I needed responded to my magic. I beckoned with my fingers again, and they flew from their shelves, soaring through the air towards me.

A mild curse caught my attention as one of the books swooped over the head of Central Archivist Mariam. A cat, black as night and with golden eyes, swatted at a scroll that disturbed his slumber. I smiled and continued calling the ink to me.

Another moment passed, then several books and about fifteen scrolls *whooshed* into the atrium, landing in a neat pile at Rosaria's feet. I opened my eyes, releasing my magic and rebuilding my mental walls. The books all started whispering again, no longer bound by me, and I lowered my arms, suddenly tired.

"Thank you," Rosaria said, already waving over the novices to help carry the books for her. "Dinner, I promise!"

Then, without a second glance, she bustled off, leaving me alone in the atrium. The smile faded from my lips.

I smoothed my shaking hands over my skirts and tried to centre myself again. It always took a few minutes after opening myself to the entirety of the Great Archives, but I catalogued the pieces that made me human and not ink.

Hair, white-blonde strands messy, hanging loose over my shoulders.

Dress, tight at the bodice and loose at my legs, with a large pocket sewn into the side seam to carry a notebook or pencil. Two red lines at the cuffs to indicate my magic.

Shoes, the left one a little worn, my toe just about breaking through the supple leather. I sighed. I would need new shoes, which meant shopping, which meant leaving the Great Archive building.

Paper cut, still stinging. It had been a particularly deep one, and my first paper cut in *years*. I had been horrified to know that I'd bled on a book, but it was old, dusty and hadn't been touched in ages before I reshelved it and told no one. Besides, I'd blotted the blood away with a handkerchief as quickly as I could. I was a scribe and an Archivist, not a terrified noviciate who would get rapped over the knuckles for even wrinkling a page. No one would mind, surely. Would they?

I opened my eyes and found myself looking directly into the deep brown ones of Beltran.

"I wondered when you would awaken," he teased. I flushed, my face heating and surely showing a bright red.

Beltran, he of the sculpted features, olive skin and curly

hair that was common to the original Vazeri citizens, was a city guardsman assigned to the Council building. He wore the copper-brown breeches and tunic of the guard, shot through with gold where the threads caught the light. It was a mage-woven piece, and almost as good as armour. At his waist, he bore the cudgel and short sword of his station. The two golden stars at his shoulders indicated his rank. He was, in essence, nothing more than an ordinary guardsman patrolling the streets around the Council building, including the Great Archive.

Except when he smiled. His entire face lit up and joy poured from every movement. He had a fierce sense of humour and was quick with a joke and a helping hand. He also had taken the time to learn sign language so he could talk with me.

One day, I vowed I would use my real voice with him, prove that my anxiety wouldn't keep me from normal relationships, from sharing my soul with someone. From belonging to a world outside of ink and paper.

There weren't many I spoke vocally with, but I knew that one day, Beltran would be one of them. My throat would no longer close and the words would just escape with ease. No sweat down my back, no fear, no trembling hands. Just me, my voice, and him.

That day, though, the words stayed trapped, so I raised my hands. *"Do you need something from the Archives?"* I asked, trying to keep my grin demure and friendly rather than overeager. *"I just found a book about lemon trees, if you want to improve your garden."*

Beltran winced even as he laughed. "No, no, dear gods above no. My garden will remain empty and bare so long as I have anything to do with it."

I'd teased him about his gardening skills since he brought me a bouquet of flowers a year ago on my birthday and asked if they came from his garden. Beltran was, apparently, the only person besides myself in all of the hills and terraces of Vazeri who couldn't garden.

I waited for him to give his reason for being here. He'd never come into the Archives before without an excuse, usually fetching some small document for the guards' station, or deciphering a written report that had handwriting so appalling that most Archivists wept in frustration. I liked the small tasks that Beltran brought; there were many other Archivists that could have helped him, but he always asked for me.

"My sister, Carine, has her first performance with the Vazeri opera this weekend. I was told that she would be embarrassed if I made a fuss, so naturally, I am inviting everyone I know." Beltran produced a square of parchment written in gilded ink, bearing the official crest of the Vazeri Operatic and Artistic Guild.

I hadn't known that his sister was in the opera. I wondered how long she'd been rehearsing. Maybe it was a secret, a surprise. *"I would be delighted,"* I signed. *"What part does she play?"*

Beltran grinned, handing over the invitation. "She's been an apprentice with them for years now, but this is her first performance outside her apprenticeship. They've given her second lead!"

I blinked. How had I not known his sister had apprenticed with the opera?

"That's amazing!" I tried to convey my enthusiasm in my smile and a quick bob of my head, but my fingers faltered in their dancing. Beltran didn't seem to notice. I shook off my confusion. It wasn't like we had spent a great deal of time together outside of the Archives. Occasionally, he would walk me back to the building if I were out on an errand. Once, we even crossed paths in the market after I'd purchased some fennel for a soup I was making. He'd carried it home for me. But time enough to discuss our families? No, we had never had that.

This could be our chance to change things.

"Thank you," Beltran said. "It will mean so much to have people there for her, even if I am making a fuss. It is the prerogative of brothers, after all!"

He started to turn away and my heart lurched. I wasn't ready for him to go quite yet. I moved my fingers in a flurry of movement, making sure he had to stay to see every word. *"How are things in the guard? I heard that the quartering of Makhierian soldiers was making things difficult."*

Beltran's expression darkened. He looked around the atrium, watching the artists as they returned to their paint and a couple of novices scurried about their business like the Great Archive cats after a mouse. He took a step closer. My throat tightened and my cheeks grew warm.

"Just between you and me, the whole thing's a mess," he

said in a low voice. Distaste twisted his features. "They've brought in the Makhierians for protection against raids from the Northern Reaches. Supposedly. There have been reports—no, *rumours*—of raids making it past the mountains and into some of the smaller villages in the hills. No harbour cities have been hit yet, but Vazeri has only the guard and..." He shrugged expressively.

"*And they can afford the protection,*" I signed. Vazeri was notorious for its wealth, from the concentration of mages to the trade of goods and crafts that were mage-made. It was, undoubtedly, the most influential of the harbour cities.

"It's hard enough policing the streets given the unrest with the missing people, but with Makhierians wandering about?" Beltran shook his head, running a hand through his dark curls. "We've had to arrest at least a dozen already, and our jails aren't big enough for this. Some people blame them for the missing people, though that started months before they arrived. No new ones in a fortnight, thank the gods. But the Makhierian presence does not help with suspicions, or the fact that we have no evidence. Not to mention the fact that they brought horses, the fools. Everyone knows that the hills of Vazeri are too steep for horses. They have to go around the entire city just to get from the Council building to the harbour. There are proposals with the triumvirate right now to open up part of the boundary wall!"

I winced, more on his behalf than any real opinion of my own. Certainly, it was nearly impossible to get a horse to climb the hills and switchback streets of the city; that was why we had the mage-powered lifts, for the goods and people who couldn't easily climb the streets. I wouldn't want to deal with that logistical nightmare. Beltran studied me and sighed.

"You don't want to know all this," he said, reaching out and squeezing my arm. My face burned with heat, and I'm sure I was the colour of the poppies that ringed the boundary wall. My arm all but tingled where he touched it. He shook his head. "Besides, these fools are worried about raids from the Northern Reaches when they should be worried about the Imaran Empire. No one ever believes they'll cross those mountains, I suppose, what with the magical barrier. But there's always the sea. Ah, what do I know? I've never even been beyond the boundary wall except for that ill-fated fishing expedition with my father."

I gave a sympathetic smile, but I hadn't heard that story, either. I tried to quiet my restless thoughts by telling myself that we would have time for that at the opera. And afterwards, there would be time for a lot of things.

Beltran took a step back. "Thanks for letting me talk your ear off, Elyria. You're such a good listener."

Without appearing to see me flinch, he turned and left the Archives, looking more frustrated than he had been before. I thumbed the gilded invitation in my hands and listened to the whispers of the ink. Then, before I shifted the ink into something foolish like a love letter I would never be brave enough to send, I tucked it into my pocket and tried to forget about it.

The invitation sang to me for the rest of the day.

CHAPTER 2

I spun around my small apartment in the light blue dress before facing the other Archivist. Margarethe wrinkled her nose and shook her head.

"That's more suitable for Temple Day than it is an opera," she said. I huffed and reached behind me to undo the laces.

"That's the last one I have besides Archive uniforms," I said, voice quiet. Margarethe was a year older than me, tall to my short, muscular to my willowy frame, and with rich mahogany skin and a mass of curly black hair. She had also been a noviciate at Liral, sent there from the Akopa Islands after her father suffered a fishing accident and her parents couldn't afford to keep her any longer. She'd been irritable and sullen as a child, and had been sent to keep me company as punishment while I lay in the sickbed during my months of recovery. The two outcasts of Liral, both from elsewhere, labelled difficult—she for her anger, me for my silence—we became best friends. She was also one of the only people with whom I felt comfortable enough to speak.

"We'll have to go shopping tomorrow." She took the dress from me and hung it back in the armoire. I pulled on my nightgown and hugged a worn wrapper around me. "There won't be any time for tailoring, but it will have to do."

My heart dropped. "I hate shopping," I said, speaking to the floor. Margarethe snorted inelegantly before shoving a glass of wine under my nose.

"Your hatred of shopping is a well-known and indisputable fact. However, if you want to inspire poetry from your beloved Beltran, then shopping it will be. Or would you rather he see you in the dress you wear to the Temple of Night every Temple Day?"

I drank the wine and ignored the question. "Fine," I said. "But you do all the talking."

"Don't I always?" Margarethe asked with a smug expression. "How else are we to get the best bargains?"

She sank into one of the chairs by my small window. I lived, like most Archivists, as near to the Great Archives as possible. In my case, because I was both scribe and mute to all the world but a couple of trusted people, I was allowed to stay directly next door in a small collection of apartments reserved for those Archivists who could not manage the walk across the city, or were important enough to be called on at midnight. Unfortunately, I was one of the latter, especially when an urgent message came from the triumvirate for a book or record. I never had the heart to refuse and had spent many nights in the Archives searching through texts.

The apartment was only now, after two years, beginning to suit my tastes. The furniture was simpler than most found in Vazeri, and though I kept writing supplies close at hand, there weren't more than a half-dozen books in the rooms. I liked having the voices of my favourite texts at hand, but too many would keep me from sleep.

Some of my better drawings were tacked to the walls. I especially liked my study of a lemon tree on the hills of Vazeri. But the sharp ink spines of trees laden with snow remained my best work, no matter the pangs it gave me. I turned away from that particular drawing and sat on my bed.

The invitation sat on my desk, whispering in dulcet tones and making my stomach clench in anticipation.

"I see you got another letter," Margarethe said, nodding to the folded parchment beside the invitation. I had been ignoring the whispers of that particular letter for about a week, shutting its voice down beneath the pleasant murmur of my other texts. It would only wait so long, though.

"Yes," I said, lifting a hand and calling the letter to me. It unfolded with disturbing eagerness, the ink fairly shimmering as it started to tell me its contents.

"Do you want me to read it?"

I hunched my shoulders. "You don't need to do that for me."

She snorted. "Trust me, you've dealt with plenty of my

own letters from family, or my lack thereof. The least I can do is be there for you."

Seven siblings kept her parents busy, I knew. She received a letter about once a year for her birthday, and the last one had been sent three months late. She always said I was her sister, that she didn't need anyone else, but I knew how her dark days could swallow her whole. My family problems were nothing in comparison. I smiled weakly, then shook my head. "I'll do it this time."

She waited patiently for me to open the parchment and begin reading. It began as it always did, in a looping, coarse hand that was easy to read and very clear as to the abrupt nature of its writer.

Dear Cousin,

In response to your last letter, which I received two months after sending my own, I have the unfortunate task of telling you that no news has been received from your parents. They have ventured on an expedition into the barren Great Plains and have not been heard from since.

There is, I believe, no reason to think that they have been brought to any harm. It is more likely that there is no easy way to send post except by falcon, and that they are saving that for an emergency. I realise now that it has been nearly fifteen years since you have seen your parents and am sorry that their ventures keep them away.

Should you wish to return home, I will be more than happy to receive you. Summerfell is always open to you, for you are to me as a sister.

Yours in affection,

I snorted and shoved the letter at Margarethe. She took the parchment and smoothed the wrinkles before reading, an aspect of Archivist training that was instinctual to us all. Then, she too snorted and tossed the letter in the general vicinity of the window.

"What an ass," she said. "To call you out for not writing, then telling you about your parents like that. No expedition to the Great Plains has ever been heard from again, yet he dismisses your concern like it's nothing!"

"That's Alar for you," I said. "Ever proper, ever unconcerned."

I hadn't seen my cousin for fifteen years, either, but at least he didn't mention that. He'd only started writing me after his father died some seven years back, and I'd been both pleased and confused by the renewed contact with my cousin. Since then, I'd given up all hope that communication between us would be anything more than stiff and formal. His occasional invitation to return to Summerfell was always ignored by me; his letters gave me no desire to return. My less common invitations for him to visit me were also ignored. I was obviously not wanted there. Besides, I had Margarethe and my work and, hopefully, soon, Beltran to keep me company. I didn't need Alar and his disapproval.

I stared at the crumpled ball of paper, calling to it with my magic. It rose into the air and smoothed, every wrinkle disappearing. The ink warped on the page, twisting and shifting until it read an entirely different message than the one that had been sent. I let it land on Margarethe's lap. She picked it up and read.

"Dear Cousin, Kindly remove the stick from your ass about my family. Yours, Elyria." She barked out a laugh and happily let the paper go when I had my magic shred it into tiny pieces, floating them out the window to be picked up by the breeze off the ocean. "You could just shorten that sentence and remove the bit about your family."

I downed the rest of my wine. "I'll write a proper to him after the opera. Maybe some inane chatter about the wonders of Vazeri will have him stop asking for me to return to Summerfell."

Margarethe reached for my hand and squeezed. "I am sorry about your parents."

I waited for the familiar squeeze in my heart at my anxiety for them, but there was only emptiness. "I think…" Tears filled my eyes and my throat closed up. I lifted my hands to sign. *"I think that maybe I mourned for them a long time ago. I think that maybe they were lost to me from the moment I was sent away from Summerfell. Maybe they deserve their fate. And maybe that makes me a terrible person for thinking it."*

"Oh, Elyria, no," Margarethe said, bright eyes wide. "You have every right to be angry with them. To want nothing to do with them. They were your parents and they left you. Abandoned you. After what happened…well, you have every right to distance yourself from your family. Don't let their expectations twist you into something you're not."

I wrapped my arms around myself, forcing the words out. "And if I don't want them to be dead?"

Margarethe moved from her chair and slipped her arms around me. I leaned into her and let the tears trickle down my face even as I tried my best to hold them back.

"I don't think wishing someone, anyone, not dead, is a bad thing, Elyria. You're a good person, okay? It's annoying sometimes," she said. I laughed weakly.

"Now, let's discuss our plan for tomorrow, because if we don't pick out the right places to go then we can't plan our day around the best bakeries."

I laughed again and let the subject change, fears for my family, frustration with my reticent cousin, all of it fall away.

"You could try something other than blue," Margarethe said as I fingered the sleeve of a navy blue gown with sheer panels at the back. I shot her a glare. "There's green. Or, look, that purple is lovely!"

The shopkeeper, a bent old woman with wild white curly hair and wrinkled brown skin, nodded eagerly. "You would look stunning in the purple. Such a rare colour, and with your light hair, you would be the most beautiful crea-ture at the opera."

I studied the purple dress. It was, as they said, very beau-tiful. Dark purple, with cap sleeves, and a bevvy of imprac-tical skirts, it would certainly draw attention. And I did want to draw attention, but only Beltran's. Having other people's eyes on me made me nervous, exasperated the anxiety that had stolen my voice. I hated it when people stared, even as I longed for their acknowledgement, their approval.

I shook my head and reached for the green. It was simpler, similar to the blue, with long sleeves, a high neck, and skirts that wouldn't trip me. There were some gold beads at the cuffs and collar, which was enough to add more of the interest I hoped would draw Beltran's attention. Draw and hold it. I held it up for Margarethe to examine.

"It's very nice," she said, but there was a frown line between her brows. I tilted my head, not wanting to sign. "Well, it's just a little...plain."

First she dismissed the blue and now the green. This was our third stop after the first one was too busy for either of us to even look at the gowns, and the second had nothing within my price range. This was our last stop, our last chance before we had to actually get back to the Archives for the evening shift.

"What you need is to dazzle," the shopkeeper agreed. "You are so striking that the other beauties of Vazeri can hardly compare. Make sure that they look at you with jeal-ousy or desire, not..."

I could fill in the gaps and barely hid a scowl. I hated being sold to. My neck started to ache, spreading tension into my shoulders. I was quickly running out of patience. I took a deep breath and turned to look at my other options. There were gowns more fit for a ball than an evening at the opera. Gowns for a wedding. Gowns for the elegant and rich and those who sought out the attention. I just wanted something simple. Something that wouldn't draw too much attention.

Blindly, I pointed to the end of a rack containing simpler things. The shopkeeper frowned, then at Margarethe's stern look, shuffled over and pulled out a black piece. It looked like velvet, and had the same long sleeves and high neckline I preferred, but the back dipped low and the skirts were fuller than the others.

"*Fine,*" I signed in a flurry, not caring about whether it was plain or boring. "*That's fine.*"

The shopkeeper blinked at me in astonishment. She whirled to Margarethe. "She's deaf? I thought that she was just quiet, but—"

"She's right there," Margarethe snapped, snatching the dress. "She can hear you. Not everyone who signs is deaf, and even if she were, she's still *right there.*"

I dug out the appropriate number of coins while the shopkeeper fiddled with her apron and spluttered any number of responses, none of which was an apology. We fled the shop soon after, the dress tucked into my basket without a care for wrinkles.

"I hate it when people do that!" Margarethe seethed,

glaring at a group of teenagers as they gathered outside a bakery. They scattered as we passed and I ducked my head so they wouldn't look at me. "They're perfectly fine to talk with you while they think you're just shy, but as soon as you start signing, as soon as you are even the slightest bit different—"

I put my hand on her arm and she stopped, eyes squeezed shut. "I'm fine," I assured her in a whisper only she would hear. No one in the busy street even bothered to look at the two Archivists paused at the edge of the bakery. "It was just a dress."

"I could tell you were uncomfortable," Margarethe said in a huff. "And I hate that people treat you differently because of your silence."

Of course I was uncomfortable. I was always uncomfortable. I flinched at the slightest unexpected sound and I scurried away when people touched me. These same reactions were part of why I didn't speak except in select circumstances with select people. I *knew* I was different, and I accepted I was different. People treating me as such was unsurprising. I tried to make myself useful so they would look beyond my differences, and in the Archives, I liked to consider myself invaluable.

"*I know you care,*" I signed. "*I know that you want everyone to treat me normally, but some people just...won't.*" I hesitated, then pulled my fingers together in the unique sign for her name. "*Margarethe, you are a generous soul, and you wish the world better than it was. I love you for that.*"

She sighed, some of the anger melting from her shoulders. "I love you too, Elyria. You're my best friend. Just...I wish you wouldn't make yourself smaller for those fools. I wish you could be accepted for yourself."

"*I know,*" I signed, then slipped my arm through hers and tugged her back up the hill towards the Great Archive building. Within a few steps, the confrontation was forgotten and Margarethe described a new pastry she had tried at a bakery by the harbour. By the time we reached the summit, my legs were burning and I was trying not to gasp for breath. Even two years in the city hadn't made me accustomed to climbing to the highest point nearly every day.

I left Margarethe and stowed the dress, taking some care to smooth out the fabric as I hung it in preparation for Saturday. I hoped that Beltran would like it. Well, I hoped that he would more than like it.

The Archives were reasonably quiet that evening. It was a Wednesday, and most people were returning documents without checking anything else out. The clerks handled that, preparing carts for me to shelve. I did so automatically, letting the whispers of the ink guide my hands while my thoughts drifted.

As night fell and the city of Vazeri grew quiet, I retreated into the depths of the stacks, shelving books and records in a quiet meditation. The last clerk pushed a cart towards me when I emerged again, looking weary.

"This is the last of them. We're going home for the evening. The monitors are locking everything up. You'll be okay?" he asked. Jeremiah, I thought his name was. He was relatively new, despite being near his fifth decade of life. He must have transferred from one of the other harbour cities, or perhaps from one of the small hill villages.

I nodded and smiled as I took the cart. He didn't question me further, for which I was grateful, and then I was left to my own devices.

Nighttime, after all the other Archivists had left, and the monitors locked up for the evening, was when I felt truly relaxed. I lowered some of the barriers surrounding my magic and let the whispers of the books fill my mind. Sometimes, I just sat in the section with great novels and epics and folklore and let a book tell me a story. Sometimes, I shut all of the noise out and focused merely on the task of reading. Or, at times like that night, I walked through the building, straightening spines, fixing misshelved titles, organising the vast collection of records to make it easier for the other Archivists.

I descended the steps to the lowest levels of the Archive, humming quietly. This was where they kept the oldest documents, those that needed a controlled climate and lighting. These documents and books and scrolls whispered to me in tongues that had long been forgotten, translating in my thoughts with ease. I shuddered at some of the things that were written there, some of the terrible histories that were oft forgotten.

I turned the corner to a small collection of shelves designed with a honeycomb pattern, perfect for storing scrolls. The last item for shelving slipped neatly into the topmost honeycomb. Done. Everything was in order and, with aching feet, I was ready to go back to my apartment and collapse.

I turned, letting out an audible curse when I saw a great black cat with long fur and bright golden eyes staring at me. He flicked his tail.

"Apologies," I said, inclining my head to the cat. "I'll let you get on with your mousing."

The cat—one of many that roamed the Archives and kept them free of vermin—yawned, showing sharpened fangs. Then, flicking his tail again, he twitched an ear, and said, "I think it time that you and I talked."

It was the first time I could recall that noise escaped me in a fit of fear instead of being pulled inside. I screamed.

CHAPTER 3

I stumbled backwards, slamming into the honeycomb shelves. Only a flare of my scribe magic kept the scrolls from falling on the floor, though there was nothing I could do about the wobbling shelf. I slid to the floor and gaped at the cat.

He twitched his whiskers in what I could only call amusement. Indignation flared in me a moment later. He was *laughing* at me. Confusion followed indignation and I could do nothing but stare.

"You humans are such a dramatic species," he said, licking a paw. "One would think you had never encountered magic before."

"It's not magic I'm concerned with," I said, too startled to be silent. "It's the fact that you're a *talking cat.*"

He heaved a sigh. "I can only talk with *you*. And it is a recent development, thank goodness. I'm not sure I could stand dealing with your ridiculous prattling for the last two years."

My jaw dropped. Perhaps I had slipped on the tile flooring and hit my head. Perhaps I was in bed in my apartment, dreaming. Or perhaps I had just been insulted by a cat. As unlikely as it was, the latter scenario was the most probable, given that I wasn't prone to slipping or hysterical dreams. Though, I wouldn't entirely rule out simple insanity.

"How?" I asked.

"I am bound to the Archives, and I have been for longer than you can comprehend. It is my sanctuary, and the home of my magic. Now that you, too, are bound to this place, then we are able to communicate."

"Bound to this place?" I wasn't bound here; I'd been in and out of the Archives for the last two years, and before that I had been in and out of the Archive in Liral. I was bound nowhere.

"You are possessed of scribe magic, are you not? And you bled on a book, did you not? You are bound." The cat flicked an ear at me, sounding almost bored with this discussion. But there was something in those golden eyes that was intent. Far more than I would expect given his tone.

Then, I realised what he had said. I bled on a book. My paper cut, which still stung when I moved my finger wrong. I had bled a single droplet onto a book. I'd cleaned it up, but apparently that didn't matter. With my magic, rare as it was, it must have been enough to do exactly as the cat said. I was bound to the Archives.

What did that even mean? I could leave freely; I'd done so earlier that day without issue. Was my magic bound here? My soul? My fate?

"Oh gods," I said, burying my head in my hands.

I felt the pressure of paws on my legs. "The gods will not help you," the cat said. I lifted my head and found myself nose to nose with the feline. He studied me, pupils narrowed into slits, then nodded.

"Well, at least you're not completely useless," he said, dropping back to all fours. "It will be good to have someone with thumbs around. You will require training, of course, but that can't be helped. Now, get up. The monitors will have heard you scream."

"I can't believe I'm listening to a talking cat," I muttered to myself as I stood and brushed off my skirts. I desperately hoped the monitors hadn't heard my screams. Telling them that I'd been startled by a cat was not something I wanted to explain.

"Ah, yes, that is the other thing. I will not be referred to as 'cat'. I am the more capable species, and my knowledge is certainly greater than yours. I am Claw That Writes With Ink. Since you are a foolish human who can barely remember a century's worth of history, you may call me Ink."

I could recall several history books with considerably more history than a century's worth, but I didn't want to argue with a cat. No more than I already was, that is. "Ink, then," I said, following him up the stairs. "I am Elyria Trevain."

"Charmed, I'm sure," he said drily, tail lashing.

The monitors had heard me scream, as it turned out. They were running for the stairs with magelights extended, ready to battle whatever demons haunted the Archives at night. They skidded to a halt before me, nearly trampling Ink, who hissed.

I tripped over the cat, I signed to the younger one, whose shoulders sagged with relief. He turned to the older one.

"Just a cat. Again. That's the third time this year that we've had people tripping over them."

Ink sneezed, wrapping his tail over his paws.

The older monitor glared at him, stuffing his magelight into his belt. "We should just get rid of the lot of them, given how much trouble they cause. We can't spell the place against motion at night like most buildings because they roam around. It makes our job so much harder. And for what?"

Cats are sacred to Night, I signed, naming one of the four gods. *They are creatures of silence and death, and they have guarded the Archives for centuries against vermin. Or would you rather deal with rats?*

The younger monitor flushed before muttering a translation to his companion. The older man huffed, glared at Ink, then jerked his head in a nod at me. "If you don't mind, Archivist, we'll let you out for the night and get on with our rounds. You are the last one in the building."

I nodded and followed the monitors to the side entrance which led into the shared courtyard of my building. Ink followed behind, stopping at the door and staring out into the night, eyes glowing faintly.

"Have a care, Elyria Trevain," he said as the monitors closed the door on him. There was none of that dry arrogance in his voice now. Just an intensity that had shivers running up my spine. "Rarely do circumstances such as these come about by chance."

The doors to the Archives slammed shut and I was left in the courtyard, the scent of lemon and mint filling the air where parchment and paper had done so only moments ago. I shivered, though the night was not cold. Ink's words felt like a warning. But a warning about what, I didn't know. No, I must have been dreaming. That was all.

Saturday came with a bundle of nerves tightening my stomach and closing my throat almost entirely. By the time I had put on the dress and fixed my hair on the top of my head with a hair stick, I was almost nauseous. Margarethe had offered to help me get ready, but I'd refused. I was too excited. Too nervous.

As I passed by the Great Archive building to the nearest lift station, I could have sworn I saw the glittering golden eyes of Ink. He hadn't spoken with me since our first encounter, and I almost believed that I *had* dreamed the whole thing, but he was always there in the Archives when I worked. Silently following me, hiding in the shadows. His presence did *not* help my nerves at all.

The lift attendant opened the small gate to the wooden platform, smiling pleasantly as I stepped on. I lifted a single finger to indicate one level and the attendant nodded. He closed his eyes and raised his hands. I could see sweat beading on his brow as he called to his magic and lowered the platform down the stone walls that held up the tiered city. A weaker mage, then, or exhausted by the day's work. I inclined my head in thanks, paid with a coin, and departed into the Arts level of Vazeri.

This level of the city was as fine as the governing level at the crest of the hill. Finer, perhaps. Everywhere there were carvings of angels or dragons or hounds on a hunt, or dancing mages. Stories played out in stone all over the buildings, flowing from one intricate piece to the next. Frescoes peeked out from between the buildings, indicating secret grottos and gardens where more beauty could be found. Artists sat on the street corners or at cafes, talking about art, performing simple dances. A few art mages plied their magic, drawing quick charcoal sketches of passers-by in the hopes of earning coin. It was a hive of activity, even as the sun dipped below the horizon. My nerves shifted more to excitement.

I climbed the rise to the end of the Art level and found myself gaping up at the opera house. It towered above the other buildings, domed and gleaming with gold plating. There were dozens of statues along the roofline: the four gods, Night, Day, Dawn and Dusk; horses drawing dark coaches; roaring dragons; singing angels. I passed through the towering columns holding up the entrance and was greeted by decadence and excess. The ceiling had been painted in a vast mural. The walls were colourful silk paper. The floor was polished marble. The building itself, though, could do nothing to compare to the myriad of people that filled the space.

They milled about, greeting each other and talking while they waited for the bell to tell them to take their seats. They wore finery the likes of which I couldn't fathom; certainly what I had seen in the shops were almost drab compared to this. Sheer fabrics and decadent silks, velvets in a range of vast colours. Gold and silver beading, crystals on hems, jewellery at every throat. The men wore tunics and jackets that were just as colourful as the women, and preened just as much.

I was vastly underdressed. I didn't even have any jewels to gleam and glitter. Just my black dress. Beltran would never notice me in all of this.

"Elyria!"

I spun around and saw Beltran in a corner by the entrance, jumping up and down and waving frantically, grinning widely. He wore a green tunic that was—thankfully—far simpler than most of the other attendees. There were a few people beside him, including a man with slicked back curly hair that surely had to be related to him, and a golden-skinned woman with soft curves and the swell of pregnancy beneath her blue-and-gold robes. His family.

I hurried over, slipping through the throng of people

until I was drawn into the family circle. I smiled widely and, to my surprise, felt words on my tongue. I was about to greet them, greet *him*, when he wrapped his arm around the pregnant woman and beamed at me.

"Elyria, I'm so glad you came. This is Sabine, my wife, and my brother, Augustus. Everyone, this is my Archivist friend, Elyria. The one I told you about."

My heart shattered. My vision swam. The words on my tongue vanished. Even my hands, always the reliable means of communication, trembled.

Augustus took my hand and bowed, formal and stiff. "A pleasure. You are the reason he learned the signed language? We must all thank you for that; it earned him a promotion just yesterday. Works directly with the triumvirate, now."

I stretched my mouth in a smile, but it didn't feel right. I hadn't even known he was up for a promotion to work with the triumvirate. There had been no mention of such a thing during our lessons and conversations in the signed language. But that wasn't the most significant thing about this situation. Not by far.

Sabine batted playfully at Augustus, a touch of familiarity and familial bonds. "What a thing to say at a first meeting! Elyria, my dear, there's no need to be nervous. Augustus means well, but he has absolutely no sense of decorum. We are all of us so grateful you came. You will have to stay with us after the performance to meet Carine. She wanted to come out beforehand, but has to get into costume."

I waved a hand, hopefully indicating that I didn't mind. My movements felt like treacle and the world swam around me.

Beltran was married.

Married.

In all our conversations, all the friendly gestures and eager smiles, I had never even *considered* this possibility. But it all made sense, now. Why he never invited me to meet his family, why he never bothered to meet me anywhere other than the Great Archives building, why his smiles were only ever friendly and not...more. Why, for all my hopes and eagerness, the shattered emotions were all one sided.

He never even realised that I cared for him like that, I saw. I could see it in the open affection as he looked at Sabine, in the way he caressed her shoulder with one hand and brushed her pregnant belly with the other. His eyes flicked to me for a brief instant before turning back to her, warm.

Oh gods, I was such a fool.

I was saved from further conversation by the bell for us to take our seats. I debated leaving for a moment, but I had already come, and there would be questions if I feigned a sudden illness. Questions I couldn't bring myself to answer.

I shoved down my emotions like I had so many times before. I ignored the sweat at the small of my back, the tension in my neck and shoulders. I ignored the churning of my stomach, the bile in my throat. Instead, I straightened my shoulders, smiled politely as Augustus offered me his arm, and followed along docilely as Beltran led the family up the grand staircase to our seats.

The opera was beautiful. Had I been paying any attention to the story, I would likely have wept, as Sabine did. I tried to focus on the brightly coloured costumes, the lament of the lovers on the stage, the deceit of the villain. My thoughts, though, wandered, and I had to force myself to focus on the stage every few minutes.

Not once, during the whole performance, did Beltran seem concerned at my inattention. Before that night, I would have thought he could spot any anxiety in me. I would have thought he knew me. Now, I realised that we barely knew each other. I was nothing more than his friend from the Archives. And I wasn't even sure I was that to him, now I knew of his promotion.

To think, I'd been so pleased that he wanted to learn to sign. I'd thought it a symbol of his affection.

He'd *used* me. I was worse than foolish. I was an idiot. So determined to please people, to be noticed, to have that affection that he had with Sabine. I wanted someone to see me for me, and instead I was here, thoughts racing, stomach churning, and completely invisible. Invisible and silent.

By the end of the opera, I was exhausted. I'd barely eaten that day due to excitement and nerves, and now I was practically shaking every time someone turned to look at me or brushed by me. I stood dutifully as the cast bowed, applauding without really hearing the sound. Then, finally, I was released from the prison of the seats and Beltran's family.

"You must stay to meet Carine," Sabine said again, putting a gentle hand on my arm and smiling warmly. I imagined she was a lovely person. The tiny lines at her eyes were from laughter, and the way she rested her hand on her unborn child was tender and loving. In another lifetime, I would have been happy to be her friend. At that moment, though, panic threatened to overwhelm me.

"*I must return home,*" I signed quickly. "*It is late and I have the morning shift.*"

Lies. I was scheduled for evening shift at the Archives, having switched with Rosaria in anticipation of spending a joyous evening talking with Beltran. I was going to be sick.

Sabine wrinkled her brow in confusion. She tugged on her husband's arm. "Beltran, we need a translator."

He turned from his conversation with Augustus and I swiftly repeated my signing, not slowing down to make certain he understood. I needed to escape. Immediately.

"You have to leave? That's a shame. Carine will be sad she missed you, especially after all the effort you made to be here." He looked a little disappointed, but only a little.

I shook my head. "*I have to leave,*" I insisted. Then, remembering my manners, I smiled at Sabine and Augustus. "*It was lovely to meet you both. Thank you for the invitation.*"

Beltran had barely finished translating before I slipped through the crowd and left him and his family behind. I made it all the way to the heavy wooden doors of the opera house before a tear fell from my eyes. From there, I made it up the hill to the lift before my eyesight grew watery. The lift mage didn't ask me any questions, just spared a sympathetic glance as I paid my fare, then I was racing along the street towards my apartments.

I saw a light glowing in the window next to mine and froze. Margarethe. She would hear me come in. She would know I was home. She would have questions.

I slipped into the courtyard and tried the Archive door. Locked. Sobs catching in my throat and stopping my breath, I fumbled in my bag for the small key. I had been issued it by the Central Archivist after three late night summonings by the triumvirate or council when they wanted a document not easily found. I was the only Archivist outside the ranks of the Central Archivists with a key, and until that moment had never abused it. I wanted to prove myself worthy of such a responsibility.

They had likely given me a key so I wouldn't interrupt anyone's sleep when I needed to work on a last-minute request, I thought bitterly.

I fumbled with the key, but the door swung open with ease, and I fled into the stacks. The whispers of the books were loud, too loud, pushing past my barriers as my emotions overtook me. I fled farther, deeper, ignoring the census counts and the entire section on taxes and tariffs. I kept moving to the depths of the Archives, nearly stumbling down the stairs until I was in the ancient section. Until I was in a room with scrolls and books so old that their whispers were barely audible.

There, I collapsed to the ground, wrapped my arms around my knees, and sobbed into the fine velvet dress.

A moment later, I felt the brush of fur against my fingers.

"What's wrong, Elyria Trevain?" Ink asked, pressing into my leg with his paw.

"Everything," I said in a stuttering voice. Ink said nothing, asked no questions, just curled up next to me and let me cry.

CHAPTER 4

*T*hree days passed in the blink of an eye and the slowness of time. I told no one but Ink the truth of what had happened that night, the true depths of my folly. He appeared to think that all humans were ridiculous, but whenever Beltran came to the Archives, Ink managed to be there and hissed at the guardsman.

To Margarethe, I had said only, "He's married," and then moved on. She tried to pry more out of me, tried to get me to talk about the opera over breakfasts of pastries or reshelving books or just in casual conversation, but I was an expert at avoiding unpleasant conversation and eventually she just let it drop, though she still watched me carefully, as if waiting for me to be ready to talk to her.

I tried to distract myself with other things, like research projects on binding magic, or trying to pry answers out of Ink. The cat, though keen on remaining my shadow, offered very little information. He preferred to order me about, requesting that I open doors or shoo other Archivists away from him. When pressed about the magic that now bound me to the Great Archives, he just sniffed, twitched his whiskers, and yawned. Most of the time, he acted very much like a cat, which is to say he was independent, taciturn, and particular. He also watched over me like a hawk and his constant presence was a balm to my anxiety.

In between keeping the books and dealing with the irascible Ink, I managed to piece together some of the broken pieces of my heart. The two times Beltran came and requested a document for the triumvirate, I was still there and still conversed with him. Somehow, holding him at the arms' length required to have a signed conversation was enough to keep me from breaking down again.

To him, nothing appeared to have changed. He smiled at me the same. Talked with me the same. He did not seem to notice anything. And why would he? After all, I had been the foolish one, not he.

One day, in the middle of a damp, grey day that had everyone in Vazeri grumpy at the loss of summer, Beltran came in looking more upset than could be explained by the weather. Ink wove around my ankles as I approached the guardsman.

"Elyria," he said, shoulder slumping in relief. "Thank the gods you're here."

Where else would I be? I signed, though thankfully the bitterness I felt at his question didn't come through my dancing fingers. It was one downside to the signed language; all tone had to come through facial expressions and I was too practised to let my real feelings show through. My fingers would never falter the way my voice did. I hoped.

"I need you to...do some research for me. Pull some books." He grabbed my arm and dragged me off to the corner of the Archives, looking grim. "Fast."

He wanted me to do a calling. To use my magic and find what he sought. It was common enough for the other Archivists to ask such things, but they usually prepared the way, clearing out unnecessary people or making an official request with the clerks. It wasn't a comfortable thing for the other Archivists when I took control of the books, and I was always weary afterwards. I was always happy to help the other Archivists; it was part of my job and I wanted to be helpful, show them why I was at the Great Archives instead of in one of the other branches in some small town. That Beltran wanted me to do a calling without any formal request or notice though, was not a good thing. I was tempted to turn away and leave him there. In spite of my anger, I couldn't bring myself to do it. Some habits were too ingrained to ignore.

Ink let out a low growl in his throat. Beltran glared at the cat.

"Damn that creature. It's dangerous to let a feral cat like that wander around where people might get hurt."

Ink took a menacing step forwards, claws scraping the marble floor.

"*What information do you need?*" I asked, ignoring his comment about Ink. If Beltran provoked Ink, I would not be held responsible. A small part of me wanted him to try something, to face some consequences for his actions. I squashed that thought down immediately.

Beltran dragged his eyes from Ink and frowned at me. He shifted, obviously uncomfortable. "I need...I need the information on any raids from the Northern Reaches."

I reared my head back as if he'd struck me. "*Why do you want that? Is it for the triumvirate?*"

They already had that information, I knew. The Great Archives kept copies of such reports on the top level, but the triumvirate never asked for them. At least, they hadn't in my time in Vazeri. They didn't need to. Most of it was hundreds of years old. There hadn't been a recent raid from the Northern Reaches in...well long before I was born, certainly. Alar and his father before him had managed the watch expertly. Nothing got through Summerfell, and the magical barrier on the mountains kept anything from crossing over them. No, the only way out was through, and that was impossible.

And yet, a small part of my mind said, the soldiers from Makhier were being garrisoned here. If not for a threat from the Northern Reaches, then why? Surely no one *actually* believed that the Imaran Empire to the east of the boundary mountains was a threat.

But then, Vazeri had no standing army apart from the guardsman. They were obviously preparing for something. The question was: what?

Beltran watched a clerk fill out a request slip from a

teenage girl, likely for some poetry or love story. My heart twisted at the thought. Beltran shook his head.

"Please," he said. "Just do it for me."

I scowled, not even dignifying that with an answer.

"Look, I can't *tell* you. Not everything. It's just…there are some things going on with the Makhierians and threats from Imara and—" He broke off, running his hand through his hair, obviously frustrated. "Please? For me?"

I folded my arms and waited. I wasn't going to do anything without an answer. He knew it.

"There have been more people going missing," he said under his breath. I blinked. Even Ink twitched an ear. "The other station houses have been ordered to keep it quiet, but there was a fourth just yesterday. A little girl."

"What does this have to do with the Northern Reaches?" I signed. *"Or the Imaran Empire?"*

"Nothing. Everything. I don't know. There were some runes at the places the people were taken and, well, everyone knows that runic magic died out when the Northern Reaches were sealed off except for Summerfell. It would be best if I could talk with the Baron of Summerfell, or even a soldier, but they're notoriously close lipped on such things. So I figured that I would look at the record of the raids and see if I could find a correlation. Because if there's no correlation, if there's no outside threat…Come on, Elyria, I need you. Please?"

I could fill in the gaps easily enough. If there was no outside threat, then it must be internal. And that was unthinkable.

Beltran, to my knowledge, rarely investigated crimes. He was tasked more often with protection and observation than investigation. That he was coming to me with an investigation now meant he was likely going behind the backs of his superiors. He truly did want to rule out any outside threats. Just in case, because the alternative…

My resolve softened. If he was coming to me for help, then it was important. And for all my misplaced hopes, he was a good person. A friend. Right?

"*I can look,*" I signed at last. Ink's eyes snapped to me and his tail lashed. "*I don't think you'll find anything. Raids haven't happened in a generation at least. And runic magic is an old topic, not often researched even by magic historians or Archivists.*"

"But you'll try?" Beltran put his hands on my shoulders as if he were going to hug me. I nodded. He grinned, a flash of his normal self, and then pulled away. "Thank you, Elyria. I'll come back later this afternoon for whatever you've found, okay?"

Before I could agree, he had turned on his heel and marched out the door into the rain.

"I don't like it," Ink said, the very tip of his tail twitching. "He's obviously doing this without permission. Not to mention the trouble you'll get into for this, which he absolutely knows."

"*Perhaps,*" I signed surreptitiously, hands by my skirts in case someone was watching and might think it strange to see me signing to a cat. "*But I can at least look.*"

Ink sniffed, flicked an ear, and stalked off, tail still

twitching. I guess that meant he disapproved. I wasn't surprised.

I waited until the lunch hour to perform the magic, and I did so subtly, quietly. While all the Archivists were out getting their food and eating far away from the precious books, I remained behind, ostensibly to be on hand should anyone need something. It was just me and a few clerks at the front desk, leaving the building remarkably quiet.

I started wandering about, brushing my fingertips over the spines of the books, directing my magic into a question. It was a longer process than simply demanding the information from the books all at once, since I had to listen to a thousand stories whisper in my head, the words running through my mind. It used more magic, too, meaning I would be beyond exhausted later. But I didn't have evening shift or morning shift tomorrow, so I could sleep.

The entire first floor was completely useless. There were a few histories on the Northern Reaches, and even one that delved into some theories about the magical barriers that existed in the two mountain ranges of the continent. It was generally known that it was a byproduct of whatever magical disaster had turned the Great Plains into a wasteland. The theories on that particular phenomenon were varied and vast, many of them ridiculous.

My parents had ventured into the Great Plains, I remembered. I ripped my hand away from the book and glared at it. It quieted immediately, almost apologetically, as if it knew the hurt it had caused for bringing up that particular memory.

"Researching Old Magic, are we?" Ink asked, padding towards me along the top of a shelf, tail held high. I looked around to be sure I was alone before I responded in a whisper.

"Looking for information about raids from the Northern Reaches," I said. "As Beltran asked."

Ink sat and liked a paw. "Pity. Knowledge about Old Magic would be more useful to you than favours for that snake. He cares naught for you, only what you can provide to him."

"What is Old Magic?" I asked, pointedly ignoring his comments about Beltran. Damn that cat, he had piqued my curiosity. "I've never heard of it."

Ink scoffed. "Of course you haven't. It existed before your four gods. Why *would* you know about it?" He blinked, long and slow and sad, then looked away. His tail twitched a moment too slow to feel natural.

Before the gods? Now he was being ridiculous. Night was the oldest of the four, followed by Dawn and Day and Dusk. They divided the world into equal parts, from the seasons to the stages of life, to the living and dead. There wasn't anything *before* them.

I shook my head at Ink and started walking again, listening for anything about the Northern Reaches. Apart from the few history books, though, there wasn't anything. I started for the upper levels, where a lot of the mundane records were kept. Ink followed on silent paws, practically radiating disapproval. I ignored him.

I ignored him all through the tax records, the conscription information for soldiers going to the watch, the various trade agreements between Summerfell and the harbour cities, all of it. It was useful only to clerks and bureaucrats, and had absolutely nothing to do with raids. The entire second floor was empty of information on any raids at all, past or present, and I was getting a headache.

"You should rest before you burn yourself out," Ink said, stopping me before I started down the stairs. He stood in the middle of the landing, lashing tail making it impossible for me to descend.

"I need to check the basement," I said, trying to step around him. The cat stood and arched his back.

"If you try, I will weave between your legs and make you fall down the stairs."

"Don't be absurd," I snapped. "I'm fine. I have done much more with my magic than this."

Ink glared, narrowing his golden eyes. "That was before you were bound to *my* Archive. To *me*. You are my responsibility, now, and I must make certain you take care of yourself." For an instant, he sounded as though he cared. "Scribes are extremely rare; I have no desire to wait around for another. Or are you so determined to help a man who lied to you that you will burn through your magic without a second thought?"

I blew out a breath and ran my hand through my hair. This cat was beyond exasperating. But, having been tripped by other mousers before, I wasn't in the mood to test him. I'd once nearly given myself a black eye and a sprained wrist from dodging an over-eager tabby. Ink stared, muscles tense and poised to pounce. I believed that he would do it, too.

"Fine," I huffed and sat on the stair beside him. Ink lifted his chin and gave me a smug look. I rubbed my chest, trying to relieve the ache there, though I knew it wasn't physical.

"You will discover that I am only looking out for your wellbeing, Elyria Trevain."

I scoffed, fiddling with the red stripes at my cuffs. "Oh, yes, you're looking after my wellbeing by keeping me in the dark on this binding to the Archives situation. I've done research, and there is *nothing* in any of the books on magic about binding. Well, except early scribes learning the art of book binding."

Ink crouched down, tucking his paws beneath him. He nudged my hand with his head and I started scratching his ears. "I told you that you should look into Old Magic."

"Yes, exactly ten minutes ago," I countered. "And, trust me, I've looked. There isn't anything in the Archives on Old Magic. I don't understand what's going on, but if I'm to be *bound*, I would like to understand what it means, and why."

The cat studied me for a minute, eyes narrow slits, ears back. Then, he sighed, and he sounded sad. "The Old Magics come from before your four gods. It came from the beings before. Gods, if you will, though the true name for their kind was lost long ago."

"There were other gods before the four?" I was aghast and disbelieving. I thought he'd been joking before. Now, I wasn't so sure. The four had created the world. They had divided the day. Made the cycle of all things. How could they have a before?

Ink merely twitched his whiskers. "Belief and truth are two sides of the same coin, scribe. If enough people believe something long enough, it becomes their truth. Such it is with the gods."

"But you're saying that Night and Day and Dawn and Dusk didn't—"

"They were not the first," Ink said. "Nor will they be the last, though whoever comes afterwards will likely usurp their place as the first."

My headache was getting worse, and it had nothing to do with magic use. I felt like something fundamental had been torn out of me. Not my heart, for that was still broken on the floor of the opera house where I'd left it. No, this was like seeing my home burn down around me, even though there was no one inside. I wasn't particularly devout, certainly, but I attended Night's temple every Temple Day. This was a fundamental truth of life as I knew it, that the gods had created everything.

"How can you just say that the gods are lying?" I croaked.

"I never said they were," Ink mewed. "I said they depend on belief, which is an entirely different thing than lies."

"Speak plainly, cat, or I'll leave right now."

Ink hissed, ears flat. "I *am*," he said, standing, fur rising on the back of his neck. There was something distinctly un-feline about the fury in his eyes. The disappointment. "You are the one who does not listen. The Old Magic that existed before, that shaped the barriers of your world and the Fall of which disseminated magic to your people, is what binds you to the Archive. To *me*. And me to you."

"I can leave," I said, though surely I'd used that argument before. "I can go out into Vazeri. I'm not bound."

"Foolish human!" Ink was practically yowling. Surely one of the clerks would hear and come running. Just about everyone in the Archive was fond of the resident cats and to hear one in distress always drew attention. "The Archive is not a place. It is an idea! A collection of knowledge. A place of learning. Of paper and ink and books. Of secrets. You can go anywhere, because you, with your scribe magic, hold the idea of the Archive within you. I, on the other hand, am stuck here."

He hunched his shoulders and flattened his ears.

This was getting me nowhere. I didn't understand it, and frankly, if it didn't force me to be in one place, then I didn't really care. My life felt as it did before, excepting the situation with Beltran, which was of my own making and therefore my own folly to work through. Ink could say that the gods were false, that magic had come from before, but that didn't mean I had to believe it. I didn't know anything about him except that he was a cat with surprising ability to speak. I had more important things to do.

I stood, ignoring the incredulous look that Ink threw my way. Without paying him any mind, even as he tried to do as he threatened and trip me down the stairs, I marched to the basement. The clerks at the front desk looked at me with concern, one of them standing and preparing to see what the yowling was about.

"*Got his claw snagged,*" I signed. The clerk's shoulders sagged in relief. I glanced at the clock and cursed silently. There were only twenty minutes left of the lunch hour. People would be returning shortly, and if I wanted to find Beltran's information without being seen, then I had to hurry.

Gods, why was I doing this?

I went to the basement and performed the same task, running my fingers over books and records, the scrolls in their honeycomb shelves and the cabinets with their single-sheaf parchments. There were a few references to the Northern Reaches in correspondence, in discussion of the structure of the watch, but there weren't any records of raids. Not even historical ones.

My fingers fell from the last possible book. Nothing.

"You look disappointed," Ink said, a hint of anger still in his voice.

"You're still talking with me," I retorted. "I would have thought you would leave me to my own failures."

Ink flattened his ears. "As I said, I do this for your well-being. I do care about you, scribe."

I ignored the honesty in his words.

"There are no records of any raids in the Northern Reaches. I *know* we used to have records. I remember hearing their whispers. But they're gone, now." I turned and looked at the vast array of shelves and cabinets. "How could an entire collection of history be missing? I know the triumvirate has their own copy of things. Maybe I can get a pass to their records."

"Don't do that," Ink blurted, sounding more than a little panicked. I frowned.

"Why? More concern for my wellbeing?" I snorted and shook my head.

"Have you ever thought about *why* there are so few scribe mages? There are hundreds of thousands of other mages. Artists. Mechanical mages. Animal speakers. Water wielders. Fire wielders. Weavers. Growers. So many that the various disciplines are impossible to count. They follow no family lines, but are distributed widely. Why, then are there no other scribes?"

"There are other scribes," I said. Footsteps were at the stairs, moving downwards. People had returned from lunch, and I was left talking with a cat.

"Really? Where? Tell me one other scribe that exists right now, not decades or centuries ago." Ink leaped to the top of a low shelf and stared right into my eyes. I cast my mind back, but nothing in my training at Liral had told me of other scribes except that they existed, and that the Archives were the only ones who could deal with them. My teachers had all been without magic. I'd had to figure out a great deal myself, through experimentation or reading on histories. I'd never met another scribe, though I just thought that was because of our relative rarity.

"This is too much." I pressed my fingers to my eyes. When I opened them, I signed at Ink. *"There are other scribes."*

"There are not," he insisted. "Why? Because they were killed. All of them. Think about it. A person who can know any written text just by being in the same room? Who can know any secret put to paper? Who can decipher any written language, any code? Missives are no longer secret. Strategies are no longer safe. Scribes make the best spies. And are universally killed because of it. The triumvirate tolerates your magic because you are *here*. In the Archive. Where they can manage the texts you have access to and keep any secrets for themselves. If you go to them..." Ink cast a glance to the stairs, where Margarethe appeared, smiling and welcoming.

"There you are!" She came up and slipped her arm through mine. "I think we should go to dinner this evening. There's a lovely little place down by the harbour, and I met the cousin of the owner while picking up some old books from an estate sale. They're supposed to have the *best* fried fish."

I was meant to meet Beltran that evening. Not that it would do any good, given that I hadn't found anything. I would just write him a note, I decided. It would save my bruised feelings not to have to see him in person. To see his disappointment in me.

I turned my back on Ink and heard a huff in response. He was just a cat that could talk. That didn't make any of his theories valid. I could go to the triumvirate in the morning and request the records. And if that didn't work, I would just write to Alar and request them directly. Even if that meant an uncomfortable letter to my cousin. No, I would do this to help Beltran prove that there was nothing untoward going on in Vazeri. The missing people were missing for other reasons. They ran away from their families. They wanted to start a new life. I would even accept the more terrifying thought of them having been murdered, though there were no bodies, no signs of blood. It was better than the conspiracy Beltran suggested.

"Fried fish sounds lovely," I said to Margarethe. She beamed and dragged me up the stairs to go help the Central Archivists in cataloguing some of their research materials. I left all ideas of gods and magic and raids behind.

CHAPTER 5

*T*he fish was delicious, as promised, even if it was tinged by my guilt at not being there for Beltran. Margarethe and I lingered over the meal, talking entirely in the signed language between us and baffling the other diners. I caught more than a few glares when Margarethe burst out laughing, as if it were unreasonable for someone who used the signed language to make noise. But neither one of us payed too much attention to the stares of the diners. Or, well, Margarethe didn't. I pretended not to pay attention.

We walked back to the Great Archives arm in arm, making it about halfway up the many twists and turns and hills of Vazeri before our legs were trembling and we hailed the services of a lift mage. He took one look at our stumbling steps and barked out a laugh.

"Tried to make it all the way to the top?" he asked, raising his hands to perform his magic.

"We made it halfway from the harbour," Margarethe protested. The mage laughed harder. Those who grew up in Vazeri were either accustomed to the many hills or smart enough to make use of the lifts. Transplants like us took years to acclimate. Or so I'd been told by Beltran when once I complained about the lack of carts to take supplies up the hill.

I frowned at my thoughts and shoved them aside, leaning against the railing of the lift and massaging my sore legs. Margarethe joined me, groaning in discomfort.

Then, we crested the stone retaining wall of the Archival level and the lift juddered to a halt, the mage's hands falling to his sides.

"Gods above," he breathed, staring at something behind Margarethe and myself. Heart in my throat, I turned.

The sky was orange against the blackness of night. Where it wasn't orange bleeding into red, it was spotted with great plumes of black smoke, making the air acrid and thick. Fire.

Margarethe and I exchanged a glance, panic welling up in the silence between us. I thrust a few coins at the mage and took off running, Margarethe a few steps behind me. She was the faster, having longer legs and a more muscular build, so she made it to the source first. It wasn't the Great Archives themselves that burned, thank Night, but several of the surrounding buildings had caught from sparks that travelled from the source of the fire. The main fire was one level up and, even from our poor vantage point, I could tell that it had consumed most of the crest of the hill.

The triumvirate building, the council building, the justicar, the various governmental buildings, they all burned. Margarethe grabbed my arm as I made to run.

"Where are you going?" she demanded. "They'll need us at the Archives!"

"There is fire protection woven into the very stone of the building," I retorted, adrenaline loosening my vocal cords. "The buildings around the Archives are already catching. There's nothing we can do here."

"And there's something we can do up there?" Margarethe was incredulous, and I didn't blame her. Running *into* a fiery maze of destruction was anything but logical. I still needed to do it.

I closed my eyes and spoke the words that betrayed me. "Beltran is up there," I murmured, knowing them to be true. After receiving my note, he would have stayed at the triumvirate building, searching for any records. I doubted he would find anything without my help, but he would have tried.

Margarethe stared at me, wide-eyed. "Elyria, you...Gods, even after what he did?" She shook her head. "Be *careful*."

I gave her a weak smile and ran off, past the Great Archives, past the building where I lived, where my drawings and belongings were likely catching flame, and up the hill. A moment later, I noticed a shape at my side. I skittered to a halt.

"Ink!" I cried, staring at the cat. "What are you doing here?"

"Going with you, obviously," the cat snarled. "If you're

going to be so foolish as to run into fire, then someone needs to watch your back."

"But the Archives!" I protested. The cat curled his lip, revealing one fang. "I thought you were stuck there?"

"You are part of the Archives, now. I am just as secure in my binding as ever, so long as I remain with you."

I stared at the cat, part of me longing to return him to the Great Archives, knowing that he would be safe there behind the protection spells. With the fire, though, they would have called every available Archivist to help secure the building anyways, and if I returned Ink, I would be roped in to help. I needed to find Beltran. To make sure he was alright.

Fury and fear tightened my throat. I signed at the cat in sharp, jerky motions. *"Fine. But stay close!"*

Ink ducked his head in a nod and raced alongside me as I pushed my legs and crested the hill.

It was worse than I could have imagined. Part of me thought that the buildings wouldn't be that bad, given they were mostly made of stone. But there were countless wooden accents, countless pieces of furniture, of art. The roofs were secured with pitch, which burned readily, cracking the tiles and sending molten pieces flying to the ground. Flames leaped from windows and licked eagerly at all the plant life that made the hill its home.

It was a picture straight out of the depths of the underworld.

I ignored the justicar and the council building, assuming that Beltran would be at the triumvirate building in all its monumental glory. I saw plenty of guardsmen about, as well as some fire mages and water mages who were doing their best to either redirect the flames or put them out entirely. The conflagration had grown beyond any single mage, and unfortunately, they could only focus on one area at a time, forced to sacrifice others.

The smoke was thick and made it difficult to breathe and see. The fire's heat was blistering. In minutes, I had already sweat through my blue dress, the fabric clinging to me with an uncomfortable weight. I pushed past some of the guardsmen keeping a perimeter; they saw the bands of red at my wrist and assumed I was there to help. That I was *able* to help. But as I drew closer to the burning building of the Vazeri government, I realised that there wasn't anything I could do.

I saw the arm and shoulder of a corpse, but it was burned to a crisp, impossible to identify as anyone but a nameless human, and even that distinction was being eaten away as the heat warped the bones. It was an unnatural heat, even for fire, and I could feel my skin starting to become impossibly warm, despite my being some twenty feet away.

"If your Beltran was in there, then he is surely dead," Ink shouted. The cat leaped for my shoulder, his fur scorching hot and his eyes narrowed against the smoke. "This place isn't safe."

I was about to agree with him, no matter that I desperately wanted to help Beltran. I started to nod, started to turn away, when I heard them.

They were like the whispers of ink on paper, of words

taken physical form, but more. Sharper. Louder. Full of pain. I whirled back to the triumvirate building and gaped in horror as I realised what I was hearing. I was hearing the *screams* of books, papers, scrolls, words, burning.

"Oh, gods," I breathed, a wave of nausea cresting over me. I swayed where I stood, a hand pressed to my stomach. Words swam before my eyes, hundreds of them. Thousands. Stories of ancient times. Reports of the day-to-day. Letters. Scraps of lists. Secrets. They burned, and they died, and as they did, they reached out to my magic and seized it. Seized me.

"Elyria!" Ink cried, digging his claws into my shoulder. I couldn't ignore it, though, the impossible draw to those texts begging to be saved from their deaths. "Resist!"

Instead, I raised my arms. Ink, pulled from the sooty water that ran over the streets, pulled from vials not yet burned, pulled from the moisture that remained in the leaves of plants, swirled into the air. A few gasps from people around me were all I heard of the real world before I was dragged completely under by the words. They subsumed me, directing my movements.

I pulled paper to me, unburned or barely touched, from the deepest depths of the buildings, from the level beneath, from scraps of cloth that would hold ink in a pinch. The words filled my thoughts, screaming at me. I fell to my knees.

"Elyria, listen to me—"

I ignored Ink, unable to do anything other than what the magic directed me to do. I knew that my skin was burning, probably peeling. I knew that my hair was singeing at the ends. I knew that the fire crept closer, drawn by the hundreds of pages I had called to me. I could do nothing, though.

With a wave of my hand and a thought, the words that shouted in my mind were put to paper, filling the pages in neat, minuscule letters, small enough that I could fit thousands of texts onto the few pages I had managed to call. I didn't know if the words made any sense. I didn't even know how to sort through the ones that still screamed in my mind. Later, perhaps, they would come to me in a dream. Now, though, the last letter was inked onto the page and my magic abruptly went silent.

I fell to the ground, face first, and landed on a pile of pages that surrounded me. On the last page, the one closest to me, I saw a line of letters that were like none I had ever seen before. The last spark of my magic flared to life, translating the runes:

We shall sleep, lest the world fall to their hungering grasp. When we awaken, perhaps we will be better prepared for the demons. The angels—

I closed my eyes, Ink yowling in my ear, and slipped into unconsciousness.

I woke to cool hands on my head and a flurry of voices. My

eyes fluttered open and I tried to sit up. Dizziness overtook me.

"Don't move," a soothing female voice said, strong and worn. "You've delved too deeply into your magic, and the fire burned you a little. I've healed you as best I can, but your body will take time to recover."

I nodded vaguely at the healer, noticing a sturdy shape but little else in the chaos. I lifted my hands. *"Where...?"* It was the only sign I could manage before exhaustion filled my limbs.

"You're on the second tier, in one of the healer tents. We had to set up three for all the burn victims." The healer shook her head, form coming more into view as my head stopped swimming. She was tall, well-muscled, with warm brown skin and kind eyes. Her hair was in a long braid over her shoulder, beads tied throughout. A healer mage, then. A rare and desirable form of magic. Almost as rare as scribes.

That thought brought back the events of the day, starting with Ink's fear, and then trying to find Beltran and the magic that took over when I heard the screams of dying books. I sat up again, this time successfully.

"Careful," the healer warned, looking me over while she washed her hands in a basin. "You'll be weak for a few days."

"Elyria!" Margarethe pushed through the healers and their assistants in the tent, falling to her knees before me. "Thank the gods you're alright. When I heard they'd brought the victims here, I started searching for you. The entire crest of the hill has been destroyed from the fire.

Except for the...you saved most every document from the triumvirate building."

She looked horrified rather than impressed and I frowned, fingers slowly forming their signs. *"Margarethe, what's wrong?"*

"You nearly *killed* yourself! You should have just let those books burn!"

"I agree with the frantic one." Ink jumped up on the bed and fixed the healer with a glare. Margarethe and the healer didn't react to the cat's words; they truly couldn't hear him, then. Part of me was relieved to see him, though I didn't know why.

"I couldn't," I signed. *"I heard them screaming as the flames encroached, and, well, they...they demanded I save them."*

Margarethe drew her head back. "Elyria...the books can't—"

"They did! They screamed and then my magic just flared without my control." I shuddered at the memory of my body moving without my will, doing things I didn't ask of it. I wasn't particularly sorry that the books had been saved, but I was terrified that my magic might do this again.

"In extreme circumstances, magic can take over," Ink said, curling up next to me. He hissed at Margarethe as she tried to pet him. "It's not common, and usually there has to be some sort of disaster related to the mage's ability, but it has happened. Healers are the most susceptible, given their need to preserve life in all circumstances."

I wanted to reply. Wanted to ask questions. But I didn't

need to be seen as crazy. That wouldn't help my case. Instead, I asked a question of Margarethe.

"How did the fire start?"

She flinched, eyes darting to the side, counting the various listeners. To my surprise, she shifted to the signed language. There were likely a few people who knew it, but it was relatively uncommon outside of the Archives. No one would see the words she signed, except for me.

"They won't tell anyone definitively, but I heard the Central Archivists talking when a message runner from the triumvirate came. They're saying it was raiders."

I recoiled. *"You're sure? From the Northern Reaches?"*

Margarethe nodded. *"There were runes left behind. Like you said Beltran had found. And there are people missing. Only two people died, and they've been accounted for. There were many injured, but everyone has been named. Ten people are missing."*

Ten! I held my fingers still even as I wanted to ask, even as the words crept up my throat and caught there. Margarethe wrapped her hands around mine as if she could sense my dismay.

"He's among the missing," she murmured.

"No," I mouthed silently. It was like the night of the opera, but so much worse. So much more painful. It was like the nightmares of my past had reached out and taken something precious from me.

"He was already lost to you," Ink said, ears back. I wrapped my arms around myself. Tired, hurting, afraid. Not sure where to turn from here.

"Come on," Margarethe said, standing. She looked at the healer. "Can she leave? Find a place to sleep for the night?"

The healer nodded. "Her body will heal itself now. I have done what I can for the smoke inhalation and burns. The magic...I can do nothing about that except to advise rest."

Margarethe helped me stand, waiting for me to find my feet again. Ink twined around my legs once before standing at my side. The world was still fuzzy, still spinning, but it wasn't as bad as the turmoil inside. Beltran. Gods above, *why*?

"Our building burned," Margarethe said as she led me from the tent. It felt like hundreds of faces with darkness in their eyes and hollows in their souls stared at us as we passed. I ignored them as best I could, focusing on the words my friend was speaking. The building was gone. My things. My clothes. The few books I possessed. My drawings.

It was just another hurt to add to the ones already flaying me from the inside out.

"They've set up cots for the displaced Archivists in the atrium," Margarethe said, already leading me to the Great Archives, which—apart from some soot on the carved stone —was untouched by the flames. Why had the fire protections around the Archives not been penetrated while all the buildings on the crest of the hill had burned? Surely they had fire mages build protections into their foundations as well.

Then, as we crossed the threshold of the building, I nearly doubled over. I clapped my hands to my ears, gasping as all the voices of the books inside started to fill my head. My magic was so depleted, so raw that I couldn't even begin to grasp at the fragile threads of control to block out the words. It was as bad as it had been that day when I was eight, when my magic manifested.

Something tugged at my skirts, pulling me with surprising amounts of force. I followed, unable to do anything else but stand there under the unrelenting pain of too many words inside my head. I passed beyond the threshold and my mind cleared. I wavered and fell to the ground, the bark of my knees against the flagstone enough to jolt me to reality. Ink stood before me.

"Are you well?" he asked, tail lashing. I nodded.

"Gods above, Elyria! What happened?" Margarethe was by my side. I tried to lift my hands to sign, tried to communicate that my magic was raw, but they trembled too much to move. And speaking was not possible. My voice was caught in my throat, stunned into silence by memories of the past, of the aftermath of responding to the words as a child. Memories of the Baron, and the beating he gave me for my magic.

I'd been sent to Liral shortly afterwards and was told by the healers there that my bones had barely begun to mend and I was lucky not to have rebroken something on the journey. A rare visit from a healer mage a year later had erased most of the scars from that beating, though they remained etched in my mind.

Ink pressed against my side, purring very faintly. He watched me, worried, but I couldn't even manage a word for him. I dragged myself to the building and leaned back against the stone. The cool material seeped through my dress until I was shivering, but I would much rather have the cold than the voices in my mind. I was born to the cold. I could handle it.

Margarethe studied me, mouth tight. "I'll...I'll see if I can find temporary accommodations on one of the lower levels. That's probably best."

I watched her go numbly, mind blank, staring at the spot where she'd been long after she vanished into the night.

CHAPTER 6

A night's sleep on a bed far from the Archives seemed to restore some scraps of my energy. Enough that I could explain to Margarethe over breakfast what had happened with my magic. She looked as tired as I felt, with dark circles under her normally bright eyes, her curly hair limp and a slight grey tinge to her skin. I was too afraid to ask what I looked like, given that I'd had no bath and was still wearing my soot-stained dress from the night before. Ink had spent nearly an hour grooming the soot from his fur the night before, so at least one of us looked refreshed.

"I received a message from a runner this morning," Margarethe said, sipping at her coffee, imported from one of the other harbour cities. A luxury on a good day, today it felt like a necessity. I raised my brows at her and took a deep drink of my own coffee. Ink, never farther than twenty feet from me, sniffed at the cup from my lap and made a disgusted face.

"I'll never understand how you could think that tastes good," he mewed, seemingly unconcerned with the message.

"The triumvirate—all accounted for and well, thank the gods—have summoned us. You. They've summoned you."

I reared back in my seat. *"Why?"* I signed.

She shrugged, tucking a strand of hair behind her ear. "Probably something to do with the display you put on last night. Saving all those documents?"

Oh. Right. Ink's warning flared to mind again and I wondered, not for the first time, if he'd been right. If being a scribe wasn't inherently dangerous, given the secrets that the world wanted to keep but not forget. My coffee sloshed a bit in its cup as I set it down. My hands were trembling.

"When?" Even my signing looked sloppy. The stares that we were getting from the other customers of the cafe weren't helping. They watched us, looking at my dirty appearance and my dancing fingers and they whispered. Stared. Watched. Prickles of anxiety ran down my spine, making it stiff. My stomach churned around the coffee, and I wished I'd had more than a few bites of bread before giving up on eating.

"As soon as we can get to the Great Archives. They've set up temporary headquarters in one of the research rooms," she admitted. I gaped at her.

"It's been an hour since we got up!"

"You needed the food. We both did." Margarethe sighed

and stared at her own half-eaten biscuit. She shook her head. "I can't eat any more. Can you?"

I pushed my plate aside and stood, already dropping a couple of soot-darkened coins from my pocket on the table. Then, cat at my heels, we started for the Archives. It was almost as bad walking through the city as it had been at the cafe. People stared, rumours of my exploits no doubt already having spread throughout the entirety of Vazeri. I tugged at my sleeves, wishing for a change of clothing and knowing that everything I had was lost.

The whispers grew in number until I was certain that every eye was staring at me, that every person was talking behind my back. My vision tunnelled and the heaviness of my breathing had little to do with the steep climb. I couldn't focus, couldn't breathe.

Fur brushed over my ankle and then a moment later a heavy weight settled on my shoulders as Ink leaped up. He perched there, tail wrapped neatly around my neck, claws digging in just enough to bring my reeling anxiety to bear, grounding me in that tiny sensation of pain. I could breathe again.

I did my best to ignore the looks and attention that we got as we hailed a lift and continued on our way. The soot-stained dress I wore was a blatant sign that I had been at the fire, and that was the only news in the city that people were discussing. Only an invasion by the entirety of Imara would top the news of the fire.

People milled about outside the Great Archives. Some were near the healer tents, still up and bustling. Others lingered near the rise to the top tier of the city, staring at it with wide-eyes, as if their thoughts alone could undo the horrors of the night before. Margarethe squeezed my hand as we approached the Archive.

"Are you going to be alright? Your magic?" she asked under her breath. I hadn't considered the pain my magic might put me through again, only the triumvirate's summons. My magic still felt depleted, raw, but the night's sleep had done me a world of good. I nodded despite not being sure of the outcome, and we kept going.

A hand lashed out and snagged my arm, tugging me to a stop. I whirled, heart leaping into my throat. Sabine, dressed in a green gown that was smudged at the hem with soot, eyes red and with deep circles beneath them, let out a sob of relief and wrapped her arms around me. Augustus was just behind her, looking mildly irritated. Or concerned. I wasn't sure which.

"Elyria," Sabine said, pulling back. "Thank the gods. The rumours of what happened…?"

I shrugged and flinched as she tightened her grip on me. Ink, still on my shoulders, growled low in his throat. Sabine didn't seem to notice; she was too wrapped up in her distress. "Beltran is missing," she cried, more tears filling her eyes.

I winced and nodded. I was well aware, and trying very hard not to think about what it meant.

"They say you're being called to the triumvirate," she said, glancing back at the Great Archives. I turned my head and, for the first time, noticed that there were several brown-clad guards outside the building, keeping people at bay. Sabine tightened her grip once more, and I twisted out of her grasp. Ink's growl became a full-bodied snarl as Sabine reached for me again. Augustus stepped closer and put his hands on her shoulders. She trembled, sinking against him.

"They won't let us in," Augustus said in a cold voice.

"You have to help us," Sabine pleaded, stretching her hands out again. "Please, Elyria, you have to help us. They're saying they won't send anyone after the missing people. After Beltran. They're saying that it was raiders and that... that...that they're most likely dead."

I took a subtle step back, ready to shake my head, to refuse. Sabine sobbed, the sound catching in her throat and making her double over. She pressed a hand to her pregnant belly and a stab of sympathy filled me. She was due within the month, I guessed. And Beltran, the father of her child, was gone.

No child deserved to grow up without their family.

Ink dug his claws further into my shoulder. "Don't be foolish," he hissed in my ear, whiskers brushing my cheek. "You should be concerned with protecting yourself, scribe. Not worrying about the foolish husband of a desperate woman."

"Please," Sabine breathed, hunched over, staring at me as if I held all the answers. Augustus, too, watched me, something hollow and empty in his eyes. I gave a nod. Then again. Sabine fell into Augustus's arms and started crying in earnest. I turned my back on her and felt the weight of this new burden settle in my chest.

"You will regret this," Ink said, but there was no real heat to the words. I already regretted. I hesitated at the door to the Archives, wavering, afraid. Ink shifted his paws against my shoulder and I braced myself for him to leave now he was back home. Instead of leaping away from me in disgust as we entered the Archives, he wrapped his tail tighter around my neck and settled his weight more evenly on my shoulders. Tears welled in my eyes.

There was no time to adjust as we walked into the building. My mind swirled with myriad whispers for a moment, buffeting me back. Margarethe started towards me in concern, but immediately, two city guards appeared at my sides and started ushering me to the stairs. Margarethe followed with a glare at the guards. I took several deep breaths, forcing the whispers back, forcing the words to quiet.

My magic settled.

My anxiety did not.

The triumvirate and council had taken up residence in one of the larger research rooms available to Archivists for various research projects. This one still had some paper diagrams on the wall of lift mechanisms in various stages of completion. The rest of the room, though, was transformed.

What had once been a space for study, with a few tables about to spread papers and books, was now rearranged, with three long tables forming a "U" at the back of the room. The triumvirate members sat at the back table, so intimidating and imposing that I barely noticed the council members seated at the other two tables, looking uncertain.

The triumvirate was more of an idea to me, a governing body, something that existed to perform a task—to rule over Vazeri—rather than something made up of people. Yet there they were. Three people, two men and one woman, all in their middle to older years. I knew them by description only, and being in their presence was enough to steal my breath away again.

The woman, Tri Luciana, was olive skinned with dark hair streaked in white, wrinkles around her eyes and mouth appearing to be anything but laughter lines. Despite the soot smudged on her cheek, she wore a pristine dress in pale purple, the sheer sleeves floating delicately around her hands, which fidgeted with a quill and ink pot. She stilled as I entered, dark eyes widening.

Tri Fidelio was the oldest of the three, with hair entirely white and frown lines inscribed deep into his skin. He was heavy set, with beige skin tanned in the sun, a nose that was too large for his face, and finery of gold silk smudged with soot.

Tri Ottario looked to be the youngest, his brown skin unlined and smooth. He wore his long hair in a tail and had the simplest of the three costumes, with a green tunic and yellow overrobe. I realised a moment later that the buttons of the overrobe were emeralds, and that the brooch at his throat was made entirely of pearls.

More wealth than I had ever hoped to possess sat before me with stern expressions. Compared to them, the council members in their fine wools and linens and even silks, looked provincial. I, dressed in singed linen covered in soot, unbathed, still trembling from blocking out the whispers of the Archive, felt like nothing more than a bug beneath their fine slipper.

The look that the triumvirate gave me, as one, was scathing. Only Tri Ottario looked mildly curious.

"You are Elyria Trevain, Archivist?" Tri Luciana asked in a rasping voice.

I nodded.

"You are the scribe mage?" she continued.

I nodded again.

"Speak, mage, so your responses can be noted down for the official record." Tri Fidelio slammed his fist on the table, making me jump. I saw a small man to his left raise his quill, ready to write out the words that would never come to my tongue in a situation such as this.

I raised my hands to sign, trembling though they were, and all three drew back in alarm. The guards behind them immediately drew their swords and pointed them at me. I gasped and fell to the ground, covering Ink's head and my own as best I could.

"Wait!" Margarethe leaped forwards. "Please, wait!"

The guards didn't attack, watching for instruction from the triumvirate. Luciana curled her lip.

"She doesn't speak. She uses the signed language to talk. That's all she was doing, I swear," Margarethe said, voice trembling.

"Is this true?" Ottario asked, peering down at me with a sneer. I managed a brief nod, but nothing more.

Luciana waved a hand, that fine fabric fluttering around her wrist. "Very well. You can translate for the scribe? Good. Do so. Stand up, scribe. We're not done with you."

Ink growled quietly, so quietly that even I could barely hear him. It was enough to jolt me back to the moment and let me stand on shaking legs. I was getting that tunnel vision again. Margarethe gave me an encouraging smile, so weak it barely flashed across her mouth.

My stomach dropped even more.

Before I could sign anything, Luciana frowned. "Is that a cat on your shoulders?"

"One of the Archive mousers," Margarethe explained quickly, stealing a look at Ink, who twitched his tail. "He's taken a liking to Elyria. Hasn't left her side since the fire."

Fidelio leaned forwards, narrowing his eyes at me. "Ah, yes, the fire. We're told that you are the one who…*saved* the documents in the triumvirate building. How?"

In as few signs as possible, I told them about the books screaming as they burned, how they took over my magic and everything else that came from that. Margarethe translated, voice uncertain but steady. I said nothing about the runes that I saw, nothing about the rumours of raiders.

"And what exactly, of all these documents, do you remember?" Luciana asked. I blinked. Ink had been right. These people were worried about the secrets they held. Had they been the ones to remove mention of the raids from the Archives? Why?

I signed, my movements becoming more steady as my thoughts solidified. Margarethe translated. "Very little. It was too much of a jumble, all the words coming at once."

Fidelio leaned back in his chair, the wooden claw footed seat creaking under his weight. "Interesting," he said, though I got the distinct impression he was more relieved than interested in my magic.

"Interesting? It's more than that," Luciana said with a sniff. She peered at me, looking as if she'd sucked on a lemon. "What, exactly, can your magic do, scribe? I know little of such things; scribe mages aren't exactly common, now are they?"

Ink dug his claws into my shoulder, but I didn't need the warning. I saw the gleam in Tri Luciana's eyes and I knew, now, how dangerous they considered me to be. Margarethe cleared her throat, obviously waiting for me.

I lifted my hands and hesitated.

"Careful," Ink warned. "Tell them only what you must. Your life depends on it."

I took a breath to try and settle my nerves, but it only served to set my hands trembling. I signed as rapidly as I could to hide the shake. *"I work with words, paper, and ink. My magic can let me manipulate the written word, or write something without needing to hold a pen. I can summon books to me. It doesn't work with drawings, though, unless they are labelled diagrams."*

I indicated the piece of paper pinned to the wall. The triumvirate members studied the paper and the diagram, then turned back to me.

"Is that all?" Luciana asked in a sweet voice. Margarethe pulled her brows together, the slightest indication of her discomfort with the situation.

"Say no more," Ink urged, and for once, I obeyed.

"That is all," I signed. Margarethe translated without hesitation, though she knew full well that my magic was a great deal more than that. I quickly added, *"Last night was an anomaly,"* which was not a lie. At the translation to that, Luciana settled back into her seat, mouth still pursed but that gleam vanished from her expression.

"Indeed," Ottario mused, nodding. He studied me from beneath his long lashes. "What, exactly, made you run to the top tier of the city? From what I understand, the fires were already burning when you arrived."

I winced. *"I was looking for a friend."*

Ink dug his claws into my shoulder, though as warning or comfort I couldn't tell.

"Ah, yes, well that makes sense," Ottario said evenly. "Very good. That will be—"

"He's missing," I signed rapidly. Margarethe coughed. I signed the words again, raising my brows. Finally, at the expectant looks from the triumvirate, she translated. *"My friend is missing, and nine others."*

"Burned, unfortunately. It is a great loss, but—"

I shook my head. *"Not burned. Only two bodies were found, and they were accounted for. There are ten people missing."*

"This is dangerous ground, scribe," Ink murmured. "Tread carefully. People with secrets want them kept. They may have turned their focus from your magic, but there is more here than meets the eye."

The triumvirate didn't answer me immediately. The council members seated on either side looked at each other uncertainly, and the clerk tasked with recording the meeting pursed his lips, quill poised over the page. A single drop of ink fell from the nib to the paper, sounding like an explosion in my head.

"*They were taken by raiders, weren't they?*" I signed. Margarethe hissed at me through her teeth, eyes wide, but she translated dutifully.

Luciana rose, shoving her chair back into one of the unfortunate guards watching over the triumvirate. "What do you know of raiders?" she asked sweetly, though there was a dangerous edge to her voice.

"Careful," Ink cautioned. It was too late for careful. The words had been said and the promise made. I had to help if I could. Not just for Sabine, either. For me. For what remained of my shattered heart.

"*I am from Summerfell,*" I signed. "*I know of raiders.*"

"Do you?" Ottario asked. "Then you should know that their lives are already lost. It is truly tragic, but we must shore up our defences here. Vazeri is vulnerable, and though the deaths of those ten will be mourned, we have other things to see to."

I reared back. They didn't know that the missing people were dead. If they were, then why didn't we find their bodies amidst the rubble? Why would the raiders go to the trouble of taking them only to kill them anyways? I had been only a child at Summerfell, and so ignorant of all the goings on, but I wasn't a fool now. The triumvirate was lying.

Why?

"You're not going to send anyone after them?" I asked.

"No," Ottario answered. "Now—"

"Then I will go."

Margarethe spoke the words before fully realising what she had translated. She spun to face me fully. "Are you out of your mind? Elyria, you can't do this!"

"Smart," Ink said, ears twitching. "Escape this place before they can imprison you for having seen their secrets. Or worse, kill you. They may suffer your existence for now, when the story of what you did is whispered on the tongue of everyone in Vazeri, but they will not suffer you for long. Especially not when they learn the truth of your magic from the other Archivists. As soon as your story has been forgotten, you will disappear."

"I am from Summerfell," I repeated, trying to ignore Ink even as I saw the calculation in Tri Luciana's eyes. *"I have family there. I can travel there and discover the true situation. Perhaps I can find the missing. Or ask the watch for help."*

From the expressions on the triumvirate's faces, they didn't expect me to find anything. They expected me to fail. It surprised me, then, when Luciana sank back down into her chair and propped her head on her chin. "Very well."

"Tri—" Ottario started, gaping at her. She lifted a finger and he fell to silence.

"We haven't the messengers to spare to send all the way

to Summerfell, and no mage-trained birds will go to the gap in the mountain barriers. And, as you said, you have family at Summerfell. They will surely know the status of the Northern Reaches better than anyone." She lifted her chin slightly, a hint of a cruel smile at her lips. "It will be dangerous. Are you sure you're up for the task?"

Margarethe coughed pointedly and shook her head, staring at me in an obvious attempt for me to reconsider. Instead, I nodded.

"*I will need supplies,*" I signed, "*as my belongings were burned in the fire next door.*"

"It will be done. You will have funds. We will send a messenger bird to Makhier to have them prepare you a horse." She rested her elbows on the table and folded her hands together. "Anything else?"

I thought of asking for some of the records on raiders, but I knew that it would be refused. Just as I knew that asking about the runes that the raiders had left behind would be akin to waking a sleeping volcano. Ink was right. These people had secrets, and they wanted me far, far from them.

Whether that was to do with my magic or my newly revealed connection to Summerfell, I didn't know. So I shook my head, sank into a curtsey, and thanked the triumvirate for their kindness, the tremble in my fingers gone.

PART II
INK DREAMS

INTERLUDE I

The palace was quiet that night. Quiet enough that even slipping through the halls seemed to produce an unnatural amount of noise to Keir. He tucked his shadowy wings in tight and stepped carefully, doing his best to avoid scuffing his sandals on the stone.

He had a right to be there, he reminded himself as he passed yet another torch with flickering flames and no guards beneath it. He was a servant of the gods, highly respected, his voice valuable. He had every right to wander the palace. Even at night. Even when most everyone else had gone to the Midwinter festival to mingle with the mortals and celebrate the birth of a new year.

He swallowed down the hum that came to his lips, a song to soothe his nerves. Now was not the time for singing.

Keir paused at the end of a hallway where a statue taller than any human man or angel stood. It was female in figure, with six wings at her back, her arms outstretched, a single foot forwards. Tani, the Over-watcher, spreading her arms for the adulation of her people. The benevolent expression carved onto the statue's face was a stretch, Keir thought, but he bowed slightly to the statue anyways. Just in case someone was watching. Just in case someone would wonder why the black-haired, black-winged servant of the gods would fail to bow at one of their images.

Then, lifting his wings to shield the movements of his hands, he reached around the base of the statue and pressed into a divot in the back. He caught the latch with the tip of his finger and flicked it open. The statue shifted, a puff of dust filling the air as it moved. Keir coughed, then looked around again to make sure no one was watching.

He saw nothing, the illuminated hallway behind him empty.

Relief had him sagging his wings before he slipped behind the statue and into the dark staircase it concealed. Another latch had the statue moving back into position, sealing Keir into the blackness.

This was a place untouched by light for untold years. Dampness filled the air and there was moss growing on the stone walls, soft and pliant beneath his fingers. He could smell mildew and the coldness that came from dark, empty places. His knee-length tunic, belted at the waist with a length of leather, felt suddenly inadequate for this place.

After blinking a few moments into the darkness, his eyes began to adjust. There was no light, yet he could see just fine. One of the benefits to being a creature of shadows and night.

His steps were light down the stair, even and easy though his heart pounded in his ears. When he reached the bottom, he wasn't winded, but he was still breathing heavily. Heavier than he should from physical exertion alone.

Gods, he realised, rubbing at the tightness in his chest, he was afraid.

He hesitated before the stone-and-metal door at the base of the stairs. If he turned back now, he could join the others at the Midwinter festival. He could get drunk on star wine and perhaps coax one of the mortals into taking a shadowy, dark angel to their beds. He could sing the songs of the season and dance until dawn. He could enjoy the favour of the gods for a little while longer.

He shook his head. No. This needed to be done.

Keir pressed his palm against the door and it swung open, recognising his right to open such a portal, recognising his authority with the inherent magic woven into the palace of the gods. There were few others who had the authority he had, few others who were trusted enough to know these secrets.

He wasn't sure if the gods were the fools, or if he was.

The light of a torch beyond the door had him wincing. He pulled back, letting four humans through the door into the darkness, sealing the stone behind them.

"Are you alright?" Of course she would be the one to ask. Honeyed voice as soothing as any balm. Flaxen hair, bright eyes, body thin and worn by the years of labour for the service of the gods. Keir relaxed at her voice, though his eyes still watered. He reached out and took her hand, brushing the tips of her fingers with his.

"I'm well," he said on a smile. "Did you run into any trouble coming here?"

"No. Everyone was at the festival," her brother said. He was tall, his body showing the years of hard labour. He scowled at Keir's fingers but didn't say anything. The other two humans, both male, one dark and the other light, shifted the torches they bore uncertainly.

"Come," Keir said, looking away from the flame. "We have little time."

"And you're certain that it will be unguarded?" her brother asked. This was not the first time he had asked that question, and Keir hoped it would be the last. This whole plan was moving ahead because of him. Did they doubt him so much that they would believe him incapable? Did *she* doubt him?

"The only guards remaining are at the doors to the palace," Keir said, taking the lead and starting back up the stairs. The others followed, their torch flames warming his feathers uncomfortably. "Everyone else was given permission to go to the festival."

"I suppose they never thought anyone would be foolish enough to trespass on the palace of the gods," she said. There was no small amount of bitterness in her voice and Keir flinched. He hated when she spat venom, even if circumstances well deserved it. Then again, wasn't that why he was doing this? So no one would need to rage at the gods again? So they could choose their own lives?

"Be quiet," her brother hissed as they climbed the stairs. "I don't want anyone to hear."

Because he didn't trust Keir. That much was obvious. Had always been obvious. Why, after all, would a trusted servant of the gods deign to lower himself to help the pathetic humans? Why would he, of all people, want to help them better their lives? Want to help them create a history for themselves, to hold on to knowledge, to build upon what came before? To improve things?

Keir tucked his wings in close and finished climbing the stairs in silence. When he reached the spot where the statue latched shut, he paused, waiting. Listening. There was no movement on the other side of the statue, not that his heightened senses could hear. The humans behind him held their breaths, their hearts racing. That was the loudest noise Keir could detect, so he unlatched the statue.

It moved in another puff of dust and everyone held their breath again until he emerged, looked around, and waved everyone through the passage. He closed the passage behind them, and when they were standing there, staring at him expectantly, waiting to be led to their target, he froze.

Wings of the gods, what was he doing? He had brought humans to this sacred place! He had violated the sanctity of his masters' home, letting in those beings who should be worshipping them, not plotting to steal from them. The potential consequences had his throat tightening in panic.

His wings flared slightly and the humans started to look uncomfortable, started to look alarmed. Afraid.

"Keir," she said, stepping forwards and taking his hand. Almost immediately, he relaxed. "Is everything alright? Do you hear something?"

As if that could be the only possible reason for his hesitation.

"No," he said, smiling weakly. "This way."

She exchanged a glance with her brother, who frowned.

He led them through the palace, never once looking back. He led them around the chambers meant for listening to glorious music, through the pavilions where star-blooming flowers swayed gently in the breeze, protected from the harsh winter weather by a spell. He led them by the quarters of lesser gods, past sitting rooms and dining rooms and spaces meant purely for entertainment. The torches were still unguarded, and eventually, Keir began to relax. Began to believe that everything would work.

That this wasn't such a crazy idea.

The room he sought was at the end of a corridor whose ceiling was made of spelled glass. It was painted with ice crystals, diffusing the starlight into a soft glow. There were no torches here, and for good reason. When he stepped into the room, he was faced with the most precious of the gods' possessions.

Books.

Thousands of them.

There were shelves along each wall, illuminated by that celestial glow. There were places for scrolls and tomes and loose parchment. There was a cabinet full of inks and dip pens, quills, pencils. It was a room for the collection of knowledge. For the writing of words. For learning.

The humans gasped.

"I never believed they would be so...beautiful," she said, reaching out to run her fingers over the gilded spine of a book on the demesne of the god of winds. Her brother glared at the collection with a tense jaw, his hand gripping the torch. Keir watched those flames leap into the air and his stomach clenched. He should have made them leave the torches in the passage.

"Where is it?" one of the others asked, looking around with a desperate hope.

"Here," Keir said, stepping lightly to a pedestal. Upon the pedestal were three items. A piece of paper, curling at the corners, foxed with age; an inkwell half-full of rich black ink; a quill, plucked from the feathers of the goddess of knowledge herself. Hirana.

"And you're sure this will work," her brother said, an eager gleam in his eye.

"Pierce your finger with the quill, mix your blood into the ink, and put it to paper," Keir said. "Traditionally, one writes their name on the paper, but since humans..."

"Have been forbidden from writing?" she asked, that same bitterness lacing her tone. "Have been forbidden from learning the craft of preserving knowledge? Have been forced to depend on the gods for things that we should be managing ourselves?"

"Just so," Keir said, swallowing a wince. "Any mark should do."

Her brother didn't hesitate. He plucked the quill from its stand, stabbed the metal tip into his finger, bled into the inkwell, then dipped the quill in the resultant ink. With a swift, but clumsy, movement, he gripped the quill and pulled it from the well. A single mark on the paper, and Keir could feel the magic take effect.

The gods power, the gift of knowledge, had now entered the blood of humans. They were forbidden no longer.

"Did it work?" she asked her brother eagerly. He stared at the paper, at the mark that was already fading, and shrugged.

"I don't know."

"Look at a book," Keir offered. "You won't be able to read it right away, but at least it shouldn't hurt anymore. The learning will come later."

The man did as suggested, plucking the first book he saw from a shelf, ignoring the blood he smeared on the cover. A treatise on war, Keir noted. It seemed fitting.

"There's no pain," he said, flipping through the pages and staring at the words. "None at all."

She took the book from him and started looking at the pages. Slowly, an effervescent grin grew, turning her into a beauty that took Keir's breath away. Maybe now he could tell her the truth about how he felt. Maybe now that he'd helped her, helped them all, she would be willing to accept him.

"It's done," she said, snapping the book shut

triumphantly. She put it back on the shelf, looked around the room once more, then turned to her brother. "Let's get back and share the news. Before the gods realise what we've done."

"Let's," he said. Then, with a nod at the other two humans, he drew his sword and raised it at Keir.

"What are you doing?" Keir demanded, wings already flaring, his shadowy magic rising to the fore.

"What we should have done a long time ago, angel," he said. Sharp, stabbing pain flared through Keir's wings and he spun around. It was too late. The two humans behind him had come up and done the one thing that would cripple his power. They'd clipped his wings.

Keir turned back to her, hoping to gain some understanding even as betrayal wound through him. She watched with a satisfied look.

"Did you think that we would welcome you with open arms?" she asked. "After all you have done at the behest of the gods to enslave us? To bind us to them?"

"I helped you!" Keir protested weakly. He was more the fool for it, too. He never should have brought them here. He had broken something fundamental in the relationship between the humans and the gods. He had thought he knew what would happen next, that he had helped usher in a new, brighter future, but that was the thing about knowledge. Knowing wasn't everything.

"As we deserve," her brother said. He jerked his head to the other humans. "Leave him here. Let the gods find him. We need to get out of here."

They left, sparing only a triumphant grin for the books that were no longer forbidden to them. They didn't look back at Keir. Not one of them.

He knelt on the floor, wings useless at his sides, his magic curbed, and found himself feeling something he'd never felt before. Certainly he knew betrayal; no servant of the gods was without that emotion. He knew despair. He knew pain. But this feeling that consumed him, weighing down his limbs and simultaneously setting fire to his thoughts, was new.

In a room dedicated to the goddess of knowledge, though, the word for what he felt sprang to mind within moments.

Regret.

Keir closed his eyes and let the regret overtake him. It would serve as a companion until the gods discovered what he'd done and came for him.

CHAPTER 7

$\mathcal{I}$ woke from a dream of shadows and wings to the motion of a ship. My stomach recoiled and I lurched from the small bed to a bucket on the floor. Once I was done emptying my stomach, I turned to Ink, who remained on the bed, looking at me with pitying distaste.

"How much longer?" I rasped.

"You slept for a couple of hours. We'll be in Makhier as soon as the tide changes," Ink said. He stretched, showing his claws, and leaped to the floor. "There are far better ways to travel than by boat."

"I know, but the triumvirate only promised me a horse from Makhier onwards, and this was the fastest way." I had left the day after meeting with the triumvirate, taking enough time only to buy supplies, prepare a map and notebook, and rest before leaving. Margarethe had argued with me the whole time, saying that it wasn't my responsibility.

Finally, I had snapped and said it was better than dying at the hands of the triumvirate for knowing their secrets.

She and I hadn't said much after that. I hoped she was alright.

"You have escaped the triumvirate. You are safe, so long as you keep your magic hidden," Ink said. "There is no need to be in such a rush."

"There were ten people kidnapped," I retorted, not sure if the churning in my stomach was from seasickness or anxiety. "Do you honestly think that me taking my time will help them?"

"Why do you care so much? Those that took them are likely long gone, and also likely travelling under the protection of runic magic, if they truly did come from the border mountains beyond Summerfell. The only thing that comes through the magical barrier there is bad news. Even *I* know that." Ink had taken it for granted that he was coming with me, and he'd complained almost the entire time without actually providing useful information. I hadn't protested his presence, though. It was nice to have a companion, even if he was hardly quiet in his opinions.

I rubbed my eyes blearily. "If there's even a chance that they're alive, that Beltran is—"

"What, do you think haring off after this man on your foolish quest will solve all your problems?" There was a dark gleam in his bright eyes. "That you'll rescue him and he'll fall in love with you, forsaking his wife and child so you can live happily ever—"

"No!" I cried. Alarmed at my tone, I quieted myself. "No. I would not want that. He loves his wife, and she him."

"Then what? Why do you do this, scribe? When you are hardly qualified to go racing into danger."

"Because it is the right thing to do. Surely that is enough?"

The cat studied me, whiskers twitching. For a moment, I almost thought him sad. It wasn't the first time I'd seen that look in his eyes, either. It made me want to reach out and touch him, but I didn't think he wanted my poor attempt at comfort.

"Not for many, no." He shook himself and went to the door, tail twitching. "The tide is changing. We'll be docking soon. Grab your bag and let us be off this miserable boat."

It was hardly a miserable boat, despite my seasickness, but explaining to a cat that a small fishing vessel was going to be faster than one of the bulky merchant transports seemed pointless. Besides, my throat was tight with anxiety and I couldn't help but wonder if Ink was right.

I was woefully unprepared for this quest. Yes, I could return to Summerfell and face a cousin I hadn't seen since I was eight, with whom I exchanged remarkably terse letters every few months. I could find out if the raiders came from the Northern Reaches. I could probably track down who took Beltran and the others. But then what?

Would I fight them?

I didn't even know how to hold a sword or bow or axe or any other weapon. I could use a knife, but only on food, or for sharpening quills. I had little political sway. I couldn't hold a conversation unless the other person knew the signed language and was willing to deal with my anxiety. I spoke only rarely, even to those I trusted.

I was far from useful, except regarding books.

I thought of the Order of Ter Avest, to whom my uncle had tried to sell me before my magic manifested. They were reasonably well known throughout the harbour cities and spoken of in whispers. Women, all, who were trained not only in the usual expectations, but in politics, in sciences, in war. They were useful. They could turn the tide of a situation with a word or two. They might have been considered witches by most common folk, but I would have bet the coins in my bag that they were trained to fight.

But, no, they didn't take anyone with magic into their order, and besides, that was a long time ago. That was behind me. Finding Beltran was in front of me. He needed me. I would have to figure it out as I went.

That was all.

I tripped on my way up to the deck of the boat, stumbling into the arms of a large, broad-shouldered fisherman. He smiled at me, one of those flirtatious looks that are bandied about by people who don't choke on their own words.

"The goddess Day has favoured me," he said, "to send such a beautiful woman falling into my arms."

I righted myself and was about to pull away as politely as possible when Ink arched his back and hissed, glaring at the fisherman. The man blanched and muttered a curse under his breath, scurrying away. Ink scoffed.

"Humans," he sniffed, pressing close to my leg. "They're so easily swayed."

I wanted to scold him for his remark, even if I was grateful for his actions, but there were too many people about and my jaw tightened enough to make words difficult. Instead, I wandered to the railing and watched as we sailed into the harbour.

Makhier was not nearly as grand as Vazeri with its tiers and beautifully sculpted buildings, but it was much larger. It was a city built for practicalities, with most of its infrastructure centred around the harbour and its residential quarter in the distance. It was a flatter city, also, settled in a gentle dip to the sea. I could see farms off to one side, and what looked like a neat grid of buildings on the other. It was too regular to be anything but military. I shivered.

"That smell is repulsive," Ink complained, leaping onto the railing and wrinkling his nose. "What *is* that?"

I covered my nose with my hand, trying not to breathe too heavily. A rash of seagulls circled around a building off to the right, their cries drowning out most of the other noises of the harbour. I saw a pair of workers wearing heavy leather aprons and gloves toss something into a heap next to the building, the lower-half of their faces covered with cloths. A tannery? But, no, why would they be dumping things outside the building?

"Never been to Makhier, I take it?" a wizened older lady asked, drawing up beside me. She leaned on a cane and tugged a shawl close around her. "It's startling the first time you see it. Smell it, too. Thankfully, the way the wind blows it doesn't much come inland except on rare still summer days."

My disgust and curiosity worked together, as did the fact that she was a stranger and knew nothing of me or my...oddities. I could speak. "What is it?" I asked.

"Refinery," she said. "There's some sort of mine to the north. Don't ask me what ore they mine, for I don't know. Nor does anyone else you'll come across, excepting those who keep secrets close to their chest. Mmm, yes, plenty of those about. Regardless, they refine the ore and infuse it into products for sale to mages. Helps enhance their magic, see, though some call it unnatural."

"It *is* unnatural," Ink spat, the fur on his neck rising. "If she's talking about what I think she is, that's bloodstone. It can enhance a person's magic, true, but the consequences are vast, and almost everyone who comes into contact with the raw material dies."

I raised my brows at the cat. He shuddered.

"The industry is the most profitable in Makhier," the woman continued. "Even the hiring of our soldiers doesn't compare anymore. Soon, we'll be the most economically powerful of the harbour cities, no matter how nice Vazeri looks."

"If any of the runoff from the refining process makes it into the water supply here, it will hardly matter how valuable the Makhierians think it. They'll all die horrible, gruesome deaths," Ink snarled, standing and digging his claws into the wood of the railing. The woman seemed to notice him for the first time. She reached out a hand to pet him and he swiped at her, only barely avoiding drawing blood.

I winced out an apologetic smile, scooping Ink up and walking briskly to the other side of the boat. The woman huffed as I walked away.

"How will they die?" I whispered to Ink before depositing him on the ground.

"It looks a great deal like the yellow plague," Ink said as though he'd seen it before. "Blisters form on the skin, then burst and become infected. Inside, though, you start to bleed from coughing so hard and eventually drown on your own blood. God blood isn't meant to be handled by mortals."

God blood? I gaped at the cat. For the first time, I wondered who, exactly, he was. What he was. I'd assumed that he was no ordinary cat, long lived, perhaps a spirit bound to the Archives some centuries back, that his knowledge came from the books held within. But this? He talked as though he knew firsthand. He talked as though he'd seen it, and worse.

I closed my eyes and bit down on my lip. No. I needed to focus on finding Beltran, not what—who—Ink was. Not this bloodstone refinery in Makhier. Nothing but finding Beltran and the others, bringing them home. That was it. The world did not rest on my shoulders. This was not the Archives where I offered pieces of myself to keep good relations with the clerks and Archivists and monitors. This was me helping one person, not the world. I had chosen my burden and I would bear it, but the rest were not my own.

I felt a little more grounded, even if the task before me was difficult enough. My anxiety eased slightly, enough that I managed to relax my death-grip on the railing, settle my pack on my shoulders, and wait for the fishermen to tie off the boat to the dock and lower a gangplank for the few passengers. I stepped off into Makhier and deliberately turned my back on the refinery.

Thankfully, Ink followed behind me, though I could see agitation in every lash of his tail. He kept turning to look at the refinery, and his nose twitched with every few steps.

The farther we got from the harbour, the easier it became to breathe. People were more numerous and I saw couples linger outside of cafes, families walking along the streets on the way to market. They looked much like the people from Vazeri, and my heart clenched at the oblivious way they went about their lives. As if a portion of Vazeri hadn't burned, as if people hadn't been taken.

Did they not know? Or was it just so far away, a distant place, not their home.

Finally, I found myself outside the livery where I had been instructed to stop and get a horse, the end of the triumvirate's help in getting me out of the city. That was when things started to go badly.

I stepped inside and wrinkled my nose at the smell. Horses were used around Vazeri for farming and overland transport, but were rarely, if ever, found in the city thanks to the steep streets. Therefore, the smell was something I could easily avoid. I remembered this smell from the stables at Summerfell and Liral, and I remembered how much I disliked it. I'd never been one for riding, either. That was about to change.

There was a large, overweight man at the counter, leaning against it and looking deathly bored. At my entrance, he perked up, smoothing his canvas apron. "Welcome to Dawn and Day Liveries," he said with a smile that set Ink to lashing his tail. "How may I help you?"

I pulled a piece of paper from my pocket and handed it to the man. He took it and frowned. "What is this?"

I waited, expecting him to read it. Instead, he stared at me, his frown deepening. I realised a moment later what the problem was. He couldn't read. *Oh gods*, I thought. I was going to have to *talk* to him.

I licked my lips, took a breath, and splayed my hands over my belly to settle the anxiety there. Thankfully, the words came. "Horse...set aside by Vazeri triumvirate for me."

I spoke as clearly as I could, but it was still quiet, perhaps too quiet. My anxiety built. I wasn't sure I could repeat myself, wasn't sure I could dredge up more words without completely panicking. The stare he was giving didn't help; he looked at me like I was a freak, an oddity, something to be ogled or laughed at.

My throat closed. I thought a silent prayer to Night and waited.

"You're the messenger, eh?" he said at last, stuffing my note into a small box on the counter. "Don't look like you're from Vazeri, but what do I know? Sign the ledger there. The horse won't be ready until tomorrow, seeing as we only got the bird this morning."

Tomorrow? I wanted to protest. This was a livery! I could hear horses in the back. I could—unfortunately—smell them, too. But I had no more words. I was barely able to get air into my lungs enough to keep the world from spinning. I signed the ledger he pointed at, ducked my head in thanks, and fled.

Outside, the air was clear and I was able to regain enough of my senses to feel desperately embarrassed by what had happened. I wanted to run away and hide, but I had nowhere to go. I was in an unfamiliar place with no one but a magical cat to help me. I couldn't leave until tomorrow, and I needed to find somewhere to stay.

Panic began to take hold of me again, an influx of new things and people and places overwhelming me. I couldn't panic right then. I had to find a place to stay, then I could lose control of my muscles, my mind. I clenched my hands into fists so tightly that my nails dug into my palm. Focusing on the pain, I looked around, picked a promising direction, and set off to find the nearest lodgings I could.

Two hours later, after walking halfway back towards the docks, feet sore, back sore, and my head spinning, I had managed to secure lodgings from a deaf old woman who didn't much care that I couldn't talk since she couldn't hear me anyways. She had no signing language skills to speak of, so settled for shouting everything that came to mind while I nodded. She led me to a room that was small but clean and I gratefully closed the door behind me, dropping my pack on the floor and collapsing on the bed.

Ink sprang up and lay beside me.

"I didn't realise that your...muteness was tied to anxiety. I thought it was just do with strangers and how well you knew people," he said, licking his paw. If I didn't know better, I would suggest he was embarrassed to be discussing this.

"Normally, yes," I murmured, my hands too heavy for signing. "I find it easier to talk with people I know well, but sometimes even then the words just get swallowed up. I think them. I want to say them, but this pit opens up inside me and any sound is devoured. I can sometimes talk in scripted interactions, like ordering food or purchasing a single item, but anything off-script and I just...freeze."

"You managed to say a few words at the livery," Ink mused. "Because of necessity, or because it was a scripted interaction?"

I shrugged, rolling onto my back. "Sometimes, I can force out a few words if I really have to, but they always go away."

"Not with me," he said. I turned my head to look at him and found myself gazing into those amber eyes. They were deeper than any feline eyes, more intelligent. What was he?

"No," I murmured, looking away. "Not with you."

Ink moved closer, pressing against my side. I closed my eyes and let my mind wander far from the events of the last few days. Moments away from drifting into sleep, Ink said, "We have to destroy that refinery."

I sat bolt upright, gaping at him. "What?"

"Can you honestly tell me that you're alright with people dying from exposure to the byproducts?" Ink asked, his ears back. "That you're okay with the consequences of a few wanting to increase their power?"

"No, of course not, but—"

"But what?" Ink narrowed his eyes. "They're using *god blood* to achieve magical enhancements. It's dangerous, Elyria. Deadly, even. Mages have the power they're meant to have; more can cause harm to the mage, not to mention the exposure to any who handle the raw product or its offals."

My stomach turned and I focused my attention on the floral design of the bedding. "It's..." I swallowed and licked my lips to smooth the way for the words. "It's not my concern."

The words tasted like ash on my tongue.

Ink exploded in a riot of claws and fur, shredding the duvet with ease, his back arched and tail twice its normal size. I felt a pressure weighing down on me, like some great force was filling the room, forcing me back to make space for it. Ink snarled, fangs bared. "So, what, the great scribe will only do something if it affects her? If her beloved is missing, taken? If her life is involved? I thought you were trying to do the right thing, Elyria. Obviously I was wrong."

"That's not fair," I protested, though the barb had struck true. "It's one thing to track down some missing people when they might have come through my family home. It's another thing entirely to destroy an entire building! If anyone were to find out, it could cause *war* between Vazeri and Makhier and—"

"You would rather let people suffer and die than take steps to prevent suffering," Ink hissed. I flinched.

"No." I shook my head, then raised my hands so I could get the words out more clearly. Instead, my hands trembled so badly I could barely form any word at all. I shook my head again and lowered my hands. "I don't want people to suffer," I murmured.

"Then do something!"

"Why don't you do something?" I snapped.

Ink lashed his tail, a growl rumbling low in his throat. "Because I am bound by Old Magic to the Archives. To *you*. I cannot be separated from you or…"

Suddenly, he seemed to deflate. That pressure filling the room vanished in an instant. His fur flattened and he sat down, wrapping his tail around his paws. He looked defeated. Sad. Like I hadn't been what he expected. "It doesn't matter," he said after a moment. "You obviously made up your mind. We can leave in the morning for Summerfell."

I reached out my hand, still trembling, for Ink. He hunched his shoulders but allowed me to brush my fingers against his head. It wasn't a pet, just a gesture of comfort. "I don't want people to suffer," I repeated, barely audible. "You understand, though, that this is so much more than…than anything I ever expected to be involved with. I just wanted to have a quiet life in the Archives, surrounded by books."

Ink let out a dry laugh. "I know all about quiet lives gone

awry," he said. Quieter, he said, "And it's not wrong to want a quiet life. But it's not always a choice one has."

"Do you know how to destroy the refinery so people won't get hurt?" I couldn't believe that I was even asking. That I was considering this. It was absurd! Sheer stupidity. And yet, I asked.

Ink studied me again with those not-quite-feline eyes, and nodded. "I do," he said. "It won't be easy."

As if anything these days was remotely close to easy. Instead of voicing that particular doubt out loud, I just nodded. "Tell me what we have to do."

CHAPTER 8

I felt remarkably suspicious walking around Makhier after dark. It didn't matter that there were other people about going to their houses or to taverns or to work in the shadows. I felt like everyone was watching me, taking note of how I walked towards the docks, what I looked like. Ink all but disappeared into the darkness, only the reflection of his eyes in the occasional lantern revealing his constant presence. I tried to take comfort in it and failed.

Once again, I was bound by my inability to say no to people. This time, though, it felt different. It felt like the right thing to do. That only increased my nerves.

The closer we got to the refinery, the stronger the smell became. The wind had shifted directions slightly, bringing the scent of whatever they were doing inland. By the time we reached the water, I was all but gagging, my eyes watering.

Ink hissed a warning before I stepped into the lamplight surrounding the harbour. I ducked behind a building and peered out.

"Guards," the cat whispered. I saw the gleam of metal a moment later and nearly gasped. There were guards all but swarming around the harbour docks. They wore leather armour studded with metal plates, nothing like the mage-crafted tunics of the Vazeri city guard, though I imagined it was just as effective. They had swords at their belts. Some had a crossbow nocked and ready to fire, watching for every movement in the shadows.

"Why is it so guarded?" I breathed. The harbour at Vazeri was protected by mage spells, certainly, but even then they rarely had more than a handful of people on duty. Given the bloodstone refinery, I had no doubt that there were mage spells laced everywhere. So why the extra force?

"To protect from sneakthieves like yourself."

I whirled around and found myself face to face with a guard, her armour painted a dull black, a baton in one hand and the other resting on the hilt of a short sword. She had three bright stars on her shoulder, likely an insignia signifying rank. Significant rank, if I were to guess. My breath hitched, my stomach dropped, and the hair on the back of my neck stood on end.

"So, are you going to try and run, or can we walk to the guardhouse?" she asked, eyeing me. Ink pressed against my leg, hiding in my skirts; I could feel him vibrating with agitated energy.

I said nothing, only stepped back from the building and

waited, fear sparking through me. The guard smiled. "Good. I hate running."

She grabbed my arm and dragged me forwards, nodding her head to the guards at the harbour. They smirked at me, some even whistling mockery. The smell of the refinery grew stronger that farther we walked until I was holding back my gorge, a hand pressed to my mouth.

"You'll get used to the smell eventually," my captor said as we approached a low-slung stone building. It was fitted with bright lanterns and narrow windows, both approachable and defensible. The guardhouse, I assumed. I was pushed through the doorway and dragged past a room full of guards either waiting to go on duty or making reports. Ink darted behind me in the shadows, walking with his head up and his tail high. If anyone noticed him, they didn't care. What was one more cat in a city likely full of cats? One of the guards even reached down to scratch Ink's ears, which he ignored.

I, on the other hand, received stares, some interested, others bored. My captor led me down a narrow hallway and shoved me into a dim room, bereft of all furniture but a table and two chairs. The stone seemed to reflect the cold, making me shiver. The door closed behind me with a heavy *thud*.

I was well and truly snared, and I hadn't even done anything. Tears filled my eyes unbidden.

"We'll get you out of here," Ink said, voice thin through the heavy wooden door. I jumped and hissed a curse, then sat in one of the chairs, suddenly exhausted.

"How?" I asked.

"You haven't committed a crime. They won't keep you for long. Just tell them the truth. Well, leave out the bit about wanting to destroy the bloodstone refinery."

Again, I asked, "How?" This time with more bite.

Ink made an exasperated sound. "Write it down?" he suggested. "They should let you have a paper and pen. Just don't use your magic, okay? We need to keep that particular talent a secret."

I looked at the cuff of my sleeve, half-expecting to see the familiar stripes of red against Archive blue, but there was nothing but plain brown linen. Ink had advised me to leave behind all traces of being a scribe or an Archivist, and I had agreed without thinking. All of my clothes had burned, anyways; it was all too easy to forget to ask for the red stripes when buying supplies.

The door swung open a moment later and my captor walked in, a tired-looking man bearing a bundle of papers, ink, and a quill shuffling behind her. I expected Ink to saunter in after them, but she shooed him away while the man curled his lip in disdain. He had dark circles under his eyes and his face was sallow, but there was something unsettling in the way he studied me. It was predatory, dangerous, more so than any of the other looks I'd gotten from the guards.

My magic flared to life, the words on those papers whispering softly in my ear. It was mostly data, likely taken from other prisoners or people being interrogated. Height, sex, general appearance, crime, their responses to being questioned. But there was a maliciousness in the words, in the reports, that had my adrenaline spiking. And there was something else, too. A whisper that didn't match the data. One that was old, ancient even. So ancient that my magic didn't translate it, only let the harsh words sing through my mind as an undercurrent to the reports. It came from a small book in the man's right jacket pocket, the pages made of parchment, the ink an unfamiliar tang on my tongue.

My fingers twitched as if to call the book to me. I clasped them to hold them still.

"Omar, you sit there," the guardswoman said, gesturing to the chair across from me. "I'll go fetch another."

She left me alone with the man—Omar—and he sat down as if preparing for a simple meeting. He arranged his ink pot and pens neatly, centring his papers between them. He fussed with the items for a bit longer before settling back into the chair.

"We might as well get started while Guard Amery finds a chair," Omar said, voice reedy and even. As if he were trying to be soothing in a situation that was anything but. I wanted to be far, far away from this man.

"What is your name?" Omar looked at me, pen poised above a blank sheet of paper. I said nothing, not even trying to find the words, not bothering to sign or mime asking for something to write with. I knew, instinctively, that silence was my best choice here, so silent I remained.

My heart pounded loudly in my ears.

"Hmmm." He tilted his head like a raptor sizing up a

mouse. "Guard Amery said that you were found lingering near the entrance to the harbour, is that correct?"

I kept perfectly still, my eyes focused on his paper. That strange language whispered louder in my mind, pulsing from that little book with an energy I'd never felt from words before. It was almost alive in a way that no other book was alive. And it was beginning to pay attention to me.

Omar pinched his lips. "I assure you, miss, we are not trying to cause you harm or frighten you. But you were found near a restricted area, and we must take note of it. For our records, you see."

I tried to identify the ink of that strange book, for it was like nothing I'd encountered before. It had the bitter coldness of iron and the texture of soot, but there was something else, something providing a depth that had a metallic, coppery tang to it. The ink was smooth, as smooth as the words whispering in my ear were harsh and foreign.

"If you do not cooperate, then I will have to move on from simply asking questions and enter this incident in as a more formal interrogation." Omar leaned forwards, dark eyes glittering. "I think you would prefer not to mark this incident down as a formal interrogation."

The door swung open and Amery returned, dragging a chair behind her. It scraped on the floor in a harsh counterpoint to Omar's soft-spoken questions. I flinched. Amery straddled the chair and leaned her arms on the back.

"That damned cat out there just won't leave. Well?" she asked Omar, peering at his blank paper.

"She is surprisingly reticent," he admitted, setting his pen down. "I was informing her that we would have to make this formal."

Amery frowned, looking mildly surprised. She fixed a friendly smile on me. "Come, now. You weren't breaking any laws. Yet. We just have to be careful of all people we find in the vicinity of the harbour after dark. For the safety of Makhier, you see. All we need is your information. Name, residence, that sort of thing."

I returned her stare and kept silent. I believe that she was honest in her desires, and that all she wanted was my information—all of which I would have gladly given, had it not been for Omar, the malice in his records, and that book in his pocket.

My fingers twitched again, ready to call the book forth, desperate to call the book forth. I clasped them tighter, so tightly that surely no blood would flow.

Amery's frown deepened. "I said you haven't broken any laws, but if you do not provide us with your information, then I will have to charge you with interfering in an official investigation. Things will get much, much worse if I have to do that."

Omar leaned forwards in his chair, barely enough to convey his eagerness. It was harder to disguise the obvious interest in his eyes. Amery waited, but when I was not forthcoming, she sighed and shook her head.

"Very well. You are hereby officially charged by the lawkeepers of Makhier with interfering in an official investigation." She stood and wiped her hands on her tunic, as if sweating. As if nervous. She cast a glance at Omar, then at me, her mouth flat. "In keeping with Makhierian law, you are now to be formally interrogated."

She turned and left the room, kicking at a black shape just beyond the door. Ink growled loudly, but was cut off once again from entering the room. "Elyria, just wait! I'll figure out a way to get you out of there," he called through the door. I hoped that he would, because in that moment, I was truly afraid.

Omar picked up his pen and licked the tip before dipping it in the inkwell. He started scratching out words on the paper, their forms coming to life before my very eyes, practically singing in malicious glee.

The subject, who refuses to give her name or place of residence, is charged with interference in an official investigation. This is a record of the formal interrogation as carried out by Omar Miris, Interrogator of Justicar House Seven.

He paused in his writing, glancing up at me. "I don't suppose you've been interrogated before, have you?"

I remained still, silent.

"No, I imagine not. They used to use mages for this sort of thing. Healers, at first, because they could manipulate the human body. But it became too much of a strain on their magic, using it in a way that runs contrary to its primary calling. They tried material mages next. Stone mages. Metal mages. But their magic is meant for crafting, not breaking. Elemental mages were the most flexible, given they could control their elements quite thoroughly, but finding them and training them to this sort of work is expensive. Yes, very expensive." Omar kept his pen hovering over the paper, seemingly forgotten as he watched me. "It turned out that regular people, ordinary people, were the most suited for this work. And I am one of the best."

He waited for me to make a move, a response, anything, then hummed softly and continued writing. *Subject remains entirely silent. I will begin by seeing if she is capable of sound at all, or is simply mute.*

He set the pen down, pulled out a small cloth from his pocket, and began cleaning the device. He took care to polish the metal nib thoroughly, removing any trace of ink, as if he were done with his report and starting to pack things away.

Without warning, he lunged, stabbing his pen into my left hand where it was twined with my right on the table. I was too startled to do more than suck in a breath before pain blinded me. A strangled sound escaped my throat, but no more than that. My mind flew away from the pain, from the horror of watching my blood pool on the table.

Omar pulled out his pen and dipped it into the inkwell, my blood still on the tip. It diluted the ink, changing the whispers of that liquid to something else entirely. I realised, between the throbbing beats of my heart now bleeding from my hand, that this was why that book in his pocket was so different, so strange.

So wrong.

It wasn't written with normal ink, even ancient ink. It was ancient, yes, but it was written in ink mixed with blood, just as Omar was now writing with a similar substance on his paper.

Subject made a noise when subjected to unexpected pain, but it is unclear whether that indicates if she can speak. A more concentrated effort is required.

I retreated into my mind, into my magic. It was the only thing that wasn't going to hurt, wasn't going to cause pain. I knew pain. I had dealt with terrible pain. I knew how to remain silent even when my bones were breaking and my vision swam. I knew how to let the world fade away into terrible nothingness, leaving me alone in my mind. I loathed doing it, but I was adept. Instead of focusing on the sensations of my body, I let my conscious thoughts turn to my magic.

I let myself be swallowed by the whispers of the words.

The reports beneath mine were all the same, all facts and figures until they became records of how people reacted to pain. I ripped the life from those words and silenced those terrible reports. The papers in front of me became quiet just as the ink now mixed with my blood began to dry up. There were no more words left, though, and Omar was stalking towards me, his hands reaching and his expression twisted in joy.

So my mind dove into the place I knew, instinctively, that it shouldn't: the ancient book in his pocket.

It whispered to me in that strange language, surrounding me, soothing me. Even as Omar drew closer, snatching my injured hand from where I cradled it, that language of the long dead past wrapped around me, offering calm in the midst of pain, power where I was powerless. All I had to do was reach out and take it.

I locked eyes with Omar as he prepared to squeeze my hand. He recoiled.

"Gods above," he breathed, staggering back until he was pressed against the stone wall. I stood, not entirely of my own volition. "Guards! *Guards!*"

The door slammed open behind me and people rushed in. They were of no concern to me, not when those words were within reach, not when I could just take hold of them. Omar reflexively reached into his pocket and pulled out the book, clutching it tightly to him. He started muttering in that same language that whispered in my mind, but it was too late.

The book would be mine.

"Elyria, *no!*" Ink screamed.

I lay my hand on the book. I didn't even take it from Omar; I just touched it and the world around me exploded in blood-forged ink and magic that hadn't seen the light of day since before remembering. The magic made a joyful sound, one of escape, of freedom after imprisonment, and then my own magic took hold.

The ink screeched, twisting into the shape of a dragon and snapping its fangs at me. But it was still ink, and even as I was still in its thrall, it too was in mine. It flew towards me, that strange, ancient magic. I reached for it, some part of my mind awake in this nightmare. I had to contain this magic or the world would fall apart. I didn't know how, I didn't know why, but I knew it to be so.

The ink-dragon touched my skin and I was engulfed. It pulled me into the air, attacking me even as I seized control. But there was nowhere for the ink to go. The book that had held it was ash. The papers that Omar had brought in were dead at my hand. The ink demanded freedom. I refused to let it go.

What happened next was a blur of needle-sharp pain over my entire body. I remember taking the ink into myself, controlling it with iron will and my scribe magic. I remember the pain. Then, I remember nothing but darkness.

I woke to the feeling of phantom fingers brushing my hair back from my face. For a brief instant, I thought I was engulfed by wings, but when I blinked to clear my eyes, all I saw was Ink's face pressed too close to mine.

"That's twice I've watched you recover from the effects of your magic, scribe," Ink said, pulling back slightly. "Let's not make this a third attempt."

"What happened?" I groaned and sat up, looking around the room. The table and chairs were overturned and there was dust from damage to the stone everywhere, but otherwise the room was empty.

"No time for that now. You've been unconscious five minutes or so. They cleared out the place, but I doubt that will last for long. We need to move. *Now.*" Ink leaped for the door, the fur on his tail puffed out. He looked back over his shoulder when I didn't immediately stand and follow him. "Now!"

I scrambled to follow, my head spinning. I *hurt*, my muscles aching and my skin tingling with a strange heat. My hand ached where I had been stabbed, though when I glanced at the injury, all I saw was smooth skin. But I could move, so I did. I didn't even question the destruction of the guardhouse as we left, noting overturned tables and chairs, destroyed papers and inkwells smashed. There were gouges in some of the tables and on the walls, which I was certain my scribe magic couldn't have caused, but there wasn't time to question.

Instead, I followed Ink into the darkness. We managed to avoid any people—they had well and truly disappeared, leaving behind an eerie stillness—and ran towards the empty places closer to the water. The foul smell of the refinery added to my headache and made my mind split with agony. I staggered to a stop behind a small boatman's shed.

"Elyria?" Ink asked, putting his paws on my knees, whiskers twitching. "What is it?"

I sank to the ground, pressing my palms to my temple. "My head is killing me. It's that *smell*."

Ink looked around, then darted off, returning a moment later with a rag carried delicately between his teeth. He looked severely disgusted by it. "Smell this instead."

I took the cloth, wincing at the stickiness. "What is it?"

"Pitch," Ink said, but only after I had already taken a

whiff. I gagged, then managed to reach the edge of the dock before vomiting into the water. I retched a bit more then sat back against the shed. My hands were shaking.

"Are you better?" Ink asked. Meaning, *Can you move?*

"I need a minute." I no longer had a splitting headache, but I was dizzy and sore. I rubbed my temples again, eyes closed. "What happened, exactly?"

"It's complicated," Ink said. I cracked an eye and glared at him. He gave a movement that was so like a human shrug that I looked at him fully. He sighed, wrapping his tail around his paws. "It's Old Magic."

"As if saying that is supposed to explain things? What *happened?*"

Ink's ears went back. "There are some things, old things, that are better left forgotten and—"

"Claw that Writes With Ink, if you don't tell me what happened to me back there, then I swear I will throw you in the water." I sat up and reached for him, just to prove my point, though all I ended up doing was making my head spin. I groaned and leaned back again, waiting for the world to stop moving.

"I would have kept you from this knowledge," Ink murmured. "It's safer that way."

"Safer isn't always better. Ignorance..." My mouth went dry as I remembered Beltran and the things I hadn't known about him. "Ignorance isn't always bliss, Ink. I would rather know."

"Very well. That book the vile man had was ancient. Before the time of your gods, certainly, and full of magic

148

that was wielded by people who were not bound to any specific domain. These people—sorcerers—could shape the world itself to their whims. They raged war against the gods and when the war went badly for them, tried to seal the knowledge of their magic away for future use. They sealed it in books like that. Grimoires. All were lost. Or so I thought."

Sorcerers. Grimoires. The words were unfamiliar to me and yet I felt as if I'd been hearing them my whole life and only now just understood what they meant. I closed my eyes again, my thoughts spinning nearly as fast as the world. "I thought you said this was before the gods."

"I have explained to you already about the gods, Elyria," Ink said, sounding annoyed.

"But who were these other gods?"

"A tale for another time. All you need to know right now is that your magic must have awoken the spells in that book somehow. I doubt very much that small, vile man could have managed to unlock that sort of power. I doubt he even knew what he had; he was probably just drawn to the innate power held within. Unfortunately, when you did awaken the magic, it tried to attack. To control."

"I felt it," I said, remembering the intent behind that ink dragon. It was almost alive. "It wanted to be free. To destroy those who had...bound it?"

Ink was suddenly pressed close to my side, his fur warm against my hands. Without opening my eyes, I buried my fingers in that warmth. "Yes," he said. "That sounds right. I thought...I thought you were dead. Part of the reason that the grimoires no longer exist is because they destroyed those who tried to wield them. The sorcerer's power was too strong for most."

"But the power was bound to ink," I mused. "My power is of ink and paper and words. It wanted out. I kept it in."

Ink stiffened. "In…where?"

"There was nowhere for it to go, no paper to bind it again, so I contained it within my own magic."

Ink moved away, then I felt sharp claws against my sleeve. My eyes flew open in time to witness him shred the fabric like tissue paper. The forearm of my sleeve fell away. It was hard to see, given the darkness, but there were enough lamps on the dock to provide a little illumination. And what I saw was not my skin. Not as it had been.

Minuscule words scrolled over my arm in intricate patterns, looking like scales and twists of claw. I touched the scale pattern on my arm. Power unlike anything I'd felt before—warm, strong, alive—flowed through me and my scribe magic, making the ink shine with a gentle orange glow, like living flame trapped beneath my skin.

"Blood of the Gods," Ink breathed. "You have a sorcerer's dragon trapped within you."

CHAPTER 9

I was prepared to panic, to start tearing off my clothes to see the whole beast now inked on my skin. Now that Ink had named it, I could feel the ink of the dragon beneath my skin as if it were breathing. Its antlered head and neck were on my right shoulder, and it twined over and down my entire body, one arm over my left shoulder, one leg down my right leg, the others holding me as if in an embrace. Its tail curled through every empty space, long and sinuous, scales alive with power.

I could feel it, and I wanted it *off* of me.

A scream built up in my throat, wanting escape, but the sound of heavy footsteps had me swallowing it into silence again. I let the silence wrap around me, a blanket, comforting, safe. The glow of the dragon faded and by the time the guards jogged by, murmuring to each other, I was shrouded by shadows and all but invisible.

They ran right past.

"We don't have time to explore this right now," Ink said, tail lashing as he stared at the place the guards had been. "We need to get to the refinery and destroy it before they find you."

"Still?" I gaped at the cat. "After all that has happened, you *still* want to destroy the refinery?"

Ink hissed in response. I took that as a yes.

"Can you just tell me why this is so important? Not the preventing people from being sick, not the danger of god blood or bloodstone or whatever, but why this is so important to you."

Anything to keep from thinking of that power now entwined with my own magic. Trapped on my skin. Alive. I stared at Ink like a lifeline, waiting for an answer to ground me.

He paced a short circle, claws digging into the wood of the docks. Finally, he stopped and said, "I have been trapped in those Archives for time beyond counting. I have heard stories and reports of things in the world that should have been left to a different age, but I haven't been able to *do* anything about it. Now, I can."

He didn't say it outright, but there was a plea in his voice. He was begging me to help him, because if I didn't go with him, he couldn't go. He was still bound, still trapped, just to me rather than a physical place. I had felt trapped before, often, and knew the way that it chipped at your soul. Normal life became a myth, and everything was dictated by someone else. Something else.

"Then let's go. I have a feeling that this place will be crawling with guards before dawn."

Surely I had gone mad. I was truly insane, after all that had happened, to be running after a magical creature towards the refinery. There was a being of living magic inked into my skin and I had no idea what it was or how to deal with it. I feared I was going to explode at any moment, but the plea in Ink's eyes had me shoving all of that aside. I took several deep breaths and stood. It wasn't far, even with ducking down to hide behind crates or sheds when guards moved past. My body still ached and I had no idea how we were even going to destroy the refinery, but I followed Ink.

After our previous run through the harbour buildings, I hadn't expected the refinery to be so close. The smell permeated everything, so it was impossible to tell when we were at the source until Ink skidded to a stop before the low building.

"This is it," he breathed, ears flat against his head.

It didn't look like much, blending in with the other buildings around it except for the various barrels stacked against one side, smelling of something rotten. Waste products from the refining process, I imagined. My eyes watered from the smell.

"How do we destroy it?" I asked in a whisper, searching over my shoulder for any sign of guards. The building was silent, though, not even a single lantern or torch providing light to see by.

"Burn it. It's fairly volatile and should burn easily."

"A fire will bring the entirety of the Makhier city guard

down on us, not to mention their military. And what if it spreads?"

"They won't be able to rebuild," Ink said, sounding so sure that I wanted to believe him. I wanted it to be that easy. But if this bloodstone truly did enhance magic, then I had no doubt that if we managed to destroy the refinery, they would rebuild. They would keep rebuilding over and over again.

"Ink—" I started to bring up my concerns, but the cat let out a hiss and leaped for the sealed barrels, clambering his way up. I wanted to complain, then quickly scrambled after him when I heard footsteps coming our way. Pain sang through me with every movement; thankfully, panic was the stronger motivational force. I made it to the top of the pile with a swiftness that I had never before achieved. Ink had his teeth around the latch of a window and was pulling it open. He leaped inside.

"It's safe. Hurry!"

I crawled through the window, my hair catching on the frame.

Once inside, I let out a series of curses in every language I knew.

"Gods above. Ink, I thought you said this was a refinery!"

He stared solemnly at the rows and rows of cots that filled the floor of the refinery, each one with a still form. On one side of the beds was a bucket of reddish-grey stone. Suspended over each bucket was an arm of one of the unmoving people, blood dripping slowly, steadily, into the buckets. This looked more like a torture chamber or a drug house than any laboratory, any refinery.

"Petrified god blood," Ink said, nodding towards the buckets. "Activated by the blood of humans. The magic of the human blood reacts with the magic of the god blood. The byproduct drains out and the resulting stones—bloodstone—are ready for use."

If I hadn't already emptied my stomach by the dock, then I would have done so again.

"Why isn't anyone tending them?" I asked. "Are they... dead?"

"No. Drugged, possibly. And why bother tending them when they're going to die anyways?" Ink's voice was quiet, sad, as if he had expected this and was disappointed to not have been wrong.

I shook my head, backing up until the wall held me up, until I was staring at the floor of the catwalk and not the blissed expressions of the people down there. "How could anyone do this?" My words were choked. Soon, I wouldn't be able to speak at all with the bile rising in me.

"The pursuit of power can be a cruel thing. My guess is that these were transients, the poor, the already ill. Those that society wouldn't miss." Ink padded to the edge of the catwalk and peered down. "Won't miss."

"And you just want to burn them?" It was a whisper and all the words I had left. Perhaps all the fight I had left, too.

Ink snarled at me, baring his fangs and arching his back. "You would let them suffer for the benefit of someone else? These people aren't the only casualties of this...this...*cruelty*,

Elyria. They are merely the first ones who will die. Or have you forgotten that the byproduct is toxic? The bodies drained to activate the god blood are toxic? They cannot be cured or saved. There is no other end. It must be done!"

Tears filled my eyes. I lifted my hands. *"You're asking me to kill them."*

"For the greater good. For their benefit. For the benefit of all those who might otherwise be affected by this."

"There has to be another way!" I insisted.

"Tell me that other way," Ink said, voice cold. "Tell me and we will leave right now."

I cast my thoughts about desperately. *"What if I brought a city official here? The guards! They were chasing me. I could lure them into the building and—"*

"Do you honestly think that this is happening right under their noses? That they aren't aware of what's going on here?" Ink scoffed, tossing his head. "You really are a fool."

I shook my head again.

"Think, Elyria! How did a snivelling, weasel of a man, a lowly interrogator in a guardhouse in Makhier, come to have a grimoire? Why is the harbour guarded with nearly fifty people? Why is the Makhierian military being quartered in Vazeri? You can't honestly believe that some ridiculous threat from Imara is the cause. That empire is *bound* by the magic in the boundary mountains, you ignorant human!"

In the end, after being flayed by Ink's words, I didn't have to muster the will to respond, to argue back. The door below us burst open and five guards entered. I could see them only by the faint glow of the buckets and the light coming in from the moon through the windows, but their armour glinted all the same. I froze, Ink pressing against my leg.

"No one came in here," one of the guards said.

"You sure?" Another looked around. "They could be hiding."

"You honestly think that chit is hiding amongst the living dead?" The first guard barked out a laugh. A third backed towards the door, holding a hand to their mouth.

"Dusk and Night, I hate this place. It reeks."

"They say they can start shutting this place down and moving production nearer the Great Plains. They've managed to use some of this stuff to neutralise the magic around the encampment. They can stay long term."

The second guard nodded, light glinting off their helm. "Thank the gods. People are going to start asking questions if this place stays much longer. The smell alone could fell a horse!"

They all chuckled at that, then slipped back out again. Not one of the people on the cots had stirred. They just lay there, oblivious to the world.

"Elyria," Ink said, all the anger drained from him. "Please."

"*They're mining this...petrified god blood from the Great Plains?*" I signed.

"There are various divine graveyards there."

I would ask how he knew that later. My thoughts were

consumed by something else entirely. *"My parents...they disappeared on an expedition to the Great Plains."*

Ink said nothing, only lashed his tail. He knew.

"You knew?"

"Your friend Margarethe's voice carries," Ink said.

I closed my eyes, tears filling them. How had my life gone from the simple life of an Archivist, shelving books, collecting information and tending to paper and ink, to *this*? On a quest I was woefully unprepared for, facing the murder of about forty people, supposedly for the greater good.

"I don't think I can do this."

I waited for Ink to scold me, to chastise me, to tell me again the cost of my refusal, but instead there was silence. I opened my eyes and blinked back the tears. Ink was gone.

Panic set my skin aflame. I spun, looking for him. There! He was running across the catwalk, steps light as the wind, heading for the stairs on the other side. Clumsily, I staggered after him, my steps anything but light, my movements tempered by pain. By the time I reached the top of the stairs, Ink was already at the bottom, searching for something.

I stumbled my way down the steps, clutching the railings. I tried calling after Ink, but I was in the grips of adrenaline and panic. Words were the last thing I could manage just then. By the time I reached the bottom of the stairs, Ink was sniffing along a wall, pawing at some wood, some metal.

"You should leave, Elyria. I don't want you getting hurt."

I thought he was bound to me. Did that mean I couldn't leave without him having to come with me? I stepped closer.

"Go to the door. Now. I will meet you there."

Was he trying to find a way to make fire? To burn this place to the ground? Given that not even the guards had entered this place with a torch, I doubted very much that the workers would have been so foolish as to leave something easily caught by flame nearby. There weren't even candles here. Or paper, for that matter, I realised, my scribe magic entirely dormant.

Just thinking of my magic had the dragon now enmeshed in my skin stirring. It was alive, in a way, attuned to my panic and thoughts but without thoughts of its own. My scribe magic had bound it, yes, but it was powerful in an entirely different way, one that rippled through me like spilled ink on paper. My skin began to glow with its design, shining through the tear in my sleeve. Ink whirled to stare at me.

I pawed at the inked dragon, trying to turn it dormant again like I had before. Only this time, it didn't work. The dragon rumbled, power gathering in those tiny inked words on my skin. My brushing at it only produced sparks of magic. Sparks of fire.

A single, solitary spark landed on a bucket that had started to overflow, the body bleeding into it either dead or so near to death that it wouldn't be alive long. Before I could do more than suck in a breath, the puddle of human blood mixed with god blood burst into flame, an inferno that started consuming everything in its path.

The dragon shifted on my back and the scales glowed brighter. It whispered in that same ancient language as the grimoire, singing through my scribe magic as though it were still on a page. Sparks flared again.

"Elyria, run!" Ink shouted. He raced towards me, leaping over the rising flames. I turned and fled towards the door that the guards had entered on the other side of the building. Fire teased at my ankles, hotter than anything I'd ever experienced, even the fire at the triumvirate building. I heard shrieks and thought I saw one of the people sit up and scrabble at their skin, but the fire arced and leaped and consumed faster than I could comprehend and the vision was gone.

"Faster!" Ink was at my side once again, legs eating up the ground. I ran, fire licking at my back. The dragon on my skin rumbled, and for an instant the fire retreated, long enough for me to get to the door and escape into the cool air. Ink and I burst into the open and kept running.

"This way," he called, leading me away from the fire now consuming the entire building in a roar so loud that it echoed off the hills of the Makhierian valley. I didn't hesitate, didn't question, didn't *think*, instead following Ink until we were back at the inn where I'd booked rooms for the night.

I dug into my pocket for the key, ran into my room, and closed it behind me with a heavy thud that echoed the beating of my heart. The world around me seemed to spin; the colours were too bright, the sounds dull compared to the rush of blood in my ears. I was vaguely aware that I shook, but was otherwise insensate to the world.

"...it wasn't your fault, I swear. I know what I asked of you and I was wrong. I'm sorry. I will spend my days atoning for that mistake if only you talk to me. Please, Elyria—"

"Ink?" I blinked blearily at him. He was sitting before me, paw outstretched and touching my arms, which still glowed softly, though there were no more sparks. Strange, but it felt more like a hand providing solid comfort, not the soft velvet of cat paws. "What...?"

"You've been...are you alright?" Ink flicked his ears and that phantom touch on my arm tightened a bit before relaxing and all I felt was that gentle paw. Had I imagined it? Attributed it to Ink's touch when it could have been the dragon living on my skin?

I rubbed my eyes. "P-panic attack. I sort of shut down."

"Then, you're not hurt?"

I had the feeling he was asking something else, but I didn't have it in me to try and read into the subtleties of his conversation. I wrapped my arms around my knees. "What happened?" I rasped, tears beginning to choke me voice. "Oh, gods. Those people—"

Ink cut me off with a growl. "It was *not* your fault. They were dead when they were put into those beds. You merely ended their suffering."

The shriek of the dying man echoed in my mind. The

ink-scales on my arm fluttered with light and I recoiled, hitting my head on the door. "What is happening to me?"

"I don't know, precisely. I can guess, but I've never actually encountered a mix of magics like this." He shifted his tone to sound rational, reasonable, almost like the scholarly cat in the Archives who lectured me on the metaphysical nature of gods. It was enough to ground me, just a little, to the room. I became aware of my surroundings enough to go through my further grounding exercises.

I could see the bed, my pack, the window coverings, Ink, and a bedside table. I could hear my breathing, Ink's tail swishing against the floor, the shouts of people outside, the murmur of voices in the room below. I smelled the faint acrid flavour of smoke, the wood shavings from where the door had been repaired, and stale baking, likely from a dinner served long ago. On my tongue, I tasted ash and salt from my tears.

Grounded, I let my body relax a bit, just enough to crawl to the bed and lie there, pulling the bedclothes tight around me. "What can you guess?" I breathed, wiping away tears.

Ink leaped to the bed and lay beside me, that same phantom touch encircling me like wings. "Your unique scribe magic let you trap the power in the grimoire. I'm not sure how a sorcerer managed to bind one of their dragons to the pages, but that magic was volatile and world-changing; I can't imagine it would be impossible. The combination of the two magics, though—the vast, star-strong power of sorcery's Old Magic and the specific nature of modern magic—that is what I'm unsure of. I don't know how they

will react together. Already we've seen that there are...
unusual effects of having the dragon attached to you."

I scoffed and turned my back to him. "Unusual effects? I
produced sparks that killed probably forty people."

Ink pressed close to my back, those comforting, invisible
wings tightening in an embrace. "If I could spare you the
blood on your hands, Elyria Trevain, then I would. I should
never have asked that you be the one to burn the building
down."

Tears slipped down my cheeks, wetting the pillow.
"Then why did you?"

Ink was silent for a minute and I feared he would not
answer me. Finally, he said in a voice that was dark and sad
and full of pain, he said, "Because I am a coward. And you
are anything but cowardly."

He said nothing more, even when I waited for an explanation. I couldn't find anything to say, either, and my hands
were tucked beneath my chin, so I remained silent as well. I
fell asleep like that, with unspoken words filling the space
between us, and for the first time in years, I doubted that
silence was the answer.

INTERLUDE II

*K*eir's feet dragged on the floor as he was hauled through the corridors, his wings useless at his sides. He tried to struggle, tried to fight back as he'd been taught, but those bearing him had been taught as well, and they hadn't had their magic shredded by human swords. The doors to the Hall of Thrones swung open on a silent wind, revealing the imposing chamber.

It was open to the sky, illuminating the stars that began to fade with the coming dawn. Spells kept the room warm against the chill, enough that the flowering plants in gilded pots bloomed happily. Seven golden thrones spaced evenly throughout the room loomed over Keir. Three of them were occupied, with several pedestals behind the thrones bearing less powerful gods.

Hirana, goddess of knowledge, sat in the centre throne, her six wings flaring in agitation. Tani, the Overwatcher, was in the throne to her sister's left, and Maris, god of the underworld, sat on the right, his shadowy wings revealing the darkness of the universe.

Keir felt the weight of his own now-useless wings even more.

"You," Hirana said, voice cutting and cruel. "What is your name?"

The goddess of knowledge and she didn't know him? Keir was suddenly aware at how small he was, how foolish. What was he but an insect compared to these great beings? And he had presumed to defy them. For what? A human woman who despised him for being a servant to her oppressors.

Before Keir could answer Hirana, Tani leaned forwards, leering at him. "Black wings. He must be one of yours, Maris."

The god of the underworld lifted his head, looking bored. "No, I don't recognise him. Perhaps he belongs to one of our lesser cousins."

Hirana huffed. "Tell me your name," she thundered, the top pair of her wings flaring wide, blocking out some of the light from torches along the wall.

Keir felt a kick in his side. He flinched away, but the second guard stepped on his wing, pinning it to the ground just a fingerspan away from the place where the humans had clipped it.

"Speak!" Hirana snarled.

"Keir," he gasped, barely able to lift his head as he quaked at the goddess's power. The goddess of knowledge reared back, blinking. Her wings fluttered and folded.

"Keir. *You* are Keir? The servant trusted with the keeping of knowledge?" She shook her head. "You lie! Guards, pierce his wings. Perhaps that will entice you to the truth."

The guards exchanged a glance, but they could not disobey a direct order from their goddess. They knew Keir to be speaking true, knew him by name, yet still they drew their swords and brought them down, the tips shattering bone and driving into the marble floor. Keir screamed, thrashing.

"I am Keir," he sobbed through the pain. "I swear it!"

Maris sighed, sounding bored. "He could be telling the truth, sister. Now that he says it, I do believe he is marginally familiar. Do you not recall seeing him fetch books for you?"

Tani peered at him, gripping the arms of her throne with barely concealed glee. She, more than most of the gods, delighted in pain. Perhaps that was why she was one of the most despised by the humans who were forced into worship and labour. "Yes, I remember now. He helped me find that piece on the proper care of breeding humans."

Hirana frowned, mouth a thin line. She waved a hand and sank back into her throne. "Yes, I believe you're right. Guards, release his wings."

The swords were freed and Keir collapsed. His vision was blurred by pain and he could feel only the throbbing agony in his wings. He gasped on the ground, watching his blood pool and trickle into the stone shattered by the sword points. These were the masters he had sworn to obey and uphold? They didn't even remember him, though all had presided at his ceremony of appointment.

Even Hirana, whose domain was knowledge, didn't remember him. And he had been punished for her poor memory.

Fire bloomed bright in Keir's chest, pushing back some of the pain. He planted one hand on the floor, then the other, and with what felt like the last scraps of ability in his body, pushed himself into a seated position. His wings lay in ruins at his side, the fine bones shattered, the muscles severed. He knelt in a slowly growing pool of his own blood, and he let every drop that fell fuel the fire now burning bright inside him.

Betrayed by both sides, Keir knew now he stood alone.

Hirana stood, towering over him, her wings spread wide to emphasise her stature. A bird posturing for dominance, Keir thought with a sneer.

"Not an hour ago, I was returning from the Midwinter celebration and I was *attacked* by a band of humans. They were swiftly dispatched, but the fact of the matter remains that never before have humans dared to attack us, their gods." Hirana stepped towards him, forcing Keir to crane his head back to look at her. He pressed a hand to his sore ribs and held them while he laughed once.

"You dare to laugh at me?" Hirana snarled. Her wings flapped, filling the room with a whirlwind of air, but apart from ruffling his hair and broken feathers, it did nothing to Keir. Another useless display of power.

"How can you not realise?" he asked, mocking. "You, a goddess of knowledge, and you don't even know!"

"I know that you were found in the Hall of Knowing, your wings clipped and your magic with them," Hirana said in a low voice. "Given that you were found directly after I was attacked, I cannot imagine how you can deny the connection."

Keir nodded, laughing again. "Oh, yes, there is a connection. But do you know what it is, Great One?"

Hirana hissed. Maris rose and spread his own wings, blocking out even more of the light. Shadows played around his feet, but Keir held no fear of them, not anymore. His faith in these creatures was gone. They could but break his body, not his soul. Not anymore.

"What have you done?" Tani asked, her grip tightening on the arms of her throne so that they creaked, bowing under the pressure of her anger.

"What should have been done a long time ago," Keir said, smiling. "I freed the humans from their bindings. I gave them the power to know."

Hirana staggered backwards, stumbling until she fell into her throne. "You added human blood to the inkwell," she breathed. "You—"

"I made it so they don't need you any longer," Keir said. His head was starting to swim with fatigue and loss of blood. His injuries were more serious than he'd thought. He couldn't much bring himself to care. He sneered at the gods. "I made it so they can raise themselves up out of the muck where you keep them. They can learn how to improve their own lives. They can learn to write and to read and to collect knowledge, to build upon the past and look to the future. No longer will they depend on you to guide their every step, their every move. They don't need you for knowing when to harvest, for knowing when to plant, for knowing who to love and who to ally themselves with. They can learn, Hirana. They don't need you anymore."

Hirana screeched, raising a hand to strike Keir down. He tossed his head back and laughed, the sound cruel and furious and broken, yet satisfied in the knowledge that he had freed the humans, and in doing so, freed himself.

Pain woke Keir, sharp and stabbing, radiating from his wings to his toes. He could feel the magic in his blood slowly knitting him back together, but when one is beaten by gods, there is only so much innate magic can do. He knew, from a quick stretch of his wings that had him gasping in agony, that they would never recover. The left one was twisted in an unnatural way, feathers brushing the ground. The right one was folded by his side, unable to extend. With the loss of his wings, all of his magic but the little healing in his blood was gone.

Crippled. His folly had left him crippled, and he had no one to blame but himself.

The price, he decided with wrathful glee, was worth it. It was all worth it to watch the gods falter for the first time.

To know that the humans would rise up and burn the gods to the ground. That they would dethrone those pretenders, who claimed power and yet were so blind, so ignorant, so confident that they ruined lives with a flick of their hand and no regret.

Then, as the pain receded and Keir was able to take better stock of his surroundings, he heard the screams. They filtered to him through the bars on the lone opening in his cell, bringing with them a trickle of light so he could be aware of his dismal fate. The screams were horrified, full of terror and pain. There were some that held rage, but they were quickly extinguished.

Where were they coming from? Keir tilted his head, his neck protesting the change in position. He must have been near the secret tunnel, the one that led almost directly to the human encampments. Because those screams weren't angelic, and they weren't god-kind. They were full of the desperation of humans, full of feeling that only humans could accomplish.

The gods were likely slaughtering them.

Keir rose to his feet with a cry of fury, rushing the door and throwing his whole weight against it. His crippled magic flared, pushing at the wood, the iron bars, the stone. His magic was repelled, almost ignored. Aching and feeble, Keir fell back against the far wall, his useless wings crushed beneath his weight. His vision turned white, pain blinding him.

The gods had made this cage for angels. For their own servants. Nothing was resistant to his power, what scraps of it were left, not unless it had been specifically crafted as such. Keir buried his head in his knees. He'd been so sure of his success. So pleased at his actions, even if betrayal loomed in their wake.

The cruel humans and the crueller gods, fighting each other because of him. Somehow, he hadn't considered that people would die.

A gentle light filled the chamber and Keir pulled his head deeper into his arms, hiding from its glow. Some magic of the gods, set to destroy the humans. He wanted none of it. But the glow didn't fade, didn't disappear, and it didn't have the acrid smell of god-magic.

Slowly, Keir lifted his head.

There was a woman in his cell. A *human* woman if he was any judge, though she was dressed unlike any human he'd known in a fitted, well-crafted gown of some fine fabric, her white-blonde hair cascading over her shoulders, her eyes a bright, warm brown. She gaped at Keir with astonishment, but there was no anger, no disgust, none of the usual expressions of humans when looking upon angel kind.

Keir struggled to his feet again, swaying. "Who are you?" he snarled, trying to flare his wings to intimidate her. He failed, the agony such a simple action caused bringing him to his knees. The woman rushed forward to help him, catching his weight before he could meet the stone-and-sand floor. He groaned.

The woman helped him lean back against the wall, wincing every time her hand brushed one of his wounds and bruises. Keir studied her, watching the way she automatically reached for her skirt and started ripping it apart, binding his larger wounds.

"Who are you?" Keir asked again, quieter. She couldn't know that his magic would heal him eventually, not with the concern she showed over his blood dripping on the floor. She pulled back a bit and opened her mouth, then flinched and raised her hands. They fluttered through the air in quick motions. What was she trying to do? Summon help?

A moment later, the woman huffed, lowering her hands. She looked around, mouth flat, noting the door, the confines of the cell, the tiny square of light that provided such weak illumination. Finally, she smoothed out a bit of the sand on the floor and traced her finger through it.

Keir sat up straighter, ignoring his discomfort, when he realised that she was *writing*.

Humans couldn't write! They had only gained the ability to know that day. The magic was strong, but there was no way that it would let them learn to write in such a short time. No, they only had the ability to learn how, to craft a written language. It wasn't something that would come magically, and yet this woman was writing with such ease that Keir could only assume she had known the shape of words for her whole life.

Elyria, she had written.

What did that mean? Keir frowned, trying to figure it out. The woman tapped her chest and then pointed to the word. He blinked in astonishment. It was her name.

"I'm Keir," he responded, awash with uncertainty. "How...?" He didn't even know what to ask. How long she'd been writing? How she came to be in his cell? Who she was, really?

The woman—Elyria—seemed to interpret his unasked question for herself, though, because she smoothed out the sand in the floor and wrote a few hurried words. *I think I'm dreaming.*

Keir shook his head. "This is no dream."

Elyria shook her head. *Not you. Me.*

A whole world of questions opened up for Keir and he found himself so overcome with them that he couldn't even think to form words. His mouth hung open like some fool witnessing magic for the first time. For what else could this be? She was no human that he knew, so she must come from somewhere else. Must possess some other magic than god-magic or the magic that ran through his own veins.

Further screams filtered in through the window in the door, accompanied by something that sounded like the roar of fire. Keir flinched. Elyria spun, facing the door, eyes wide and afraid.

What is happening? she wrote.

Keir scoffed, a cold sound. "The humans are learning to stand on their own, and the gods are doing their best to knock them back down."

Elyria's face twisted in confusion. Keir waited for her to ask another question, but she remained silent. Watching, studying, taking in far more than he wanted to share.

Finally, when the silence grew to be too much to bear, he spoke.

"I don't know where you come from, that you write so well, that you...have understanding, but here, the humans are slaves to the whims of the gods. They are—were—totally dependent on them, and now they are not." He laughed sharply. "The gods have decided to take issue with their independence. You hear the result of this."

Still, Elyria said nothing. Something in her seemed to deflate. She leaned back against a wall and slowly sank to the ground, her torn skirt revealing her legs. There was a flash of black, of ink, and Keir stared.

"What...what is on your skin?" he breathed, sending tendrils of his power out to sense it, to taste it. To ink one's skin in the tiny words he saw, well it was impossible to fathom. To hold knowledge on one's form instead of trapped by the gods, it was blasphemy to even think it. Keir could know, he could write and understand, but even he hadn't considered such a thing.

Elyria, though, seemed to shrink back, folding her torn skirts around her legs and tucking them beneath her.

"I won't hurt you," Keir said, though his growl was likely anything but soothing. "I just want to know what—who—you are."

Elyria seemed to fold in on herself, cloaked in a shroud of silence that Keir's words and questions couldn't break. Her entire body was still, now, no finger dancing, no writing in the sand. There was definite fear in her expression, now, directed at him as well as at the door where the sounds of destruction still rang out. She swallowed once, shuddered, and closed her eyes, hands clenched into fists.

"Please," Keir said. "Tell me. It…it could matter. For the humans here. Please."

It could matter for *him*. The humans had earned their fate.

Her eyes snapped open and she studied Keir. She took in his wounds, his broken and twisted wings, the way he trembled on the floor. Her hands unclenched, relaxing just enough for him to hope. She rubbed at her sleeves, tugging them down, shuddering as she brushed bare skin.

Then, she reached for her left sleeve and undid the lacings on the cuff enough to push it up. Keir leaned forwards eagerly, drinking in the sight of thousands upon thousands of tiny words inked into a pattern of scales and talons. He could almost make out the overarching shape, if she just lifted her sleeve a little more, if he could get close enough—

Footsteps, heavy and furious, charged down the hallway. Keir and Elyria straightened in alarm. He leaped forwards, spreading his wings as wide as they would go and gritting his teeth against the pain. She was barely hidden behind them. Whoever was coming, and he had a few guesses, they would not be kind nor merciful to Elyria if they found her there.

"However you came to be here, I need you to leave," Keir hissed, bracing himself on the ground. Elyria's eyes widened, panicked. She brushed the ink on her arm and it glowed, magic flaring to life and pressing against Keir's senses. She remained in the cell.

"You said you were dreaming," he suggested. "Wake up, then! Wake up!"

Elyria closed her eyes again, wrapping her arms around herself, and moving her lips. He couldn't hear her, but he knew she was trying to wake herself up.

"Come on, wake up!" Keir snarled, spreading his wings as wide as they would go. The right one barely moved and the left only twitched in agony. Tears filled his eyes as he fought the pain, as he fought down panic at the steps getting closer.

Elyria's eyes flew open as the door rattled, then in a flash of that magic bound in ink, she was gone. Keir was alone.

Relief warred with desperation as the door swung open, revealing Tani. She looked as though she had fought a war and come out on the losing side. Her arms were drenched in blood up to the elbow. Her wings were missing feathers; the bottom left one hung limply at her side. Her hair was matted with gore and she held the spark of violence in her gaze.

"There you are," Tani said, grinning. Her teeth were stained with blood as though she'd used them to tear the throats of her enemies. She likely had. "I thought you might like to see the fruits of your labour, traitor. Might like to see the destruction your actions have caused."

She lunged, faster than anything Keir could hope to counter given his injured state. Her hand latched onto the back of his neck and she dragged him out of the cell, heedless of his wings or other injuries. At first he tried to fight, tried to struggle, but Tani shook him, making the world spin and his head ache, so he sagged, limp in her hold.

The Overwatcher dragged him to the highest point of the palace, overlooking the human settlement and the lands beyond, where the gods liked to play. Tani squeezed his neck, forcing him to look up, to see.

"There," she snarled, waving a hand over the burning fields and houses, the piles of corpses and blood-stained ground. "Are you satisfied?"

Keir spotted a shape, far away and separate from the other destruction. It looked familiar. Winged. He squinted, his vision blurry from Tani's grip. Then, he realised what it was. Keir started laughing, the sound building up in his chest and spilling out like bile. "Satisfied indeed," he sneered. "For I see one of *you* dead on the ground."

Tani screeched, turning to face the battlefield. Judging by her shock, she hadn't known. She must have left when she thought victory assured, come to gloat over Keir. He laughed all the harder, the sound echoing over the palace, even knowing what his laughter would bring him.

So *this* was what victory tasted like.

CHAPTER 10

I woke with the memory of that cell burned into my mind, a scream caught dead in my throat. I sat up and gasped, vertigo making the room swirl around me. Closing my eyes, I silently counted until I felt more steady. When I opened them, Ink was sitting in the corner, tail wrapped neatly around his paws, eyes wide and intent.

"Are you well?" he asked. I got the impression that there was a second meaning to his question, some mystery that I was meant to unravel. I shook off my paranoia and shrugged. The image of that ruined angel remained in my mind, the piercing intensity of his gaze making me shiver.

"What time is it?"

"Four bells past dawn," Ink said. He leaped to the window sill and looked out. The sky was grey and sooty, though whether from impending rain or the remains of the fire at the refinery, I didn't know. The refinery.

Tears pricked my eyes at the memory of what I'd done,

the screams of the dead mingling with the terror of being in that cell in my nightmare. I stood and shuffled to the window, braiding my hair messily as I went. The town was oddly still, except for the few figures going about their morning business, looking over their shoulder and walking with hunched posture. I saw no guards, no officials, and only a faint plume of smoke in the direction of the harbour to indicate our nighttime activity.

"Things quieted down about an hour ago," Ink said, watching me rather than the outside world. "I haven't seen any guards or soldiers for quite some time. I don't think they're looking for you."

I was the only logical suspect. After that sorcerer's dragon had destroyed a guardhouse and been bound to my skin, after a fire at the refinery that destroyed all their supplies of bloodstone, who else could they blame but me?

Gods, I had so many questions. I was terrified of the answers.

"Are you alright?" he asked quietly, flicking his ears towards me.

"We need to leave as soon as possible," I said in a whisper. Ink didn't argue, just sighed, then leaped from the sill and stalked towards the door, the tip of his tail twitching. I felt again that phantom pressure, that agitation and power that filled the room, suffocating me for a moment before vanishing. This time, I was sure; it had come from Ink. I wanted to ask what that was, what sort of magic he bore, what he *was*, but we were far from the Archives, and such questions no longer felt like theory, like losing oneself in a tale of the past. They felt dangerous.

The deaf proprietress of the inn squawked at me as I descended, launching into a shouted description of the terrible events that had befallen Makhier during the night. She didn't seem to suspect me, only expressing concern for my well-being, seeing as I was travelling alone. Still, I winced at her shouting until I was able to get away. Head beginning to pound, I made my way to the livery.

It was busier than it had been when I first arrived, with several people milling about, whispering, one at the counter arguing with the illiterate man about hiring a horse.

"I'm sorry," he snapped. "All our horses are spoken for. If you want to leave Makhier, I suggest you do it on foot!"

The man grumbled, but persisted, offering higher and higher prices until the others in the livery began whispering louder, eyeing each other. Were they trying to escape the aftermath of the fire, or was it something else? I saw a young boy, perhaps seven or eight, clutching his mother's skirts. His eyes were sunken and his expression was weary. He coughed, lifting a hand to his mouth. I saw a flash of a blister beneath his sleeve and the world seemed to still.

"I told you bloodstone was dangerous," Ink said.

Had I caused this by burning down the refinery?

"This wasn't your doing, scribe," the cat said softly, flicking his ears even as he pressed closer to my leg. "The offal from the refining process must have already escaped into the city through the water or some other way. The burning cleansed things. You did not make him sick. In fact, you may have saved countless others."

The boy coughed again and his mother pulled him closer, glaring at me as I stared. I looked away, shuffling towards the wall. The man at the counter spotted me, and a look like relief passed over his features. He waved me forwards.

"The messenger from Vazeri," he said loud enough to draw the attention of everyone in the room. "You came at precisely the right time. Your horse is waiting for you. Last one available."

People grumbled at that, and the man trying to buy his way to a horse gaped at me, face turning red. I ducked my head and followed the worker to the side door and stable, the stares of the people prickling the back of my neck. I knew I had to get to Beltran and the others, knew that my path lay ahead, so why did I feel so much like I was running away?

"Good thing you came when you did," the man said, grumbling as he pulled open a stall door and led out a sturdy-looking brown horse. "We've had more people trying to leave the city in recent days, but after the fire..." He shook his head. "An omen sent by the gods for meddling with their god-given magic."

I shrugged and nodded before putting my bag in one of the saddle bags. Memories of learning to ride as a child were not quite enough to have me swinging in the saddle gracefully, but I managed without help. Ink leaped up in the saddle behind me, ignoring the way the horse stomped and snorted.

"Take good care of Storm, okay? I know your people bought her outright, but she's always been a favourite and I wouldn't mind buying her back once your journey is done." His tone was suddenly quiet, tender, and the way he brushed the horse's cheek was familiar and sad.

"I'll try," I whispered, all I could manage. Then, I was off.

I had just left the stable yard when I saw two guards enter the livery. There were yells a moment later and they ran back into the street, shouting after me.

"Damn," Ink hissed. "I knew we should have tried to dye your hair. You're too noticeable."

"What do we do?" I squirmed in the saddle, the horse dancing beneath me as she sensed my unease. I was many years removed from being able to ride well and was already at the limits of my meagre skills. If she bolted now, I would fall. "If I turn myself in—"

"They'll just kill you. Or worse." Ink's fur fluffed out until he was twice his usual size. "Keep riding. Don't gallop, just keep going. There's only the two guards. We might be able to find a place to hide before they can get reinforcements."

I did as he asked, my hands clutching the reins of the horse so tightly that I soon lost feeling in my fingers. I tried to keep my gaze ahead, but often found myself looking over my shoulders. The shouts of the guards persisted, and the closer we drew to the edge of the city, the more likely we were to meet resistance; that was, after all, where their military was camped. There were few stories in which the Makhierian soldiers were not effective.

"Ink," I said, nudging Storm with my heels to pick up the pace. She tossed her head but complied, my nervous energy making her movements jerky and twitchy. "They're still following. And we're running out of city."

"I'm thinking!" the cat growled.

"Think faster!"

"There's no choice. Time to run, scribe." Ink climbed around me, settling in my lap before the pommel. He hunched down, claws digging into the saddle, bracing himself. "Let's see how swiftly this Storm can fly."

At the idea of flight, the dragon on my skin shifted, an eagerness flowing through the ink. I cried out, pain flaring as it tried to move, tried to summon power enough to fly away or take me with it. This magic, whatever it was, existed beyond my ability to control it. To understand it. All I could do was demand that the ink on my skin remain still. The dragon fought me, ink-scales glowing. A faint scent of burning cloth filled the air.

Storm smelled this and, ears back and eyes wide, panicked. She burst into a gallop without any warning, throwing me back in the saddle. I barely managed to hang on with my knees, thighs screaming in protest. The dragon was startled by the sudden change and settled, seeming to hold on to me just as I clutched the saddle, which was a relief since I could do nothing but hold on.

The city came to an end and we were through the regular buildings of the military before anyone could stop us. I heard a few shouts behind, but no one leaped onto a horse and ran after us. The guards were left well behind, and if the soldiers knew I was wanted, I doubted they could catch me with the sheer panic that filled Storm's stride.

The countryside blurred past, not that I was paying much attention with my eyes held in a squint and my focus on staying seated. Ink yowled something that was snatched away by the wind and I just shook my head, hair whipping around me. Just when I thought I would have to let go and risk whatever injury came from falling to the ground, Storm ran out of energy.

She slowed to a stop, sides heaving, head low. When I made to pat her neck, she shied a bit, but that appeared to be all the fight she had left in her. Ink meowed, something I couldn't quite understand, and the horse's ears twitched. She tossed her head, whickering, then stopped entirely, just breathing.

"Are we safe?" I rasped, certain I could feel some threat approaching behind me. Ink peered around, ears flicking forward and back, nose twitching. The fur on his spine flattened.

"If there is any pursuit, it is distant."

"T-the dragon," I said in a shaking voice barely louder than a whisper. "It...it reacted on its own. And she must have felt it and been scared and—"

"Hush," Ink said, tail whipping. He turned on the saddle

so he was facing me, eyes glinting. They softened a bit. "It's not your fault. I have dragged you into this, into all of this. If I had never wanted to destroy the refinery—"

"But you said it was making people sick," I murmured. I hunched my shoulders and tried to rub some feeling back into my numb hands. "I saw the boy. You were right."

As much as the screams of the dying, of the already-dead, haunted my thoughts, I couldn't deny that Ink had been right. Even just spending a few minutes in that refinery had made me woozy, though I wasn't sure if it was just a reaction to the sorcerer's magic that now lived in me or something more. I had seen the lack of care those guards had shown. I knew that death lingered in that horrific smell.

Ink sighed, head lowering. "Are you regretting leaving the Archive now, scribe?"

I considered, then shook my head. "No. I couldn't stay there any longer, not with the triumvirate watching me. And Belt—those taken from Vazeri are still out there. They need my help if nothing else."

He studied me for a minute, seeming to look so much deeper than the surface. I shivered. "You are a strange creature, Elyria Trevain."

"You, too," I said drily. "And I know you're not a cat. Or, well, not just a cat. Don't deny it."

Ink said nothing, only leaped from the saddle and stretched, rubbing up against Storm's leg in the most cat-like movement I'd ever seen him make. I sighed and swung my leg around to dismount. That was one mystery I certainly wouldn't be solving anytime soon.

We walked well into the evening, stopping only when dusk threatened to turn into deepest night. Storm settled after a few hours, seemingly content to be led by the reins. Ink would occasionally trot by my side, but he often darted off to go investigate something, or rode on Storm's back, watching for danger. I asked no more questions about him or my new magic, and he offered no answers. I passed one family with a wagon heading into Makhier, but the road was otherwise quiet. Strangely quiet for the main thoroughfare into a harbour city. Even with the villages in the hills leading to Summerfell being small, there should have been more traffic than this.

Still, I was grateful for the solitude. It let me relax a bit, and when my legs were sore and weak from walking, I focused my attention on my thoughts, trying to make sense of everything that had happened in the last few days.

It seemed like only yesterday that I had been in Vazeri, pining over my lost love for Beltran. Now, I had bound a sorcerer's dragon to my skin, killed more than two dozen people while destroying a trade in god's blood, and was on the run from Makhierian authorities. My destination, my quest, had seemed so clear. Now, I wasn't sure.

We camped a little ways off the road under a few trees bent by the wind and time. Ink coached me in making a fire without the use of magic, the dragon restless under my skin the entire time. Then, my eyes refusing to stay open even a moment longer, I fell into sleep.

There, I dreamed.

The cell was colder than it had been the first time I visited, or perhaps that was my stressed body bringing its reactions into my mind. The light was dim, not nearly so bright as it had been. I could barely see into the corners, and what I could see was mostly an accumulation of dirt and feathers dropped from angel wings.

Then, a shape made of rags and shadows that had been curled in the corner moved.

Keir, the angel from my first dream, straightened. I recoiled in shock.

"Elyria?" he croaked, blinking at me. When I didn't move, didn't retreat or go to him, or disappear, his expression cracked a bit. He smiled, the look a mixture of joy and relief. "Elyria. You're really here."

I nodded. For better or worse, it would seem that I really was there in that dream world again. A world of angels and vengeful gods. Keir's shoulders sagged and I did gasp this time. His wings, which had been twisted and injured before, were now little more than stumps with feathers sticking out. They looked like they'd been torn off. Violently.

I knelt before him and took him in. His black hair was longer, shaggier. He had the start of a faint beard that failed to hide bruising along his jawline. His clothes were little more than tatters. But his eyes, they were the most changed. Before, they had been dark and fervent, full of some hidden power and strength. Now, they were tired. Empty.

I wanted to reach for his back, for the wounds on his jaw, but I hesitated. Keir lifted a hand, knuckles bloody and raw, palms cut from where his fingernails must have cut into them while clenched in a fist, and took mine, shuddering.

"You're real," he breathed. Then, without warning, he launched himself at me and wrapped his arms around me. "You're real."

Hesitantly, I returned the embrace. A shiver ran up my spine and something inside me seemed to warm. I hadn't realised how worried I'd been about the angel in this cell until I was back, cradling his bruised and broken form in my arms. I didn't know if this was dream or vision or something else entirely, but it felt real. More real than the past few days.

Keir clung to me for several minutes until his breathing evened out and he no longer trembled. I let him pull back before gesturing to his back. He hunched his shoulders.

"Torn off...it must be a season ago, at least. It's so hard to keep track in here when nothing ever changes. I never know when they'll come for me, to gloat about their progress in the war or to beat me for the losses they've endured." He let out a dark laugh, and I realised that his eyes weren't quite empty. They were tinged with madness as well as pain.

That madness kept me silent, so I wrote swiftly into the sand and dirt on the floor. *War?*

Keir blinked. Pulled back and studied me. "You don't know, do you?"

I shook my head. The weight of my ignorance in so many things was enough to crush me.

He slumped a bit, leaning against the wall in such a way that the stumps of his wings must have been in agony. Not a stitch of it showed in his expression, only astonishment. "I should wish that you would return to wherever you came from, if you know nothing of the war. I can't wish you away, though. I'm too selfish. I've been here for too long."

I reached out and touched his hand, even now mildly surprised to find it solid and real and not as ephemeral as a true dream. He closed his fingers around mine and I tried to smile comfortingly.

Keir leaned his head back against the wall and watched me, tracing the places of my face with those eyes. I flushed, suddenly too warm, but couldn't look away.

"Ten seasons ago, I think, though it could have been considerably more, I angered the gods." Keir's expression turned wicked, satisfied. "I gave the human slaves that laboured for them, worshipped them, the ability to know. To learn. I gave them the ability to break away from their dependency on the gods. Naturally, the gods weren't pleased with me when they discovered that their devoted slaves weren't as devoted as they thought."

The gods...I wrote swiftly in the sand, *Dawn, Day, Dusk, Night?*

Keir frowned. "The...times of day? What is that to do with this?"

The gods, I wrote. His eyes widened and he straightened slightly.

"Your gods aren't...They aren't Hirana? Miras? Tani?"

I shook my head.

Keir rose onto his knees in a swift movement that had me leaning back even as I so desperately wanted to lean in. I tried to keep still as he lifted his hand and reached out to touch a strand of my hair, the fabric on my dress. He trailed his fingers down my sleeve to my wrist, then took my hand. Carefully, he brushed his fingers against mine. Then, he froze.

It took me a moment, heart pounding in my ears and breath shallow, to realise that he was staring at the ink on my wrist. It was one of the dragon's claws, wrapped around my arm in a five-toed embrace. My sleeve had pulled back so the dragon's hand was visible, pulsing with a quiet power.

Keir touched the ink and I flinched, feeling the power surge through me in a barely controlled wave. The inked claws shifted, tightening their grip on me.

"What are you?" he breathed. His eyes flicked to mine. "Who are you?"

I didn't know how to answer, didn't know if I even had a good answer. So I remained silent, still. Trying to convey my thoughts by looking into someone's eyes hadn't ever worked for me before, but maybe in this dream-place, with the dragon's magic running uncontrolled through my veins, it would work.

Keir kept his gaze on mine and just a hint of that dark madness crept to the surface. Before I could move, he closed the distance between us and kissed me, hard and brutal and full of a heat that flooded my veins.

The magic of the dragon flared, bright enough to blind, and when I opened my eyes again, I was staring at the dying embers of the fire where I'd fallen asleep.

CHAPTER 11

*D*awn had barely begun when Ink prodded me awake again and insisted I pack up the meagre camp. He grumbled as I moved, agitation showing in the lashing of his tail. I had barely covered the fire and started work on Storm's saddle when Ink leaped to the horse's shoulders.

"Can't you move faster?" he asked.

I kept quiet, tightening the girth strap on the saddle and taking care in placing the saddle bags so as not to be uneven. The dream—if it was a dream—had unsettled me, so much so that any other sleep I'd gotten had been irregular and interrupted. Dealing with an irritable cat was not high on my task list in the midst of my tumultuous thoughts. Finally, I swung into the saddle and clicked my tongue at Storm, setting her into motion.

"We'll have to avoid the main road as much as possible," Ink said as soon as we passed out of sight of the camp.

"There is only one road to Summerfell," I said, "and we are on it."

"I, too, have looked at the maps, scribe, but there is a great deal of open country between the villages of the hills and Summerfell. I suggest we make use of it." Ink settled down in front of me, his warm fur pressing against me despite the already building heat of the day.

"Why? We haven't got enough supplies to travel across the country without stopping in towns, and in case you haven't noticed, I am not a hunter. I am an Archivist!" I gestured to the saddle bags. "I have exactly one knife and can barely start a fire. The closer we get to Summerfell, the colder it's going to get, too, which means that we need to camp in inclement weather, which I am not prepared for. I have no tent, no furs, no—"

Ink let out a sound that was half-meow, half-exasperation. "Alright, alright! I get it. I'm sorry." He huffed and hunkered down, staring at the back of Storm's neck. "Those guards will be hunting us down, you know. They've probably already enlisted soldiers and will be travelling this road —the only road—in search of you. I just thought that if we could avoid dealing with other people then we might be safer. You might be safer."

I relaxed slightly, stretching my back. "The farther north we go, the less likely people are to talk to soldiers from the harbour cities. But...you're right. For a while, we should probably stay off the main road. We can stop for supplies in a few days."

Ink flicked his ear in acknowledgement of my words,

thankfully not berating me when I turned Storm from the well-worn path to a divide between the hills. The horse looked at me for a moment before snorting and obeying the nudge of my heels. Even she seemed to think that this was a bad idea. I couldn't blame her.

I followed what memory I had of the maps of the region, and the more recent memory of travelling from Liral to Vazeri to start my position in the Great Archives. Granted, that had been along the main roads, but my teacher at Liral had made Margarethe and I memorise the maps before our trip, both out of prudence and as a mnemonic exercise. So I directed Storm north and followed the hills. There were a few smaller trails, out to farms and for more remote people to travel, but most were little more than cowpaths that meandered through the hills at a snail's pace.

After a few hours' riding, I finally brought Storm to a halt at a stream. Dismounting, I groaned. My muscles ached in a way that they hadn't for ages. I was strong from walking up and down the streets of Vazeri, but sitting astride a horse was an entirely different task.

"We should be able to reach that tor on the horizon by nightfall," Ink said, nodding in the direction of a large hill in the distance. The thought of riding for any longer made me want to weep.

"I need to take a break," I insisted. "I haven't ridden this much since I was a child, and I hurt."

Ink's ears pricked then flattened. He sniffed me and I got the sense he was frowning at me. "Why didn't you say you were in pain?"

"It's just part of riding. It's just pain." I paced back and forth before the stream to return some of the feeling to my legs, then sat against a rock and wondered what I was doing here. "Do you think Beltran and the others are alright?"

Ink sat, wrapping his tail around his paws. "We don't have enough information to know. They were taken by someone with runic magic, which can only have come from the boundary mountains that Summerfell guards. But who? Why? Were they taken as slave labour? As hostages? Or were they just the consequences of a raid? We don't know how the attackers travelled to Vazeri—I doubt they took the main road, or we'd hear reports of attacks. This means we don't know how they travelled back, and—"

Ink broke off, staring at me. I was trembling, barely able to keep my breaths even and my eyes from watering. I *knew* all of this. I knew precisely all the questions we had no answers to. I'd run over them in my head more than once. It still hurt more than I could express to have them voiced aloud.

"I'm sure they're fine," Ink murmured. "For all his faults, Beltran is a guardsman to the triumvirate. He is not... useless."

I snorted. "What a compliment."

"He hurt you. And don't you dare say it wasn't intentional. He came to you every day for months to practise his signed language. He became friendly with you. He invited you to see his sister at the opera. Yet, in all this time, he neglected to tell you that he was married with a child on the way? No. That was intentional. And for that, I cannot bring myself to compliment him as you would like." Ink sniffed and lifted his chin, the picture of the haughty cat. His words might have been sharp and angry, but they soothed some wound I didn't know I had while simultaneously digging in a knife to another sore spot.

I leaned my head back against the rock. Three birds lazily floated in the sky, black against the vibrant blue. If I squinted, I could pretend they were griffins or dragons, something magical.

"Ink," I said slowly, bringing my hand up to block out the birds. There, just at the base of my wrist, was the tip of the dragon's claw. "Is there some way I could learn to control this...sorcerer's magic?"

Ink made a sound like a growl deep in his throat. "Why would you want to do that?"

I lowered my hand. Then, because the words caught in my throat, I signed, *"So it doesn't control me."*

Ink didn't answer at first. I turned to find him watching Storm graze on a bit of grass, his attention so fixated I almost thought him an ordinary cat for a moment. I stood and brushed my skirts off, ready to ride on and drown out my thoughts in the pain of my aching muscles. Just when I had mounted, Ink called out, "Wait. Elyria. Wait."

He leaped lightly into the saddle and put a paw on my hand. "I...don't know if there is a way to control it now that it's been combined with your scribe magic. It was dangerous enough back when sorcery, when Old Magic, still roamed free. Now..."

I frowned. "But it's not just when I use my scribe magic

that it reacts. It sets off sparks or glows or shifts when I think about flying. It doesn't feel like normal ink, yet I know that it is ink on my skin."

The blood-tinged ink of the grimoire, I thought. I shivered.

"As I said, I don't know. This is unprecedented. It is not a living thing, yet it acts independently. It is tied to your magic, yet it is sorcerous. I just don't know. If there is a way, we will find it. I can try to modify some basic magical exercises for you. I will give it some thought." With that, Ink turned his back on me and settled in, the conversation obviously at an end. I wanted to ask how he knew magical exercises from a time whose magic had been entirely forgotten, but the words lay heavy and unspoken on my tongue. I nudged Storm into motion and we continued our journey in silence.

The tor turned out to be a series of craggy cliffs and hills that melded together into one menacing figure that dominated the skyline. It wasn't quite a mountain, but I had no doubt that climbing it would have been a nightmare. Still, it felt nice to have something at my back when setting up camp; the threat of guards and soldiers from Makhier searching for me had made me uneasy.

I'd never been a wanted criminal before.

I'd never done anything like any of this before in my life.

The thought unsettled me a bit, as though I was coming untethered from the docile centre that had been myself for all these years. I had worked so hard to be pleasant and helpful and wanted, yet now I was a murderer and a fugitive. I felt like a stiff wind could blow me away and remake me into something new. What I wouldn't give in that moment for a book to read, to hear whisper in my ears rather than the empty notebook and pencil in my bag, brimming with potential yet utterly silent.

Instead, I made the fire and was treated to a lecture by Ink about the nature of magic.

"Old Magic is the magic of the world around us. It is taking energy from the fundamental forces of the world and shaping that energy into a useable form. Unlike the innate magic you hold as a scribe, it doesn't depend on your own body's power." The cat sat on the other side of the fire and wrapped his tail neatly around his paws. "Close your eyes and try to picture the energy of the fire that surrounds it."

I raised my brows. His task was nebulous and imprecise, which was not particularly helpful. Still, I did as he asked, closing my eyes and settling my hands on my knees. I took a deep breath and, half of my mind on the dragon that I now bore, pictured the fire before me. I tried to feel the energy around it, tried to imagine the heat as a tangible thing. I could feel the dragon become restless, shifting. Tightening its claws around my wrist, around my ribs.

Then, like a wall broken down by time, something shifted and tumbled. There, invisible but for a slight glimmer, was a thread of ink between the dragon and myself, between my centre and its heart. No more was it a prisoner, bound against its will to my skin. It was a piece of me now, and we were tethered together by my scribe magic.

A vision appeared in my mind's eye without prompting. It was the campsite, dark and barren but for tiny sparkling ink motes like stars that made up the rocks, a myriad of brightly coloured filaments surrounding the fire. When I turned my attention to Storm, I saw ripples like the ocean, warm and red. A thousand patterns drawn in colours of ink that very nearly sang to my magic. A smile split my mouth until my cheeks hurt.

"Ink, I—" Eyes still closed, I turned to the cat. The vision in my mind changed and I stumbled back with a gasp, eyes flying open. My hand caught on a rock and I cursed as the sharp edges bit into my palm, making me bleed.

"Are you alright?" Ink bounded towards me, standing on my leg with his paws while he sniffed my hand. Silence twined around my throat, choking me.

I'd seen him. I'd *seen* him. Unlike the bright specks and dancing motes and threads of fire, he was stark against the backdrop of the night sky as nothing but shadow. Empty. Dark. A pool of obsidian ink so thick that it blotted out everything else. That emptiness stretched around him like massive wings folded around a single orb of amber the same colour as his eyes. Energy—impossible, boundless—had coalesced there, but could not expand, could not fill that emptiness.

It was horrifying, enough that tears sprang to my eyes. It was like looking into the abyss and seeing nothing but endless reflections. Loneliness. I was filled again with loneliness, that same feeling that had consumed me when Beltran exposed his truths.

"It's just a scratch," Ink decided, sitting back with relief. "It should stop bleeding soon."

I nodded and stared at the blood welling in my hand. The dragon cocked its head where it rested on my shoulder and I felt that line of ink go taut between us. Some of the filaments from the fire lifted and floated to rest over the cut on my hand, then settled. It burned at first, and I hissed. Then, in a blink, it was done. The filaments were gone and my hand was smooth and unbroken.

Ink lashed his tail. "I see that the visualisation exercises went better than anticipated." His tone was dry, and I sensed something else there. Was that fear?

I shook my head. *"I don't think I did that,"* I signed. *"I think it was the dragon. Maybe we're coming to an understanding?"*

Ink blinked slowly. He shook his head, fur fluffing out a bit. I couldn't quite get that vision out of my head, the darkness that surrounded him. I tried to tell myself that he was the same as he'd always been, that I was just learning something new, but it didn't change the racing of my heart.

"Enough magic for one night. We don't need to bring down the hills on us if you sneeze while trying to tame your dragon." He spoke as if he were just that mildly irritated creature I'd met in the Archives, but the words fell flat. He continued to watch me with the sort of concern that would have been touching had it not come from a creature I couldn't quite comprehend. "You should eat something. You haven't eaten all day."

I nodded and reached for the saddle bags, more for something to do than anything else. I wasn't even remotely hungry. I needed to eat to keep up my strength, but the thought of eating the bread and cheese, the dried meat, didn't sit well. Ink watched me nibble half-heartedly for a while before sighing and slinking off into the night. To hunt, I assumed, though it occurred to me just then that I'd never seen him eat or even hunt like a regular cat.

I put the food away and wrapped my arms around my legs, staring into the fire.

A vibration in my spine like the growl of a mountain cat alerted me to the attacker moments before the boot came down on my shoulder. I cried out as I was shoved forward, face inches from the fire. I flipped over, away from the flames, and saw the wide, eager hunger in the eyes of the man before I saw the bandolier of knives he wore.

A bandit. And, judging by his size and bulk, by the fine leather armour he wore, a successful one.

He was tall enough to blot out the moon, with skin that glowed gold in the firelight. His long brown hair hung loose around his shoulders and the half-grown beard barely hid a long scar on his right cheek.

Before I could scramble to my feet, he had a knife out and thrown. It landed point down in the ground beside my head so close that I could feel the metal tremble from the force of the throw.

"Don't even think about it," the bandit purred. He flicked

some hair out of his face and leered down at me. "Now, what would a creature like you be doing out here all by your lonesome? Don't you know that this is dangerous country?"

I hadn't, actually, but then I hadn't paid much attention to reports of bandit attacks for years. It had always seemed so far away from my life in Vazeri, or Liral. Just another fact to be filed away with other census data in the Great Archives. Now that I was actually travelling through the countryside, I cursed myself for my stupidity. Here I was trying to hide from Makhierians and I'd all but lit a flare for someone to see by camping here.

Obviously, someone had seen it.

I looked around desperately, but Storm was still tethered where I had left her by a patch of grass, and Ink was nowhere to be seen. Hunting. The only weapon within reach was the knife by my head, and I had the sickening feeling that if I reached for it, the bandit would be on me in an instant.

"Playing coy, are we? Well, I can have fun with that. It's been a while since I've seen someone like you out this way." He pulled another knife from his bandolier and spun it in his fingers, the blade flashing in the firelight. He smirked at me. "Interesting, isn't it, that you're not moving south like most of you lot. No, you're heading the opposite direction far from the main roads, which tells me you're running from something. What are you running from, little mouse?"

He knelt on one knee and leaned over me, breath rancid, eyes too interested. If he got much closer, I wouldn't stand a chance. I reached my mind towards the dragon on my back, but the thread that had been so easy to find earlier was gone. There were no filaments from the fire, no multitude of ink-wrapped sparks in the stone. The world was just as it had ever been to me, and any sorcery that I might have had remained silent.

"Come, now, little mouse, I won't hurt you. Just tell me," he said, leaning closer. He braced one hand on the ground beside my head and traced the knife down my face, my throat, my chest. "Just tell me," he whispered, leaning closer still.

Panic leaped through me, igniting me. I lashed out, squirming and fighting. My nails raked down the bandit's cheek. He roared with fury, rearing back. I took my chance and scrambled to my feet, trying to run to Storm, trying to flee.

I was too slow.

He caught me from behind, slamming me into the ground. His hands went around my throat and squeezed, choking me. I clawed at the dirt, kicking as best I could, but I was no fighter.

I saw a shape in the distance, a cat. Ink, standing just outside the firelight, his eyes wide with horror. "Help me," I mouthed, reaching for him.

He leaped, yowling. The bandit snarled and threw a knife before I could rejoice at being rescued. It caught Ink in the shoulder, knocking him flat and all but pinning him to the ground.

"Elyria," he gasped, struggling to move. Tears filled my

eyes at the realisation that this was going to be not just my end, but his. "Your magic."

I shook my head as much as I could, my breath starting to come in choking gasps.

"You're going to die here, and I'm gong to enjoy it," the bandit said in my ear, squeezing just tight enough to cut off my air without killing me quickly. I saw the glint of a knife out of the corner of my eye and knew that he wanted me to suffer, wanted my death to be slow. I looked at Ink, desperate.

"Your scribe magic," Ink said, a plea in his voice. With the paw not injured, he scratched something into the dirt. If he wanted me to read it, I was too far away to see, not to mention distracted. Besides, my scribe magic needed ink to work and —my magic flared into being and a sickening feeling filled my stomach even as the edges of my vision blurred. He was using blood as ink; it was enough for my scribe magic to grab hold of, the words clawed into the ground as clear to my mind as quill and iron gall ink on parchment.

Black book in the bag.

Why would I care about that? I was being pinned to the ground, a knife at my neck, my attacker slavering over me, demanding I give up my secrets. A blank notebook in my pack would do nothing. not without ink.

Blood from my attacker's scratched face dripped onto the ground beside me and the world stilled.

Oh.

My heart beat once, and I closed my eyes, shuddering.

I reached for the magic of ink and paper that lived in my bones, then linked it to the living ink that flowed from the being beside me. The dragon shifted on my back, lending attention to my actions, as if it was as tied to my scribe magic as Old Magic. I called the notebook to me, opening it to a blank page. Then, using the blood of the bandit, I began to write.

He screamed and fell back, nearly crushing me beneath him. I kept hold of my magic, ignoring the stab of pain in my leg that couldn't have come from anything but a knife. I kept writing, the words flowing from my mind without hesitation, until the man went silent and the ink source began to dry up.

The words slowed to a trickle, the pages of my notebook full of what I was sure were insensible ramblings. My magic sputtered, then gave out entirely. I wiped away blood and tears from my eyes and, not daring to look back at the dead man behind me, crawled to where Ink lay on the ground.

"You're going to be okay," I swore, my voice catching.

He opened one amber eye. "I know, Elyria Trevain. I know."

CHAPTER 12

I kept wiping my eyes with the back of my hand as I tended to Ink. Every time, water came away, glistening red in the light of the fire. Ink lay on his side, as still and calm as possible, though the very tip of his tail twitched. I had removed the knife and cleaned the wound as best I could, but it was still open and bleeding and I was no healer. I had, however, read many books on the healing arts.

"This will hurt," I said, voice choked. The shape on the other side of the fire taunted me, a dead man that laughed in the face of my misery.

"Don't tell me it will hurt, just fix it!" Ink said, finally starting to sound exasperated, though I got the impression it was more for my benefit than his. I squeezed my eyes shut and took a steadying breath before lifting the needle and thread.

No matter how I tried, the dragon on my back didn't answer my call to heal Ink again. I closed my eyes and sought the energy signatures of the world around me. They came with surprising ease, a swirl of ink and blood that made my stomach churn; when I tried to use that energy, though, the dragon shifted and broke my concentration. Again and again I tried until I was weak with weeping and couldn't bring myself to fail again. Now, I carefully pierced the skin around Ink's shoulder, stitching the wound shut. He flinched with every pass of the needle, panting, eyes glassy. I managed to keep the trembling out of my hand until the thread was finally tied off. Then, I collapsed backwards and started crying in earnest.

"Don't cry," Ink said, struggling to his feet. He limped towards me on three legs, a rumbling sound in his chest. I realised a moment later, as he climbed into my lap and pressed his head against my hand, that he was purring. It only made me cry harder. "Hush, now. I will be well. Do you think that I could have survived this long if a simple knife wound could put me down?"

I flinched and pulled my hands back, chest heaving as I tried to gulp in air around my sobs. Ink reached out with his good paw and brought my hand to his head again, purring louder. I gave in, stroking my fingers down his spine, rubbing his ears. This was the first time I had petted him as just a cat, the first time he had acted as such, and I knew that it wasn't for his benefit. He was doing it for me.

"I-I—" I tried to speak, but the words were caught up in my tears. I couldn't sign, either, not with my hands entwined in Ink's fur. I felt the blood, there, drying in the night air. My stomach recoiled and I barely had time to move Ink from my lap before I crawled to the edge of the camp and retched. The dragon shifted, its tail wrapping around my ribs in what felt like a poor imitation of a hug.

Suddenly, I wanted to scrub myself clean. To scour my skin and remove the dragon from my body with the blood of a dead man and my friend. I scrambled to my feet and stumbled blindly to where a small stream ran by the base of the tor. I'd used it earlier to fill my waterskins and knew that it was icy cold. I didn't care.

I stripped out of my dress with shaking hands and practically fell into the water. The ice set my blood to screaming, my skin immediately going red before turning white with cold. I grabbed a fistful of sand from the bottom of the stream and started scrubbing at my hands, my legs, my ribs, anywhere I could feel the ink stained into my skin.

"Elyria, you have to stop," Ink said, voice muffled as though I were listening to it from underwater. I looked up at him, a blurry shadow through my tears. My teeth chattered and I didn't understand why I trembled so. "Come out of the water. You're clean. I promise."

"I-I killed him," I breathed, not daring to look back towards the camp where the man's body lay. I shivered and collapsed completely in the water. "I knowingly took his life! It wasn't like with the refinery, where the people were already dead. That was an accident. This was..." I gulped for air as the memory of how *easy* it was to pull his blood for ink on my paper. How easy it was to kill him.

"You were defending yourself!" Ink limped closer. I blinked and he became less blurry, though he blended into

209

the darkness so easily. "He would have killed you. Worse, even. If you hadn't done what you did..."

My teeth chattered uncontrollably now, and I was shivering so hard I wasn't even sure I could stand up. Still, I cried. Ink took a step closer until he was close enough to touch the water.

"Please, Elyria," he begged. "Don't make me get my paws wet. I don't think it would be good for me with my shoulder the way it is. If I slipped, well, that would be bad."

I nodded dumbly, realising the truth of his words even as part of me saw through his ploy. I didn't want him to put himself out anymore for me than he already had. I crawled from the water on my knees and stared at Ink blankly, not sure what to do next.

"Come, gather your clothes and sit by the fire with me," he suggested in a low meow, the sound as soothing as his purr. I glanced to the camp, where I knew the body lay, and Ink meowed again. "It will be fine. I swear it, upon your gods and mine. Come, Elyria. Come sit by the fire."

Later, I would wonder if there was some sort of magic in his voice jus then, because I stood in a daze, dressing again with numb fingers and floating after Ink as he limped back up the hill. The fire was enticing, fingers of warmth reaching for me, comforting in their brightness. Storm grazed contentedly, tail swishing. I blinked slowly, suddenly so terribly tired and cold. Ink gestured to a spot by the fire with his tail. I sat, then lay down, unable to stand any longer. Then, purring loudly, he lay beside me.

I didn't even notice that the bandit's body was gone and

the notebook was nothing but ash until after I had already closed my eyes and was halfway to dreaming.

The cell was as I had left it when last I visited. The light was a little brighter and the floors were a little cleaner, but everything was otherwise the same. Including Keir.

He sat up when I appeared, a flash of a smile appearing amidst the despair on his face. He moved for me eagerly. I flinched.

"Elyria?" He paused, then crouched before me. His wounds seemed better healed and there was a little more flesh on his bones than before. Details I noticed to keep myself from looking into those eyes. "What happened? You're trembling."

I was freezing here in the dream as well as in life. The thought that my trauma could cross into this realm of dreams was enough to bring further tears to my eyes. In an instant, Keir was beside me. He hesitated for only a moment before wrapping his arms around me and brushing his fingers through my hair.

"Hush, now," he murmured as I wept into his shoulder. "You're safe here."

I clutched at his tunic and let myself cry. Slowly, the tension leeched from my muscles and the soothing movement of his fingers against my scalp reduced the trembling until it was no more than the occasional shiver. He was warm. So warm. So *real*, though I knew this to be a dream. It had to be a dream.

"I thought it would be ages since I saw you again," Keir admitted, shifting so that I was in a more secure embrace. "It's been less than a week since you last came, and I can't be anything but grateful. Gods—no, never them." He shook his head. "I thought—I think..." He sighed, then closed his eyes and leaned back against the wall. "Every time you disappear, I'm afraid I'll never see you again. I fear that you're the only thing keeping me sane in here."

I squeezed his arm and he pulled back enough to let me sit up and face him properly. I signed, "*I think you're the one keeping me sane out there.*"

He watched me intently, focusing on the movements of my hands. "It's a language, isn't it?" he asked. "The movements. They mean something, don't they?"

I nodded.

"Will you...will you teach me?" He reached out and touched my hands. "I want to be able to talk with you. Please."

The last time someone asked me to teach them the signed language, it was when Beltran came into the Great Archives with a charming smile and a glint in his eyes that I mistook for interest. Now, though, there was no possible ulterior motive. Just communication.

I touched my fingers to my lips as the memory of that kiss sprang to the forefront of my thoughts. Just communication? When he kissed me like that? Enough to send my heart racing, to spread fire through me, to make my magic sing, however briefly?

I looked up to find Keir watching me with a half-smile. "I couldn't help myself, if that's what you were wondering. I couldn't let you disappear on me again without tasting you at least once."

"And?" I signed. Keir's brows furrowed slightly before he smiled wider, a wicked glint in his eyes.

"You taste of meadowsweet," he said. He leaned forwards. "Meadowsweet and summer dew. And—" His lips brushed mine. "And a hint of fire."

Before I knew what I was doing, before I could question it, I surged against him. He let out a sound of surprise, then put his hands on my waist and pulled me closer. We tangled together, kissing, devouring. His hands tightened on my waist and I let my hands roam over his shoulders, his neck, his jaw. He groaned and finally pulled back, panting.

"Blood of the gods," he swore, pressing his forehead against mine. "I wish I knew where you come from. Who you are. I wish—no. It doesn't matter. You're here. You tried to bandage me and you provided comfort in the dark. I only wish you could *stay*."

I smiled and kissed him again. I wished I could stay, too, though this was a prison cell and the things that Keir told me were so impossible as to make no sense. I knew that I would wake up eventually, that I would have to continue my search for Beltran, and that Keir would once more become a dream.

I pulled back, my skin finally warm and my heart

pounding in my ears. I lifted my hands, starting their familiar dance. One letter at a time, I spelled out my name. I tapped my chest. Keir brightened.

"Your name? Elyria?"

I nodded.

He signed the motions back to me, only stumbling over the letters a few times. When I nodded, he signed the letters again and again. "Elyria."

So I began to teach an angel without wings to sign, and for a while, forgot the worries that awaited me when I was awake.

After three more days travelling without roads, Ink directed me back towards the main road to Summerfell. He had been healing well enough, taking it easy and riding on Storm's back, even when I walked to stretch my legs. Every night, I checked the wound and applied a basic poultice I'd learned from a healing manual long ago. Ink never complained, never snapped at me. Just quietly let me tend his wound. It was, frankly, a little unnerving, though at least it kept my mind off the shadows in the night.

After returning to the main road, I twitched and jumped at every person that passed, wondering if they were going to attack me or arrest me as a criminal. I decided that my trail must have been well and truly obscured coming from Makhier. I still saw danger in the eyes of people I passed, my thoughts a swirl of bloody ink. Ink swore that I was safe, but I still wondered. I began to miss the humid warmth of Vazeri, and the pleasant, friendly smiles of its people. Those I passed watched me with wariness, each of us keeping to ourselves, sharing no news.

Several more days passed until I crested a hill to look down on a village that sat at the base of the place where the foothills turned into mountains. I knew this village. I had visited it twice before. Once when I was about six, on a journey with my cousin Alar, his tutor, and my parents. We'd gone to bid them farewell as they left for their latest journey, and also to pick up some needed supplies at Summerfell before the winter. The second time I'd visited, I'd been insensate with fever and pain.

"Aviena," I said in a low voice. "A long day's ride from Summerfell, if the weather holds. And if the pass hasn't had any rock slides in a while."

Ink flicked his tail. "*Will* the weather hold? I haven't been this close to the boundary mountains in quite some time."

Just the mention of the magical boundaries that divided the continent by two mountain ranges had my skin tingling. The dragon had been blissfully silent since I'd failed to use it to heal Ink. I hadn't tried to meditate again, nor had I tried to pull on any magic, scribe or sorcerous. I'd been glad, frankly, when the creature had been silent. Now, though, it was awake and aware. Something about the boundary had the thing on edge. The tattoo itched.

"Summerfell may guard the gap in the boundary, but Aviena is the last true bastion of civilisation this far north.

We can get all the supplies we'll need for the pass crossing here." I didn't answer him about the weather. Summerfell wasn't known for mild weather, even in the height of summer, and we were past that. Already, I was starting to shiver and I had donned my heaviest dress and cloak that morning.

Ink sat up a little, his ears back. "Are you well, scribe?" he asked cautiously. "You don't sound like yourself."

The dragon dug its claws into me, making me flinch a little. "Something about the boundary magic is making the dragon upset."

"I'm not surprised. A creature born of sorcery would likely react to a boundary created by the clash of gods and magic. But that's not all, is it?" Ink asked. He narrowed his eyes. "Talk to me, please. I want to help you. I want to—"

Scrams cut across the quiet afternoon. Storm's ears pricked and she shifted nervously. I scanned the outline of the village, hoping to find where the sound originated. Because if we had to avoid the village entirely, we would never make it to Summerfell unscathed. I couldn't risk capture by the Makhierians, though. I would never be able to help Beltran and the others then.

Muscles tense, I prepared to wheel Storm in the other direction when I spotted plumes of smoke rising from the edge of Aviena closest to me. Smoke, just like that night when Vazeri burned.

"The raiders," I breathed. Ink's fur fluffed out.

"Elyria, wait—"

It was too late for his warnings. I kicked my heels into

Storm's sides and urged her towards the flames. Storm shied the closer we got, but something about my insistence —or the intense interest of the dragon—kept her moving until we were right on top of the fires.

Several houses had caught, with at least two barns and one grain storage shed already burned down to the ground. A woman wearing dark trousers and a bear skin over her shoulders was directing people with buckets. At the sight of me, she waved over an older man with black skin and a beard down to his waist to take her place, then stalked towards me.

"We want no strangers here," she snarled. "We've had enough problems with—wait. I know you."

Did she? I didn't recognise her. Instinct had my hackles raising, enough that I wanted to run away again. But I'd been through too much to run away now. So I dismounted and faced her, fiddling with the fabric of my skirts.

"You're related to Lord Alar, aren't you?" she asked. "You have the same eyes. The same nose."

Relief pooled in my gut even as her statement left me winded. I nodded. *"My cousin,"* I signed on the off-chance that she might know the signed language. When her brows furrowed in confusion I winced. I swallowed and hunched my shoulders, but mustered up the will to speak. "My cousin," I rasped, the words as hoarse as if I'd been breathing in the smoke of the dying fires.

The woman's eyes widened. "You're the lost lady?" she asked, drawing attention from the line of people hauling buckets. Whispers started up immediately. I flinched and shoved my hands deep into the pockets of my skirts. "My apologies, Lady, for the rude reception. I'm Ursa, head hunter of these parts. What can I do for you?"

"What happened?" I asked quietly, nodding my head to the fires.

Ursa curled her lip in disgust and spit on the ground. "Monsters happened. Raiders from beyond the Gap. I don't know how they got past Lord Alar and the watch, but this is the third one in so many years. Every year, about the start of harvest, they come down. Make a ruckus. We've held them off every time until this year. They came earlier than expected. A lot earlier. Came through about a month back. Made it through, since most of our people were off hunting. They came back this morning and you can see the destruction they caused."

Alarm prickled down my spine. Three years in a row something had gotten past the gap, past Summerfell, and tried to escape into the countryside? Why hadn't I heard about this? I had seen the reports, surely, before the triumvirate had them moved. I had talked with travellers and traders alike and hadn't heard even a rumour of such things. And now Vazeri had been attacked, Aviena was burning, and Beltran and who knows how many others had been taken.

"Were there…" I licked my lips and looked around at the destruction. "Were there people with them?"

Ursa looked at me with sympathetic eyes, even as she wiped away a smudge of soot on her cheek. "It's why they were so careless with their destruction. They threw torches at anything that would burn so that we would be busy dealing with the fires instead of stopping them and the people in chains that they took with them. Me and a few others tried to stop them, but we still have a month left until harvest and so many are out hunting to supply Aviena and Summerfell before the pass closes."

I nodded vaguely, the world spinning around me. Beltran was alive. The others that had been taken from Vazeri and maybe elsewhere, they were alive. The raiders, whoever—whatever—they were, hadn't killed their captives along the road. My legs felt weak at this news and I realised that I'd been thinking they might be dead since departing Vazeri.

"Elyria, look." Ink hissed in my ear and I turned, spotting a patch of glowing fire on the ground. Only it wasn't fire. It was those selfsame runes that I'd seen in Vazeri, before my magic took hold of me completely. Even as I looked at them, their meaning sprang clear in my mind.

For the gods' hunger must be appeased.

I reached out and grasped Ursa's hand, desperation making the words clear and strong. "I need supplies to get to Summerfell. Fast."

CHAPTER 13

$\mathcal{U}$rsa personally led me to a store where I could purchase supplies, then helped me load Storm up for the perilous journey. The passes were open, she said, but riding right on the heels of the raiders? It was likely I would meet resistance, or at least destruction. I purchased a dagger and short sword, though I had little idea how to use either. Ursa suggested a bow, but I knew that there was no way I would be strong enough to draw the bowstring, let alone aim with any accuracy. I tried to protest when she pressed a crossbow into my hands, but the fire in her eyes coupled with her soot-streaked face had me giving in.

Finally, dressed in two layers of skirts with woollen hose, a fur-lined cloak over my shoulders and further supplies should the weather turn unfavourable, I rode Storm through the streets of Aviena. Smoke still choked the air, but it was the whispers of the people at my backs that made me ride faster.

"Why do they call you the lost lady?" Ink asked once we were into the pass. Stone walls started rising on either side, studded with trees at first then fading into nothing but hardy grasses and lichens. I shivered, and not from the cold.

"I don't know," I admitted after a few moments. I studied the ground for any sign of the raiders' passage, but all I saw was scree and stone and dirt. I was no tracker. "Can you smell anything?"

Ink lifted his nose to the air and twitched his whiskers. "No. The wind is blowing the wrong way. Everything smells like smoke from the fires in town." He settled deeper into the saddle, pressing against me and fluffing out his fur. I rearranged the cloak to cover him, mindful of his shoulder, though it barely seemed to bother him. "You said you were from Summerfell," Ink said. "And the villagers call you the lost lady. Then you said that Lord Alar—" He sat up abruptly and gaped at me. "You're *cousin* to the Baron of Summerfell?"

I hunched my shoulders. "His uncle was my father's brother. The title goes back countless generations."

"It goes back to the creation of the boundary mountains!" Ink shook his head as if in disbelief. I couldn't see what was so special about such a claim. Then, he said, "No wonder you were able to bind the sorcerer's dragon to you. An ancient power runs through your veins."

The dragon growled, a rumbling sound that I felt in my spine more than I heard it. I stiffened. "Magic doesn't follow family lines. It's random."

"Perhaps now. But it was not always so with Old Magic," Ink said.

"Oh, yes." I could taste the bitterness in my voice. "Old Magic. Exactly what got me into this mess to begin with. And I know no more about it now than before. Perhaps you would be so kind as to explain—"

The dragon growled again, deeper this time. The back of my neck prickled. Before I could think about it, the world shifted into its web of energies drawn in vibrant inks. Some of the stars from the rocks surged towards me and an ink-blot shield formed a quarter dome just above Storm's head, protecting Ink and me.

An arrow, barbed and made of some strange, glistening black metal, slammed into the shield. A second one impacted a moment later, sending reverberations up my arm.

The dragon on my back roared, loud enough to shake the walls of the pass. That line of ink which bound us, which seemed to link my will to the dragon's, glowed brightly before rearing up as if the dragon had reared its head then dove into the back of my neck. I cried out in agony, dropping the reins to scrabble at my neck.

The shield grew stronger, and I noticed through the fading of my vision that three more arrows struck. Pain, though, had me doubling forwards.

A roar echoed again through the pass, as much in the world as in my mind. The roar was at once ancient and powerful, full of the brimming potential of fire combined with the steadfast nature of stone. It reverberated through my mind, drowning out any other sound. I clawed at my ears to try and silence the sound. A pinprick of bright pain in my arm drew my attention and broke some of the terror at the new noise.

"—you have to breathe!" Ink shouted. His claws were deep in my arm, bright blood welling up to stain the fabric of my dress. Another arrow hit the shield and clattered to the ground. Storm pranced in place, obviously frightened, but she didn't bolt, thank the gods. "Breathe, Elyria!"

The dragon rumbled a threatening growl, hissing as though drawing in breath to breathe fire. I focused on the pain of Ink's claws in my arm and pushed the distraction of the dragon's terrible sounds away much as I pushed aside the whisper of books. The ringing in my ears lessened and the energy of the world shone brighter. A thought, a single thought, had me lifting my arm and directing the air just as another arrow flew towards me. I clenched my fist and the arrow burst into flame, bright sparks of energy filling the air.

"Good," Ink said, breathing heavily. "Now draw your sword!"

I didn't have time to argue that I couldn't even use the sword. I pulled it from its sheath at my waist and held it in front of me. The metal of the sword was full of quietly glowing stars, like the stone, but with more trapped in its form. I barely had time to notice this new vision, this new energy I saw, when two figures leaped onto the path before me.

My heart leaped into my throat and I nearly gave in to the desire to run.

They were clad in a myriad of furs and armours that were covered in soot and rot. Their stature was more or less human, but their shoulders were too broad and their backs were hunched. The one on the left's face was covered by a massive helm with two curling ram's horns, but I saw unnatural claws gripping the crossbow that pointed directly at my heart. The one on the right, however, was un-helmed, and it was this that had me freezing in panic.

Its face was, in a word, angelic. Having spent so many dreaming nights in that cell with Keir, I recognised the inhuman beauty of the sculpted features and sensual mouths. Their skin, though, was split and oozing black sludge that coated their armour. And their eyes were bright orange, feverish, insensate.

"Blood of the gods," Ink cursed on a breath. I felt him trembling against me, and for all the yelling he had done to protect me from so many things, this was the first time I thought he might have actually been afraid. "If there is anything you can do to control that sorcerer's dragon, do it now. Kill them. Please."

I tried to do as he asked. I called upon the stars bound to the metal of my short sword as I would to write a letter by scribe magic and sent them forth in a spear of light meant to pierce the heart of the helmed warrior. The beast flew back as my attack hit, but they started rising to their feet almost immediately afterwards. I had barely winded them.

"Maybe the crossbow?" Ink suggested, panicked. I

scrambled for the bow, nearly dropping the short sword in the process. The un-helmed warrior didn't waste a moment; as soon as I was distracted, they leapt as if gravity meant nothing to them, flying through the air and raising their own sword to strike at me.

The shield still glowed, and that was the only thing that saved me. The creature slammed into the shield, spooking Storm into rearing, her eyes wide, whites showing, her scream piercing the air. I dropped the sword in my scramble to stay on the saddle, and I still failed in that. I slid to the ground, slamming my back against a boulder. The vision into the energy of the world necessary for sorcery vanished with a burst of pain. Storm bolted. The creature took a step towards me, grinning as they raised their sword.

Ink leaped in front of me, back arched and fangs bared. He snarled viciously, but no matter what he had once been, he was only a cat now.

The creature paused a moment, then laughed, throwing back their head. Despite the rot, the laughter only made them all the more beautiful, striking. My breath caught in my throat.

Then, an arrow fletched with red feathers whistled through the air and struck the creature in the chest. They screamed, a horrible screeching sound, and turned to find their hunter. Before they could do much more than turn, another arrow slammed into the creature. They fell, and unlike when I'd struck them with magic, the thing dropped and did not get up again.

The second beast let out a snarl, crouching and looking

around. A man wielding what looked like a copper knife leaped out from behind a boulder and sliced the creature's throat. Black, oozing blood sprayed everywhere, obscuring the man's face. The creature fell, their helm rolling down the pass to stop at my feet.

I could barely breathe I was so startled. Adrenaline coursed through me, preparing me to run back towards Aviena even though logic told me I would never make it. Then, the man wiped his face on his sleeve and a flicker of recognition sparked to life inside me.

"Are you alright...My gods. It can't be. Elyria? Is that you?" Alar leaned over and helped me to my feet, crushing me in a hug before I had a chance to blink. I let him hold me for a moment and the shock seemed to bleed out of me. I started crying.

Alar recaptured Storm while I stood, trembling, by his own horse with Ink pressed against my leg. As he approached, Storm's reins in hand, I stared at my cousin through bleary, red eyes.

I hadn't seen him since I was eight, since that terrible day, yet I knew him immediately. I had been sent away without ever being able to say goodbye, and it was years later before his letters reached me. Since then, despite numerous invitations, I had done my best to avoid returning to Summerfell. Now I was here and I found that the memories were buried under the weight of years and the aftereffects of what had just happened.

He was tall and broad-shouldered, with muscles built from years of fighting and hunting. He wore no furs, likely thinking the weather quite warm, and his clothes were as well-worn as they were well-mended. His skin was sun-kissed into the slightest tan, with more red from sun burning than golden colour. His hair, the same white-blonde that I had, was cropped short, unlike so many of those who served up here and kept their hair in long braids and twists. He had a scar on his left jawline, but otherwise his strong features were unmarked.

He looked, I realised, remarkably unlike his father.

"Come on," Alar said as he approached. "We can make it back to Summerfell by nightfall if we hurry."

It was past midday, and if I knew the pass, then there was no way we were going to make it. Still, my cousin was more familiar with this place than anyone else. So I mounted, left room for Ink to ride before me, and followed Alar into the pass.

"I was coming down this way after we had a messenger bird from Aviena about the raiders. We've had dozens more attacks in recent years, so a few get through, but they've rarely done such damage before. I'm glad I found you!" He turned and grinned at me, obviously still coursing with energy after that battle, though I trembled with shock.

Alar studied me, taking in my shaking hands, and frowned. His gaze slipped to Ink, who let out a low growl.

"Elyria," Alar said in a low, soothing tone, "what are you doing out here with a magical catkin?"

I blinked. Catkin? I ran through the books and tomes and papers I'd seen on legendary monsters, cycling the words through my mind. None of them had mentioned such a thing as a catkin, and the only other time I'd heard of such a thing was something to do with flowers. Ink was many things, but flowery was far beyond him.

"Catkin?" Ink snorted and flicked an ear, still not taking his eyes off Alar. "Foolish human. He's spent too long guarding the gap to think I am of such ilk."

Alar frowned and leaned forwards. Had he heard Ink? Fear and shock seized my chest, making it hard to breathe for a moment. "It is certainly tame for a catkin. But how you came across one is very much of interest. They're notorious for stealing washing off the line, and they eat birds and squirrels and small dogs with no reservation. But they're boundary creatures. Not lowland creatures."

Lowlands. That's right. That's what we called everyone not from Summerfell, not from the mountains. Lowlanders. How had I forgotten? I wondered, then, how much more I had forgotten.

"Elyria?" Alar asked. "How did you find him?"

I shrugged, and pulling my still-shaking hands from the reins, signed, "*He found me.*"

Alar's frown deepened. He shifted in his saddle. I remember one of the letters from my cousin detailing that he had learned the signed language as part of his training to lead the watch, so I knew he understood. But my use of it seemed to make him distinctly uncomfortable.

"Why are you here?" Alar asked a moment later, not meeting my gaze. He stared instead at my hands. Stared a little too intently.

"It's a long story. Those...raiders attacked Vazeri and captured a friend. I came to get him back." My hands fell to my lap as if those few words had wrung out every last drop of energy I had.

"Attacked *Vazeri*?!" Alar cursed. He looked at the sky and let out another curse. "Come on. We have to hurry if we want to make it back before dark, and I don't want to run into one of those monsters without the sun at my back."

He dug his heels into the sides of his horse and drove it off the main path and up the side of a mountain. Storm followed with a powerful surge, her ears pressed flat to her head. She obviously wasn't going to be left alone in the pass.

We rode a much harder path than the pass road afforded, nearly slipping a few times on some scree and ascending so rapidly that the horses were both breathing heavily by the time we reached the summit of one small peak. Alar didn't wait for his horse to recover, just urged it onwards down the other side. I noticed that we were riding hard enough to avoid further conversation, but whether that was by design or just incidental, I couldn't tell. I didn't know my cousin anymore, not really.

The trees started increasing, thinly at first, then leading into the tall, thick forest that covered the mountains. Lichen and moss covered the trunks and their branches stretched high in the thin mountain air. They were a species of ever-green not found anywhere but Summerfell, and they wrapped themselves around me like a familiar blanket. The trees with their spiny needles and glossy leaves that reminded me so much of home. Suddenly, I wasn't an adult returning to a childhood home after so many years, I was a girl of eight, running through the forest to exchange lessons with my tutor for a day of glorious sun.

The tattooed dragon on my back, though exhausted as I was, noticed my agitation and shifted against my skin, tail wrapping around my ribs, claws tightening their grip. Ink hissed at the sparks that flashed on my skin.

"Elyria? Are you—"

"Don't," I murmured under my breath. Alar was moving too fast to hear me, his horse a length ahead of Storm. "Don't ask if I'm alright. Because if you do, I may very well not be."

Ink ducked his head. "Very well, then. But I won't leave your side."

I nodded, a lump forming in my throat. The paths before me suddenly seemed familiar, as though a ghost of myself ran ahead to lead me the way home. I knew that once I passed the massive oak tree up ahead, I would see—

My breath caught, and if I had been walking, I would have faltered. Summerfell. It rose before me, as sudden and imposing as a creature emerging from the fog. Its stone walls were exactly as I remembered, as was the space empty of trees around the fortress. The portcullis was open and the gates were thrown wide, with so many people moving in and around the fortress. They carried firewood or practised with arrows and swords. Some rode back on horses from deeper in the gap, looking weary, while others left from Summerfell itself, fresh eyes for the watch.

Oh gods, I'd come back to the very place I'd sworn to forget.

I was shaking so badly that Storm danced under my guidance, snorting with agitation. Alar twisted to look at me.

"Cousin? Are you well?"

My skin felt clammy and I knew that I was moments away from a panic attack the likes of which I hadn't had in years. If I entered that place and found it unchanged, found it just as it had been, the demons that haunted my nightmares still roaming free, I wasn't sure I wouldn't take my chances with the angelic monsters in the gap.

"Elyria, listen to me." Alar was suddenly there, right beside me, his hand on my arm in an iron grip. I gasped and flinched, some part of me expecting to be pulled from the saddle as I had been as a child when I wanted to go adventuring and was expected to learn the harp instead. Alar pulled back, alarmed. "What's wrong? Is it...is it this place? Is that why you ran away?"

My panic shifted in an instant, turning from wildfire to ice. My trembling became stillness and my ears rang as though the world was suddenly one step removed from myself. The words tumbled from my mouth in a sharp, bitter laugh. "Ran away?" I scoffed. Alar gaped at me as though I'd sprouted wings. "Is that what *he* told you? That I'd left of my own volition?"

For the first time since he'd leaped onto the path and fought off monsters, I saw uncertainty in my cousin's bright eyes. "You left after the representative from the Order of Ter Avest rejected Father's petition."

Did he think I followed her? "Indeed," I said darkly, baring my teeth in a loose smile. "After the Order rejected me. After my scribe magic manifested. After the Baron beat me until I was more broken bone than whole person. Until I could neither walk nor move, until I could not *speak*. Yes, I left, cousin, but I did not do it under my own power."

I urged Storm onwards, my declaration leaving tears in my eyes and silence creeping up on me once again. This time, it was a defence. It was safety. It was comfort. And it was a weapon I would wield against those who stood in my way, my own family included if need be.

Pressed against me, Ink shuddered and buried his head in my side. "I'm sorry, Elyria," he breathed. "I did not know."

INTERLUDE III

*S*ome days, the memory of Elyria's visits were all that kept Keir sane in his endless imprisonment. Some days, those memories felt more like illusion. The time between her visits felt interminable, and there seemed no rhyme nor reason to them. Sometimes, she came multiple days in a row, dressed in the same garb as though no time at all had passed for her, as if she were within the same dream. Sometimes, it was many seasons between visits, and she held a haunted look in her eyes. Each time, he held her as though she were the only thing holding him in this world, the only thing that was real. He kissed her, touched her hair, mimicked her signing. He loved her, and then he waited for her.

This time, Keir hadn't seen her for years.

The war between the humans and gods had not been going well. Hirana, Tani, Maris, they had seemed to believe that the war would be over in a matter of hours, days maybe, when all this began. They had practically gloated to Keir as they beat him and threw him in the cell.

Then, the first gods had fallen.

The humans were a resourceful species, which was why the gods had desired them so. They could fight long past what they should have done. They used their newfound ability to know things with an alacrity that had taken everyone by surprise. Yes, the gods were mighty and with their angelic servants at their side, they wiped vast swathes of humans from existence. But the humans had fled to the mountains, fled to the caves, hidden themselves in nomadic groups. They had scattered, and they had fought, and they had planned.

Now, Maris was dead. That had been the cause of Tani's tearing Keir's wings from his back in her anger. All the healing power he possessed could do nothing to regrow his wings, no matter how he jumped whenever he tried to flex them. His other magic had died with his wings, leaving only scraps and tatters, barely enough to lift a pebble, enough only to heal himself, and that only barely. He still dreamed he could fly, sometimes.

Maris's death had not been the first, and it wouldn't be the last. The angels were diminished in number, fighting against some new sorcery that the humans had discovered in the energy of the world, taking what they knew of the gods' magic, the angels' magic, and making it their own. The gods had suffered as well, their numbers already few and now fewer.

Yet even with all of this, as certain as the rising of the

sun, Tani would drag him from his cell at the zenith of the year, haul him to the roof, and recount the war as they looked out upon the field of destruction. The victories and the losses, she told him everything. It was as if she told Keir because there was no one left to tell. Her servants were dead. And Keir, for all he was branded a traitor, had once been a servant of the gods.

Now, though, he lay on his side, cold stone making him shiver, and knew that two days had passed since the zenith of the year. Tani had not come for him.

He was thirsty. So thirsty. His tongue was rough and his lips were cracked, constantly healing and using up what little energy he had. His tunic had long since become rags and tatters; had Elyria shown up at that moment, he would have been embarrassed, but without her, he could not bring himself to care about his clothes. He could not bring him to care about much at all without her presence.

Fool. Always a fool, and this time twice. He had once again fallen in love with a human. The first time had been a mistake that cost him everything and opened his eyes to the faults on both sides. The second time, well, he could only hope that her lack of visits was not because she didn't want to see him. Not because she wasn't real.

Maybe, Keir thought, if he closed his eyes and managed to sleep deeply enough, he could be the one to visit her. She had, after all, signed that she came to him in her dreams. He could show her how much he'd practised her signed language, how smooth his movements were. He could touch her face, kiss her, let the burning desire warm him when he was constantly so desperately cold.

He could—

The door to his cell creaked open. It had the sound of finality, and Keir knew instantly that one way or another, he wouldn't be returning to the cell. He hoped that Elyria would find him wherever he went. And then he stopped hoping at all.

The shadow that stood in the doorway wasn't Tani.

"Hirana," Keir rasped. The goddess of knowledge had a bitter weariness about her. Her six wings drooped, the feathers ragged and disarrayed. Her dress, once a pure white with a purple sash, was almost as grimy as Keir's own tatters. She held a sword in one hand, but the point nearly dragged on the floor. Her eyes were dull.

She studied Keir for a minute, saying nothing. Then, she turned. "Come with me."

The goddess walked away without a backwards glance, leaving the door open. Keir could have gotten up and run away, free of the gods and that bitter cell. Part of him—the part that still burned with anger at the gods and the humans alike—wanted to do just that. Wanted to escape to some remote place and build a life for himself, waiting for the moment when Elyria would return to him. Instead, he pushed himself off the cold floor and staggered after Hirana.

His legs were weak from lack of use and he was panting for breath by the time they reached the rooftop where Tani liked to bring him and remind him of his treachery. His magic kept him in reasonable health, but after uncountable years living in that cell, he had lost so much conditioning. He was as weak as the humans whom he had first tried to help, and far less cunning.

Hirana let her sword fall to her feet. Her wings drooped, and for the first time, Keir could see that there was blood on her feathers, streaked across her skin. "What do you see?" Hirana asked, nodding out to the landscape beyond.

What had once been a hospitable, inviting landscape of lush grasses and plains that teemed with life, was now a barren, desolate place. Heat lay over everything like a blanket, suffocating, and the grasses were dry and brown. There were a few birds in the distance. Keir thought they might be vultures. It was an empty place. A silent place.

"The land is dead, angel. It will never be as it was, not with the blood of a thousand gods watering it. The humans that lived here are gone, now, scattered to the corners of this world. We were a great civilisation, and now..." Hirana shook her head. "I am the last. Do you know what that means?"

Keir started to smirk, but it faded. He was not proud of the destruction that he had caused. He had not served the gods as the other angels had. But that didn't mean he wanted *this*. "All I wanted when I put the human blood in the inkwell was to see them prosper. They were so beaten down by the casual cruelty of the gods. Their lives were joyless. They had no freedom to choose their mates, their talents, nothing. They slaved away for the whims of the gods, and for what? At least the angels had lives to live."

Hirana cast a glance at Keir before turning back to the dead lands before them. "Do you think I don't know that? I will admit that we were wrong to treat the humans as we did. It was our own arrogance that led to our downfall, though you were the catalyst. And perhaps it was our arrogance in that, too, which led this to happen. Did you not... did you not love us, Keir?"

He stiffened, the muscles in his back that had once borne wings screaming in loss. "*Love* you? I was your devoted servant, ready to uphold your slightest whim. I wanted the humans to have that, too. I wanted them to love you, not to fear you." He had wanted more from the humans, from one in particular, but that was his own foolishness talking. The cell had at least granted him clarity on that, even if madness overtook everything else. "When I was found, when I was dragged before you and Tani and Maris, you tortured me because you didn't know me. You had forgotten who I was, despite my having been assigned to the archives by you personally. Any love, any devotion, that I held for you died that day."

Hirana studied him, and Keir was surprised to find sadness in her eyes. "It is a difficult thing to believe oneself all powerful, infallible, and to discover that you are just as flawed as anything else in the world."

Keir curled his lip. "This dead place is what your ignorance has brought you," he bit out. "And I cannot find myself sorry for what has happened."

The goddess sighed and turned back to study the horizon. "I am the last."

"You said that before. Do you want me to weep for you when you're gone?" Keir eyed the sword on the ground, wondering if he should be the one to drive it through Hirana's chest. Wondering if he should be the one to kill her. There would be a certain symmetry to it, as he had been the one to start the war, even indirectly.

Hirana smirked, though it was half-hearted. "You could kill me," she said. "I wouldn't fight you."

He took a step backwards. "Why did you bring me up here?"

"The gods are gone but for me. Oh, there are ways a god can disappear from the world without being killed. If the ones who know them, worship them, forget, then a god can fade away. Many ages of the world have been brought about by this very method. The slaying of gods, though, is another matter entirely." Hirana nodded to the dead lands. "Our magic lives in our bones and in our blood, and instead of slowly fading back into the ether, we are absorbed into the land. We are left to rot. There will be repercussions for this war that will last long after the next gods have come and gone. All those who come to this place will be affected by its magic. I have put certain…measures in place to protect the lands not yet touched by this war, but it is all I can do."

Keir frowned. "So, what, you want me to warn people to stay away? To keep a watch over whatever measures you've enacted?"

"There will be a boundary around this place, from mountains to mountains and northern sea to the edge of the plains. My blood will fuel it and my bones will see it endures." Hirana sighed and deliberately turned her back on the empty landscape. "It will have nothing to do with you."

Keir took another step back, the first hint of fear crawling up his spine. "Why did you bring me here? Why didn't you let me rot in that cell, if you are the last? If all my brethren are dead and gone and all the gods but blood and bone."

Faster than he could anticipate, Hirana lashed out and grabbed him by the throat. There was enough power in her grasp to remind him that she was a goddess, that she had once held the power of life and death in her grasp. "Because you must pay for what you've done."

Keir scrabbled uselessly at her hand.

Hirana laughed drily. "Oh, yes, I grant you that the gods crafted their own downfall, but that knowledge cannot change the fact that it began by *your* hand. That you were the one to start it all."

His heart pounded in his ears. He couldn't get enough air to speak. His hands started to move of their own volition, shaping out words. He froze. No. He wouldn't give Hirana the satisfaction of seeing Elyria's beautiful words. He wouldn't betray Elyria like that. He might have betrayed everything else in his life, but not her. Keir grasped Hirana's wrist and snarled wordlessly at her.

The goddess laughed as he struggled, that cruelty she'd displayed in the throne room showing through. She brought him close enough that he could smell the blood on her skin, sickly sweet and sharp. "Why did you do it? Why did you betray us?"

He thought of her, the human woman whose name now seemed as inconsequential as the countless stars above. Beautiful, enticing, but easily forgotten when not in view. He had loved her once. Truly loved her. But it was the love of a devoted servant to the gods, who could not forget where his first loyalties lay. It was the half-love of a creature who had not understood himself so fully as to be able to give his heart. He wanted blind love in return for such a foolish offering and he hadn't questioned her even once.

What would Hirana say if she knew that Keir had betrayed her for such a broken love?

Instead, he bared his teeth at her and laughed.

The goddess screamed in fury and tossed him aside. He rolled on his ruined back, bruising his ribs, his little remaining energy hardly enough to heal him. He sat up on his knees, cradling his ribs, and laughed again. "The goddess of knowledge. Who knows not the answer to her own question!"

In a huff, Hirana turned her back on Keir. Her hands were clenched into fists at her side and she trembled with suppressed rage. She stared out at the dead plains beyond her and made no move towards Keir, even as he started to his feet, ready to turn his back on her and the memory of the others forever more.

"Stay where you are, angel," Hirana said in a dull, dead voice. "Your punishment is not yet complete."

"You've torn my wings from my back, you've tortured me until I had no skin left to flay. You've left me on my own for seasons without end, barely even seeing fit to remember to feed me, to water me. I've seen animals doomed to slaughter get better treatment than me." Keir shook his head, full of bitterness and fury and that spark of satisfaction that he had done the right thing. For once in his life of servitude and submission, he had thought for himself and done the right thing. What's more, he had granted that right to the humans as well. "Whatever punishment you devise, I'm sure it cannot be worse than knowing the beings I served and *worshipped* were nothing more than cruel, ignorant monsters wearing a facade of power and knowing. That you were not worth all that you were given."

For a brief instant, Hirana stiffened. When she spoke, her voice was soft, almost regretful. Almost. "I had not realised you held us in such contempt."

"Only as much as you held us," Keir spat.

She turned, and there was a look of sympathy in her eyes. It was false, surely, for what sympathy could Hirana hold for Keir? "You poor, ignorant angel," she murmured, taking a step towards him. He was rooted to the spot, mesmerised, unable to run as he should have done when she first threw him to the ground. "Your punishment shall be to see and to understand what you have done."

"What *I* have done?" Keir laughed. "I am aware of what I have done, have no fear of that."

She smiled, all traces of sympathy gone. In another blur that Keir couldn't quite follow, she was before him, a knife in her hand. She grabbed his right arm and held it out, drawing the knife down a vein in a single precise stroke. As his blood dripped to the roof, Keir could feel a deep magic start to form around him.

This was deeper than his own power, deeper than the magic that the humans had created and conquered. This was power woven into the fabric of the world. The power of the gods, what little of it remained.

"For your crimes, you are to be forever bound to the knowledge that you would give so freely to lesser beings. For eternity, you will be present, unable to speak to them as they keep your precious knowledge, hoard it, misuse it for their own purposes. Silent and useless. Until the knowledge you so *cherish* sings to them as it does—did—to us." Hirana leaned in and smiled fiendishly. A single teardrop of blood rolled down her cheek and landed on Keir's open wound.

Pain as he'd never experiences blossomed through him. His vision turned red with agony and a fire was lit through his bones. He contorted and twisted, trying to escape, trying to run. A moment later he realised that Hirana wasn't holding him any longer; the pain was coming from within him as the deep magic took hold of him and devoured. Keir folded, screaming. Only the scream was more the sound of an animal. He drew a breath and tried to claw at his skin as it split around him. More pain.

Finally, he could do nothing but give in, riding the waves of agony until he was nothing but a trembling shape on the ground. His body felt different, wrong. Every breath was a struggle and his vision seemed to have lost some of its colour. Finally, panting and shaking, he lifted his head to seek out Hirana, to chastise her and to salvage some of his dignity at whatever punishment she had meted out.

Instead, he saw her on the ground, body contorted in a pose that was anything but natural. Her eyes stared vacantly at a distance beyond Keir's shoulder. Her fingers were curled and stiff around the hilt of her knife, which had been plunged into her belly.

Had he done that? Keir dug his fingers into the roof, though they felt more like claws, and dragged himself towards Hirana's body.

"Serves you right," he said, the sound a hiss of laughter as he rasped for air. He had killed the last goddess. Dead. He laughed again as he collapsed to his side. A strange feeling settled in his belly, one he'd never known before. He thought it was joy, true joy, at finally being free.

It would be many lifetimes before he renamed it as sadness.

CHAPTER 14

Summerfell had indeed changed in the years since I'd been away. Where my childhood memories were full of an organised chaos that seemed to constantly roll through the fortress, now things were precise and orderly. Where outside had been a constant stream of activity, inside was a bastion of calm and quiet. There was no unspoken tension in the air. People went about their tasks with a surety that spoke of no fear of the inhabitants of the fortress.

The stones on the floor were clean, gleaming between the colourful rugs on the floor where rushes used to be. The walls had been plastered over with a thick layer of wattle and daub for insulation, tapestries I recognised has having been in storage for years now hanging proudly, displaying scenes of dramatic Trevain family lore. The fortress was no longer a picture of war inside as well as out, but comfortable, a place that people could call home. It was entirely unfamiliar to me.

I was ready to admit that I had expected my uncle's ghost to linger in this place. I still looked for it, for him, and tried to ignore the shivers running up my spine. Ink walked at my side, prowling with his head down and his ears back. He curled a lip at any who dared to stare at me as the obvious relative of their Baron and let out low rumbling growls when any got too close. Oddly, his overprotectiveness made me feel better.

Alar reappeared after having ordered the horses seen to. He didn't look at me. "I've sent your bags to your room. You are welcome here for as long as you would like, cousin, and you…you don't need to tell me any more of what, ah, transpired."

I nodded my head in silent thanks. Some of the tension in Alar's shoulders melted away, though he still did not look me in the eye. A moment later, though, the crackling awkwardness between us didn't seem to matter.

A woman stepped into the hall, her step light and her every movement graceful and sure. She dressed in a simple gown of blue wool like my own, if a bit finer, and her brown hair was done in a simple braid, but from the tilt of her head, the way she held her shoulders, the gentle smile on her face, there could have been no comparing her to me. She was beautiful in manner and face and every eye in the hall seemed to turn towards her.

My neck prickled with immediate discomfort and I took a step back. I remembered a woman with those same movements, that same impossible draw. She had stood by while the Baron had beaten me for the magic in my blood. This woman, whoever she was, hailed from the Order of Ter Avest.

"Husband," the woman said, gliding over to Alar and greeting him with a kiss to his cheek. "I take it your journey was successful, then? Did you best the creatures? Is this one of those whom they stole?"

She smiled at me, all benevolence and charm, with just a tinge of sympathy that showed through her fluttering lashes. I took another step back, nearly stepping on Ink as he pressed against my leg. He growled low and deep at my discomfort, glaring at this woman—Alar's *wife* was of Ter Avest. How could he have done such a thing? Why?

Alar squeezed the woman's arms in that familiar way of lovers. "My dear, this is my cousin, the Lady Elyria Trevain. Elyria, this is my wife, Jessamine."

Jessamine's smile widened just enough to display delight. She reached for me, obviously intending to embrace me. Ink's growl grew louder until it echoed throughout the hall. Jessamine faltered, but only for an instant. She bowed her head at me and made no move to come closer, as if she'd never reached out at all.

"I am thrilled to meet you at long last, Lady Elyria," she said. "Alar has told me so much about you that I feel as though I know you already. And who is your companion? Not a catkin, surely?"

"*Claw that Writes With Ink is not a catkin,*" I signed with more fervour than was truly necessary. Alar winced at my lack of speech, but translated dutifully. His translation was a little slow, but it was accurate. I expected no less. It was a good way to communicate with soldiers when silence was necessary and had been required of the watch for countless years. Jessamine didn't blink at my muteness, just inclined her head at Ink.

"A beautiful name for a beautiful creature," she said. "Now, you must have had a long journey through the pass. Please, come, let me show you to your room. I will call for some refreshments and you can rest before supper." She swept her arm in a graceful movement that made it clear I was to proceed her. I did so begrudgingly, trying not to show my discomfort at having her at my back. The dragon stirred but lightly, still exhausted from earlier, though more awake now that I was so agitated.

Jessamine guided me through the once-familiar halls of my childhood home, neatly avoiding any talks of what my life must have been like when living there, instead discussing such banal things as the tapestries and the upcoming harvest. She led me to the guest wing of the fortress, where the rooms were larger and finer than any in the family quarters, meant to show off Summerfell's prowess to visiting dignitaries who liked to view the protections of the gap for themselves. Even refurbished, they were grand, opulent. I was placed in the meadow room, a light and airy room at the circular corner of the fortress, decorated in whites and spring greens with tapestries of ladies frolicking through meadows with angels at their side.

I shuddered, the image of Keir in his prison cell flashing into my mind.

"How fortunate it is to have not one but two guests so close to harvest," Jessamine said. "We had a traveller up the pass just yesterday, such a shocking thing in these times. Perhaps it is the increased activity beyond the gap that draws people forth. Well, I'll leave you to get settled, and—"

The door opposite the meadow room swung open, revealing a person I thought I might never see again. Dressed in loose trousers and a woollen sweater that was more patches than whole, she looked the worse for wear but was as unmistakable as the fire burning in her eyes. I went weak at the knees.

Margarethe.

"Elyria," she cried, sweeping me into a bone-crushing hug. I returned the embrace, crying into her just as she did for me. Jessamine seemed startled at our familiarity, a glint of something sharp and cunning in her look for an instant. She blinked and the look was gone. With a bow of her head, she swept off. Alar remained, shifting his weight awkwardly.

"Do you...know each other?" he asked, watching Margarethe with wide eyes.

"We work together at the Great Archives in Vazeri," Margarethe said, a surprising amount of bite to her tone. "She is my *friend*."

Alar coughed and nodded. He turned to me. "If you...I would like to talk with you later. Alone, if you, that is... before dinner if you have the time. I'll, ah, be in the library."

He turned on his heel and walked away, back stiff and a hurry to his stride.

Margarethe snorted as he left. "As uptight as his letters," she said, making me laugh. Gods, it had been so long since I laughed.

"Come on, let's get you settled in to your room. No offence, Elyria, but you stink and there is a *wonderful* bathing system here." She grabbed my hand and pulled me into the meadow room. My bags were already at the foot of the great bed, and a dress that was likely Jessamine's had been laid out for me to wear. Ink leaped onto the bed and kicked the garment to the floor, settling into the spot where it lay with a blink.

"What are you doing here?" I asked once we had reached the bathing chamber. Margarethe was already pouring me a bath, unstopping several glass bottles with various scented soaps and pouring them into the water. "You were going to manage the mess at the Archives and—"

Margarethe winced, nearly dropping one of the bottles. Foam started forming, a thick layer of bubbles that smelled divine after having been on the road for so long. She buried her head in her hands. "Gods, Elyria, I don't know what to say. I watched you ride off and then everyone tried to go back to normal, as if Vazeri hadn't just been violated in the worst way, as if no one had been taken. It was awful. And the triumvirate, they kept sending these mysterious missives to Makhier and whispering behind closed doors. They stopped giving public forums and, well, it took about two days for things to devolve into paranoid chaos. I left after that."

Two days? How had she made it to Summerfell before me? We must have passed each other when I strayed off the main road from Makhier to Summerfell. She must have barely stopped, barely slept, to get here so fast.

I peeled my clothes off and left them in a heap on the floor, then stepped into the water with a grateful sigh. The warmth was a gods-sent blessing, and it was a pleasure to watch the dirt sluice off of me.

Margarethe gasped.

"Deepest Night," she cursed on a breath. I turned and found her staring at my bare back with horror. The tattoo. The dragon. I had forgotten.

Fear spiked through me for an instant as I scrambled to come up with a reasonable explanation. The dragon, though, woke up a little more with that fear and shifted on my back, turning its head and tightening its tail around my ribs. Margarethe let out a quiet scream.

I turned so quickly that water splashed over the edge of the tub. Margarethe was watching me, wide-eyed, her hands covering her mouth.

"*It's not what you think,*" I signed immediately, then cursed to myself. If I'd seen someone with a body-sized tattoo made of innumerable tiny letters only a short time after having sent them off on a quest, then witnessed the tattoo *move*, I would think I was going insane. I wasn't entirely sure that I hadn't already. "*It's okay. I can explain,*" I signed.

Margarethe took a deep breath, still staring at me. "Gods

above, Elyria. You have a tattoo of a *dragon* on your back. And it *moved!*"

I winced. If Ink weren't asleep on the bed, he would likely be scolding me for my carelessness and urging me to lie to Margarethe for her safety as well as mine. Instead, I felt all the resolve I'd built up since leaving Vazeri shatter into shards that cut to the quick. I wasn't meant for grand magics and quests to save people, no matter how I cared for them. I was a scribe. I had trained for a life in the Great Archives and I had been happy there amongst the whispering books.

How quickly my surety vanished into nothing.

I told Margarethe everything. I signed so rapidly that I thought she must have surely lost the thread of the story a few times, but she kept watching, her mouth hanging open as I signed and signed and signed, my arms getting tired and the bathwater growing cold. Finally, I let my hands grow still, dropping them into the water and shivering.

"And, well, here I am," I rasped.

I expected her to run screaming from the room. I was half-tempted to do so myself. I'd killed people, some unintentionally as a product of the strange magic inhabiting me, others intentionally. I'd bled a man dry with scribe magic. I'd been attacked by angelic monsters in the pass. I was no fighter, no huntress, yet I had blood on my hands as surely as I sat there staring at Margarethe.

She closed her eyes and rubbed her hands over them. "Okay, let me get this straight. Since you left Vazeri with the triumvirate all but ready to kill you for unintentionally reading their secrets—which are apparently vast, if the world is as insane as you say—you have bound a sorcerer's dragon to you with your scribe magic, burned a refinery of god blood to the ground, been attacked and killed your attacker, dreamed of an angel in some other place or world or something, and dealt with actual, literal monsters trying to kill you."

I nodded.

"Out of all of this, you didn't once think to tell me that you could *talk* to a *magical cat* before you left haring off on some fool's errand to rescue that…that…idiot, Beltran!" She exploded to her feet, full of fire and fury and concern for me. "Gods above, Elyria, don't you know that things that talk that should definitely not be talking, are nothing but bad news?!"

A bark of laughter, nearly hysterical, escaped me. I clapped a hand over my mouth, but the laughter escaped again. Margarethe stared at me, then she, too, broke out into hysterical laughter. I waved my hands vaguely in the air. "Out of everything, you think *the cat* is the problem?"

Margarethe laughed harder, sinking to her knees on the wet floor and wrapping her arms around me. "I was so worried about you. And now it seems I was absolutely right to be!"

"I'm okay," I breathed. "I'm worn and weary and I've seen and done terrible things, but I'm okay. I promise."

She pulled back and wiped at her eyes. "You had better be. Now, drain that water and draw a new bath to clean off. You still smell. I'll see you at dinner."

She hurried from the room before I could see her cry properly, see the truth of what my tale had done to her. I did as she asked, draining the dirty water and sighing in pleasure at the freshly warmed water. I washed and scrubbed until I was raw, then sat back and soaked some of the tension from my muscles. After I felt a little more human—though still less than myself—I wrapped my hair in a linen towel and dressed in a robe, emerging into the bedroom.

Ink was still on the bed, sleeping. As I approached, he lifted his head and cracked his eyes open.

"Are you alright?" I asked, hovering my hand over his shoulder. I hadn't had a chance to see how the wound was healing since we'd been in Aviena. Gods, was that only this morning?

Ink stretched, claws raking the air, and yawned. "I'm fine, scribe. I heal swiftly. Just needed a proper sleep."

"Well, you stay here, then, and keep sleeping. I'll go down to dinner—"

"Not a chance." Now he was wide awake, on his feet and pacing. "I saw the way you reacted to that woman. I won't leave you with her if she's dangerous."

Jessamine. I sighed and sat on the bed, all the tension that had melted away in the bath returning with that single thought. "She's not…dangerous per se, not that I know of. I just have bad memories of another member of her order."

"Her order?" Ink asked, his voice carefully bland. I watched him watch me.

"The Order of Ter Avest," I murmured, sinking back on the

bed and wrapping the robe tighter around me. "It is an order for the daughters of nobility and the wealthy, those who are not heirs, sometimes those who are. What they are taught, exactly, is kept carefully secret, but rumours abound. How to walk gracefully, how to speak in exactly the right tone to draw the attention of everyone in a room, how to whisper in someone's ear so they take the course desired. They are versed in politics and warfare, diplomacy, poetry. Some say they are even trained to kill, should the need arise to further their goals."

The tip of Ink's tail flicked once. "What, exactly, are their goals?"

I shrugged. "I don't know. No one does, or if they do, they keep quiet. They weren't very well-known twenty years ago, but now, they are married into or connected with many of the powerful families of the continent."

"And you have bad memories of...you said your uncle tried to sell you into the order," Ink said with dawning realisation. I nodded. "But they wouldn't take you—"

"They don't take anyone with magic." I shivered. Ink sat beside me, his fur warm and a subtle purr making me relax again. For a brief moment, I thought I saw something familiar in his eyes, something I'd seen only in a dream, but it was gone with a blink. "Some call them witches, though they have no magic of their own. Many think them dangerous, even as they think them desirable."

"There are many different types of magic, as you have learned," Ink said slowly. "I had heard whispers of such an order during my time in the Great Archive, but I admit I didn't pay much attention. I should have. My interests in the outside world lapsed during my time there."

It was an admission of guilt, one I didn't quite understand. I turned a little so Ink was cradled in the curve of my body. His purrs increased slightly. "How did you become bound to the Great Archives?" I asked softly. The purring ceased.

Ink heaved himself to his feet and padded to the edge of the bed. He hesitated there a moment before springing down and wandering over to the window. There was pain in his walk as there hadn't been when asking about his wound. He hunched his shoulders as though the weight of the world rested on them, and his tail dragged on the ground.

"I was a fool," he said at last, looking up at the window as though it were a glimpse of the sky in the midst of a cage. "I did something that needed to be done, but I did it out of selfishness. And I had to watch the world that my actions brought about. Never able to interfere, never able to tell anyone, for no one could hear me unless they were bound by the same Old Magic."

The Old Magic that I'd initiated when I bled on a book and some of my scribe magic bound me to the Great Archives. Bound me. I sat bolt upright.

"That was how you knew I could...I could save myself from that bandit," I breathed. "Because I was bound to the Great Archives by blood."

"Blood that sang as ink," he said, ducking his head. "Blood that sang as ink even as you were silent."

There was that pain again. I could almost feel it as an oppressive shape that filled the room, vast and powerful and completely incapable of affecting the world. It had, almost, the shape of wings. Those wings that I had seen in the firelight and the threads of the world. I sucked in a sharp breath.

"Ink," I started slowly. "How long have you been bound?"

Ink leaped onto the windowsill and stared out at the wall of the fortress, and the trees beyond that. I almost didn't hear the words when he spoke them, for they were so quiet as to be less than a whisper. But they were spoken and I did hear them. "Since the gods fell."

CHAPTER 15

I went down to dinner in a daze. Ink's words pounded in my ears, reverberating through the air like tangible thoughts. It was a piece to a puzzle that I didn't quite understand. Didn't quite *want* to understand. It was impossible and yet felt so right and I still couldn't wrap my mind around it. Instead, I stumbled my way through half-familiar corridors to the great hall, following the smells that set my stomach rumbling.

The hall was little changed, thankfully. There were still large tables running throughout the room, various people sitting at the benches and eating together without concern for rank or position. Some of the watch sat together, laughing over a goblet of wine, but otherwise everyone was integrated. Except, that is, for the head table at the back of the room. It was the only one with chairs instead of benches and they seemed to overlook the room with a quiet sense of superiority.

I remembered sitting in the chair at the very end of that table and eating as quickly as possible without being scolded, fearful of everyone's eyes on me. Now, as I stepped into the great hall, my fears were realised. Voices quieted and people stared, watching me walk by with an interest that made my spine prickle and the dragon shift on my skin. As I passed, whispers broke out, sounding very like the whispers of books in my mind.

Jessamine was already seated at the head table, Margarethe to her left. My friend looked unnerved by whatever quiet conversation Jessamine held with her. She sat up and smiled at me with palpable relief as I approached. Jessamine, too, straightened and smiled, though there was no relief there. Only what she wanted me to see.

"Elyria, come, sit by me. I'm sure Alar won't mind being put out of his usual seat for the evening." Jessamine patted the central chair. I remembered the Baron sitting there, watching over his hall with pride, and shuddered. Still, it was not a request I could easily refuse. I wished for a brief moment that Ink was there to wrap himself around my ankles, to press that power of his around me in a comforting embrace. To—no. I needed to put that from my mind, to breathe, to *think*. He had gone off somewhere; I didn't ask where.

I sat. A plater of food was immediately set before me. Roasted venison, potatoes and carrots by the look of it. Typical winter food for Summerfell, but unusual before the harvest.

"I hope the accommodations were to your liking,"

Jessamine said, pouring me an overfull goblet of rich red wine. I inclined my head. "It is fortuitous of you to come now. A few days earlier, and you might have been caught up in the raider attacks!"

My attention was caught, though I had no doubt that was what she wanted. Margarethe had likely told her why I was here as it wasn't some great secret. I turned to Jessamine and tilted my head to show my interest. She waited a beat, that selfsame smile gracing her features. She waited for me to speak, to ask, though she knew I would not. When I did not, her smile widened almost imperceptibly.

"A whole troop of them came through at the start of summer. It was so unexpected, and they were many. The watch was at its summer levels, which as I'm sure you know is diminished for those who serve as farmers and labourers during the warmer months. Still, many were defeated." Jessamine speared a piece of venison with her fork and nodded to the back wall, just above the doors to the hall. I turned and my breath caught.

Wings.

At least a dozen pairs of angel wings like I'd seen on those twisted monsters, like I'd seen on Keir's back, were pinned to the wall with metal spikes. Some of the feathers were missing and there were stains on them that turned my stomach. What, exactly, had come through the gap in the boundary? And *why*?

Jessamine's tone turned solemn, and a quick glance at her showed a single careworn line at the corner of her mouth. "Some made it through, despite our best efforts. And I'm sorry to say we didn't have the forces to spare to follow after them. We did send missives to all the towns and cities. Many were returned unopened."

At the start of summer. I thought back to Vazeri, then. I'd been smitten with Beltran and content to spend my time with the books, so I hadn't paid much attention. But I vaguely recalled that the Makhierian soldiers had arrived around that time, supposedly in response to rumours of an invasion from Imara.

The records from Summerfell had also disappeared at the start of summer, I realised.

The wine turned to ash in my mouth.

"What...what *were* they?" Margarethe asked, looking as horrified as I felt.

Jessamine lifted one shoulder, the movement somehow ungraceful for one of her order. "We thought them angels at first. The wings, you see. And they sort of looked like the angels of legend." She took a sip of wine and shook her head. "They were monstrous, horrible creatures in the end. Just like every story that's ever come out of Summerfell."

It was then that I heard it. A whisper. It was so like the other whispered conversations in the hall that I hadn't noticed it at first, but as the conversations changed and people no longer whispered about me, this one persisted. I should have recognised it earlier, even with the dragon's magic singing through my scribe magic. Ink on paper. A letter. It whispered at me from Jessamine's pocket, unfinished and hurriedly written, the ink still fresh and young.

*She has returned. I don't know if she knows the truth, if she knows of her power here, but I cannot discount that fact. If I do not find a way to dissuade her, all our plans regarding Summerfell may be—*The text stopped there, aching with its unfinished potential. The whisper sounded almost like Jessamine, in the way that some letters reflected their writers. I would have bet everything I owned that she wrote the letter. And that it was about me.

A weight settled into my stomach, growing heavier with each moment. Gruesome wings to the front, potential enemies to the side, and whispers all around. It was enough to set my heart beat soaring. Sweat began to trickle down my back, though the room was not warm enough for that. When I picked up the fork, my hand trembled.

Margarethe shot a look at me over Jessamine's shoulder, but with Alar's wife between us, it would be impossible to talk freely. Impossible to sign without being seen, and I didn't trust that she wouldn't know what I was saying. The Order of Ter Avest was, according to rumour, very thorough in their education.

The door to the great hall swung open, hitting the wall with a loud *crack*. I jumped in my seat, nearly upending my goblet of wine. I heard more than one person curse and laugh nervously at the interruption. Until, that is, Alar strode through the door. He was carrying a heap of feathers in his hands and he was splattered in blood, the colour not quite right to be human. I realised a moment later that he was carrying a pair of wings, hewn roughly from their owner's back, still dripping with gore. Several members of the watch cheered and rushed to help Alar pin them to the wall. One must have been a metal mage, because the spikes moved of their own accord, a ghostly dance that impaled the wings to the stone with grim delight.

I was going to be sick.

I jumped from my chair and rushed to the side entrance to the hall, a small door meant for servants that led directly to the kitchens and then to the walled kitchen gardens beyond. It wasn't quite freedom, the peace that came from wandering beneath the trees of the mountains, but it was close. I heaved a few times, though there wasn't enough in my stomach to come back up.

A hand rested on my back and I jumped, the dragon's magic flaring so that I could see the ripples of ink-as-energy in the world. I spun.

Alar stood there, watching me. He was still covered in gore, still the triumphant watchman returned from his hunt, but outside the hall, he looked little more than sad, reflected in the slow shimmering of energy that flowed within him.

"Are you alright?" he asked gently.

I nodded, stiff.

"I'm sorry. I went back out hunting after I brought you to the fortress, to see if I could...I didn't realise that such things would upset you." He sighed and ran his hands through his hair, heedless of the blood. "Apparently, I didn't realise a lot of things. Gods above, Lyr, I didn't know what my father did. You must believe me. I thought—"

"You thought I ran away," I signed.

"You always hated it here, with your lessons and Nissa and her small cruelties, and Father's demands," Alar said. "I knew that, and I always assumed that it would get better. Then, you were gone. I thought that the Order was your way out and you took it, even if they rejected you at first. I didn't know until I married Jessamine that you weren't a member. I didn't think about why you…I swear I didn't know what he did to you."

I believed him. I never thought he had any part in that, or the years of silence that came after them. I knew that Alar had been as under his father's thumb as I was, more even, because he bore the weight of expectations that I would never have.

I reached out and touched his hands. They were still sticky with blood. Alar pulled away, but I held tight. "I forgive you," I breathed. Alar sucked in a breath and shuddered, then closed the distance between us and wrapped his arms around me again.

"Gods, Elyria, I missed you so much."

I had missed him, too, the only real friend of my childhood, the single bright point in a myriad of shadows and fog. His letters had always been stiff and formal, as if dealing with a stranger, but standing here with him beside me, he was nothing more than the boy I knew, only older.

Finally, he pulled back. "I've ruined your dress," he said with a wince. I fingered the fabric and shrugged. Alar sighed, perhaps at my silence, perhaps at the dress, and tugged me back towards the fortress. Instead of going to the great hall, he pulled me in a different direction. I didn't realise until too late that he was bringing me to the library.

Panic set me alight and my breath caught. The dragon roared and the ground shook. I grasped onto the specks of inklight in the stones all around me and forced them to stay put, to steady me. They obeyed. Alar gaped at me.

"What was that? Was that you?" he asked. I said nothing. Telling Margarethe was one thing, telling Alar, especially when he was connected to Jessamine, was another thing entirely. "No, it doesn't matter," he said, shaking his head. "Not right now. Come, I have something to tell you."

The library. He was still going to the library. The place where everything had been taken from me. It had been months before I could stand to be in the same room as a book without breaking down into panic attacks. I'd spent the first year in Liral slowly building up my tolerance to being around the written word, to accepting the whispers and my scribe magic. That is, after I had healed physically.

I clenched my hands into fists and shoved them into my pockets, but I followed my cousin. The specks of energy and the flowing rivers within Alar continued in my vision, even as the dragon settled down on my shoulders to wait. But the closer we got to the library, the fewer traces of magical energy shone. Alar threw open the doors, and then the energy changed, sparking and shining and rippling every-where except for the array of shelves on the back wall.

Dead. A rot spreading from the void of the bookshelves.

"Something about this room..." He shivered, giving a dramatic shake. "It always gives me the strangest feeling.

Like something terrible has happened here. But that's silly. It's just a bunch of dusty old books. Like your Archive."

I stepped forward to the shelves, which were exactly as I remembered, unchanged even a little bit. I brushed my hand over the spine of those books. Something terrible *had* happened here. I had killed these books as surely as if I'd burned them. I had stolen their voices. Silenced them. Unknowingly, perhaps, but it was still a cruelty I wouldn't soon forget. I would give so much to return their voices. Maybe it would help me find my own in the process. But it was impossible. They were dead, nothing but paper and leather and ink. They could be read, but they would never again tell a story.

My cousin watched me, waiting for a reply, perhaps. When I continued to say nothing, he sighed and turned to the desk, to the papers strewn there, stacked with abandon. These were newer, and they whispered with the voice of their author. Yet they were subdued, as if they sensed the wrongness of the room, of the words stored there. No wonder my cousin preferred to be outside, hunting, patrolling.

Killing.

I shuddered and wandered to the window, wrapping my arms around myself.

"I'm sorry to have to tell you this, Lyr, but…it's about your parents." Alar grimaced as I spun to face him. "They were lost to the Great Plains."

I frowned. *"I know that from your letter. Have you found their bodies?"*

Alar shook his head. "What letter?"

"The one you sent at the height of summer? You told me they were lost to the Great Plains, their expedition vanished." I wondered vaguely if my parents had also been searching for god blood, if they had been involved with the Makhierian endeavour to enhance magic.

My cousin sat in the chair at the desk and studied me. "Elyria, I sent you no letter. I've never sent you a letter."

"You've been writing to me since before I arrived in Vazeri at the Great Archives. Since your father died," I signed, insistent. His letters hadn't been all that friendly, certainly, but they were done in Alar's hand, the same messy scrawl of childhood, the same scrawl that littered the papers on his desk now.

"No," he murmured. "I haven't. I only received news that you were still alive when the Great Archives petitioned Summerfell for your records. I never wrote to you. I assumed that you...that you didn't want to be reminded of this place. Of me."

It was my turn to gape at him. I'd been getting semiregular letters from him for years. Yet here he sat before me, claiming he had never written because he didn't want to interfere with my decision to stay away. Blood roared in my ears as I ran through my mental archives, going over the contents of the letters. They were formal, from an indifferent cousin to an indifferent cousin, almost as if we were strangers rather than bound by blood. They never brought up the past except in general terms. Yet they had been done in Alar's hand, familiar to me.

I reached out and called one of his papers to me, the ink responding to my demand with a swiftness that nearly tore the paper. Alar flinched.

"My gods," he murmured. "You said you had scribe magic, but I never imagined…"

More proof that he hadn't written me. The shock on his face was real, true. I'd told him about my scribe magic in the second letter we'd exchanged, and it had never been brought up again.

The letter rustled in my fingers, the ink demanding I pay it attention. I did, studying the formation of the letters, the depth of the pen strokes, the jab of punctuation. The whispers of the words. It was an older piece, so the voice of the ink was nearly neutral, without much tone of the original writer. But it was enough.

The letters that had been sent to me were forgeries. Good ones. Ones that were close enough in hand to Alar's writing to be a facsimile of the original. Letters whose original voice had faded due to the time between writing and reading, leaving only the whispers of ink. And, having been away from my cousin and his writing for so long, I had swallowed the false letters without questioning it. I had *laughed* at them, thinking my cousin grown stiff and formal and unsure of me.

The paper in my hands fluttered to the floor.

"Whoever wrote the letters knew enough to fool even one with scribe magic. They were careful," I breathed. Alar was on his feet in an instant, hands on my arms, steadying me.

"Who would do that?" he asked. "And why?"

I shook my head and shrugged. "I don't know. I don't. My scribe magic was well known in Liral and at the Great Archive, but no one there cared enough about my past to inquire, let alone send letters from a long-lost cousin."

"What did they say?" Alar asked.

"Nothing important. News of Summerfell, in general terms. Reluctant invitations for me to return whenever I wished it. News of my parents." Legs weak, I leaned against the bookshelf of dead books, my fingers brushing against the cold leather of their spines. "Letters designed more to keep up the appearance of a relationship between us than to forge one. To keep me content where I was."

"Why?" Alar asked again, pacing the library. He cursed under his breath. "The upswing in raids, these new creatures emerging from the gap, the rune magic left in their wake, and now this?"

I stilled, and the quiet whispers of words in the room stilled with me. The dragon on my back was now awake, listening with the same rapt attention that seized me. "Rune magic?" I croaked.

Alar pressed his mouth in a thin line. "Perhaps you had better come with me. This is something better shown."

CHAPTER 16

*A*lar snuck us through the servants' door in the kitchen gardens, peering over his shoulder as though he expected to get in trouble for going out. No one had pursued us or even paid us any attention as we walked through Summerfell. The news of the mysterious letters had obviously thrown him. He jumped at every sound and reached for the sword at his waist as if reminding himself that it was there. He had even pressed a small dagger into my hand despite his assurances that we would be perfectly safe.

His anxiety was infectious.

I wondered again where Ink had gone, and this time I didn't dismiss the thought. Unease gripped me as we stepped into the twilight forest. The dragon awakened again and sparks of ink flared in my vision.

Trees loomed over us, a slight breeze sending their leaves and needles fluttering. The night air was chill and I knew that in another week, the leaves would likely be falling. Autumn was coming and it rarely did so quietly in Summerfell. I shivered.

Alar picked his way through the forest with the precision of one who had travelled these paths often. To my surprise, I slipped into the familiar step of walking through the forest as though it hadn't been more than a decade since I'd done it. I was able to avoid stepping on loose sticks and I passed through the trunks of the trees like they were my old friends. Maybe it was the sorcerous magic and dragon that I now possessed, the ability growing easier and easier with each use. Maybe it was the memories of childhood reasserting themselves, a sort of muscle memory I didn't know I had. Or maybe it was that ancient magic in the Summerfell line that Ink had talked about.

After about five minutes, Alar slipped from the forest path. The undergrowth here was rougher, the trees closer together, competing for light. The ground became rockier until we were standing near the edge of a small cliff, looking down on a slight valley. The edge of the gap, I knew, though I had never been there myself. It had been forbidden and it was one rule I had never broken. But the magic of the boundary tingled against my skin, frayed and sharp. Broken.

The gap seemed to sing, and the singer was furious.

"Do you see?" Alar asked, pointing into the darkness. I followed his direction. The breath froze in my chest.

Runes. They were identical to the ones carved in Vazeri, in Aviena, only more numerous. With my magical vision, I could see the energy that was woven into them like a cloth. It was intentional. Someone had crafted these runes from magic and done so with great deliberation.

My scribe magic translated them with ease, the whispers in my head pressing against my temple with gleeful viciousness.

Burn. Explode. Stab. Bury. Kill. Kill. Kill.

"We tried to get past them," Alar said in a low voice. "They appeared after our first battle, glowing in the dark. I lost seven members of the watch before we realised that touching the runes, even slightly, was a death sentence."

"They're spells," I signed. I pointed. *"That one is set to burn someone alive. That one will open a sinkhole in the ground and bury a person. That one explodes the boulder on which it is written. And that one there..."* I faltered at the rune that looked so much like an eye, staring. Watching. *"That one is different. It's not a spell set to kill, but more of a...scrying, I think. For someone to watch what goes on here."*

Just the mere thought of someone watching me had my hackles rising. The dragon was fully awake, now, offering its power for my protection, for my command, that magical ink-thread between us now a rope of steel.

"How do you know these things?" Alar asked. He fairly shone in the faint moonlight that was overtaking the twilight, his white-blonde hair giving him an ethereal look that was reflected by the tiny strands of magic within him. I imagined I shone in the same way, but when I looked at my hands, I saw no magic. Only darkness.

"Perhaps you shouldn't ask me these things," I signed, my

hands nearly invisible in the darkness. Alar stilled them with his own.

"Elyria, please. For the sake of the watch, for everyone here at Summerfell, I need to know."

I pulled back and strode away, turning my back on the killing field below us. "My magic—my *scribe* magic—it translates any written word." I didn't tell him about my other magic, though perhaps he already knew. He had to have seen it during the fight with those monsters. Right?

"Okay," he said. Then again, "Okay."

I got the impression he was telling that to himself more than me.

"Lyr, something is going on, isn't it? Something is happening. Here, at the gap. Maybe even out in the Great Plains where your parents were lost. I've heard rumours about people trying to enhance their magic. About sickness. About…I don't even know. Nothing real, nothing substantial, but they never are this far north, this close to the boundary. But there's something going on, and I think you're involved in it." He took a deep, shaking breath. "Or else you wouldn't have come back, would you?"

I was saved from answering only by a noise coming from the cliff behind us. I whirled, my vision picking up sparks and strands of magic that lived in the trees and the rocks and the runes. There was motion at the edge of the cliff. A hand reached over the edge, digging its claw-like fingers into the dirt. A second followed it, hauling the owner over the edge.

Hunched over with wings that shone nearly white, beautiful angelic features, orange eyes that wept with rot.

My heart plummeted in my chest. "Alar," I breathed, not sure how I found the ability to speak.

"Lyr," he answered, sounding just as shaken as I. "Run. Back to Summerfell. Now."

He drew his sword. The angelic creature laughed, the sound disjointed somehow. Wrong. The creature drew its own sword, longer than Alar's. Heavier. It grinned at us as if daring us to attack. To fight.

"Elyria, run!" Alar begged, already stepping forward to protect me. He had no armour, only the sword to protect him, and there was barely a sliver of a moon to light the way. Darkness had fallen too fast.

I knew, logically, that my cousin had been trained to fight monsters from the gap his whole life. I knew, logically, that he had already killed many of these creatures, pinned their wings to his wall. I knew, logically, that he was a far better fighter than I, who could barely hold a sword properly. Yet I stayed where I was.

The angel, the monster, whatever they were, laughed again. They lunged.

Alar had killed the previous monsters with a bow, perhaps laced with magic of some sort to kill them the way my short sword hadn't. Now, though, he was fighting up close with the monster and I began to see just how outmatched my cousin was. He was obviously a talented warrior. His movements were fluid and practised, swift enough that they happened without thought, but the angel was faster. More fluid. The sword had a longer reach and when the blades clashed together, the angel bore down and drove Alar to his knees.

"Elyria, please," Alar begged. "Run."

His sword cracked, shearing at the hilt. The angel's sword sliced through the air towards Alar's exposed neck. I threw out my hand, a scream stuck in my chest.

The world stilled.

Magic filled my eyes, glowing so brightly that it was nearly blinding. The words making up the dragon on my back itched, their whispers almost deafening. I held the inkstars trapped in the angel's sword within my hands, their energy mine to control. Alar's blood dripped from a small cut in his neck, flashing bright with energy before fading as it hit the ground. The trees were strong with numerous weavings of a brownish-red ink so complex that it would have taken me an age to unravel it. The rocks held their galaxies and the ground was brimming with multitudes of minuscule twinkles of inkblots of light.

The angel, too, swam with energy, viscous and rotten, the same insidious colour as their eyes. Just the thought of touching it had me recoiling.

The angel turned, still holding their immobilised sword. Interest flashed in those terrible eyes. They smiled, showing rot. "Sorcerer," they hissed. "At last."

Before I could react, the angel had dropped their sword and leaped for me, wings scooping the air and propelling them forward. I gasped and stumbled backwards. Grabbing onto the sword had been instinctual, but I didn't actually know how to fight with this magic. And I had no paper with me, so I couldn't kill them with scribe magic, even if I could bring myself to manipulate that rotten blood. In a blind panic, I called the angel's sword to my hand and raised it with shaking arms. It met the very tips of the angels' feathers, but did little more than shear off a few inches.

The angel danced backwards, laughing again. I raised the sword between us and they just laughed all the harder. "Incompetence! To find the last sorcerer and be met with such incompetence! I will enjoy this."

They danced around me with a few quick movements. I could barely track them, the sword too heavy in my hands. The angel was at my back and buffeted me with a wing. I flew forwards, dropping the sword and barely catching myself on a tree. The angel deliberately ignored the weapon and walked towards me at a casual pace. In a blur of motion, they had buffeted me again and leaped on top of me, straddling me, hands gently wrapped around my throat.

A bit of that rot dripped down onto my skin, burning like acid. I screamed that time, unable to contain the sound as pain tore through me.

"Perhaps I should take you back with me. A gift!" The angel leaned forwards, rancid breath brushing my face. More rot fell, each drop burning through me.

The dragon writhed on my back as if trying to escape the pain, the whispers of those ancient words rising in volume, but if I expected it to do something, *anything*, then I was sorely disappointed. It seemed trapped.

Or afraid.

I tried to grasp onto the magic that still lingered in my vision, reaching for the bursts of light in the ground. It swelled at my command, reaching to claw at the angel with sharpened rocks and stones. The angel hissed, squeezing my throat tighter. More than that, though, fear had me in its grasp and I trembled.

"I'm going to enjoy dismantling this world piece by piece," the angel said in my ear. "Starting with your friend there, who so enjoys hunting my kind. I think it's time to show him who the true hunter is."

My fear turned brittle and shattered, emerging instead as rage. I let out a roar that echoed the dragon's roar on my back and the forest shook. I slammed my hand into the angel's chest, sending the energy of the ground through them so that they flew back and slammed into a tree. Their wings crumpled. I clambered to my feet. The dragon shifted, claws stretching out to embrace my fingers until I had phantom claws of ink and magic and blood at my command. Horns of that same insubstantial magic formed at my brow. I felt fire tickle my throat, warming me with a dragon's wrath. The dragon melded into my scribe magic until I was it and it was me and we were one and the same.

The angel didn't even have time to scream before I slashed my claws across their throat and whispered, the words lost to the dark, "Burn."

They burst into green flames and were nothing more than ash in seconds. Not even a feather remained.

"Lyr?"

I whirled, the magic falling from my body and my vision.

Alar stood there, leaning against a tree, eyes wide with awe and fear. "My gods," he breathed. "What was that? Was that *you?*"

My eyes couldn't fix on his, couldn't meet his questioning gaze. I could only look around at the destruction wrought by the brief battle. No words even tried to get stuck in my throat, instead eaten entirely by silence. Unease churned my stomach.

"It's okay, Lyr," Alar said. He straightened and winced, rubbing at his side. "You...you saved me. You have nothing to be afraid of. I swear it upon Dawn's bright light."

I laughed, the sound harsh. *"Nothing to be afraid of?"*

"If you signed, I can't see. It's too dark." He moved closer. I tried to take a step back only to find my muscles frozen. I stiffened as his arms wrapped around me, strong and steady and sure. "Thank you, Lyr."

Cautiously, I wound my arms around him and tried not to panic when it felt good. Familiar. Like something I'd been missing for so long.

Alar let out a soft grunt and went stiff. His arms fell from around my waist and his weight collapsed on me. I saw a gleam in the dark, sprouting from his shoulder before we both fell to the ground. A crossbow bolt, one that matched the ones those other creatures had used earlier that day.

I tried to reach for the magic again. I could *feel* it at the edge of my reach, a living thing that danced away when I tried to grasp it. I could still feel the sorcery, but the dragon was silent and still, as if summoning its shape to enhance my own had changed something. Even the whispers of the tattoo's ink were silent, though I could still feel the shape of the words. There was no time to explore or consider. Two other angels were upon us, bolts loaded into their bows and eager gleams in their eyes.

I curved my body over Alar's. I tried to grab onto the magic again, tried to do something, anything, but it was too late. I was emptied out. Tears filled my eyes and I mouthed, "I'm sorry," to Alar. He blinked, as if in understanding, as if in forgiveness.

Then, I closed my eyes and wished beyond sense and reason, that I could see Keir one last time. My magic, what little of it there was, sang out, blood and ink and light, reaching for something that I wouldn't find. I expected emptiness and shadow. I waited for the final blow.

"Don't touch her."

My heart stuttered and stilled. I didn't dare look up.

"*You.*" A hiss, a snarl, a hint of fear.

"Me." The voice was familiar, so *achingly* familiar. There was a slight accent, a slight rasp that hadn't been there. And something else. A growl?

I feared that if I looked up, the voice would disappear. I clutched Alar tighter. He tried to look around me, to see what was happening, and when he caught a glimpse, I saw awe widen his eyes. "By Night's Sword," he murmured.

I couldn't resist any longer. I turned.

Three beings fought, illuminated only by moonlight. Two had claws tipped with rot and wings that looked ragged by comparison. Comparison to him. To *Keir*. Whose wings stretched behind him like a cloak of night. The feathers were shining, slightly translucent, yet solid and strong. They seemed formed of magic, as my own had been but minutes ago. Formed of ink and blood.

He couldn't be here. He was a *dream*. And yet I had known he would come, somehow. I had known when my magic called out, yet still I doubted.

Keir tore the other two angels apart with a predator's skill. He didn't waste time with small blows to tire them; he attacked with the intent to kill. The other angels, though obviously prepared to fight Alar and myself, hadn't counted on him. They seemed poor, weak creatures by comparison to Keir, a shadow of what they should have been.

They died easily, falling to the ground one after another, their throats slashed to ribbons, their eyes empty. I stared at them because I couldn't bring myself to stare at him. He turned to face me, those wings gleaming. He didn't come any closer, though. Waiting.

"Lyr," Alar said, shifting beneath me. I felt his wince of pain and sat up, scrambling away from him. His shoulder was bleeding heavily, the blood flowing more than it should have. Poison?

I turned desperately to Keir. "Help him? Please?"

He inclined his head. I thought I saw a flicker of sadness there, but it was gone too quickly for me to be sure. He approached and I could see him clearly for the first time in what felt like a lifetime. His features were so beautiful, sculpted of golden marble and the pain that life had dealt him. He looked healthier than I'd ever seen him, his skin whole and free from bruises, his posture strong and proud. His hair was black, as long as his shoulders and mussed only from the fighting. His eyes, though, they were the same. Grey and deep and sad.

He passed by me, those wings of his fading away until they were a shadow and then nothing at all, sprouting from the protrusions on his back where true wings had once been. He knelt before my cousin, still not looking at me. I put a hand on his arm. He flinched.

"Keir?" I breathed. He looked at me, untold pain swimming in his eyes. Pain and hope. Just a spark, but hope all the same. Then, I spoke again. "Or Claw that Writes With Ink?"

He recoiled, shaking off my hand. In a swift movement, he had Alar in his arms as if the weight meant nothing. "We have to get him back to Summerfell. Those arrows were tipped with heartsbane. I recognise the effects."

I stood, a little unsteady, a lot sore. Keir started towards me when I stumbled, but held himself back. He waited until I was standing, sure on my feet, before turning and walking back towards Summerfell. I wrapped my arms around myself and followed, silent once again.

INTERLUDE IV

*K*eir had hoped that Elyria would come to him again. That she would appear and break up the desperate loneliness that plagued his soul. That she would come and fill the empty spaces that filled the palace. That her movements would replace the whistling of the wind.

She never came.

He had tried leaving. Once he grew accustomed to his new existence, his new...body, he had padded down the steps of the palace and tried to set out across the sands. His breath had immediately choked out and his heart raced so fast he could do nothing but tremble on the ground and claw his way back inside.

It took several seasons, but he discovered that he was bound to the palace because of the books there. Those infernal books. That hall of knowledge that had been his downfall, it now trapped him and forbade him from leaving.

Hirana had been especially cruel, he realised, when she bound him to the knowledge that he had so freely given away. He was alone in the palace with nothing but the words and writings for company. He tried shredding them with his claws, but something stopped him. He tried calling on the magic that had once been his as an angel, but it was bound up so tightly within him in a mass of ink and words and blood that he could do nothing but summon the shadow of wings.

He tried starving himself. Tried throwing himself from the rooftop. He tried to end his existence, but achieved nothing except for pain that healed. He couldn't even regret that he had tried to kill himself.

"Why aren't you here?" he asked the books night after night, hoping beyond hope that Elyria would come. That she hadn't abandoned him with the onset of Hirana's curse. Eventually, he decided that it was better she wasn't there. He didn't want her to see how broken he had become. He didn't want to see her and discover that she no longer loved him, that her eyes were empty of that warmth that was only for him.

Over countless seasons, Keir adjusted to his new existence. He watched the empty lands around the palace start to bear new life, though it was stunted and strange. He watched the birds return, their bodies affected by the residual magic of the land. He watched the deer stalk through the waving grasses, their eyes glowing green and a trail of mist following in their wake. He began to forget when he had last spoken to another living creature. He began to forget what it felt like to be anything other than what he was.

He read the books in the hall of knowledge. Twice. He turned his back on them and didn't look at them again until they crumbled into nothingness. Then, he looked at them only to bid them a quiet farewell and left the palace at last, a pull in his chest leading him on. If he strayed from that pull, he was robbed of breath and thought. So he followed it and hoped once again that it was Elyria at the end of his journey.

It wasn't.

It was a small house built into the side of a mountain where three human men in long robes bent over books and wrote in precise, beautiful lines. It was the start of another hall, another scriptorium, another library. He tried talking to the humans at first, so relieved to have another intelligent being with him that he nearly went mad trying to make them hear. He tried to write, but that only earned him shocked looks and being thrown out into the cold where he couldn't help but stay, bound to that collected knowledge.

He passed through the ages this way. Following the books, the knowledge, that interminable tug in his chest that took him from one crumbling hall to the next, new and modern and full of knowledge that the humans had carved from the world. They forgot so many things and learned so many more. They started worshipping new gods, started writing new stories. They paid the black cat no mind at all.

He began to wonder at their blindness. Then he began to despair. Then, he did his very best not to think at all. He was months away from becoming nothing more than a library cat content to sleep in the sun and chase mice when a woman appeared, wearing a uniform dress of Archives blue, two red bands marking her magic at her wrists.

Keir would have known her in an instant, just from the way her hands moved. He stared. No, surely his mind was playing tricks on him, after so long doing nothing but enduring. He had dreamed her. The product of a broken mind after so long being tortured with his mistakes.

She had been nothing but a figment of his imagination to soothe his wounded soul.

Yet there she was. Elyria.

He hesitated, sorely tempted to race towards her, to talk with her and tell her everything about what had happened. But there was something in her gaze that bade him wait. It was a shadow, or rather the lack of one. She didn't look as she had when she came to him in the cell, through her dreams.

Could it be? For the first time in countless lifetimes, hope bloomed in his soul like a fire, igniting him. She hadn't come to him because she hadn't been ready yet. She wasn't possessed of that ability. She wasn't yet *his* Elyria.

So he waited. And one day, she bled on a book and the magic in her was bound to the magic in him. And he was so afraid.

"I think it's time that you and I talked."

PART III
SWORD SONG

CHAPTER 17

*a*ny thoughts of confronting Keir, of seeking answers and trying to understand, fell by the wayside as we returned to Summerfell. Our absence had barely been noted, but returning with Alar being carried by Keir—who, even though he looked mostly human, could never have disguised the sheer grace and beauty he bore—and followed by me. Both of us injured, Alar obviously suffering the effects of poison, and with a new stranger in tow? The fortress erupted into chaos.

"He needs a healer," Keir said, refusing to relinquish Alar to the alarmed watch members. "He's been poisoned with heartsbane."

One of the watch cursed before running off. The others stared at Keir and me, distrust written plainly across their features.

"We were attacked by those...things," I signed. Surely one of them would understand. Signed language was standard to

their training, wasn't it? The oldest of the group, a grizzled woman with grey streaks in her hair and furs wrapped tightly around scarred shoulders, hissed.

"How many?"

"*Two. They came from the valley with the runes,*" I signed. She cursed loudly.

"Why was he even there, and unarmed? With you?" She glared at me.

"We don't have time for this," Keir snapped. "He needs to be seen to. Immediately."

The woman frowned. "Fine. This way."

I had the distinct impression that she was going to interrogate us as soon as we had settled Alar with a healer. I didn't even know if there were any mages with healing magic at Summerfell any longer. There had been one when I was a girl, but that was a long time ago. And healing magic was rare. Maybe the other healers would know what to do, though. They just needed the right potions and herbs and—

I was spiralling. I recognised the signs, but only barely. My breath was shallow, my heart pounding in my ears. My hands trembled and the world swam before me. I stopped in the stairwell, leaning against the wall. Two deep breaths in, let them out slowly. The world stopped spinning for a moment.

"Elyria?" Keir asked, pausing at the top of the stairs.

"*I'm okay,*" I assured him, though I think I lied. "*Just need a minute.*"

He swallowed and shifted Alar in his arms, as though he would hand off my cousin and return to me. Instead, he hesitated, then nodded stiffly and continued following the watch. I was left in the stairwell for a brief, blissful moment, surrounded by quiet.

"Elyria, what happened?" Jessamine. She raced up the stairs with the grace of a leaping deer. Gods, even her panicked expression seemed contrived. "I heard that there had been an attack. Alar...he's not—?"

I shook my head. I started to sign before remembering she didn't understand. Then, still shaking and feeling as unsteady as before, I pointed up the stairs and we went to go find Alar together.

Jessamine didn't say anything as we moved through the familiar halls, but I could feel the weight of her eyes watching me. The letter that had been in her pocket at dinner was gone, not a trace of ink anywhere on her person to whisper to me. I tried to feel sympathy for her; her husband was gravely injured, after all. I couldn't. I just felt exhausted and wary.

"I know you don't like me," she said as we paused at the end of the hallway leading to Alar's quarters. "And please, don't deny it. I could see your unease the moment you arrived. I'm sorry for that, for I would dearly love to be your friend. You are my husband's cousin, and that means something. Please believe me, though, when I say that I am truly concerned for him. I care about him. I love him. I don't want to see him dead."

I said nothing, silence wrapped around me like a blanket. I believed her when she said she didn't want him dead, but everything else screamed at me as blatant falsehoods. She was dangerous, and I didn't think it was entirely to do with my bad experiences with the Order as a child. There was something else there. Something that spoke in shadows.

Instinctively, I reached for the dragon at my back and froze. It was silent. Not even the faintest whisper rose from the ink on my back. I could feel it there, feel the words and the shape of the dragon, but there was only silence. It was as if I'd killed it as thoroughly as I'd silenced those books in the library. I reached for the sorcery that was entwined with my scribe magic and nearly doubled over in pain. The panic that I'd been staving off with deep breaths and focusing on minutiae rose to the surface and took hold.

Blindly, I staggered away from Jessamine, not quite sure where I was going. My feet took me through hallways that I barely saw with the ease of muscle memory. If anyone called after me, then I didn't hear them. I didn't think to check on Alar. I didn't think to get my own injuries seen to, I just ran.

The room where I ended up was small, the furnishings covered in dust cloths, carpets rolled up. There was a single window overlooking the forest, but no other luxuries. Still, I threw myself down into the corner of the room and found that it fit almost as it had when I was small. The nook between the armoire and the wall was tighter than it had been, but my body contorted itself to fit the space and I brought my knees to my chest, wrapping my arms around them and burying my face in my skirts.

I don't know how long I sat there, tears flowing freely, unable to control the full-body shakes. The press of the armoire and the wall against my body provided a familiar comfort and slowly my panic abated. I calmed. Then, I cried in earnest, too many things having happened too quickly.

I missed my rooms back in Vazeri. I missed my books. I missed my drawings. I missed home, and the simple life that it promised.

"Elyria?" The door opened a crack. I flinched back, prepared to be shouted at, but Margarethe just slipped into the room and sat with her back to the wall. "I've been looking everywhere for you. No one would tell me what was going on, only that something had happened and you were involved. They're saying that a stranger showed up with your cousin unconscious in his arms and that he may have hurt Alar. And they were sure that you knew something about it, but no one could find you."

I wiped my eyes and sniffled. *"How* did *you find me?"*

"This is the family wing. Jessamine pointed it out to me when I first arrived. She was pretty much telling me not to come here, but I figured that you had probably grown up here and thought you might come back to your childhood room." Margarethe was smarter than a lot of people gave her credit for, including myself sometimes. She saw details and put them together in ways that most wouldn't dare. It's what made her a great Archivist. A better friend. She peered around. "Is this your childhood room?"

I nodded. *"They covered the furniture and rolled up the carpets, but this is it."*

"Huh."

"What?"

Margarethe shrugged. "I just...I expected more. I mean,

you are second in line for Summerfell. I sort of thought you would have a bigger room. Maybe more than an armoire and a bed. I thought you would have a desk, some bookshelves, something...personal."

I looked around. Compared to the room I'd been given, it was small and poorly furnished. Yet as a girl, this had been my only sanctuary outside the forest. A place where no one would punish me, where I could be safe and free to think and do as I liked. Even now, despite the comfort of the wall and armoire pressing in on me, the familiar peace of the room was more prison-like than anything.

I shrugged and shifted, suddenly feeling too small. Margarethe moved without a word so I could crawl out and sit beside her, my legs outstretched. *"Is Alar...alright?"*

"A healer saw to him. I heard from one of the watch that they got to the poison quickly enough. He lost a fair bit of blood, but he's going to be just fine."

I breathed a sigh of relief. "Thank the gods."

Margarethe swallowed and fiddled with her skirt. "What happened? One minute you leave because of the, ah, wings, and the next you're coming back with your cousin injured. Was there really a stranger? Was it something to do with your magic? I heard a roar, and I thought...gods, Elyria, I was so worried!"

I took her hands in mine. They were ice cold. Mine weren't much better, but it was nice to have that contact. A minute later, she pulled back and studied me with a quiet frown.

"Have you been in here...since returning?" she asked.

I nodded, unsure how much time had passed.

Margarethe looked like she wanted to explode. Her eyes were wide and she dug her fingers into the curly mass of her hair. She closed her eyes, took several deep breaths, then finally slumped against the wall. "Dawn and Dusk, I want to shout at you so badly right now."

"Why?"

"Because you *hid* instead of coming to find me. I know that being here, in this place, with all this magical—" Margarethe waved her hands vaguely. "—whatever it is, I know that this sets of just about every trigger you have. And if you were to be silent for days, only signing when neces-sary, that I could understand. I could understand asking for some time to process things. But this? *Hiding* without telling anyone where you were? You worried me! Alar! Even that stranger, Jessamine, the watch. None of us knew where you were."

I recoiled. *"I didn't mean to hide. I was having a panic attack and—"*

"And nothing! I have helped you through plenty of panic attacks over the years. Gods, how many of my own bad days have you helped me through? Depression so bad I could barely get out of bed? Thinking I was going to get tossed out for shelving those books wrong? Sent back to my parents who couldn't afford to keep me?" Margarethe rubbed her eyes. "The point is that you could have come to me. And instead you didn't. You just went off on your own, leaving people behind you who were worried and could have helped."

"*I'm sorry,*" I signed. Tears pricked at my eyes and I wanted to run away again. "*I...just reacted. The dragon on my back was different and the battle and...*"

"And you ran away to deal with it on your own. Like you ran away to chase after Beltran on your own." Her words were laced with bitterness. I frowned and lifted my hands to reply, but she shook her head. "No, don't explain. I get why you did it, but gods, you didn't even ask me to help you. I would have! You're my best friend. Instead, you just ran off and left me behind. And, frankly, that hurt. It was like you didn't trust me. Tonight only made that worse. You didn't come to me when you were confused and afraid. You ran to deal with it yourself. Because you don't trust me enough to be vulnerable."

Air whooshed from my lungs until I felt like I was collapsing in on myself. "*Of course I trust you! I trust you more than anyone else in the world!*"

Margarethe shrugged. "Then why didn't you ask for my help?"

I hesitated. Why hadn't I? Going after Beltran on my own had seemed like such a good idea at the time. I didn't want anyone else to get hurt, and I had a past with Summerfell so could come here and be granted admittance. But I wasn't suitable for rescue missions. I was a scribe, an Archivist. I couldn't fight. Yes, I had walked right into a powerful magic, but that was an accident and I couldn't control it. I didn't even know what it was, now, after that battle. If it still existed or if I had depleted it and achieved nothing for my efforts.

Asking for help would have been the smart choice. The logical choice. Instead, I'd run off just as Margarethe had said, only Ink at my side. And that, too, seemed especially foolish now.

"I'm sorry," I signed. I shifted closer to her and lay my head on her shoulder. *"Perhaps I'm more broken than I thought, to want to be alone even though it's...even though I'm..."* I lowered my hands.

"You're not broken," Margarethe replied, resting her head against mine. "Well, no more than the rest of us, that is. You just seem to forget that you have people who care about you. Doing everything yourself isn't commendable, it's not a sign of strength. It's okay to ask for help."

I nodded faintly. She sighed. I think I would have happily fallen asleep there, with my best friend beside me, but Margarethe spoke again.

"So what's the situation with the stranger? I heard that he carried Alar back to the healers, but he wouldn't speak with anyone. Jessamine threw him in the cells."

I sat bolt upright. *"She did what?!"*

Before Margarethe could stop me, I was on my feet and out the door, waiting only long enough for her to scramble after me before I grabbed her hand and all but ran down to the cells of Summerfell. As a child, they'd been a place that was off limits on the promise of a severe punishment. I'd explored there once and was so frightened that I ran out and never spoke of it again. To my knowledge, they hadn't been used for hundreds of years, but my uncle had kept them clean and ready for use. Just in case.

Now, I didn't hesitate. I just pulled Margarethe behind me, complaining all the way, and went down the narrow, winding stairs into the darkness. The cells were carved from the mountainside on which Summerfell stood. They were more cave than building and smelled of must and rot. There was no light but for a few torches near the stairs. And on either side of the long, damp hallway were cells carved into the stone.

They were, I realised, almost identical to the one in which I'd found Keir.

"Elyria!" Jessamine stood before a cell at the very end of the hall, in the darkest part of the tunnel. She had a lantern in hand that illuminated silver threads in her dress and the jewelled necklace that she wore, but provided very little light. "What are you doing here? We've been so worried."

She spoke evenly, smoothly, as though she were truly concerned about me. I saw a frown at the corner of her mouth, carved into high relief by the lantern light.

"Where is he?" I demanded. Jessamine started. This was the first time I'd spoken to her properly, and she obviously hadn't expected it. I ignored her surprise, instead pushing past her.

The cell was blocked off with steel bars, clear of any rust despite the dampness in the air. The cells were still being maintained, then. Inside, it was nearly entirely dark, only a sliver at the front reflecting the lantern light. I crouched down and peered into the darkness, searching, listening.

A rustle of fabric, then he stepped into the light. Keir. Ink. Gods, I didn't know what to call him, or how I felt about him, but he was there in a cell and he looked almost afraid.

"Open the door," I said, trying to meet his gaze, to make him see that it would be alright. He studiously looked at the bars.

"My dear, I cannot," Jessamine said. I stood and whirled. She spread her hands in supplication. "He appeared from nowhere with Alar injured in his arms. You ran off, also injured, and he would not answer any of my questions. He could be dangerous."

"Open the door."

Jessamine shrugged one shoulder and looked away, the picture of reluctant refusal. "No."

I spun back around and wrapped my hands on the bars.

"It's alright," Keir murmured so only I would hear. Gods, how had I not recognised his voice in Ink's? "I'll be alright."

I could see panic creeping up on him. I knew what that felt like. I wouldn't leave him there. Desperate, I tried to yank the bars open. I closed my eyes and pulled, but they were crafted to keep out creatures from the gap, not yield to scribes.

Then, in a blink, the world shifted so that I could see the magic within it. This was different than it had been before, when I felt my connection to the sorcerous dragon on my back in whispers of ink. This came from within my own thoughts. This was as innate to me as my scribe magic. And when I willed the hinges on the door to break, scattering their magical energy into the world, that was as easy to me as listening to the song of ink on paper.

The door fell. I stumbled out of the way, slamming my back into the opposite wall. Jessamine let out a cry of surprise and Margarethe cursed. Vehemently.

Arms wrapped around me. "Shh, it's okay. I'm okay."

"Keir?" I asked. He nodded, pressing his nose to my hair.

"Yes," he breathed.

"What did you do?" Jessamine demanded, cracks starting to show in her refined mask. Keir stiffened and pulled back, pushing me behind him. I touched his arm and he looked at me in surprise.

"Are you certain?" he asked. I nodded. He stepped aside.

"This man is under my protection," I signed, the words caught up in my rush of feeling for Keir, my confusion at my magic, in my anger at Jessamine. Margarethe leaped in to translate with an eagerness that was a little surprising, as if she had just been waiting to put Jessamine in her place. *"As heir to Summerfell, it falls within my authority to declare him a guest and therefore pardon him for any perceived crimes."*

"I am the wife of the Baron—"

"The power of Summerfell falls along bloodlines, not along marriage lines." I turned my back on her, knowing that I would pay for that slight later. I didn't care. To Margarethe, I signed, *"Take me to Alar."*

She grinned at me. To Keir, she said, "Are you the Keir she's told me about? From the dreams?"

He nodded.

"Hmph," was her response to that. With a swirl of her skirts, she turned and marched from the cells as if she owned the place. The darkness seemed to bend away from her as she walked, shoulders back and head held high. I shook my head and jumped when Keir brushed his hand against mine.

"Please," he breathed. "Let me touch you."

I hesitated for only a moment before twining my fingers with his. Some of the tension eased from him and the shadow of a smile appeared. For a moment, a heartbeat, I was able to forget my troubles, my fears, everything that had happened. All I could see was Keir, right there, hand in mine, and thought it was surely impossible, it was the only thing that felt real.

CHAPTER 18

*a*lar slept for two days, leaving me both in charge of Summerfell and completely at a loss as to what to do. News of my declaration of authority in the cells spread throughout the fortress like wildfire, and it wasn't long before I was being asked questions about trivial matters like where to store extra straw for the winter. Those trivial matters became larger until I had to resort to delegating the authority to higher ranked members of the watch. I knew nothing of how Alar had run the fortress in my years away, and before that I'd been a child, barely aware of the details of life there. Yet still they asked me and took my words as authority.

It made my chest ache.

No one questioned my decision to keep Jessamine out of the line of authority. They simply went about their way, deferring to me when necessary. I feared that I had cultivated an enemy in her. A dangerous one. But, frankly, she was the least of my concerns.

Keir's presence had been explained away to all but Margarethe as someone who had come up the pass after me and stumbled onto Alar and I during the battle. Jessamine likely guessed more than that, but no one else seemed to think there was anything unusual about yet another stranger appearing at Summerfell, not after the return of the line's lost lady, a name I couldn't quite get them to shake.

Margarethe was invaluable to me. She knew me well enough to perform tasks almost without prompting. She had the members of the watch organised for the next rotation before I could find the ledgers that detailed the usual situation. More importantly, she fielded questions about Keir and replied with half-truths that were more believable than reality.

Keir, however, proved to be a problem. Despite his strength and appearance of grace, he hadn't been in a human body for countless centuries. After the adrenaline of that first night wore off, he became as graceless as a fawn. He seemed to have forgotten how to use his thumbs and such things as walking required all his concentration. He practised constantly, often in full view of the sparring watch members. All this was fine, and was explained away in many different ways, but every time I tried to get him on his own, to talk, to process, to do *anything*, he managed to slip away.

Finally, after two days of him avoiding me, I went to his room before dawn spread across the sky and pounded on the door. I heard a shuffling and a quiet *thud* as he must have walked into something. He fumbled at the latch and finally opened the door with considerable force, looking surprised by his own strength. Then, he spotted me and grimaced.

"Elyria," he murmured, the sound almost a worship.

"*Are you going to let me in?*" I signed. He winced but stepped aside, closing the door behind me much more gently. The room was a mess. Linens were strewn everywhere as if he couldn't untangle himself getting out of bed. Clothes were piled on a chair and one of the doors to the armoire in the corner was hanging askew, as if the hinge had been bent.

"I apologise for the mess," Keir said, suddenly at my side. "I'm, ah, still adjusting to this new body. I keep expecting to have a tail."

I sat on the bed and said nothing, waiting. He was more used to my silence than most, but very few were able to keep calm when I used my silence as a weapon. Keir was no exception.

He broke into a bout of pacing, his movements graceful yet clumsy and a little too inhuman to be ignored. He moved too fast and too far, occasionally bumping into the bed or stumbling over the linens on the floor. Finally, he pulled the clothes from the chair and flung himself into it. "Do you want me to apologise, is that it?"

I waited.

"Yes, *of course*, I wanted to tell you that I was...that I was me trapped in the body of a cat. A cat! That was a special cruelty that Hirana bestowed upon me. It wasn't enough that I was bound to places where knowledge was collected; I had to be incapable of being taken seriously if ever I did show signs of unusual behaviour. I couldn't be anything more than a cat. And then you came along, the perfect combination of blood and ink and magic and you accidentally bound your own magic to the world of knowledge and books. Suddenly you and I could talk and it was wonderful, but would you have even believed me if I told you that I was an angel bound in the body of a cat and that I had been for countless generations? So long that I have forgotten half the lives I lived? And then to tell you that, not only that, but I was the angel that you dreamed about? Except you didn't start dreaming of me until after you bound a sorcerer's dragon, so how would you even know what I was talking about? And it was my past, but your present, your future, and…and…Gods, Elyria, you were the one bright light in that damn cell and afterwards, I didn't even know if you were real or if I had imagined you. Not until you walked into the Great Archives. I didn't know you could give me back this form. How could I tell you?"

He took a breath on a strangled cry and buried his head in his hands, silky black hair spilling forward to cover his face entirely. Half of what he said made no sense to me at all, but I heard quite plainly the anguish in his words and that was apology enough. I slipped from my perch and knelt before him, resting my hands on his knees. He made a sound in the back of his throat and grabbed my hands desperately.

"Start from the beginning," I said quietly, for once not afraid that my hands were trapped an unable to use for signing. He did.

We undoubtedly missed breakfast while he spoke, and I had to rise twice to pour him a glass of water from the pitcher by the bed, returning each time to his side, but at last, I had the whole story. The explanation of Old Magic, once possessed by now-dead gods and then by the humans they battled. The story of his imprisonment, the reason we were tied together over the impossible distance between us. What, exactly, lay in the Great Plains that was being dug up. There were still questions—there would likely always be questions—but it was enough.

"*Why did you insult me when we first...met?*" I remembered it vividly, and it felt so completely different from what I knew of Keir. To my surprise, he flushed a deep crimson.

"That was..." He rubbed the back of his neck. "I was a cat. And you were, well, you. I couldn't just tell you who I was, how I felt. So I, ah, insulted you. To make you think that I was just a cat."

The tiniest smile broke free of my control. Keir's eyes lit up. He reached for me, but I lifted my hands to speak again, trying to ground myself in what had just happened. Gods, what *had* just happened?

"*Those creatures, then,*" I signed. "*Angels?*"

Keir shrugged. "They look like angels, but I recognise none of them. And that rot is like nothing I've ever encountered. It's almost like they rot from the inside out."

"*So you don't know what lies in the gap. What's trying to... what took those people from Vazeri.*"

"What took Beltran, you mean." He pushed out of his chair and glided across the room, a little more control over his body as though disappointment in me was enough to make him forget his awkwardness.

"*Are you suggesting that I'm still in love with him? If ever I was, it was a fool's love. He's married!*"

Keir curled his lip, but there wasn't any heat behind it. "As if marriage were ever a thing to stop people who decided they loved each other."

I didn't even bother dignifying that with a response, instead rising from the floor and heading towards the door. My knees ached and I had a headache from not eating anything. I wanted to check on Alar and there were things to be seen to before—

Keir's hand snaked out and grabbed my wrist, halting me where I stood. "Please," he rasped. "Don't."

I watched him, silent, waiting once again for truth to spill from his tongue. He closed his eyes.

"I've been in love with you for lifetimes beyond measure, even when I thought you were nothing more than a dream."

His hand dropped and he let me go, turning his back on me without looking at me. "I understand, though. It's only been a few weeks for you. A few dreaming nights."

Any words of comfort I had dried up in my throat, leaving me empty and raw. I tapped his shoulder and waited until he turned to me before lifting my hands and starting that comforting dance. "*I have lived more in those few dreams than in my entire life. Don't you dare diminish that."*

He smiled, bright and broad. "You mean that? Truly?"

I nodded firmly.

Without warning, Keir surged forwards as though he still had wings at his back. He cupped my face in his hands and brushed his lips against mine. Fire sparked there, from my magic or from him or from both of us. It wasn't a devouring, as our first kiss had been. It wasn't desperate or brutal. It was as though our two souls mingled, as though the magic that had bound us spooled between us like infinite threads gleaming in the night. It was a simple kiss, a moment in duration, but it shifted something irrevocably in me. For the first time in a long, long time, I wasn't afraid of the unknown, of the words left unsaid inside me. I kissed him back, gentle, insistent.

I think we would have stood there for eternity, lost in each other, but someone pounded on the door. Keir leaped back with a snarl, shoulders hunched as if spreading his invisible wings.

"Elyria? Keir? Are you in there?" Margarethe.

"Here," I said. The door opened and Margarethe poked her head in, black hair dishevelled.

"Alar is awake."

In an instant, the spell was broken. What was I doing? I knew Keir only in my dreams, and he was right; we had only met a few times over a few weeks for me. I shouldn't be distracting myself with his touch, not when impossible things were emerging from the gap. Not when I still needed to rescue…Beltran. Yet there was a pull to the angel even as I walked away, following Margarethe to Alar. One that had me clenching my hands into fists at my side and choking on my desire to be near him.

Alar was in my uncle's old chambers, which had been done over in reds and golds, making the room both grander and warmer than it had ever been when my uncle was still alive. He sat up against a pile of pillows in the middle of a vast bed, and he looked unnaturally pale against the warm colours.

He tried to straighten when we appeared only to let out a groan. Margarethe hurried forward, scowling. "The healer told you not to get up, you fool."

"All I did was prop myself up against some pillows," Alar retorted, his scowl matching Margarethe's. "No need for you to meddle."

Margarethe crossed her arms and glared. "I fetched them, as you requested, *your Lordship*."

I winced at the scorn in her voice. Whatever Alar had done to earn her ire was unlikely to be forgiven. Margarethe was generally even-tempered, enough that I had rarely seen her snap at anyone other than myself. But this? It felt like true animosity, and it sent a crackling discomfort up my arms. I blinked and realised a moment later that tiny arcs of inkstars were dancing on my arms. I closed my eyes and recited the numbers one through ten in random order until my new, unpredictable magic was once more under control. It was the same calming technique that I'd used at Liral when first learning about my scribe magic and I was shocked that it worked with the sorcery.

When I opened my eyes, everyone was staring at me. Heat burned my cheeks.

"What was that?" Alar demanded, sitting up straight again despite his obvious pain. Margarethe, too, watched me with wide eyes, though she knew more than my cousin.

"Elyria?" Keir breathed, reaching out a hand to brush my arm. I flinched as a single spark of lightning arced between us. "How long has the sorcery been like this?"

"Sorcery?!" Alar lurched towards me and gasped, falling back to the pillows with a cough. Margarethe was by his side in an instant, holding out a cup of water, mouth in a firm line.

"*It's a long story,*" I signed uncertainly, shifting my weight and wishing that I could just run away. Being vulnerable with Margarethe was one thing. But Alar? I hadn't seen my cousin for years, and despite our productive conversation the night of the battle, he was still essentially a stranger to me. And Keir? Well, I was afraid to tell him how the sorcery had changed during that battle, how the dragon on my back had become silent, though the magic still lived in my blood.

"I'm not going anywhere," Alar said, scowling at Margarethe.

"*It's a really long story. Essentially, it's an old magic, from before the gods. And I somehow managed to gain control of it.*"

Alar gaped at me. "Before the gods? Lyr, I don't think—"

"There are a great many things in this world that you do not know, Baron of Summerfell," Keir said, sounding more like Ink than I'd heard since he changed. "The gods as you know them are a young race, brought into being after the gods that I knew were killed."

"Who *are* you?" Alar asked, narrowing his eyes.

"I am Keir," was the response, accompanied by a slight bow. "You knew me as Claw that Writes with Ink."

"So, what, you're some sort of skinchanger? From the gap? How long have you been beyond the boundary borders?" Alar's attention shifted to where a sword lay propped against a dresser. Keir let out a dry laugh, sharp and dark.

"My lord Trevain, you are in no shape to do battle with me, even with my issues controlling this body," he said. "And believe me when I tell you that I have been in the world a long time. Longer than your people's memory can recount. I mean you and yours no harm."

Alar looked to me for confirmation. I nodded. My cousin sighed and sank further into his pillows. "Well, then, you are welcome here as my guest. I owe you my thanks anyways for coming to our aid. And I'll get that long story out of you sooner or later. But we have other matters to discuss."

I nodded again and lifted my hands to speak. Alar spoke before I could start signing, a sting that I shrugged off. "My cousin has informed me that she has received letters that were purportedly from me. I'm not sure why someone would write to her pretending to be me, but there are serious political implications to such a thing, namely that she is my heir until such time as I have a child."

"A letter?" Margarethe scoffed. "You have actual monsters attacking you from the boundary mountains and you're worried about some letters that someone wrote pretending to be you? I read them; they weren't exactly trying to get Elyria to take over the world. They can be dealt with at another time."

Alar looked irritated, a line forming between his brows. "If someone were trying to manipulate Elyria into giving up her rights to Summerfell, then they could be trying to take control of the gap. Which might be connected to those actual monsters you're so worried about, given they've been increasingly active these last years. Or do you think I go out to hunt them for sport alone?"

Margarethe scowled and huffed. She tossed her hair over one shoulder and wandered to the window, where I could practically see steam coming off of her. I wanted to go to her, but Alar was right. There *were* matters to discuss, and it wasn't to do with the letters.

"*I am less concerned with the letters,*" I signed. Alar blinked. "*Whoever wrote them obviously has long-term plans, which of course must be dealt with, but there are more immediate concerns.*"

"Such as? If Summerfell falls, then there is no way to contain what lies beyond the gap. We will be overrun, as will every other village and town from here to the boundary mountains on the other side of the country." Alar, injured and weak though he was, seemed to possess a sort of strength to him that I had never seen in my uncle. It was the strength of purpose, and of righteousness, and it suited him.

"*I have to get back the people that were taken,*" I replied. "*They were taken for a reason.*"

"Oh? And what reason would that be?" Alar shook his head. "It doesn't matter. You can't go. You're needed here, not to mention the fact that you can't fight. You worked at the Great Archive's for Dawn's sake! What do you think you can do that—"

"After all that Elyria has done in coming here, in taming a sorcerous dragon, in destroying a supply of god's blood, more, you doubt her still?" Keir asked in a rumble. I saw the faint outline of inky shadows form at his shoulders, his wings starting to take form. Alar didn't seem to notice, only glared and shifted his attention between the two of us. "No wonder she never wanted to return to this place if you were so eager to clip her wings."

Alar recoiled as if Keir had struck him. "I *never*—"

"Enough." Margarethe turned back towards us from the window. I saw a shadow in her gaze, a quiet hurt that had replaced her temper. "I agree with Elyria. She needs to go after those people. They were taken for a reason, and if doubt that, you are more foolish than ever I thought."

"She can't," Alar insisted. "She doesn't know how to fight!"

Margarethe snorted. "Didn't you see the lightning? Don't you see the angel at her side? You're blind as well as foolish."

"Angel?"

Keir stiffened under my cousin's scrutiny. I took a step towards him, drawn by that inexplicable connection. He relaxed as our shoulders brushed, enough that the shadow of wings vanished. Alar's eyes widened.

"*I am going,*" I signed. "*And before you do something like offer to come with me, don't. I need you to stay here. You, too, Margarethe.*"

She blinked and opened her mouth to argue, but I shook my head.

"*This has nothing to do with not wanting to ask for help. It's the opposite. I need you here, to investigate the letters and help Alar. To get messages back to Aviena and Vazeri and all the other towns should further attacks get through.*"

"So you want me to let you go into the gap alone," she said flatly.

"As you said, I will be at her side," Keir promised quietly. Margarethe studied him with a frown, then put her hands on her hips and lifted her chin in the air.

"No. Oh, I know how important it is to get messages back to the other towns, but you know who can do that? The people whose entire job it is who have been stationed here for exactly that purpose." She glared at me so fiercely that I nearly backed down right then. "You are going off into the unknown, full of monsters and magic that hasn't been seen for centuries. Yes, you are perfectly capable, I'm not denying that, but even perfectly capable people need help. I'm going with you."

I lifted my hands to argue, but Alar interrupted. Again. "As am I."

This time, everyone turned to him, wide-eyed. "Weren't you just complaining that Elyria going would leave

Summerfell vulnerable?" Margarethe asked, crossing her arms and cocking a hip.

"Because *I* intended to go!" Alar protested. "It is my sworn duty to protect all citizens of the lowlands from what lives in the boundary mountains. That means going after those who were taken."

"And who will stay here to keep Summerfell?" Margarethe asked pointedly.

"The watch," Alar said. "I'll leave my second in charge. Rikard, you remember him, don't you Elyria? He started a couple of years before you, ah, left."

I frowned and searched through my memories. The names and faces of the watch from my childhood were blurry with time, but I vaguely remembered a Rikard. He was from the Akapa Islands, tall as a tree to a child, with mahogany skin and black hair done in a multitude of long, small braids. I remembered he had a kind smile.

"You're injured," Margarethe pointed out.

"I will heal," Alar argued.

"What about your wife?" she continued.

"Jessamine can stay here and help with the household. She will be safe."

"Elyria, you can't let him—"

I threw up my hands and turned for the door, signing rapidly as I left. *"Fine! You can all come. But I will not be held responsible for the consequences."*

CHAPTER 19

We lingered at Summerfell for a further two days before setting off into the gap. I was eager to get away, but between waiting for Alar to be well enough to ride, making sure that the proper order of things could be managed while we were gone, and gathering supplies to last in any number of unknown situations, it took that long just to be ready. I was kept so busy running around on errands for Alar that I barely had time to sit and talk with Margarethe and Keir, let alone finding them on their own. Even sorting through my thoughts on everything felt impossible. Everything that was left unsaid before remained unsaid, even after we were each mounted and on our way.

The first few minutes were the easiest; we were still on Summerfell land and hadn't yet reached the gap. But the farther we went into the forest, the closer we drew to the uncharted territories of the mountains and beyond, the quieter things became.

"Gods, I can't believe you grew up here," Margarethe said at last, startling Storm beneath me. The other horses, more used to life in this place, barely blinked. "This place is creepy. And cold."

"It's the residual magic from the god blood and bones that power the boundary," Keir said. "It seeps into the land and lends it an...awareness."

I winced. Now I was going to imagine the trees watching our every movement. Alar cleared his throat.

"What do you mean the god blood and bones that power the boundary?" he asked. Keir hunched his shoulders as if trying to wrap wings about himself. Wings that only existed in magic, now.

"It's...complicated," he murmured. I directed Storm closer to his big bay gelding so that my knee brushed with his. He lifted his eyes and I nodded. "The gods you know now weren't the only gods. Before your memory and theirs, there were...others. They enslaved the humans and were served by the angels. Until one angel gave the humans the gift of knowledge. The gift to learn and to build. The humans no longer needed the gods, so they warred with them. They killed them. But there is great power in a god's blood and their bones, particularly if they have been slain rather than fading alongside the fading of their beliefs. The dead gods fuelled the land with their magic, creating crea-tures and places that defied logic. It was dangerous, so dangerous that the last god created the boundary mountains, containing the magic within the Great Plains, leaving what you now know as Imara and the Uncharted Lands on the other side empty, and the coastlands safe. But the magic remains beyond the boundaries, even if the gods have been forgotten. And it is, indeed, dangerous."

Margarethe studied Keir, then looked to me. I hadn't told her what Keir had told me, about who he really was and what the gods had done to him. But she hadn't worked in the Archives for nothing. She dropped the reins for a moment and signed to me, rapidly, *"He's the angel who gave the humans knowledge, isn't he? That's why he was in a cell in your dreams and—"*

"You do know I can understand the signed language, don't you?" Alar asked, voice dry. Margarethe's back went stiff. Her brown skin flushed and she pursed her lips in a scowl. Keir stifled a snort. I shot him an indignant look.

"You can tell me the whole story later, Lyr," Alar continued. "For now, I want to know what your *angel* knows about what we can expect."

Keir flinched at the judgement in Alar's voice. He hunched his back a little more. I wished then that whatever magic I'd used to restore his angel shape had been able to restore his wings properly, too, instead of leaving them as insubstantial ink and blood. "Very little, I'm afraid," Keir said evenly, despite the discomfort written in every feature. "I never experienced the world beyond the boundary mountains."

"But you're familiar with this god blood. What it does?"

"The Makhierians were trying to refine it down for

human consumption, to enhance the inherent magic they had. It may have worked for a while, but prolonged exposure can kill. And the refining process itself is deadly. Exposure to raw god blood has…dangerous effects, though rarely does it kill so much as it contorts what is into something else. It's unpredictable at best. Tortuous at worst."

I shuddered at the memory of those souls whose lives were being drained to refine the god blood. No matter that their screams still haunted me, I had no doubt they were better off dead.

"The…Makhierians?" Alar asked. He fixed me in his gaze, and I shuddered again. "Maybe you should tell me the full story before we continue. I have a feeling that there's a great deal I need to know."

"Would you like me to…?" Keir asked me in an undertone. I shook my head.

"Thank you, but no. I can do it." For once, I wasn't seized by a paralysing fear that kept the words inside. I was doing nothing more than recounting recent history. My recent history. There was nothing I could do to change the past, but perhaps having the full knowledge would help Alar and Margarethe was we tried to change the future.

So I told them everything. I hadn't talked so much in ages. I was shocked when my voice didn't give out as I described the death of the people in the Makhierian refinery, the binding of the dragon to my skin, the way I used my scribe magic to kill a man. It didn't even give out as I relayed what Keir had told me about how our magic, our lives, were intertwined. Silence didn't creep up on me or demand that I remain safe in its embrace. I knew it would return at some point; it always did. At that moment, though, it was safe to talk. And I did.

I had just gotten to the point where I was arriving at Aviena when the world around us shifted. My words faltered and fell off. The temperature changed, dropping so suddenly that frost seemed to form on our cloaks within an instant. The sky seemed redder, the sun peering through a haze of grey and tingeing the world. There were no birds. No squirrels. Just the sound of the horses' hooves on the ground. We were nowhere near the ravine where the runes had been carved, but I felt the magic all the same.

We had crossed into the gap. We were in the heart of the boundary.

Storm shifted uneasily beneath me, dancing sideways as she tried to turn around. I clicked my tongue and tried to soothe her. She settled a bit, walking close to Keir's steadier horse, but her ears twitched back and forth and she shivered.

"Is...is this normal?" Margarethe ventured after a minute, all of us following Alar as he rode forwards with unerring determination. "This...quiet?"

"I don't know," Alar said after a moment. He didn't turn to look at us, but I saw him reach for the sword he bore. "The watch is meant to keep things from coming out of the gap, not going in. I've never been this far in. Neither has anyone else I know of. There's a reason why we set up watch houses in the pass and not up here."

"Oh, great," Margarethe muttered. She drew her fur-lined cloak tighter around herself.

We rode in silence for a while, our hands close to our weapons. I had been issued with my crossbow and short sword, despite not knowing how to use them. Keir was similarly outfitted, and even Margarethe had been given a set of daggers and a short sword.

My friend shifted in her saddle, looking around. "Do you think—"

A screech filled the air, echoing off the rocks and trees and triggering my magic sense as though by reflex. I saw the inksparks of the trees, the galaxy within the ground, and then I saw it.

Angry, red lines glowed through the creature as though magic had replaced its blood. It was about the size of a large dog, but its feet ended in talons sharp enough to flense flesh from bone. Two whip-like tails lashed through the air and a series of spikes along its back rattled as it screeched again.

In a heartbeat, before I could so much as decide what to do with my magic, Alar had drawn his crossbow and fired, a copper-tipped arrow slamming into the creature's side and felling it.

"Ferals," he said, riding to the beast and leaning over to retrieve his crossbow bolt. "Dog-kin ferals. I hate them. One of the more common creatures to cross the gap, but they have a vicious streak. And the often hunt in packs, so—"

"Watch out?" Keir asked as three more of the dog-kin emerged from the shadows between the trees and snarled at us.

"Something like that." In a swift movement, Alar was off his horse, sword drawn. I caught the wince on his face, though it was gone a moment later. Still, before I could do more than reach for the dagger I had no idea how to use, Alar had cut off the head of one of the dog-kin and sliced deep into the side of another. The two remaining snarled and leaped for the horses, but except for Storm who neighed in fright, her ears back, they kicked and pawed with precision. They were trained for this.

The dog-kin were exactly as vicious as Alar had said. They avoided the horses' hooves and retaliated with bites and slashes of their talons. Keir's horse received a shallow gash to the flank and Storm nearly unseated me when one of the dog-kin grabbed her tail.

Before I could get control of the horse, Margarethe had slithered from hers and ran for the dog-kin, a dagger in each hand. Alar cursed and kicked away his own opponent. Margarethe was already engaged in battle, roaring as fiercely as any lion as she sank her knives into the sides of the creature. It turned and wrapped its jaws around her arm. She yelped and scrabbled back.

Alar stepped in and brought his sword down on the creature's neck, severing the head. The last remaining dog-kin turned tail and ran into the forest, disappearing in an instant.

"What were you thinking?" he demanded, sheathing his sword and dragging Margarethe to her feet. She yanked her injured arm away and winced. "You are an Archivist! You have no business being in the gap. I never should have let you come."

"That wasn't your decision," Margarethe snapped. She hissed and cradled her arm. I clambered off of Storm and went to her. "It'll be fine," she said to me, glaring at Alar. "It's just a scratch."

It was definitely *not* a scratch. The bite had been deep and there were no less than six puncture wounds in her arm, all bleeding heavily. I huffed. Keir was suddenly by my side, holding out our bag of medical supplies.

"And what of you, angel? Were you just going to sit there and watch?" Alar grumbled, rounding up the horses even as he kicked away the head of one of the dead ferals.

"You seemed perfectly capable," Keir said smoothly in the tone I'd heard a thousand times from Ink. A cat's superiority. "There doesn't appear to be any poison," he said, turning Margarethe's arm to see better. "Apply this poultice and wrap it. We'll dress it properly tonight when we make camp."

"No," Alar said, practically shoving Keir aside and snatching the bandages. "It will be seen to properly when you *go back* to Summerfell. None of you should be out here!"

"You can't make me go back," Margarethe retorted. She yelped when Alar applied the poultice and the two glared at each other. I was about to reply, to tell them again of the importance of our journey, to try and deescalate the situation as best I could, when my magical sight lowered over my vision. The stars and sparks and ripples and currents that made up the world were different here, brighter and dimmer at the same time. Then, they shuddered, flaring red for an instant. Blood red.

I swayed where I stood.

"Elyria!" Keir caught me before I could fall. "Are you hurt?"

"You didn't feel that?" I whispered, loud enough only for him. He shook his head, grey eyes wide. "The boundary," I breathed. Then, I raised my hands. "*Someone closed the gap.*"

Half-an-hour later, Alar returned, expression thunderous. He swung his leg over the back of his horse and dropped to the ground. Margarethe leaned against a tree far from the carnage of the dead ferals, her arm now neatly bandaged. I paced while Keir stood watch, his hand resting on the hilt of his short sword.

"Well?" Margarethe asked.

"Lyr is right. The gap is closed. I tried finding a way through, must have travelled nearly a mile, but it's completely closed." My cousin turned to me. "How did this happen?"

"Mind your tone," Keir growled. I raised my brow at him and he at least had the decency to look abashed as he muttered an apology.

"*I felt it. Sorcery.*" I shrugged. "*Someone else out here can use it.*"

"I thought you said the boundary was created by a god,"

Margarethe said before Alar could speak. "Doesn't that mean only a god could manipulate it?"

Keir sighed and shook his head. He ran a hand through his hair and then shook his head again. "I don't know," he snarled. "I *should* know, but for all the lifetimes I've had to study the boundary mountains, I never did. It was...too painful." He turned to me, shoulders hunched. "I'm sorry, Elyria."

I shook my head. *"It's not your fault. None of this is your fault."*

He scoffed and turned away. "Isn't it?"

I reached out and grabbed his chin, making him face me again. I saw the pain in his eyes, the guilt, the fear. I understood. From what he told me, he'd been integral to the war between the humans and the gods so long ago. Blaming himself wasn't going to get us very far, though.

"Look at me when I'm talking to you," I signed, trying to put as much snap into my motions as I could. He blinked in surprise, then the corner of his mouth twitched in the barest hint of a smile. *"What happened lifetimes ago isn't something you can change now. Nor are you responsible for the actions of others. Right here, right now, none of this is your fault. Do you understand?"*

He reached up and brushed a strand of hair back from my cheek. "I don't know if I've ever seen you angry," he murmured. "You get a fire in your gaze, like you could take on legions."

I frowned. *"Not helping."*

Keir chuckled, and just like that, the pain and guilt was

gone. Hidden away, perhaps, yet he seemed more present and aware. "Thank you, scribe."

"Oh, for the sake of the gods, can you save the love-making for when we're *not* trapped in a creepy, cold forest full of things that want to kill us?" Margarethe asked, her tone lightly sarcastic, belying the smile. Alar stiffened.

"Lovemaking?" he asked. "I thought—"

"You're blind, then," Margarethe said. "Incredibly so. Not surprising, I suppose. I'm still not sure how Elyria became such a wonderful person when raised with a pack of wolves like you."

"Don't insult my family!" Alar rounded on her, a hand going to the sword at his belt. Margarethe flinched back and pressed against the tree, her eyes wide. Alar brought himself up short. "Gods, I'm...I'm sorry. I never would have—"

"Perhaps we should move on," Keir said, taking a small step away from me. His tone brooked no argument. "We have far to travel and I would prefer not to camp amongst dead dog-kin."

Margarethe didn't hesitate, going for her horse and mounting. Alar tried to apologise again, but she ignored him, eyes straight ahead. Keir helped me mount Storm, then climbed into his own saddle. He kept glancing at Margarethe, his face pale, eyes wide. As if reaching for his knife to fight her for a moment had broken some piece of him. I wanted to reach out to him, but didn't know how. And when I turned to Margarethe, she didn't even look at me. We started off again, heading deeper into the boundary mountains, silence filling the void between us.

After a couple of hours, Alar had us stop and eat something, passing around a waterskin and letting the horses graze on what little food there was. It would be difficult to feed them, I realised, given that I'd seen very little grass and other undergrowth and we hadn't been able to pack more than a few days' supply of grains with everything else we needed. The thought had my skin itching with anxiety. It didn't improve as the day went on and Margarethe's horse began to stumble as it walked, its injury obviously inflamed.

Storm had managed to escape without more than a scratch to the tip of her tail and seemed to be coping fine, but Margarethe's gelding was breathing heavily, limping, and jumping at every noise.

"We'll stop here for the night," Alar said at last, eyeing the injured horse. "Can you three handle making a fire?"

"Is that such a good idea?" Keir asked, looking around. "A fire could draw attention."

"We're drawing attention no matter what, given we have two injured among us. Creatures from the gap have a nose for blood. And without a fire, we'll freeze."

Keir ducked his head in a nod. We set about making a camp under a stand of cedar trees, their trailing branches providing a bit of shelter at least. The fire was easy after so much practise on the road; my sorcery came to me as easily as did calling ink and paper, though it still felt odd without the dragon's inky whispers.

"Where did Alar go?" Margarethe asked, looking up from the roaring flames.

"To hunt, no doubt," Keir said. "It's better if we can

conserve our rations. We don't know how long we'll be out here."

"Do we even know where we're going?" my friend asked, pulling her fur-lined cloak tighter around her. "I mean, at first it was just us getting into the gap, but now? The maps of the boundary mountains at the Archive are huge. And almost completely uncharted."

I hadn't considered that, I realised. I'd been following Alar blindly, trusting that he knew where we were going, that he was taking us towards Beltran and the others, towards whatever terrible thing we were going to meet that wanted the blood of humans to dine on. Whatever commanded the angels. A tracker I was not, but I hadn't seen any sign that someone had come through this way, certainly not with a group of people bound in chains.

Alar returned a moment later, a skinned rabbit in one hand. "Here. This should last us the night."

None of us said anything at first, Margarethe's question hanging over us. Finally, I took the rabbit and ducked my head in thanks. It was a long, quiet night after that.

CHAPTER 20

"*L*yr, wake up."

I groaned and rolled over, but this wasn't my bed and a rock digging into my ribs pulled me from the last scraps of sleep. I opened my eyes and glared at Alar where he stood over me. It wasn't even dawn. Darkness still held the sky firmly, a lack of proper moon making the shadows even more ominous. The fire burned steadily, but it only held back so much of the night.

And it was cold.

"Come on, get up. It's time for your watch."

I sighed and stretched. A gust of wind had me shivering and pulling my cloak tighter around me. I glared at Alar as he laughed.

"You've been in the south too long if a light breeze has you reaching for the furs."

I noticed that he, too, was wearing his fur-lined cloak, but I decided to let it go. I yawned and stretched again, rising from my blanket on the ground and wincing as the various aches I'd accumulated made themselves known. *"Anything happen while we slept?"* I signed, yawning again.

"No. It's been quiet. Which, frankly, I don't trust." Instead of moving to his own blanket, Alar picked up a stick and prodded at the fire, releasing sparks that had my magical vision flaring. I winced at the sudden brightness. It seemed permanent, this overlay of ink and energy, and the dragon tattoo was still silent, even after resting. It unnerved me and woke me faster than coffee from a Vazeri cafe. "We should have seen a lot more movement, but four ferals? That's it? We get more than that on an average night on watch."

"Maybe those raiders, whatever they are, scared them all away." I offered.

Alar scoffed. "Oh, great. Because something that scares away creatures of the gap isn't at all terrifying."

I sat and scowled at the fire, pulling my blanket around me. To my surprise, Alar sat beside me, his shoulder nearly brushing mine. On the other side of the fire, Keir and Margarethe slept soundly, though Margarethe twitched in her dreams, her expression pinched. Alar followed the direction of my gaze and sighed.

"I'm sorry she got hurt," he murmured. "But I'm not surprised. Neither of you should be out here. It's not safe."

I snorted. *"That wasn't your decision."*

"I am the Baron of Summerfell—"

"If we were under your command, then perhaps that would make a difference. But we aren't. And it's not your decision."

Alar slumped a little. "Gods, Lyr, I barely got you back. I care about what happens to you. I just want to protect you."

I leaned my shoulder against his and watched the sleeping faces of Keir and Margarethe for a moment. *"I am grateful that you care,"* I signed, choosing my words carefully, *"but I am capable of making my own decisions and facing the consequences."*

"You can't fight." He winced as he said it. "I'm sorry, but it's true. There are things in the boundary mountains far worse than dog-kin. And those angel things? You faced off against two, but what if there are more? Lyr, I can't...I can't lose you."

"You won't," I promised, though it felt like a ridiculous thing to say when we were all trapped in this place. *"It will all work out."*

"I can't tell if you're being optimistic or foolish," Alar admitted. He held out his hands to the fire, revealing a few scars on his fingers that gleamed in the light and shone slightly different with magical energy than the rest of him. I blinked and rubbed my eyes, trying to push the magical vision aside. It remained, perhaps some part of the sorcery I now controlled trying to keep me safe in this place. I hated it.

I raised my hands, examining them in the light. There were inksparks at my fingers, flickering in time with the flame, like I'd smudged ink on my fingers while writing. Potential ready to be cultivated.

"Tell me about Jessamine," I murmured, tucking my hands inside my cloak to hide that inkstain light.

Alar pulled away slightly, frowning at me. "My wife? What about her?"

I said nothing, only waited for him to begin his story. After a minute, he sighed and turned back to the fire. There was a faraway look in his eyes.

"When Father died, things were a bit of a mess. Oh, he ran Summerfell well, for a militaristic operation bent on only fighting. But there were so many things about the manor house, the people quartered there, that had been left to fall by the wayside. The accounts were barely managed, supplies weren't ordered on time, forcing people to risk the pass in winter to get to Aviena. I was…despite my training, I was unprepared to take on the management of Summerfell."

Alar took a deep breath and shifted his gaze to the ground. "It would have been easier with you there, to handle the accounts and things while I managed the watch."

I froze, not daring to even breathe as I let the quiet accusation fall between us. Alar tilted his head back and laughed drily at the stars. "Gods, I was so angry with you, Lyr, for leaving. Hurt. As a child, I didn't really understand why you left, only that you did and you left me behind. When I got older, I pieced together enough tales and memories to know that things had never been easy for you at Summerfell, but that took time. I never knew what my father did, though. I swear it."

I nodded my belief and some small part of Alar relaxed.

"I got to thinking about the Order of Ter Avest, the things that you must have been promised to go with them. And I thought, well, that it would be nice to have someone with that sort of training to run Summerfell with me. So I wrote to them." Alar shook his head, white-blonde hair falling into his eyes. "I don't know. Maybe I thought that they would send you home to me. I still thought you were with them. I hadn't yet received the records request from the Great Archives. I thought that maybe once you realised you were needed here, you would come home. But they didn't send me you. They sent Jessamine.

"It was a shock at first. After a while, though, it was so nice to have someone to help. Someone to talk with. She was charming and knowledgeable. She could turn an argument between watch members into a humorous situation. She could sing and play the harp and…and I fancied myself in love with her. I realised soon after our marriage that I didn't love her, but she's a good person. I believe that. And I think she likes me well enough, even if she doesn't love me either. I know you have your prejudices about the Order, but Jessamine is…she is good."

Alar looked across the fire to where Margarethe slept, her brow creased in worry. Pain filled his expression and he turned to throw another branch onto the fire. "I'm going to get some sleep," he said gruffly. "I'll leave you to the watch. Wake us when it's dawn, okay?"

Without another word or look, he left me by the fire.

I was anxious for a while after Alar lay down, seemingly asleep within moments. I strained my ears for any strange noise, convinced that something was going to come out of the dark and attack us. After about an hour, the only noises that I'd heard were the horses swishing their tails and the crackle of the fire. We were, it felt, completely alone in the world.

I shivered and pulled the blanket tighter. My magical vision, sight, whatever it was, still hadn't gone away, and with everyone sleeping, I figured it was time for me to learn. I closed my eyes and focused on the dragon that I knew. Instantly, a shape lit up within me, the inky dragon now melded to my bones and my blood. It was no longer bound to that tattoo on my back, its power and life entwined with my scribe magic, I realised. I was a sorcerer just as much as I was a scribe.

Ink and blood. Together.

The thought was both thrilling and terrifying.

Opening my eyes had the sight returning, every scrap of energy and power winking at me from the ground, the fire, the trees, my companions. There were ripples and currents and entire galaxies in the world. I extended a hand to the fire, imagining one of those motes moving from the flames to my hand. An inkspark moved, followed by a lick of flame. I could feel the heat against my skin, warm then unbearably hot. I yelped and shook my hand out, the flames winking out with them.

"If you want to practise your magic, might I suggest starting with something *other* than fire?" Keir spoke as if he hadn't been asleep at all, no hint of grogginess in his voice. His grey eyes fairly glowed in the firelight, as cat-like as the golden orbs he'd had as Ink.

"I didn't know you were awake," I murmured. He sat up

and lifted one arm. I went to him and snuggled into his side, his arm resting around me in a comforting weight.

"I, ah, haven't slept well since you gave me back this body," Keir admitted. "I was a cat for a long time, and everything feels strange. The hard ground doesn't help."

"It's not very comfortable." I leaned in closer, inhaling his scent. Books and ink and crisp, growing things.

"So, practising sorcery, eh?"

I grumbled and shrugged. "Something...changed. That night at the ravine. Before, it was like the dragon was separate but bound to the tattoo. It moved on its own and it sort of just did the magic when I needed it. Now, it's me. At least, it feels like it's just me. Not separate. And I can see the magical energies better. All the time. But it won't do what I want."

Keir started rubbing small circles on my shoulder, an absentminded touch that sent warmth straight through me. "I am hardly an expert on sorcery—"

I snorted. He raised a brow. "Sorry. Just, you're probably the only one left who even remotely understands this. You're an expert, if only by default."

"Encouraging," he said drily. "Anyways. I don't really know how the humans came to learn sorcery back during the war, but it was derived from the gods' magic, Old Magic, and I can try to help. If you want."

I tilted my head to look at him. He was staring just beyond the fire, something like pain in his eyes. "You have already helped so much. I just wish..."

"What do you wish?" he murmured.

"I wish I weren't so useless."

In an instant, Keir was on his feet, towering over me, looking thunderous. "Who told you that you were useless?" he hissed. I could see vague shapes at his back, impossibly black against the darkness. Wings of ink, swirling in the night.

"No one!" I said, shrinking into myself. At least, no one living had said such a thing. Out loud. To me.

Keir sank to his knees and took my hands in his. "Then why would you ever think you are useless? Blood of the gods, Elyria, you have travelled across vast spaces just to rescue some...fool of a man. How is that useless?"

I shrugged and pulled my hands from his, lifting them to sign. I wasn't sure if it was because the words were stuck in my throat or if I were afraid of the feelings his touch summoned. *"It's not that I'm not capable,"* I started, staring at my fingers against the firelight. *"It's just that Alar is right. I don't even know how to hold a sword properly, let alone fight. If there were books, it would be different. Ink. Paper. But even with this magic that I've bound, I can't use it to summon fire! How am I meant to use it to save those people they took? To protect Margarethe?"*

Keir bowed his head and the shadows at his back disappeared like smoke on the wind. There was that look of sadness again, soul deep and vast as the sky. "There are more ways than wielding a sword to be useful. To be strong. And you are strong and useful and intelligent and so, so capable. If anyone can find those people, it is you."

I smiled weakly. I could see that he believed his words,

but I was more hesitant. During the fight with the ferals, I had done nothing. I hadn't been able to summon magic, to attack, to do anything. If Alar hadn't been there, we would likely be dead.

Keir brushed my chin with the tips of his fingers and lifted it so that I looked him in the eye. "You are *not* useless," he breathed. Then, he kissed me.

The sparks that surged between us were palpable, like the sparks from the fire or pieces of sorcery filled our lungs. Need yawned in me and I pressed forwards until I straddled his lap. His hands tightened around my waist hard enough to make me hiss, not sure if I felt pleasure or pain and not caring which it was. I devoured and he gave endlessly. My hand traced the plane of his chest beneath his shirt and he fairly purred when I rocked my hips against his. We scrabbled at each other's clothes, not quite ready for bare skin, but neither content with the layers of fabric between us.

"Well, well, what have we here?"

Keir and I sprang apart, him to his feet and the dagger at his belt that I hadn't realised he'd been wearing. I was slower, nearly tripping over the blanket at my feet and still tangled in my cloak. I tried to call the sorcery to my aid, focusing on a shield like I'd constructed in the pass, but nothing happened except for a few sparks from the fire crackling almost explosively.

Our assailants laughed.

There were five of them, all angels with hunched backs bearing rotten wings, their movements somehow still graceful and smooth despite the rot. Two had helms, one with horns sprouting from the sides. All wore mismatched leather armour, stitched together in a rough hand. All bore weapons of that same black metal of the crossbow bolts I'd encountered before. I had no doubt they were poisoned.

The leader, the one who had spoken, was female, tall and stocky, her muscles unnatural when combined with the delicate wings she furled and unfurled at her back. Her hair was like straw, sticking out at every angle. And those terrible, orange eyes were crazed.

"We heard whispers of intruders that made it through before we closed the gap," she said, leering at Keir and me. Beside me, Margarethe stirred. I nudged her with my foot and signed for silence behind my back. She stiffened and did not stir again. "But we never expected this!"

The other four creatures fanned out, spreading their wings and raising their weapons. They advanced a single step, stopping when a snarl ripped from Keir.

"Now, now, don't be like that. And put down the sword, foolish human, do you honestly think you can claim the wings of us all before we gut you?" She clicked her tongue in mock disappointment. Alar, who had moved so quietly I hadn't even heard, stepped into the firelight.

"I'm happy to try," he said, smiling with bloodthirsty eagerness. It was a look I'd seen before. On his father.

"Dear me," the creature cooed. "I guess we'll have to have some fun."

"Get behind me!" Keir cried, shoving me back. I tripped on the blanket and fell to the ground beside Margarethe.

She grabbed me and we struggled to our feet. By the time we were standing, the battle had already begun.

Alar fought like a man trained to it his whole life, moving with confidence and strength, his sword meeting the weapons of the angel creatures with ease. He dodged and parried and feinted, cutting deep into the arms of one, the legs of another. But he was one man against too many and I could already see him flagging.

Keir, though, fought like a man possessed. The ink-and-blood wings at his back were as much weapons as the claws he seemed to sport at his fingers. He didn't bother with the sword at his hip, nor did he seem to care that the others had weapons and therefore reach on him. He was upon them like a demon, clawing into their wings until they hung limp. One angel got too close and Keir closed his claws around the creature's throat, tearing it out in a slew of rot and gore.

He, too, was only one against many.

And, as the lead angel had said, it was futile.

Between one blink and the next, Alar's sword was twisted from his grasp and he was struck a blow that sent him reeling, staggering until he leaned against a tree, holding his ribs and gasping for breath. Margarethe let out a cry, leaving my side to go to him. I tried to hold her back, but it was too late. The angel with the horned helm had her pressed against them within a moment, a long knife at her throat. Alar froze, eyes wide. Keir let out a shout and fell to the ground, two angels bearing down on him, their boots at his back, a mace poised to crush his skull.

Through it all, I stood there, unable to move, to fight, to *think*. Now, it was too late.

"See?" the leader said, spitting a wad of rotten blood on the ground. "Wasn't that fun?"

"Elyria," Keir breathed, turning his head to me, panic in those grey depths. "It's about intention. And desire."

"What are you saying?" the angel snarled, reaching out and grabbing a fistful of Keir's hair. He groaned in pain and winced further as one of the others dug their boot into his hip.

Intention and desire. What did that—

I stilled, and so did the world around me. Magical energy swirled through the air as if blood hadn't been spilled, full of potential, ready to be shaped and used. With intention. And desire.

Fury at the capture of my friends, at all the battles I'd had to fight, unprepared and terrified, rose like a wave in me. I clenched my fists at my side. The magic answered. A roar of fire filled the air and suddenly the sky was alight with flame. It leaped for the angels holding Keir in the shape of a dragon, its teeth razor sharp, its antlers setting wings on fire. The creatures screamed and jumped away, flapping their wings uselessly. The leader bared her teeth at me and jumped away from the dragon.

Alar tackled the creature holding Margarethe, drawing the attention of both the lead angel and the dragon. I lifted my arms as if summoning books to me and demanded that the dragon fly. It flew.

"Not so fast," a voice whispered in my ear. I felt cold

metal at my throat and the magic faltered as fear replaced fury. The dragon vanished in a wisp of smoke, leaving spots in my vision. "Good. Now, everyone, drop your weapons."

Keir had barely managed to stand. He staggered a step towards me and I felt the knife bite in.

"Ah, ah," the voice said, cruel and gleeful. Blood, warm and wet, slid down my throat. It cooled rapidly in the frigid air and I shivered. Keir paled, halting his advance. Alar stood with an arm around Margarethe's waist, his hand hovering at the hilt of a dagger. A hand reached around me, gloved in black leather, and gestured. Alar dropped the knife to the ground.

"You should not have crossed the gap. You are entering into something you couldn't possibly understand. But that doesn't mean I won't take advantage of your presence. An angel reborn? The last sorcerer? The taker of wings? Oh, yes, you are quite the prize indeed."

INTERLUDE V

*I*t was strange that Keir, despite being led through the boundary mountains by abominations, despite watching Elyria flounder in her steps as a dark-winged *thing* pushed her forward, could only think about how he longed for music.

When he'd been trapped in the body of Ink, he had sometimes stood at the entrance of the Archives and watched street performers ply their craft. He would ache for the days when it grew warm enough for musicians to busk their trade, when music filled the streets and wove through the oppressive stillness of the Archives. Over the countless lives he'd lived—so many that he didn't remember even half, and even those blurred together—he could still recall the music. It had changed so much as the humans changed, their tastes and skills evolving. It never ceased to amaze him.

He should have been terrified then. He should have been

trembling, his blood as ice in his veins. The woman he loved, whose face he'd held through all of his lifetimes, was walking in front of him, captured, her eyes wide and face pale. She flinched each time her cousin or best friend tripped, each time one of the rotten simulacrum of angels jabbed a hand or a blade towards them. She caught his eye more than once, impossible questions flashing across her face and then disappearing.

He should have been afraid.

Instead, he longed for music.

He wasn't a fool. His heart beat so fast in his chest that it could have been the drumbeat of a crescendo. He watched each step of the things that had taken them, searching for weaknesses. The magic that lived inside him, formed of ink and blood where once he had possessed pure power, pushed at his mind, demanding to be let out. Demanding that he unfurl his ink-crafted wings and destroy those that had dared to hurt his loved one.

Still, despite all of this, he thought of music. Of stringed instruments singing a poignant song, of horns and drums playing a counterpoint. Of the hush between beats where a harpsichord filled the silence.

The horses had vanished during the fight, slipping their ties and running off. Smart creatures, even if it meant they now had to travel on foot. Surely, though, their destination could not be far. Keir watched the position of the sun through the trees and frowned slightly when he saw the direction. Almost directly south, back the way they'd come. A slight eastern angle, but mostly south.

Where were they going?

Alar fell to his knees, having tripped over a protruding tree root. Margarethe gasped and rushed forwards, only to be held back by the female abomination.

"*I'm fine,*" Alar signed. Margarethe's shoulders sagged in relief. Elyria frowned, a line forming between her brows.

"*They...don't speak the signed language,*" she signed in a flurry of movements. The symphony playing in Keir's thoughts stopped abruptly. Suddenly he could think clearly.

"*Where are we going?*" he signed. Alar blinked in astonishment, perhaps unaware that Keir could sign. "*They're taking us south, but there's nothing there but Summerfell. Right?*"

"What are you doing?" the dark-winged creature snarled, stepping in front of Keir and bearing down on him with a sneer. The black rot oozed from his mouth, staining his teeth like ink. Keir wrinkled his nose at the smell.

"*Say nothing,*" he ordered. "*Let me handle this.*"

"Stop that!" The creature flared his wings, showing off broken feathers and ragged plumes. Hardly something that could be used for flight. Not that Keir had tested his own ink-crafted wings for such a thing. Blood of the gods, what exactly had Elyria *done* when she'd changed him back?

He'd been too afraid to find out. Now, it was too late.

Keir fixed the creature with a hard stare. "What? Are you afraid of a few hand motions? We're unarmed."

"You are," the female abomination said, twirling a knife in her fingers. She grabbed it by the blade and pointed the hilt at Keir, ready to throw. "But what of your sorcerer? We are not so ignorant as you think. Even a *hint* of magic and you'll find my blade through your heart, no matter what she wants."

Keir ducked his head, feigning obedience while his thoughts whirled.

She. So, there was someone behind this. One entity, not many. But who?

Keir could tell Alar had the same realisation; his expression stilled into a mask of perfect calm as he righted himself, brushing off some of the dirt. He was careful not to meet the gaze of anyone else, including Keir, but Keir could tell he knew. This changed things. One more piece of the puzzle fell into place.

There were still too many questions, though. And they were running out of time.

The creatures didn't give them any more rest, pushing them onwards in a fast march no matter how often they tripped or how tired they were. He watched Elyria carefully, chest tightening with each stumble. She seemed to grow ever more weary as they walked, her breath heavier than it should be, her hands reaching for support from the tree trunks. Margarethe, too, seemed to be flagging, cradling her injured arm to her chest. Alar lingered close to her, helping her when she faltered. Keir longed to do the same with Elyria, but she was watched intently by their captors, just in case she started using her magic.

Gods, what an idiot he was for letting Elyria come here. As soon as he knew of her quest, he should have talked her out of it. Instead, he'd *encouraged* her. Told her that it was better to get out of Vazeri because the triumvirate knew what she could do as a scribe. Idiotic. As if three humans couldn't be dealt with easily. Compared to the things that now marched them through the forest? Compared to whatever awaited them at the end of all of this? The triumvirate was nothing compared to all of that.

He would have happily sacrificed this form for her safety, living out the rest of eternity in that feline body. Instead, he was watching the woman he loved be marched to an unknown doom.

A hiss against his skin crackled and Keir stiffened. There, on a rock, was the fading glow of a pattern. A rune. And while he'd never been particularly fond of the runic language, he knew what it meant. They'd set off some sort of alarm, alerting whoever lay ahead to their presence.

They continued south. Suddenly, Keir knew exactly where they were going.

Why else would these facsimiles of angels have put runes meant for killing in that ravine, so close to the Summerfell border? It wasn't just for protection; the humans were fool-hardy, certainly, but even they weren't stupid enough to climb down into a ravine and get themselves trapped on the wrong side of the gap. No, it was meant to protect some-thing. Some*one*.

The ground started falling away to their right, sloping downwards into the ravine. More runes littered the trees, the rocks, the ground, glowing faintly. Some were for killing, others were for warning and protection. They increased in number until everyone, including the false angels, were having to step carefully so as not to trigger them.

Elyria turned to look over her shoulder, just once. And what he saw there had Keir's heart freezing. She knew.

She knew what the runes meant. Of course she did. Her scribe magic would translate it for her, and while runes and sorcery weren't the same, they were compatible, used by humans in conjunction for centuries. And before the humans, they were used by—

"You're trying to raise a god," Keir realised aloud. The female creature turned, wings twitching at her back. She leered at Keir.

"You are more intelligent than you look," she said on a laugh. "Not as clever as we'd been led to believe, but not so stupid as these humans."

She wasn't speaking the modern language. She was using the tongue that Keir had used back when he had been an angel. Before he'd been Ink. Before the death of the gods. Vaguely, he realised that Elyria had gasped. But his head pounded too much to understand the implications.

More pieces of the puzzle fell into place.

"The petrified god blood," he said in that same dead language. "You introduced it to the humans."

"A devoted servant, since we were not yet crafted, but yes," the female said. The dark-winged one shot her a look and she shrugged. "What? They won't live long, they can know."

"Fool," the dark-winged creature said, but half-heartedly. As if their death were certain.

"It was a test," Keir said, extrapolating aloud to distract them. To buy time to *think*. "To see if modern human blood —mage blood—could reconstitute the blood of a long-dead god. To determine how much human blood was needed to raise a god."

"To raise a god's *body*," the female said, holding up a finger. "No need to raise the spirit, after all. A god killed by their own hand—"

"Walks in spirit through the land," Keir breathed, and he was certain then that his heart stopped. He couldn't get a proper breath in, the air catching in his throat. His stomach bottomed out and though his feet kept moving, he could barely feel them.

Hirana.

She was alive. She had *always* been alive. She had transformed Keir and killed herself, ensuring that her spirit lived and that she could continue on. And because Keir had been left alive, she would always have someone who remembered her. She would never fade due to being forgotten, even if her body was dead. She'd been so *accepting* at the end, and now Keir knew why. Because she wasn't about to give up without a fight. It must have taken all this time, all these countless lifetimes, to collect enough energy to be able to interact with the world again. To bid someone to serve her. To prepare the way for her true return.

Through all of it, the punishment, the endless years of waiting in silence, Keir had been nothing but a pawn.

Keir staggered to a halt, the world spinning around him. He leaned against a tree, breath ragged. Then, he vomited.

Elyria was suddenly there, her hands steadying him. He reached for her, only for her to be yanked back by the female, who bared her rotted teeth. Elyria said nothing, only gave a neutral, unaffected look, her gaze slightly unfocused. She stared through the creature and didn't flinch when the creature hissed again. Disconcerting in her silence, Keir's stomach dropped when he realised what she was doing. She was getting them to reveal their hand. She had understood what they said in their dead language. Just as she had been able to speak to him in that cell during her dreams, the sorcery giving her an innate ability to understand the spoken word as the scribe magic let her understand the written word.

She understood what was happening, now, and she was preparing to fight it by gathering as much information as she could.

Keir wished more than anything in that moment that he could send her away. He wanted Hirana nowhere near Elyria and her vulnerable, beautiful silence.

"The sorcerer is broken," the dark-winged angel grumbled. "Just leave her alone."

The female sniffed and leered again at Elyria. "All humans are broken. Doesn't mean I can't have some fun."

"Leave her," the other barked. "She will be wanted."

By Hirana.

Keir was hauled roughly to his feet and shoved forwards. Elyria watched with that same empty expression, but there was a spark in her eyes. Fury. Not pain, not sympathy, not even fear. Fury. A fire that burned so deep and strong that there would be no containing it. Keir looked away before he could see if the fury was directed at him or at their captors, those disgusting approximations of what he had once been.

He wasn't sure he wanted to know.

They kept walking, stepping between and around runes. The sun began to sink lower in the sky, painting the world in a splendid array of colours: reds, purples, blues, oranges. They climbed deeper into the ravine, following it along its bottom towards a large space littered with rocks and debris, some of it vaguely human shaped.

As they stepped into the camp, the place where Hirana was going to raise her body, Keir's thoughts went carefully blank, and the beginnings of a requiem mass started to play.

CHAPTER 21

*I*f I wasn't so focused on what was going on, I would have been in the midst of a panic attack. We'd been captured, taken, no easy options for escape. Terrible creatures, rotting from within, pointed poisoned weapons at our backs. And amidst all of this, a god from Keir's past was trying to be resurrected.

He had told me his story, yes, but I wasn't sure whether he'd told me everything, and I wasn't even remotely sure which god was trying to rise again. It didn't really matter, since it required the sacrifice of humans. My people.

Everything was tied together. The kidnapping of Beltran and the others from Vazeri, the refinery at Makhier, the sorcery, all of it. What other pieces of the puzzle wasn't I seeing? Just trying to figure out the unknowable had tingles in my fingers and my vision growing wobbly. I sucked in a deep breath and tried to ground myself, focusing on the world around me as I had done so many times before.

It didn't help.

The ravine had widened into a clearing surrounded by high cliffs and filled with fallen rocks. The whole place was studded with runes that whispered of death and rebirth and the transfer of energy from one being to another. Of magic that hadn't seen the light of day until I foolishly took it into myself. A part of me wished for the comfort of the living ink dragon wrapping its tail around me, but though the tattoo remained, it was inert. Dead. The magic was me and I was terrified.

At the far end of the clearing was a bier of stone carved into a thousand fantastical shapes. It reminded me of the artistic carvings that made up Vazeri architecture, but there was something twisted and angry about these shapes. They reached up for a shrouded form upon the bier like hands reaching in supplication. Or in desperation.

There were several of those rotting angel creatures milling about, guarded the shrouded form. They turned and eyed us eagerly as we were shoved into the clearing.

"More blood for our god?" a male said, wearing a tunic that was little more than patches sewn together. Surely he felt the cold? The snow that was starting to fall?

"Where is she?" the female who had taken us barked, flaring her ragged wings. "There are those who she should see."

"She's preparing," the male said, jerking his head towards a fissure in the far cliff. A faint glow flickered from within, though I'd never seen green fire before. "Not to be disturbed before moonrise."

The female clicked her tongue and leered at me, wrapping her hand around my arm. "Guess you'll have to wait, little sorcerer," she said. She cackled and shoved me forwards towards another fissure in the cliff, this one darker, a foul smell emanating forth. Behind me, Keir muttered something under his breath in that ancient language. I willed myself not to hear, not to translate, but that magic which bound us together did anyways.

"I will skin you alive if you touch her again," he had said. It was so quiet that no one heard but me. Still, when I turned, I saw the anger and the intent there. I believed he would follow through.

Alar and Margarethe were pushed into the fissure before me, Alar catching Margarethe before she could fall. I followed, doing my best to ignore the angel's touch on my arm. Silence was alternately my weapon, my prison, my sanctuary, and right then it was all three. I lifted my chin and went to the fissure willingly, Keir following behind.

It took a moment for my eyes to adjust, but when I did, I clasped my hands over my mouth to keep from retching.

"My gods," Margarethe whispered, the sound echoing through the chamber.

There were about forty people crammed in the space, leaving barely enough room to move about. Some sat nearly on top of each other, others were pressed against the walls to try and make space. They were filthy, obviously not having had access to water for some time, their clothes stained with dirt and waste. They were thin, gaunt-cheeked and dull-eyed. All ages and types, the youngest being a sniffling girl of about four with matted black hair and brown skin, the oldest a man with jowls that sagged and wrinkles on every exposed piece of his pale skin. They weren't chained then, but I could see visible wounds where they had been chained previously. Though they easily outnumbered the angels outside, they remained trapped in this space. Broken.

"We're going to get you out of here," Alar said in an undertone, looking over his shoulder. The angels had left, abandoning us in this fissure, though they likely watched the entrance. I had thought they would take me somewhere to be kept under close watch, given my sorcery, but they almost seemed not to care, instead sticking me in this place.

"Who is that?"

I stiffened and tried to move backwards, but Keir was behind me and there was nowhere to go. He put his hands on my waist, gentle, firm. A reminder that he was there. I wanted to turn and bury myself in his arms. I didn't, instead waiting.

The people in the chamber shuffled a bit until one man, not quite as thin as the rest, made his way forwards. His hair was a greasy mess and he looked like he'd been covered in soot, but I knew him. Beltran. He could only have been there for a few days, yet he looked nearly as bad as the rest.

He blinked a bit against the light from the outside, then his eyes widened and he gaped at us. At me.

"Deepest Night," he breathed. "Elyria, is that you?"

I nodded.

"What are you doing here? They must have raided

Vazeri again after they took us," Beltran said. He took another step towards me, pushing past Margarethe and Alar with little care. Keir's grip tightened on me. "I'm so sorry. Oh, gods, I would...you shouldn't be here. You shouldn't have to..."

He shrugged helplessly, at a loss for words. I raised my hands slowly to sign and lowered them again. It was too dark for him to see the signs properly. I would have to talk to him. After all that I had been through, after all that I had done, speaking aloud to him seemed almost insurmountable.

"I came after you," I said. There was a slight wobble in my voice and I could feel my throat tightening, but I managed to get the words out. "To save you."

Beltran gaped at me, swaying slightly where he stood. He shook his head, then again. Then, he started laughing. "I'm hallucinating," he said to himself. The other prisoners just watched, so still and vacant that they might have been statues witnessing the fall of man. "I've finally broken. This is my mind playing tricks on me."

"I am no trick," I said flatly, irritation rising.

"Except Elyria doesn't talk," Beltran said, barking out a hysterical laugh. "She's mute! Silent as the grave. The perfect secret keeper. Unable to—"

"Shut up," Keir snarled, the sound more animalistic than angelic. "After all the time you spent with her, you obviously know nothing. Not that I should be surprised, ignorant and unobservant as you are. Obsessed with your own life, your own tale."

Beltran reared back as if struck. He wasn't laughing any longer. "Who do you think you are to talk to me like that?"

"Elyria's lover," Margarethe broke in, sounding furious. "And if you will get your head out of your own ass for *one* minute, then maybe you would figure out that we're here to help you. All of you."

"I can talk," I said softly. "I always could. I just…don't feel safe enough to do it most of the time. The signed language is easier."

Beltran reached out, as if he were going to brush my arm or cup my chin. I shifted away. He shook his head again, still disbelieving. "You didn't feel safe enough around me?"

"Is it any wonder?" Keir asked in a low voice. "When you used her to teach you the signed language and manipulated her into thinking herself in love with you?"

Beltran flinched. "I never—"

"Yes," Keir said. "You did."

I rubbed my hands against my eyes, sparks of magical sight flashing in my vision. It was still there, even after having summoned fire to do my bidding and failing spectacularly. In this place, the energy mostly came from the walls and the floor, the stone. The people were barely alive, only a few of them shining brighter. The most recent abductees, I surmised, newly arrived from Vazeri.

"We don't have time for this argument," I said. "We need to get out of here. Before they—"

"Before they what? Sacrifice us?" Beltran scoffed. "And I suppose you know all about that, since you are so good at keeping things from people."

362

"Enough!" Alar barked. He straightened his shoulders and lifted his chin, and it was then, in the half-shadows, that I could see how much he had truly changed from the boy I knew all those years ago. He was strong, sure, but he had always been that. Now, he drew the gaze of the captives like moths to a flame. "I am Lord Alar Trevain, Baron of Summerfell. We have come to return you to your homes, and you *will* do as I say, or we will all die here. Do you understand?"

The majority of the captives just sat and stared, but a few murmured their assent and a few more nodded. Beltran glared at me.

"Trevain, huh?" he snapped. "Another secret?"

I looked away, ignoring him. He snorted, obviously taking my silence as admission.

"How are we going to get out of here?" Margarethe asked in an undertone. "They took our weapons. And these people hardly seem up for a fight."

"Lyr?" Alar asked me, looking hopeful. "You can still… you know. Right?"

I realised that he was looking to me to save them. He was looking to me to use my barely controlled sorcery to get us all out of here. I had managed to use fire offensively for a brief moment, but everything else was beyond me. I had no idea how to fight with sorcery. I had no idea how to help these people.

Keir tapped my arm and I turned, the space in the chamber so tight that I was pressed against him, his warmth enveloping me in the chill and damp. He rested his forehead against mine and murmured quietly. "It will be alright."

"How?" The word was barely a breath.

"There is another way. We just have to find it."

I pulled back as far as I could and shook my head. There was no other way. Alar wouldn't have asked me if he weren't certain. We had no weapons. The rotting angels had ones bearing poison. The captives were alive, but some of them were so weak I didn't think they could stand. I was tired, yes, but at least I had a chance to do something.

"I will try," I said to Alar.

"Try what?" Beltran asked.

"Shut up." Margarethe stepped between us, turning her back on him. "You can do it, Elyria. Just...just think of it like those times back in Liral. When you practised your scribe magic with me. Okay?"

I nodded. Surely it wasn't so different, right? Learning to control the ink and paper and the whispers of a thousand writers in my mind, and learning to manipulate the inherent energy in the world. It was similar. Surely.

I raised my hands, cupping them as if to hold water. I focused on the energy in the stone around us, the inkspecks of untold galaxies that lived in the earth. On an inhale, I called them to me, bidding them light.

Fire burst into existence in my hands.

Several of the captives gasped and started murmuring. Some of the more inactive ones began to blink and squint their eyes, focusing on us. On me. Hope began to build as I willed the flames higher, brighter, the heat so intense that I started sweating.

"Careful," Keir cautioned. I concentrated harder, pulling more of those sparks to me and shaping the fire into the familiar draconic shape I'd come to know. Before I'd even started to shape the antlers and claws, a cry from the back of the chamber broke out. Rocks started crumbling as I took their energy, falling onto the people beneath. Immediately, I snuffed out the fire. It was too late. Dust filled the air and more rocks started falling.

"Out!" Alar cried, shoving us towards the entrance.

"But the angels—" a woman shouted before being cut off as people pressed forwards. Keir grabbed my wrist, but I was soon separated from Alar and Margarethe as the captives shoved their way out of the chamber and into the open night air.

One of the angels—the female who had taken us— started laughing as we stumbled forwards and fell on top of one another, some bruised and bleeding, all covered in dust from the falling rock. "Look at this!" she crowed, sauntering towards us, a crossbow resting in the crook of her arm, its bolt dripping with poison. "We didn't even have to go in there and pull them out. They came willingly!"

Keir hauled me to my feet and I coughed out some of the dust.

"It's okay," he murmured, though that was far from the truth. I had just brought down the chamber ceiling on a bunch of injured and weak people. The energy I'd taken for the fire had to come from somewhere and I had foolishly taken it from the very thing above our heads. And now, we were out in the open, surrounded by a dozen armed angels, staring at the bier, and I realised that it was so, so much worse than just bringing down a few rocks.

The chamber had at least provided some protection to these people. Now, though, they were exposed. And the angels were ready to make their sacrifice.

"Line them up!" a grizzled-looking angel with white hair and a missing eye called out. His wings were rough and grey and he seemed to have a little less of the rot than the others, though he smelled just as bad. Half of the other angels leaped to obey, plunging into the midst of the people around me and dragging them forwards by their arms or their necks. Screams filled the air as the prisoners were lined up and shoved to their knees.

"Not you," Missing Eye said, baring his teeth at Keir. He slid his eye to me. "And not you."

Margarethe cursed loudly in several languages as the female tried to shove her into place next to Beltran. Alar lunged, grabbing the female by the wings. She shrieked and attacked, but it was too late. My cousin managed to wrap his hands around her head and snapped her neck. It happened so fast, the blink of an eye, and I barely had time to take a breath.

If it was meant to serve as a signal to the others to retaliate, to strike, then it failed. We could do nothing but watch in shock. Missing Eye leaped forwards as two other angels wearing helms reached Alar. They shoved him to the ground, wrenching his head back and exposing his throat.

"You get to be first," Missing Eye said.

"No!" Margarethe screamed. I wanted to join her.

Alar met my gaze. "Run," he mouthed. Tears filled his eyes. "Please."

Missing Eye raised a knife, black and glittering in the light of the fires on either side of the bier. He arced it towards Alar's neck and I acted without thinking.

The world exploded in my vision, all the sparks and ripples of potential energy flaring to life. I called on some of them, all of them, heedless of anything except I had to *stop that knife*. The magic obeyed.

Intent, Keir had said.

Desire.

I had both.

The knife became dust.

Keir and Alar moved before I fully realised what I had done. Alar fell backwards, freeing his hair from one of his attackers. He kicked out with one leg, sweeping Missing Eye to the ground. Keir leaped into the fray, ink-and-blood wings forming at his back, his fingers curling into claws of shadow. He sliced through the wings of one of the helmed angels; the creature slumped forwards, wings useless, a low keening sound coming from their throat. Missing Eye found his footing and joined the attack and then it was nothing but chaos.

Keir and Alar did most of the fighting, but Beltran and even Margarethe joined in as well, tearing and clawing and hitting where they could. One of the other captives, an older woman with olive skin and shorn black hair, managed to grab the crossbow from the dead female angel. She shot the bolt through the shoulder of another helmed angel. Her actions spurred others to join in. Weak and broken, they still outnumbered the angels.

We had a chance.

I raised my hands and reached for the sorcery again, focusing on my desire, my need. I aimed for wings and throats, not quite sure how the magic would manifest and not particularly caring.

Then, the fires at the bier went out and my sorcery went silent. The sparks and currents, the ripples and shadows of energy, magic, disappeared. It felt like I was a marionette with cut strings. My limbs were heavy, tired. I fell to my knees.

The fighting stopped, people flying apart as though some great being had waved a hand and demanded it be so. Within seconds, the humans were cowering on the ground, either injured, dead, or staring wide-eyed at something just beyond my shoulder. Where there had been a dozen angels before, there were now perhaps five, the others in pieces on the ground. Margarethe knelt over Alar as he pressed a hand to his shoulder, face pale.

Keir alone, it seemed, remained standing. He stared towards me. No, not towards me, beyond.

I turned, my vision darker than before. Even so, it was impossible to mistake the shining form that stood taller than everyone else, chin lifted, six wings at her back, a smile painted across beautiful features.

"Did you think you could fight your way out of your

fate?" she asked, voice slightly distorted. Her shape flickered and she took a step forwards. "That you could use *sorcery* to stop me?"

She paused just before me and crouched. She lifted my chin, her touch like ice, sending shards of frost through my veins. I coughed. "Foolish human. I *created* sorcery. Many much stronger in the art than you have tried to face me and failed. Did you truly think you could win?"

I said nothing. The woman—spirit? god?—clicked her tongue and straightened. She smiled wider and spread her wings, laughing.

"Well, this *is* a surprise. Are you still here after all this time, Keir?"

"Hirana," Keir snarled. "I had hoped to have killed you."

Hirana. The goddess that Keir had served. The frost in me spread, fingers of ice grasping my heart as I realised who this was. The goddess of knowledge. The one who had bound Keir. Who was now trying to regain her body.

She bared her teeth in a wolfish grin. "You are more than welcome to try again."

CHAPTER 22

*W*ith a flick of Hirana's hand, the fires at the bier relit, illuminating the bodies of humans and rotted angels alike. Hirana studied the carnage, shaking her head and clicking her tongue. She stepped over several of the dead until she came to a man of middling years, his brown hair matted with gore, his eyes glassy. He was bleeding out, his breath coming in sharp gasps as blood pumped from a wound on his thigh.

Hirana knelt.

Keir stood frozen, watching. Horrified. I tried to lift my hands to sign, to say *anything*, but I could think of nothing to say.

"This one. Bring a vessel," Hirana ordered. Missing Eye, his right wing in tatters and dragging on the ground, wounds on his body oozing black, shuffled forwards with a bronze bowl in his hand. He placed it under the wound of the dying man, the blood dripping into the bowl. *Plink. Plink. Plink.*

Hirana inhaled deeply, a shudder running through her. She straightened and watched, eyes bright, as Missing Eye shuffled towards the bier.

"No," Keir murmured, the word more a croak than anything. He tried to leap for Hirana, but his hands passed right through her flickering wings. She wasn't fully here. A spirit. He couldn't touch her.

I tried to reach for the sorcery in my blood, hoping I could do something to stop her, but where there had once been that magic, now all I could feel was a great pressure. Like someone was holding the lid closed on a box ready to spring open. Hirana. It had to be. She was suppressing my sorcery, and I wasn't skilled enough to know how, let alone be able to fight back.

Missing Eye took the bowl of blood to the bier and flung back the shroud. I heard Margarethe mutter another curse, this time in her native tongue, which she never used for fear of the memories it would evoke. She'd sworn she'd forgotten the language years ago, but now it fell from her tongue naturally. That was enough to send splinters of ice through my heart.

We were going to die here.

Alar was wounded, weaponless.

Margarethe was strong, but she—like me—was an Archivist. She didn't know how to fight.

Keir was in shock and I wasn't sure I could snap him out of it.

And me? Well, the one weapon I had was gone. Taken by the goddess before me, who watched with bated breath as Missing Eye revealed what looked like a skeleton carved from ruby.

"God bones," I realised aloud. The words startled me, jolting me. I straightened a bit and my muscles screamed in protest, but obeyed. The bier held god bones, petrified over many lifetimes, likely scavenged from the depths of the Great Plains. Perhaps even on the expedition my parents had joined. And if god bones were anything like god blood, they needed the inherent magic in human blood to awaken.

Missing Eye tilted the bowl over what looked to be an ordinary lump of rock just above the skull of the petrified skeleton. I didn't need to have a sorcerer's sight to know that *something* was released when the blood touched the stone. I shuddered, energy rippling through me, though the sorcery was still suppressed.

The stone bubbled for a moment, shifting, changing shape as though it were alive. Hirana sucked in a breath, then let it out again when the stone stopped moving.

I tried not to gasp, even going so far as to clamp my hands over my mouth to keep in the sound. Silence was my ally in that moment. I feared that the beating of my heart—loud and fast in my ears—would give me away. The stone wasn't stone any longer. It was glass. Worn and scratched with time, but glass nonetheless.

A glass inkwell, to be precise.

And I could hear the potential of the ink within.

It had the same coppery feel as the ink in the grimoire,

the ink that had taken shape on my skin. It had the taste of iron and soot, but there was blood in the ink, too. Many different types, if I wasn't mistaken. When ink was involved, I was rarely mistaken.

"I thought I destroyed that years ago," Keir said, voice cracking through the silence. Hirana turned to him, wearing a triumphant smirk.

"You? An angel with clipped wings?" She barked out a laugh. "You never had the power to do such a thing even at the height of your glory. *My* glory. Oh, yes, I knew full well when your useless feline shape tossed the inkwell into the fire. Tell me, did it give you pleasure to watch it burn? To watch your failure melt?"

Keir rocked on his feet, his eyes gleaming as if with tears. "It was not a failure."

Hirana tilted her head. "Oh? You started a war, angel. A war that could not be won. Not then."

"The humans deserved to know. They deserved—"

"Nothing!" Hirana spread her six wings wide, the feathers shimmering and flickering, a beautiful nightmare given shape. The surviving people cowered, drawing closer together, unable to look at her. "They deserved nothing more than what they were given. After all this time, can you *honestly* say that they haven't misused the gift you gave them? The wars. The greed. They persecuted their own kind, driving them off the mainland or killing them altogether. They slaughtered innocents for following different gods. They—"

"They learned to sing," Keir said. His eyes were fixed

firmly on the ground, and there was not even a hint of those ink-formed wings at his back. Yet, despite his obvious fear, his voice was steady. "They learned to craft music that would make your soul weep. They learned how to draw, to paint. They learned to build monuments that would never have been imagined under your reign. They learned to breed plants, to cultivate gardens full of peace and birdsong and colour."

Hirana curled her lip. "Music? Gardens? Buildings? You count those things against the truth of destruction and death?"

"We prize them above anything." Margarethe, still cradling Alar in her arms, glared at the goddess. Hirana blinked, as if unused to even considering humans as something other than her enemy, worthy of sacrifice. As if unused to even considering humans at all. Margarethe set her jaw and continued. "We value art. Beauty. A moment of love captured in song. A mother's tragedy at losing a child depicted in a mosaic. We've had wars, yes. Done terrible things. But we've grown and learned from our mistakes. We have crafted sagas to remember how we fell so that we might not do it again. We learn to improve ourselves, and we make art because it makes life worth living."

Hirana snorted. She turned back to Keir, waving a dismissive hand at Margarethe and the others. "Truly, Keir, *this* is what you were so concerned about that you set about destroying the world? That humans might make pretty things?"

Keir flinched. Margarethe looked as though she would

continue to chew the goddess out, but Alar tightened his grip on her arm and shook his head slightly. She, surprisingly, obeyed.

"It is much more than pretty things," Keir said softly. "It is the chance to govern themselves. To decide what is right and what is wrong. You bound me to books and words and knowledge so that I might see the humans mistreat it, but I never have."

"Never? Why don't I believe you?" She shook her head and turned her back on him. "It matters not. The war is over at last, now that we've come this far. Centuries wandering formless, gathering scraps of energy so that I might move amongst the world again. Now I am here and it will only take a few sacrifices that I might live again in the flesh. Then, we shall rectify your mistakes."

She stepped towards the skeleton on the bier, reaching out for the inkwell. Her fingers passed through it, but I felt a tingle up my spine, as if something in the ink reacted with the sorcery that Hirana used to hold her form together. She made a sound of annoyance, whirling to Missing Eye.

"Start with the recently dead," she snarled, "before the energy of their lifeblood fades away."

The angel scrambled to obey, dragging some of the dead humans towards the bier and starting to drain them of blood. Several others retched, crying at the mutilations that took place and knowing they were next. I had seen it done before, though, in that refinery in Makhier. My throat tightened, but I did not look away.

Hirana only watched the process for a minute before

376

growing bored with the bloodletting. She turned and wandered by the lines of captives, sneering at them as they cried and flinched away. Gods, they probably didn't understand what was happening, not really. They only knew that they were faced with some great power, some terrible thing that wanted their lives. Keir, Margarethe, Alar and I were the only ones that even vaguely understood what was to come, and even then, I think only Keir truly grasped the magnitude of the situation.

This wasn't just about vengeance. This was going to change the very shape of the world. I doubted that the four gods who currently ruled would allow Hirana to just take over. But Night and Day and Dawn and Dusk were not so involved as Hirana and her kind had been, according to Keir. They were distant, dealing with their people in whispers and small things, not ruling from a great palace.

Surely they at least knew what was going on. What was happening here in this place. This was a direct challenge. Why didn't they do something?

Hirana turned at last towards me. She sauntered towards me with the sort of curious look in her eyes that a scholar got when presented with some great puzzle. "Now, *you* are quite an interesting conundrum. I have wandered this world far and wide as little more than a breath of wind for centuries, yet I know it to be true that sorcery is dead. Modern magic is so...tidy. Then again, gods who divide their world so evenly are bound to produce tidy magic. Each person to their own little speciality. Fire. Water. Healing. Art. Metal. All so precise, so limited. Not a hint of the vast power of sorcery. Until you."

She leaned in, inhaling deeply as though scenting me. "What *are* you?"

I did not answer. Even if I had been able to force the words out of my tight throat and into the world, I would not answer her. She did not deserve that, not from me.

Hirana hummed and smiled slightly. "Oh, I see. You think to be defiant. Yes, others of your kind tried defiance with me. They died readily enough."

Fury snapped something in me. I raised my hands and signed ferociously. *"Yet you and your kind were the ones who died in the end. Who lost that war."*

The goddess reared back, bemused. "What is this? You could not have broken through my binds on your magic, but—no. No you did nothing. Then why did you...?"

She looked over her shoulder at Keir, who smirked. "I will give you no explanation, Hirana," he said on a chuckle. "I am no longer your servant. Besides, aren't you the goddess of *knowledge*?"

"Shut up!" She whirled to Missing Eye, who was busy trying to harvest blood from the dead. "Aren't you done yet?" she demanded.

"The heart does not pump," Missing Eye said, bowing slightly, though that could just have been because of his ruined wing. "It is slow and—"

"Then take it from the living! I do not care how you get the blood, only do it. Or shall I tear your form to pieces?" Hirana waved a hand and the fire sparked higher. I felt that same shudder, that same shiver down my spine as her magic flared. The inkwell. It was intrinsically tied to her and her magic.

Keir's eyes widened at me and he lifted his hands. "*Write.*"

Hirana hissed. "What are you doing?"

I shook my head. "*I can't. I don't have anything to write on!*"

For all that I could feel the ink with my scribe magic, I needed paper to do something with it. I couldn't just call the ink forth without a purpose, without writing. That wasn't how my magic worked. And my notebooks had been in Storm's saddle bags, which were likely long gone from here, if they even survived at all.

"*Parchment,*" Margarethe signed. Hirana looked between the three of us and something like understanding spread across her features.

"Oh, I see," she purred, drifting towards me again. "It's a language. How clever, a language of silence. Well, it is going to be quite difficult to use a language when you have no hands."

She jerked her head at another of the remaining angels, who shuffled closer, a gash on their left arm dripping steadily on the ground. *Plink. Plink. Plink.*

So like the sound of the inkwell coming back to life. *Plink. Plink. Plink.*

The rot inside the angel seemed to spread even as I thought it, the wound darkening and that terrible black blood flowing smoothly from the gash. Hirana must have created them recently if they were so prone to rot and so poor at healing. She must have used quite a bit of whatever magic she had managed to cobble together to craft something tangible. And if her magic was tied to ink—

"Parchment is made from skin," Margarethe signed rapidly, her hands nearly hidden by her leg so that the goddess wouldn't see. She pointed to the body of a man not two feet from where she lay with Alar. Beltran was kneeling near the man, his eyes wide and vacant, though surely he had been following the signed conversation. Shock, perhaps. His hands were coated in the man's blood as though he'd tried to save him.

Then, I realised what it was Margarethe meant. Bile rose in my gorge and I nearly heaved. Gods, no. I couldn't. That was—*"It's desecration,"* I signed, ignoring the bleeding angel that drew closer, an axe held weakly in their good hand. Hirana curled her lip at me.

"That's quite enough of that. Take her hands. Now."

The angel raised the axe. Margarethe let out a wordless cry and Alar struggled where he lay, pale and shivering. Keir froze, inky wings forming at his back between one heartbeat and the next. Our eyes locked. He could never reach me in time, even if there weren't other enemies in the way.

The axe swung for my hands.

I lifted them high.

Then, I shoved all thoughts of sorcery aside and dove deep into the magic that made me who I was. Deep into the whispers of ink and words, deep into the taste of ink on my tongue and paper under my fingers. I called forth my scribe magic and I began to write.

The angel before me faltered and dropped the axe as their blood flowed freely under my command. Theirs and all the others, swirling together with soot from the fire. I could taste it now, beneath the rot and corruption that had turned ink into blood. They were crafted from ink, from the very power that Hirana claimed as her own. And they became ink once again.

I directed the ink to the bodies of the dead, swallowing down revulsion as I started writing as I would on parchment. Parchment that was nothing more than skin, treated and preserved. As these people's skin would never be. I wrote in minuscule letters, overlapping one another. I told the stories that Keir had relayed to me about how all this began. About the gods of before, their power and their cruelties. About his treachery and punishment. About the war. About the lifetimes of silence that followed.

And when I ran out of his stories to write, I wrote my own. The realities of my childhood. The pain. The joy. Being sent to Liral, only to find Margarethe and start to build a life of my own away from my past and the nightmares that haunted me. I wrote about Vazeri, it's beauty and the fear of the people that lived there, hidden so well until crisis came. I wrote about how I fell in love with a guardsman that had been kind to me no matter that it was false because I was afraid that no one else would love me. I wrote about the fire. The decision to find those that had been taken. I wrote about Ink. And I wrote about Keir.

Hirana watched all of this with wide eyes for a minute before she leaped into action, as much as could be managed with her incorporeal form. "Stop this!" she snarled, reaching out a hand that sparked with sorcery. Rocks leaped for me and I flinched, my writing faltering for a moment.

But there was no pain of impact, no broken bones. I looked up, only to find Keir standing over me, those wings of ink and blood spread wide. He sheltered me. "Keep writing," he said softly. "I will keep you safe."

I nodded, closed my eyes, and dove deeper into the magic than ever before.

During the fire in Vazeri, I had been overwhelmed by the magic, so overtaken by the words as they demanded to be saved that I lost all sense of myself apart from the words. Here, the words that formed were my own; they emerged from that core of myself I rarely let anyone see. Raw, vulnerable, they were my pain and hopes and dreams and fears made manifest. They formed of blood and they were hardly neat, filling any available space on the bodies of the dead that I could find. But the magic wasn't endless. I could feel it draining my energy too fast. There was too much ink, and I wasn't used to giving so openly of myself.

The last angel fell, dust on the wind, and I collapsed. Keir collapsed beside me, wings fading from existence. He had a deep gash over his left eye that bled freely. There were several other large wounds on his arms, his back, and the way he cradled his side told me that some of his ribs were broken.

Hirana lowered her hands as the last angel disappeared. Keir let out a dark laugh.

"It's over," he said, coughing slightly. "You have no more

servants to harvest your blood. You don't have enough power to form more. You have lost, Hirana. Face facts."

She turned to him, burning fury etched into her features. "Oh, you foolish, foolish angel. You fell in love with another human, didn't you? Haven't you learned your lesson? Perhaps it is time I *make* you learn it."

She lifted her hands and pointed them at me. "You should never have tried to master sorcery, human. It is *my* power."

Then, I erupted into blinding agony.

CHAPTER 23

My back bowed. I felt as though I was being torn apart. A thousand pinpricks jabbed my skin. Vaguely, I felt the spells of ink on my skin pulling and twisting, as though Hirana was trying to remove the sorcery from me by force.

"How *dare* you challenge me," she hissed. A twist of her wrist and my body contorted, pushing me forwards. "You are nothing but a lowly human. Your role is to worship me. A god, power beyond your comprehension. You are made to serve me. To do my bidding. And yet you would dare to defy me? To steal power that does not belong to you? To try and take my place in the world? You are not gods, you are fodder beneath my feet."

Vaguely, I felt a hand on mine. Keir held me, grey eyes wide, his mouth moving, though I could not hear the words. Hirana moved her hands again and another burst of power surged through me, amplifying my pain. I moved again, compelled.

Keir held my hand tighter, but then he was somehow on the ground, writhing in pain as lightning arced over my skin and into him.

No. I ground my teeth and tamped down on the electricity, stifling it until only a few sparks flickered in and out of existence. Keir's body stopped twitching, but his chest was painfully still. Hirana smirked.

"Isn't that useful?" she purred, raising a hand. My own mirrored her movements. The sorcery in my blood roared as she used her own magic to bind us together and make me do her bidding. "Far more useful than those golems. I never was one for creating, not like the others. They always seemed to fall apart so easily. This, though, is much better."

I ground my teeth together and managed to get my hands beneath me enough to push myself upwards. I staggered to my feet and lifted my chin, staring her down.

"There's that defiance again." Hirana chuckled. She clenched a fist and I nearly let out a cry of pain as a lash of fire burned across my back. "Why do you not scream? Surely it hurts. Or are you a true mute? I would prefer not to have to learn that silly hand dancing language." She tilted her head, curious. "Perhaps another lash will grant me the answer I want."

Fire flared in my vision before pain laced across my back. I sucked in a sharp breath as the world went white around me. When I could see again, I was on my knees before Keir, panting for breath. He was so still, lifeless. His chest didn't rise and his eyes stared blankly at the night sky. The only movement was a slight breeze rustling through his ink-black hair.

I bared my teeth in a snarl, ice shards piercing my heart and tears filling my eyes. She had killed him. Without a second thought or an ounce of hesitation. I shouldn't have expected otherwise, but seeing him lying there, impossibly still, fractured something in me.

I staggered to my feet again and pushed against the bonds of her sorcery. I was exhausted, having used up my reserves with my scribe magic. I could barely stand. My hands trembled. But I looked at Keir, laying still before me, and I pushed back. The magic was still suppressed inside me, bound by her and used for her own malicious purposes. I knew full well that she was going to use me to kill my friends and every other person there, to pour their blood on the bones and raise her to life once more. I would be damned before I helped her.

"Your defiance begins to bore me," Hirana said, feigning a yawn. "Time for you to get to work."

She flicked her fingers and my feet staggered towards the bier, towards that bronze bowl still half-full of blood that Missing Eye had harvested from the dead man. I glanced at the man's body as I moved and nearly retched. He had not an inch of exposed skin left. It was all ink, thousands upon thousands of words overlapping until he was tattooed into unrecognisability. The other dead were no better, looking barely human in the aftermath of what I had wrought.

I nearly tripped over the step leading up to the bier, my hands fumbling towards the bowl. Hirana hissed. "Have a care, human!" she snapped. "Every drop of blood you spill will be paid back by you ten fold."

As if I were the one controlling my movements. Under Hirana's direction, I lifted the bowl and started pouring it over the skeleton, starting from the skull. The inkwell shimmered, the blood interacting with its magic and sending another shiver down my spine. I nearly collapsed as Hirana's sorcery faltered. The blood flowed over the ruby-stone skull. The red stone cracked and splintered, fragments falling away and revealing a piece of face that was almost human beneath.

It was barely a fraction of a face, a bit of temple and eye, but it was solid and possessed of the power that ran through the inkwell. Sorcery and ink and blood, all combined in one place.

Hirana tugged at the bond between us; I fought, remaining there by the skeleton, though it took every scrap of ability I had left.

"What are you doing?" she asked, her flickering hand reaching for me. It passed through and she let out a cry of annoyance. "Finish the task!"

I remained where I was, shivering. I couldn't let this continue. If Hirana returned to physical form, she would tear the world to shreds. I had killed her few remaining servants, but that wouldn't be enough to stop her. Especially not if she regained the power that being whole would bring.

She would destroy everyone here. Margarethe. Alar. Even Beltran. Just as she had destroyed Keir.

A tear slipped down my cheek.

"Lyr," Alar whispered. I didn't turn, didn't look at him. I was too busy fighting Hirana's grip on me. That bond, pulled taut.

A bond.

Bound by Old Magic. Sorcery. The magic that shaped worlds. Bound by my blood. By ink.

That paper cut seemed like a lifetime ago, and yet it was the thing that made all the difference.

"Move!" Hirana shouted. Lightning arced through me and I spasmed, unable to fight the pain. "Do you think you can defy me just because you have my power? Or did that fool angel spin stories in your head that made you think this was a good idea? That fighting me was even possible?"

I reached for the inkwell. Every inch of movement was enough to have me panting for breath. I could feel the tears on my cheeks mingling with blood that dripped from my nose. My vision swam with effort as I fought against the goddess's hold.

"What are you doing?" she asked. That was fear in her voice.

The sorcery controlling my movements tightened. I saw Hirana's form flicker even more, as if whatever power she had to keep her in the world was used instead on me. It worked. I couldn't move. Couldn't do more than stand there, reaching for the inkwell, my breath ragged and tears flowing freely. She had *killed* Keir and I couldn't do the one thing that could stop her.

"Margarethe," I mouthed, my vocal cords too tight to produce sound. "Help me."

I blinked away the tears as best I could and opened my mouth to try again, to call out, to force the words free. But Margarethe was suddenly there, tears filling her own eyes. "I'm here," she murmured.

"You will die for trying to interfere. I killed my own servant, do you not think I will kill you, too?" Hirana moved closer, form still flickering. She faded nearly entirely as more lightning arced through me. My muscles tightened, locking my joints into place. I had no doubt that the only reason my heart still beat was that Hirana used me as a conduit for her magic.

Margarethe didn't hesitate. She glared at the faded form of Hirana and picked up the inkwell. "Try and stop me," she said, then pressed the inkwell into my hand.

The sorcery that bound me and flowed through me flared like sunlight in my eyes. My scribe magic, depleted enough that it was nothing but raw magic and the taste of ink on my tongue, surged past all the barriers I had developed over the years and took control of my body in a way that Hirana's sorcery could not.

Too late, I realised that Margarethe's hand was bleeding and that a drop of her blood had slipped into the ink.

She screamed. Hirana roared with fury. My vision bloomed with energy and light. The dragon inked on my skin roared to life once again, pulling free from the sorcery in my blood, now mixed with the magic in Hirana's inkwell. The world exploded around me.

I was conscious long enough to see a dragon formed of thousands of tiny inked words tear into the ephemeral form of the goddess Hirana. She tried to fight back, using her sorcery to throw rocks and twist flames, but the ink was as much a part of her as she was a part of it. The dragon scattered her into a thousand pieces. The world shook as though the very ground was being remade. The other captives screamed, trying to flee.

The dragon turned its attention to Margarethe.

My friend screamed again as the beast roared for her. I reached out a hand, pulling on the very last drop of my scribe magic. I signed one word. *Bind.*

The world around me trembled again.

I succumbed to darkness.

If I dreamed, I did not find Keir there.

Light pressed against my eyes, splitting my head into a thousand shards. I groaned.

"She's waking up," a voice said. Was that Beltran?

"Lyr? Come on, wake up." Alar. He sounded concerned. I squeezed my eyes shut and brought a hand up, only to gasp in pain at the agony that speared through me when I tried to move. My eyes shot open.

"Gods," I rasped. "It hurts."

"Of course it hurts." I knew that voice. It was sharp, scolding, possessed of the certainty that they were right. That *he* was right. "You burned through your entire reserve of scribe magic while also trying to use sorcery. You should have tried to ration your magic a little more prudently. This is the *third* time that you have—"

I rolled onto my side and nearly burst into tears. Sitting there, his left arm in a make-shift sling, a scar like a many-tongued burst of lightning spreading from his neck up to his right cheek, was Keir. We locked eyes. Then, he smiled. "This is the third time you have blacked out from use of magic in my presence. Perhaps we could keep it from being a habit?"

"You're alive." The words were nothing more than a whisper, choked by tears, and I was certain that they were unintelligible, but Keir just chuckled and nodded.

"I'm alive." He shifted closer, helping me to sit up. "I told you, scribe, it takes a great deal to kill me."

"What he means to say," Alar said drily, "is that he was only unconscious and unable to move, especially given he'd had the equivalent of a bolt of lightning pumped through him."

I stared at my cousin. He was incredibly pale, even for him, and there were several holes in his shirt, which was stained with blood so as to be unrecognisable. I saw a hint of bandages beneath, and he moved gingerly, wincing after a deep breath. But he, too, was alive.

"I managed to patch him up after everything that happened," Beltran said quietly. He didn't look at me, instead focusing on the small fire around which we sat. "My healing skills are rudimentary at best, and certainly I have no healing magic at all, but I think he'll be alright."

Beltran was alive. Alar. *Keir.* I looked around, searching for Margarethe, but she wasn't here. We were in the forest, no sign of the runes or of the ravine. Just trees and undergrowth. There were no other people, either. Just us.

Fear stole my breath.

"She's okay," Keir said, squeezing my shoulder. I winced at the pain, but leaned into his touch. "She's bathing at a stream down the hill a bit."

I struggled to my feet, every movement sending agony through me. Keir held me still. Alar shook his head.

"Lyr. Don't."

"*Why not?*" I signed. Then I dropped my hands, trembling. It hurt, fire licking at my muscles.

"She..." Alar licked his lips and exchanged a look with Keir and Beltran. "How much do you remember?"

I glared at my cousin, not even bothering to give a response.

"My love, she was closest when the Old Magic manifested." Keir traced a shape on my skin, a squiggle with horns. The dragon. I tried not to stare at his fingers on my wrist. "Hirana was destroyed by the dragon, but Margarethe... well, it had nowhere to go. And she..."

"I bound it to her," I realised. The words fell from my mouth like stones without care to tone or volume. Flat. Empty. Horrified. "It was going to kill her, but it was still made of ink, and I..."

Alar closed his eyes. "She bears the dragon, now."

I shook my head desperately. "No. She can't. She doesn't. I just…"

I squeezed my eyes closed and concentrating, reaching for the sorcery that had lived on my back and in my blood. There was nothing, only a silence so deep that it echoed. Breath heaving, I tried again, pushing past the drained reservoirs of my scribe magic and finding ragged wounds where the dragon had been ripped from me by Hirana's magic. By my magic.

"You're awake."

My eyes flew open and I gaped up at Margarethe. She stood at the edge of the fire, wearing the same dress full of tears and bloodstains. Her curly hair was soaking wet and dripping onto her shoulders like the *plink* of blood into that bronze bowl. She looked at me with a small smile that didn't reach her eyes. And at her neck, there was the edge of a claw inked there, two shades darker than her skin.

"No," I breathed, shaking my head. Before I could fall apart completely, Margarethe was on her knees before me, arms wrapped so tightly around me that it was impossible not to bury my head into her shoulder and start crying.

"Shhh, shhh, it's not your fault," she soothed. I returned her embrace.

"How can you say that?" I whispered in her ear, so like those times when it was easier to breathe words to her rather than speak aloud. When she was the only person I trusted to speak freely with. "It's *all* my fault."

"It's mine, actually," Keir interrupted. I looked at him and he nodded. "I started all of it by giving humans the ability to know, all those lifetimes ago. Hirana...she...none of this would have happened if I hadn't—"

"Don't be an idiot," Alar snapped. Beltran frowned, uncharacteristically quiet. "You can't control the actions of others. That, well, whatever that was chose to try and enslave the world. What happened afterwards was nothing to do with you and everything to do with her."

I blinked. Afterwards? How long had I been asleep? Long enough to have been carried from the ravine, clearly. But what about the other people? Where had they gone? And what were we doing here in the middle of the forest?

"What..." I broke off, pulling out of Margarethe's embrace. I lifted my hands. *"What happened?"*

No one spoke at first, letting the wind through the trees fill the void. Then, finally, Beltran broke the silence. "The boundary magic fell," he said, finally meeting my gaze. "That thing, Hirana, whatever it was, seemed to be intrinsically connected to the boundary magic. When she—it—disappeared, then the boundary magic vanished as well."

I flicked my attention to Alar, who nodded solemnly. "The things that Summerfell was meant to contain, they're free, Lyr."

"How bad?" I signed, ignoring the discomfort.

"Bad." Alar ran a hand down his face, breath hitching when he moved too much. "I had a message from Summerfell shortly after the boundary fell, delivered by bird." He reached into his cloak pocket and pulled out a letter, badly mangled.

My scribe magic was empty. I didn't even feel the whisper of ink on paper, and there was no way that it would tell me what the letter said. So I reached for it.

It had been a long time since I'd read without the breath of my magic in my ears. So long that it felt odd, like being underwater, the sound dampened and the world distorted. And when I finally comprehended the words, understood what they were trying to say, I wasn't sure that I hadn't drowned in that water.

The boundaries on the eastern and western mountain ranges surrounding the Great Plains had fallen simultaneously. Creatures distorted by the magic of the Great Plains and the boundary mountains had flooded the country. But they were nothing compared to the rest of the news that filled the paper. Imara had invaded almost as soon as the eastern boundary fell, their army apparently waiting for just such an event. Their navy had sailed at the same time, finding all the harbour cities unprepared and vulnerable. Makhier had been taken. Vazeri had been taken. The interior villages were swiftly falling. The Akopa Islands—Margarethe's homeland—were still untouched, as of the time of the message.

Worst of all, though, was the news, written on the most torn corner of the letter. Summerfell had fallen. To Jessamine.

I let the paper slip through my fingers and flutter to the ground. Alar picked it up and tossed it into the fire, looking grim.

"The other captives went to Aviena," Beltran said, "in the

hopes that they could find shelter or be returned home to their families. It's doubtful that Imara would care about a handful of kidnapping victims, given how weak they were."

But Summerfell, impenetrable fortress that held back the monsters for countless generations, had fallen. From within.

"*What do we do now?*" I wasn't sure my hands had formed the words correctly given that no one answered. Maybe they were shaking too badly. Maybe I had formed the words wrong, being so hurt. Maybe—

Keir lay his hand on top of mine. "This goes deeper than Hirana wanting to take back the power I took from her."

I nodded vaguely.

"Someone had to have helped her. Someone from Imara, for them to have their armies waiting." Alar kicked a twig towards the fire. It missed. "And no doubt the Order of Ter Avest was involved, given that the witch took Summerfell at the same time."

Margarethe shivered at the word *witch*, wrapping her arms around herself, a hint of the dragon tattoo showing through some of the tears on her dress. Alar didn't seem to notice.

"We could give in," Keir said flatly. "But your scribe magic makes you dangerous, and no doubt they will know all about you from the triumvirate by now. All of you, if they've taken control of the Great Archives. Or—" His voice dropped into a low rumble. "—we fight back."

"How?" Margarethe asked, scoffing. "There are four of us. Against magical creatures and invading empires and who knows what else. The world isn't the same as it was yesterday. How do we fight against that?"

"We go to the Uncharted Lands," Alar said. He drew a quick map in the dirt, pointing to the tongue of land to the west. "Or, we go to the Great Plains."

Where the remains of dead gods were buried. Where my parents had vanished on their expedition to find bloodstone or worse. Where all of this had started.

I watched the last fragment of the letter curl in the fire, edges smouldering red. A single word whispered to me before it was burned away.

Run.

EPILOGUE

*A*lyse knew the moment her husband would enter the room, though she had been ostensibly doing nothing but playing the harp for the last hour. So when the gilded doors burst open, slamming into the marble columns to either side, she neither jumped nor blinked, though she knew that was the reaction her husband had hoped for. What Sitric Mallory, Emperor of Imara, hoped for was rarely what she needed. And Alyse was far more concerned with the latter, as that was what aligned with her plans.

Sitric strode in, his finest gold silk robe embroidered with cranes gleaming in the afternoon light. It was tailored to his form, lithe from hours of sword play and the benefit of being still young, as his father had not been when he inherited the empire. Alyse didn't care much about such things, but there were benefits to having a handsome face on the throne.

"I just received reports from the front lines," Sitric

announced, waving a letter with a flourish. It was stained with blood. He dropped the letter in Alyse's lap, likely expecting her to recoil with disgust.

"Which lines, my love?" Alyse asked, gently setting aside her lap harp and lifting the letter. She didn't read it, knowing Sitric preferred to tell her.

"I have taken the most valuable city beyond the boundary mountains. Vazeri!" He laughed sharply, eyes gleaming. "Is it not a marvellous prize? The jewel of the west, full of gold and art and other...valuable things."

Also home to the Great Archives. Where, Alyse knew, certain records were kept. Records her Order wanted. Had wanted since their inception several centuries ago. Finally, they were nearly in her grasp.

"A marvellous prize indeed," Alyse said. She stood and flashed a coy smile at her husband. He grabbed her chin and kissed her. Hard. She responded eagerly, though her thoughts were already calculating the next step. Not that Sitric could ever know the truth of her careful manipulations. He pulled back, shoving her aside just as roughly as he'd kissed her, pacing the room with a manic look.

"All this time and the west is *mine*. They didn't know we were coming, do you know? They were totally unprepared for our attack! Foolish, uncultured people." He grabbed a curtain and flung it aside, letting in a beam of bright light that shone directly into Alyse's eyes.

Uncultured people? Just a moment ago, he was crowing about the magnificence of his prize. Imara may have had vast resources, given the size of their holdings, but until recently, they had been a people of divided and indistinct culture. They had been nomads, hunters, more concerned with brewing their grain alcohol than gathering wealth, planning for the future. Only the capital city had been different, and the people there were buffoons, squandering their wealth on that same alcohol, laughing at foolish delights and thinking that buying things equated to power.

Alyse had helped to change all of that.

"It is just what they deserve," she said, gliding smoothly to Sitric's side. He wrapped a crushing arm around her waist, staring out of the palace windows to the city beyond. A lot had been done in five years. Improvements, all. Well, not all. There was the unfortunate incident with the Eastern Quarter, when Sitric's bloodlust had gotten away from Alyse, but she'd learned from her mistake there. "You will rule them so well, my love."

"I will, won't I?" Sitric squeezed harder. "And once they all bow to me, we can pave the path to my godhood."

Alyse smiled, suppressing the urge to roll her eyes. "It shouldn't be too hard. A whisper here. A story of divine retribution there. After all, gods are made by those that worship them. And when you control the world, how can they do anything but worship you?"

Sitric grinned. In a flash, the grin vanished. He pushed Alyse away and started pacing. "But what if they do *not* worship me? What if they think me only a man?"

"My love—"

He rounded on her, eyes wide and manic. "I have heard the whispers, you know. All around the palace, I have heard them whispering about me. They say that I overreach. They say that I am foolish for stepping beyond the boundary mountains. That doing so is a death sentence for all of Imara. I have heard them say that I do not think straight, that I am weak in the head. That I am mad."

Ah, yes, but madness was so much easier to mould. And his was truly a gift to her Order.

Alyse crossed to her husband, despite knowing that he was just as likely to strike her as to embrace her. She brushed a hand down his cheek gently. "You know that I have been by your side for the last five years. Surely, you can trust my judgement on the state of your mind."

Sitric scowled and huffed, but nodded. "Your judgement is impeccable. Everyone says so."

Alyse smiled. They had better, with how much work it was to keep up this facade of gentleness. "Then believe me when I tell you that you are not mad. Those who say otherwise are merely jealous. They wish they had your power, your *destiny*, for themselves."

Sitric's eyes flashed. "You're right. They think to usurp me."

"Do you think it so dire?" Alyse asked, putting a desperate fear into her voice. One her husband could not resist.

"They are traitors," Sitric announced. "They will die with the dawn."

"Who?" Alyse asked, hiding a grin of her own behind her sleeve.

"The Council of Families," Sitric said. He already whirled

towards the door, the thought of treason likely all he could think about. The thought so carefully planted by Alyse, who had made it so easy for her husband to hear the whispers. "They will all die. Then we will go see my new prize. You would like that, darling, wouldn't you? To see Vazeri kneel at my feet?"

"I would like it more than anything," Alyse said. Sitric was already gone. She hummed to herself and sat back down, picking up her lap harp. She was still there some hours later when shocked cries and whispers flooded through the palace. Her husband apparently hadn't waited until dawn to execute the so-called traitors. Alyse stood and walked to the door, calling for her servant.

"I need to pack. Prepare for a prolonged journey. I will be accompanying the Emperor on his voyage to the newest addition to the Imaran Empire."

Finally, it was time for the Order of Ter Avest to put their plan into motion. She just needed to get to the Great Archives, first. Then, they could begin.

ABOUT THE AUTHOR

Evelyn Grimald "E.G." Stone is an independent author, editor, and linguist who has been writing, creating and causing vast amounts of trouble since a young age. When not writing, she is off musing about the workings of languages—both real and created—or reading and sewing. E.G. reads voraciously, much to the confusion of her two dogs and two cats. Weird, nerdy, perhaps a little crazy, she is having a grand old time writing, reading, editing, musing on language, and, naturally, continuing her endeavours in causing trouble.

ALSO BY EVELYN GRIMALD STONE

In Memoriam Duology

The Wing Cycle Trilogy

On Behalf of Death Series

The Crow and the King

The Order of the Owl

Speaker of Words